Last Exit in New Jersey

Last Exit in New Jersey

C.E. GRUNDLER

THOMAS & MERCER

Text copyright ©2011 C.E. Grundler

Published by Thomas & Mercer
P.O. Box 400818
Las Vegas, NV 89140

ISBN-13: 9781612182414
ISBN-10: 1612182410

ACKNOWLEDGEMENTS

There are a few people who are due much thanks; each of you helped me along at some point in this process, and for that I am grateful. To start with: Mom, Dad, and Rachel—your feedback and priceless comments were invaluable through that first draft. Walter, for the RF guidance and all your input. For all the motivation, Frank, and Felicia for far more reasons than I could ever list. Diane, my editor on the high seas, for all your blunt and brutal comments as well as your ceaseless encouragement. To Eleni Caminis, who saw the potential in my writing and provided me the opportunity and assistance to move forward. And to my editor, David Downing, for all your knowledge and professional guidance in streamlining my story and writing.

Finally, I would like to dedicate this book to my late friend Butch.

03:14 SATURDAY, JUNE 26

38°39'51.72"N/74°34'27.40"W

NORTH ATLANTIC, 23 NAUTICAL MILES

SOUTHEAST OF CAPE MAY, NJ

Alone at the helm, shivering in the predawn darkness, Hazel Moran listened to the soft rush of water as *Witch* cut through the offshore Atlantic swells. Guided by compass she headed southeast by south while radar monitored the empty spread of ocean for unwanted company. Beyond the dim glow of the instruments, everything on deck remained black; not even running lights revealed the small schooner's position. The boat surged forward under full sail, in perfect balance with the broad waves and a steady southwest wind. The air hung heavy with a dampness that clung to every surface; Hazel knew by afternoon violent thunderstorms would rumble across the Jersey shore.

She switched a flashlight on and aimed the beam astern; it pierced the blackness behind her. The weather-beaten wooden dinghy still followed reluctantly in *Witch*'s wake, tugging against the towline like a sacrificial lamb sensing its fate. It hadn't sunk yet, but rode low as water seeped through loose seams.

Hazel checked her watch then shut the light, letting the darkness close in. Dawn was an hour away, and her twenty-first birthday in two weeks; there'd been moments during the previous evening when she wondered if she'd see either one.

Normally Hazel enjoyed the quiet solitude of the night watch, miles from shore, surrounded by an inky emptiness while the rest of the world disappeared. Normally the worn mahogany wheel would have been comforting in her hands, but adrenaline still raced through her and she fought to keep from shaking. Normally there wasn't a dead body onboard.

The deceased cargo offered one benefit: now her father had to believe her. When she'd first insisted, two nights before, that someone was out to kill her, he'd said she was just being melodramatic. Actually, "full of shit" was how he put it, words usually reserved for her blue-haired, multi-pierced cousin Micah. She should have been honored.

"I think you've been reading too many Travis McGee mysteries," her father said when she tried to explain how her ancient Miata had ended up parked beneath thirteen feet of water. He didn't buy her story of ditching the car in the river to escape masked gunmen in a Taurus. Even their friend Joe agreed she was pushing the limits of credibility.

Her father alternated between relief that she'd survived her long drive off a short pier and frustration that she held to such an elaborate lie. Just tell the truth, he insisted. Admit she was screwing around and miscalculated one of her high-speed drifting skids into the lot. It was a maneuver she'd honed to perfection and yet another driving technique her father forbid, arguing she'd either get herself killed or raise their insurance rates. Sometimes it was hard to tell which worried him more.

"Stop lying!" he had said, over and over. He wouldn't listen.

But now she had proof. She nearly said, "I told you so," but the words caught in her throat. Far better not to push the issue, not when both her little driving mishap and the corpse in her cabin were almost certainly tied to Micah's recent disappearance.

Witch plunged into a wave, taking spray over the bow as she drifted off course. Hazel turned the wheel and watched the compass as she returned to a heading of 139 degrees. Her destination was deep water, the deeper the better. The depth finder confirmed the ocean's bottom, well over one hundred feet below, still dropping away.

The companionway door banged open and Hazel jumped, heart pounding. Light spilled across the deck as Joe came above, his shaved head and thick arms glistening with sweat that made the octopus tattoo encircling one arm come alive. He staggered to the rail, gulping mouthfuls of fresh air. Her father emerged after him, his long hair slick and shoulders heavy with exhaustion. He studied Hazel. "You okay, hon?"

She nodded stiffly.

"How much water do we have?"

Hazel checked the depth finder. "One fourteen."

"That should do. Head up."

She swung the wheel until *Witch* pointed into the wind and slowed to a stop, rolling impatiently, broad sails slapping in protest. Joe hauled the plywood dinghy alongside and secured it as the small boat banged and thumped against *Witch*'s hull. The men went below, each returning with a pair of heavy, lumpy black trash bags. They seemed bulkier than Hazel expected, considering the various body parts they contained. It was likely they'd been weighted down with some anchor chain to prevent anything from floating up. One by one the bags were loaded into the dinghy, nearly to the point of swamping.

Her father stepped to the helm, checked the radar to be sure no one was near, then turned his scrutiny to Hazel. She'd cleaned up earlier, scrubbing herself with cold seawater until her skin stung, but it still felt as though she was covered in blood. She shuddered, trying to block the memory of the warm slickness on her hands and soaking her cotton nightgown.

Her father frowned, smoothing back his dark hair. "You're shaking."

"I'm cold," she said, her throat painfully tight.

They both knew better, but he only nodded and took the wheel. "You're not dressed warm enough. Go grab a jacket."

Hazel looked toward the companionway and hesitated.

"It's okay. Everything's cleaned up."

And so it was. Not a trace of the grisly mess remained: the dismembered body, the blood, her sheets, blankets, mattress, her Jay and Silent Bob poster, even the quilt she'd spent last winter neatly stitching by hand—it had all been removed. Only the "NO WAKE ZONE" needlepoint above the cabin door and some books on upper shelves had been spared. Bleach vapors burned her eyes and throat and she choked, panic building at the memory of waking to a hand clamped over her face, the suffocating grip smothering her screams. Her father had been playing poker at Joe's while this stranger stood leaning over her bunk, a smoldering cigarette pressed in his mouth, steel-blue eyes gleaming. She'd struggled to breathe and move away, but he pushed all the harder. He moved in tighter, told her if she screamed it would be the last sound she made, then lifted his hand. Paralyzed, she didn't even whisper.

Her choice, he said. Tell him where Micah was, or suffer first and then tell him.

She didn't speak. She couldn't.

"Haze?" her father called down. He leaned into the companionway. "You okay?"

She shook her head, pulled on a sweatshirt, and raced back to the fresh air on deck. Leaning over the rail, she peered down at the bags. Her quilt was in one of them, blood-soaked and bundled around assorted pieces of the late Jim Kessler of Cherry Hill, New Jersey. Beyond a name in a wallet, she had no idea who he was. There'd been no car in the boatyard parking lot; he'd slipped upriver aboard the dinghy found beside *Witch*, the same one he currently occupied. Her father untied the dinghy, now barely visible in the water, and it sank under the waves, swallowed by blackness.

Joe took a drag on his cigarette. "And that's the end of that."

But it wasn't and they all knew it.

Her father slumped back against the stern rail and turned to Hazel. "Take the wheel and bring her about. Let's go home."

She returned to the helm, swung the rudder hard to starboard, and waited as *Witch* responded. The sails ceased their banging as they filled with wind, and the boat heeled and gained speed. Hazel finally began to relax as *Witch* got into her groove, racing up and gliding down the wide swells, no longer held back by the dragging dinghy and unwanted cargo.

Her father turned to Joe. "When we get back, I want to haul her car out."

They moved away to trim the sails, their tense, hushed words carried off with the wind as they snugged the sheets. The boat responded by picking up a bit more speed.

Hazel watched the tip of Joe's cigarette, the burning ember floating in the darkness. The cigarette between Kessler's lips had glowed the same way. It was her choice, he'd said, almost as though he hoped she wouldn't cooperate. Tell him where Micah was, or he'd make her an example so Micah would understand who he was dealing with.

He leaned close and clamped his hand over her mouth again. He took a drag off the cigarette and exhaled. Acrid smoke filled the tiny cabin. His middle finger forced her lower eyelid down even as she tried to squeeze her eyes closed. "This is just for starters," he said, the glowing tip of the cigarette moving toward her tearing eye.

Pinned to the bunk with that vile hand smothering her, she let out a muffled scream as she twisted her head violently from side to side. His grip tightened, she felt the webbing between his thumb and forefinger within her mouth, and she bit down hard, fighting her revulsion as her teeth sank into the tough flesh. He bellowed and jerked his hand away.

"That how it's gonna be?" His bloody hand curled into a fist, then opened again and snapped forward to grip her throat. His wet grin bloomed in the dark. "You just made things a whole lot worse for yourself." He loomed closer, the burning cigarette held forward like a weapon.

Flailing against the curve of *Witch*'s hull, Hazel's fingers brushed a cool steel shape on the shelf behind her bunk: her sewing shears.

He'd made it clear. She had no choice.

WHERE AM I?

Hammon stared into blackness. Enveloping, gravelike, absolute blackness. He blinked several times to no discernible effect. A steady rain drummed overhead, and empty soda cans clattered around in the galley sink as *Revenge* pitched against the choppy waves.

It was raining. That was important. But why?

Oh, right. Last night he'd docked in Brielle, New Jersey. He fumbled with his Timex, squinting at the luminescent blue rectangle; 1:13 p.m., June 26. Good. He hadn't overslept. Normally he followed a nocturnal schedule, but not today. He'd been waiting for the rain, counting on it. He'd felt it coming, that familiar dull pain: every fracture, pin, and screw in his body radiated aches, the throbbing more insistent than usual. Ah, the convenience of being a human barometer.

He eased himself from the forward bunk, stepped over dirty laundry, and quietly rummaged around the drawers for a change of clothes, then padded through the dark galley into the tiny head. He could navigate around the boat blind, which, without his glasses, he pretty much was. In the dark it didn't matter. In the dark lots of things didn't matter. Darkness was good. He should have been born a bat.

Door locked, he stripped, shoving his sweaty clothes in the corner, feeling his way into the cramped shower. He scrubbed at the uneven textures of his face with the tight, grafted skin on his fingers, following the scars that spread like flames from above his right eyebrow across his neck and shoulder, past where the cosmetic repairs stopped and the real damage began.

Naked, he was as vulnerable as a hermit crab torn from its shell. He raced through his shower, dried and dressed, then combed his hair so it fell across the right half of his face. He flossed, pricking his knuckles against his unnaturally sharp canines. He scowled into the darkness at the black rectangle over the sink. Even unseen, he felt his reflection's mocking presence. He would have shattered the mirror years ago but superstition stopped him.

Not his superstition; far as he knew, he wasn't superstitious.

No, not him.

It was Annabel. She tore into him at the mere thought of destroying the mirror, insisting it would offend the mirror spirits as well as the boat they protected. At times it was hard to take her seriously, but Hammon had discovered that Annabel's guidance usually kept him out of trouble, while defying her could turn his existence into a living hell. Thus, a compromise: he painted every mirror aboard black.

The rain overhead intensified: time to get moving. Hammon shuffled over to the dinette, flipped on the dim galley light, and switched his world from black to blurry. He felt around unsuccessfully for his glasses. Up forward he heard a soft yawn.

"Annabel, you awake?"

"No, Otto. Sound asleep. Next question."

"Yeah. Where'd you put my glasses?"

She gave an exasperated sigh. "I didn't touch them." Her sleek bare shape slipped past him. "Don't blame me when you lose things in this floating disaster area."

"It upsets you so much, feel free to clean up."

"Do I look like your mother?" She stepped into the head, not bothering to close the door. "You know the rules. And you left your glasses behind the laptop."

Sure enough, there they were. He slipped them on, bringing his world into focus, and considered taking them back off. Maybe she had a point. The rules were simple: whoever made the mess cleaned it. Annabel was compulsively neat but refused to straighten up after him.

Hammon opened a curtain in the salon and contemplated the Jersey waterfront. Seated on the toilet, Annabel leaned out, looking up. "I think it's time for some new scenery," she said. "Why don't we head up to Maine for a while?"

"Yeah, sure. But first, I got things to do," he said, trying to remember what exactly those things were. He picked up the pad beside the laptop and read the notes he'd left himself. Grocery lists, memories, ideas, reminders. Ones he'd dealt with were scribbled out, but others still remained.

6/25 DOCKED IN BRIELLE
6/26 TAKE ANNABEL TO LIBRARY

Okay, he knew that. So far, so good.

GARY'S—NEW FREEZER, FUEL GAUGE

Three for three. Not bad.

6/23 M T CAR TRUNK.

He checked his watch again. It was the twenty-sixth; worse yet, unseasonably warm the last few days. Definitely not good. And where *was* the car? He searched his memory to no avail, which wasn't unusual. He probably left himself another note, a clue to its whereabouts. And there it was, further down, squeezed sideways into the space beside the spiral binding:

6/23 FAIRMONT BY GATES OF HELL

Crap. That was bad. Extremely bad. Why'd he go and leave it there?

There was one more note, a new one, written neatly between the lines in Annabel's fluid hand: *Eat something healthy.*

That he could handle. He dug through the galley for anything clean, settling on a sixteen-ounce. Mix N' Measure container, and added WASH DISHES to his list. Annabel re-emerged from the head, still not bothering to dress, and paused to regard the bowl of Peeps bobbing in chocolate milk like pastel ducks in a mud puddle.

"Should I ask?" she said, sliding into the seat opposite him at the dinette.

"Poultry and dairy." He stabbed one with the plastic spork. "It's in the food pyramid."

"Nice try." She combed her bobbed hair, the curls grazing her neck. "Peeps aren't poultry, and they have zero nutritional value."

"Okay, Mom." It amused him the way she berated him for some of his habits, yet tolerated other idiosyncrasies, like the painted mirrors, with a sympathetic smile. Mirrors distorted reality, she contended, and reflections were irrelevant. That's how she put it, insisting society would benefit from painting all the world's mirrors black. Humans, she ranted, were pathetic, shallow, image-conscious primates. She completely disregarded her own appearance, which was easy for her. He stared across the dinette table, taking in every inch of her. The wild curls and wide, dark eyes, the irrepressibly mischievous smile, the neck that begged for nibbling, the body firm and curved in all the right places, the satiny, unmarked skin. She was, quite simply, perfect. Not that he was complaining, any more than he'd complain about her preference for minimal clothing.

She gave him a wry smile. "You're crooked, dear."

"Huh?" He washed down a pair of NoDoz caplets with a swig of grape soda.

"You can't even button yourself straight. If you insist on dressing in the dark, at least check when you're done."

"That's what I have you for." He inspected the uneven shirttails and unbuttoned his shirt, revealing the T-shirt beneath, which read: "I wouldn't be so broke if the voices in my head paid rent."

Annabel scanned the galley for something she considered edible, and Hammon jotted down BUY MORE FOOD. She paused, turning back in the classic Betty Grable pose. "Oh yeah, I almost forgot. You left it in the snow."

"I what?"

"I don't know. You said it last night. You told me to remind you. You said it was important."

He scratched at his scarred arm. "Snow? In June? I must've been dreaming."

Annabel sighed the way she did whenever she was about to say something he didn't want to hear.

Hammon groaned. He knew where this was going. "And?"

Another sigh. "You said, and I quote, 'Make sure I tell Stevenson it's in the snow.'"

"Then it was a nightmare," Hammon said flatly, scratching at his wrist.

"Stop scratching. Maybe it means something. You could—"

"—talk to him? Sure. When hell—"

"—freezes over." Annabel stared up at the hatch while rain pounded overhead. "So, Otto, why are we up at this awful hour? Four hours' sleep isn't nearly enough."

Hammon took a deep breath. "I was just thinking…"

"That's my job." She did a series of catlike stretches, derailing his train of thought. "Thinking about what?"

"I figured maybe we'd—" He hiccupped.

"—take a walk down to the library?" She tucked her hair behind her ear. "Nice try, Otto. We're in Brielle, it's raining, and I saw the list. You're going to ditch me at the library and go to Gary's."

Damn. He really had to remember not to leave his lists lying around. His eyes lingered on the smooth curve of her neck, transfixed. He could watch her for hours. Sometimes he did. But not today; he had things to do.

"Just for the afternoon. The new freezer's in."

"Admit it. You're tired of me."

"No!" He didn't have to tell her. But making him sweat was her favorite game.

Annabel fiddled with her MP3 player. "You don't want me around anymore." She slipped on the headphones and danced up to the salon.

"Annabel."

She pointed to the earphones, smiling apologetically as she sang, way off-key, to "My Sharona."

"Annabel."

Eyes closed, she moved to the music, swaying before him hypnotically. Hammon watched, trying to stay focused as another train of thought crashed and burned.

"Annabel."

She paused, lifting the earphones. "What?"

Good question. "You know I can't think when you do that."

"Which implies you can when I don't. Nice try." She smiled. "It's okay. Have fun telling Gary why the old freezer's dead."

Oh yeah. Gary.

The freezer.

It was raining.

He was dropping Annabel at the library.

She never ceased to amaze him. Gary swore she was bad news and Hammon should get rid of her. Gary didn't understand. Hammon and Annabel had been together for years, starting as fellow inmates in the pediatric ICU. He was dying when he first saw her gazing down at him with the sad serenity of an angel. She stayed beside him, blind to the disfigurement and bandages as he endured ongoing surgeries. She accepted the irreparable damage within his shattered skull even when he couldn't. She refused to give up on him and wouldn't let him give up either, no matter how much he tried. Even with a few bad sectors on his hard drive, the critical programs still functioned, and that was fine with her. He didn't want to consider what she was doing with a mess like him or why she'd stayed all this time. Lifting those rocks would only bring to light some troubling truths about him, her, and their relationship. He knew better than to question why and risk losing her. Without her he would have unraveled years ago.

13:40 SATURDAY, JUNE 26

39°13'58.83"N/75°01'59.09"W

BIVALVE, NJ

Typical of New Jersey summer weather, even as isolated storms deluged sections of coastline, other stretches baked under a cloudless sky. Along the southwestern shore, an unrelenting midday sun beat down on the marshy banks of the Maurice River, cooking the low-tide mud to a pungent level. Stagnant air hung wet and sticky, ripe for a good thunderstorm. This was Bivalve: the end of the road, figuratively and literally.

Long ago there had been oysters. Freight trains full of oysters, history told. In its day, the one-time oyster capital of the world created more millionaires per mile than anywhere in the country. Oyster schooners by the hundreds sailed the bay, hauling up a seemingly limitless bounty. Oystermen crewed and dredged the bay; they built and maintained the schooners in hundreds of boatyards; jobs were plentiful on roads and rail, shipping the oysters across the country. By the late 1880s, Bivalve filled ninety freight cars a week, and by the 1920s, the annual harvest reached ten million dollars. But in the 1950s, disease struck. Oysters began dying off, taking with them the region's bustling economy. Abandoned fleets sank into neglect and into the mud. Docks collapsed and marshes reclaimed the shores. Over time nature methodically erased most traces of a once booming industry until all that remained was a building here, a twisted length of railway there. Bivalve was a ghost town, and even the ghosts had long since packed up and moved on. Only a few people, a few docks, and a few boats remained.

Among those boats were a plywood center console, an old Sea Ray, and a rust-streaked patrol cruiser. In slip F-18, the only numbered slip around, bobbed an ancient wooden Grady-White named *Kindling*, sporting hot-rod-style flames that covered the bow. Across from *Kindling*, *Witch* sat silent, all traces of the previous night's voyage and cargo washed away.

Above the docks, a faded plywood sign read:

BRANFORD'S BOATYARD
GENERAL MARINE WORK—DOCKS AVAILABLE

Along the bottom, fresh lettering in a shade of red remarkably similar to *Witch*'s boot stripe stated: GO AWAY.

Beyond the docks and past the lot paved in crushed white shells stood a sagging wood-frame building. Once a sailmaker's loft, it presently housed Joe's marine repair shop and yard amenities consisting of showers, a laundry room, small kitchen, wood stove, a sunken couch, and a pool table supported on all corners by car jacks. A carpenter's level held a place of honor in the cue rack.

Inside the shop, Hazel stared restlessly out the window at the lot. Her father had left an hour earlier with no explanation, depositing her under Joe's protective custody, and she'd spent much of that time calculating how to make a break for it. She knew she wasn't supposed to leave. Her father made that clear, even having her recite back his instructions.

"Stay with Joe while you're gone. Under no circumstances short of fire, earthquake, or nuclear attack should I leave this building."

She really did intend to keep her word, at least at first. That had to count for something.

She sat beside the workbench and picked at red paint dried on her shredded jeans. She wanted to talk about last night, but since it "never happened," that topic was off-limits. Instead she scanned the service manual for the dissected Johnson outboard currently spread across Joe's workbench, passing him tools before he asked and trying not to worry about Micah. Joe concentrated on his work, focusing harder than usual as he loosened a fuel line. With each turn of the wrench, the colorful tentacles on his octopus tattoo writhed around the anchor and skull beneath them.

If there was one thing Joe lacked, it was subtlety. She could see it in his eyes every time he glanced up. He kept studying her the same way he had last night, when she'd wandered trancelike into his apartment, blood-soaked, axe in hand, and said in barely a whisper, "I just killed a man." She wondered what Joe was thinking, but she was afraid to ask. Maybe she didn't want to know. Even with the air-conditioner straining and AC/DC screaming from the radio, the silence was intolerable.

"You think it's not getting enough fuel?" Hazel said at last, stating the obvious. She might as well have commented on the weather. Joe paused, forehead creasing like he was trying to read between the lines, and he wiped his face with a bandana.

"Yeah. Figured I'd test the fuel pump."

She could see he wanted to say more but turned his attention back to the motor, setting the end of the fuel line into an empty two-liter bottle, cranking the engine. The pump kicked to life, and the fuel line spurted like a severed artery, filling the bottle with raw gasoline. He killed the power, capped off the bottle, and reconnected the fuel line.

Silence resumed. Minutes ticked by.

"Joe?"

He looked up. "Yeah?"

Hazel knew what she wanted to say, but couldn't actually say it. Joe waited.

"What's better?" she asked, just to say something, anything. "Double-clutching or floating shifts?"

Joe chuckled darkly. "Neither, if the vehicle in question sinks like a rock."

She was never going to live that submerged Miata down. "You know what I mean."

"Yeah. *RoadKill*'s tranny's acting up again, and you want me to check it before your dad notices."

"Could you? Please? Maybe it's nothing, but I don't want to take any chances. I'd tell Dad but…"

Joe rubbed his face. "Lay off the clutchless shifting until I take a look."

Hazel smiled. Her father had bought *RoadKill* back when she'd been born; even then the Kenworth was already old and rusty. And once they finally purchased a new truck, he began suggesting what Hazel considered unthinkable: getting rid of the antiquated Kenworth. But so long as *RoadKill* remained reliable and continued to earn its keep, thanks in part to Joe's ongoing clandestine repairs, Hazel got her way and the truck stayed.

She said, "It's just that Dad really doesn't need any more aggravation right now."

"Speaking of which, I haven't seen Micah around much these days. What's he been up to?"

She gathered scattered sockets from the workbench, returning them to the gang box. "I wouldn't know." Joe was fishing, but he wasn't going to catch anything. She knew better than to volunteer any information, not that there was anything to volunteer other than the fact that last night's visitor asked the same questions. But that little detail might only make matters worse, and besides, it wasn't what Joe asked. "I haven't seen Micah." And that part of her story wasn't changing. "Or heard from him."

Joe looked less than convinced. Hazel and Micah weren't just cousins. They were best friends, confidants, and partners in crime, inseparable for as long as either could remember. Unlike Hazel, Micah's upbringing had the benefit of married parents, a picture-perfect suburban house, traditional schooling...and a home life that was anything but happy. He rarely talked about it and never suffered any outright abuse, just emotional neglect by parents preoccupied by their own dysfunctional relationship. Aboard *Witch* he found warmth, guidance, acceptance, and sanctuary from the screaming at home.

For the most part, Hazel's father treated them equally, though he tended to push Micah a bit harder, expecting more from him. And he blamed Micah whenever Hazel got into trouble, whether justified or not; either way, Micah always accepted it with a smile. Unfortunately this earned him a reputation as a troublemaker, no matter how loudly Hazel proclaimed his innocence. In the end her father and Joe simply assumed that if something went wrong, Micah was at fault. This was a perfect example.

"Maybe he's just away with some girl." Hazel said, pulling threads from the hole in the knee of her jeans. "Or lost his cell phone. Or both." She wished it was that simple—and that she believed it herself. Joe's skeptical look was reply enough.

"It's happened before," she said defensively. While her father suffered from terminal seriousness, Micah was a Labrador puppy in human form: carefree, oblivious, and prone to straying after some enticing scent. More than once she'd received a postcard or call from Ft. Lauderdale or New Orleans, where he'd wound up with a group of girls on spring break.

"Yeah," Joe said, "but those times, *Tuition* didn't vanish with him."

There was that. Their gleaming new Freightliner, *Tuition*, represented far more than merely Hazel's entire college fund. For twenty years her father had supported them by driving *RoadKill*, living frugally, and homeschooling Hazel, keeping her by his side even as he worked and saved for that rainy day when he'd ship her off to the very place he'd left in his rearview mirror when she was born. It wasn't easy convincing him her heart wasn't set on college and they should instead use those funds for a new truck. A childhood spent riding shotgun in the cab and under sail, while solitary and unconventional, was something she wouldn't trade for four walls, a yard, and every sitcom she'd never watched. She was happiest behind the wheel. It suited her far better than Micah's bustling college life. It took nearly a year to persuade her father that her mind was set; she was intent on continuing the family business, and they should buy the new truck they needed. Only now *Tuition* was gone, and so was Micah.

"Maybe it's just coincidence." Hazel turned away to examine the black-and-white photos on the walls she'd studied a thousand times before, frozen images from Bivalve's prosperous days when the river teemed with schooners. She swore she could see *Witch*'s stern in one.

Joe said, "I don't believe in coincidence."

Hazel could feel his eyes on her as she contemplated the beam of sunlight scattered into rainbows by the facetted stone in her ring. The air-conditioner whined, the radio blared, and tension hung in the stuffy air. She tried to distract herself by organizing the trophies from Joe's more interesting repairs. Bent props, mangled pistons, twisted valves, and the shattered remains of a crankshaft. She tried to calculate the number of screws in the unfinished sheetrock walls, then poked at hardened formations of over-expanded spray foam insulation spilling from the seams. She inventoried a cardboard box by the door packed with fireworks. Mortars, fountains, Roman candles, firecrackers, M80s, whistling rockets, Saturn missiles.

"Gonna be a hell'va Fourth," Joe said, his voice tight.

Was she actually making him uncomfortable? She didn't think anything made Joe nervous.

Hazel closed the box and turned to him. "Joe? Do you think there's something wrong with me?"

Joe stiffened slightly but continued to spray down the carb. "Wrong how?"

"I don't know. It's…" She closed her eyes, searching for the right words. "Like when we go hunting, and I have to…"

She didn't have to explain. He knew. She'd learned to hunt beside her father and Joe and was quite skilled, yet she detested the actual killing and would have stopped long ago if not for the fact that her kills were consistently cleaner and more humane than either of theirs. How anyone could consider hunting a sport, though, eluded her. It was an unpleasant task, necessary for filling the freezer with venison. She wasn't squeamish: she could efficiently field dress, skin, and butcher her kill, but the process left her somber for days.

"But last night…" She couldn't say it. Saying it would be admitting it, and that—that she didn't even want to consider.

"There's nothing wrong with you. You're just in shock."

"I didn't think. I just reacted."

"You had to or God knows what would have happened." He slammed the gang box drawer closed. "This is the Pierce thing all over again, isn't it? Don't listen to what anyone says; just because you defended yourself doesn't mean you're some kind of sociopath."

She understood what he was saying, but there was a difference between last night and the time Dave Pierce tried to rape her. She had been fourteen then. He followed her until she was alone, then cornered her and held her down, fumbling with his jeans as she screamed and struggled to escape. She'd been crying for him to stop, to let her go—and suddenly he did. Then it was Pierce who was screaming. He fell off her and she stumbled to her feet, backed away, and stared down at her knife clasped in her blood-slick hand. And as he lay shrieking, his gut sliced open, she stood and considered for a fleeting moment whether to cut his throat as well. Instead she ran.

"I didn't kill Pierce."

Joe rubbed the back of his neck, pressing on knotted muscles. "And last night you did what you had to. You're okay and that's what's important. Don't forget that."

She didn't think she ever would. She could still see Kessler's sadistic face every time she closed her eyes. Hazel stared down at the cracked linoleum tiles. "I don't feel okay."

"You're in shock."

He didn't get it. After she stabbed Kessler, she probably could have escaped. He was already dying—just not fast enough.

"It was so…" she started, her voice trailing off. So what? Easy? Satisfying? Why was it she felt more remorse killing a deer than another human? What did that say about her?

Joe carried the carburetor to the parts bath and began spraying it with Clean-R-Carb. No. He wasn't cleaning the carb. Hazel peeked over his shoulder, and saw *Witch's* axe soaking in a bath of carb-cleaner. Joe turned to her. "It's over. Let it go. It never happened."

But it did and she had a bad feeling it was anything but over. She stared at Joe and he stared back. Sweat beaded across his forehead, and his scalp glistened beneath the shadow of stubble. Hazel rose, checking the thermostat. It was eighty-two degrees in the shop. "Too hot," she said.

"Gonna be another scorcher," Joe agreed, visibly relieved by the change of subject. "We could use a good storm, break this heat."

Hazel glanced at the barometer on the wall. The air pressure was dropping. "It's coming."

If she'd ever needed Micah, it was now, and he probably needed her even more. She had to get out of there; she had to find him. She knew what her father said about staying put but she didn't care. Clearly the building wasn't on fire and an imminent nuclear attack on Bivalve seemed unlikely, which left one option. She turned up the air-conditioner, cranked the radio to match, then paused and looked around.

"Did this place just shake?"

Joe shrugged. "This dump's built on sand and mud. Ninety years, the foundation's still settling. I'm amazed it hasn't collapsed yet."

It might've been settling, or maybe the ground trembled, even to the slightest degree. That would qualify as an earthquake.

"But it wasn't my imagination. You felt it too."

Joe kept working but he nodded, "Yeah, maybe, I guess."

He was just humoring her, but that wasn't the point. She had confirmation; that was good enough. "I'm going to wash up and grab a soda," she said. "You want one?"

"Yeah, kiddo. That'd be nice."

"Be right back." She walked out of the shop, heading toward the refrigerator. And past, to the lot. She hadn't specified where she'd get the soda. With the radio cranked and the air-conditioner maxed, Joe wouldn't hear a bomb go off. He'd be so absorbed in his work it'd be some time before he realized she left.

Seriously, he should have known better.

I'M HEADING OUT

Time to go. Step outside, shut door, lock up, walk.

Simple on the surface, but wasn't that the case with so many things?

No. First Hammon had to check every system aboard from bow to stern. Check the stove, make sure it was off, not that he'd used it in years or even had propane tanks aboard. Double-check each knob anyway, confirm they were off. Everything unplugged. Every circuit breaker off. Every hatch locked. Step into the pelting rain, lock the cabin. Yeah. Definitely locked. Hammon slid his fingers along where frame met door, verifying there was no gap. He pushed a bucket up against the door. That meant it was closed and locked. He wouldn't have done it if it wasn't closed. Check again, just in case. Try to open the door, jiggle the handle.

"The boat is locked," Annabel said. He checked again, and again Annabel reassured him. Of course it was locked. The bucket was there. He wouldn't walk away if it wasn't.

Climbing off, he checked each dock line. Exposed to a stiff chop, the boats on either side churned and fought their lines while *Revenge* rode out the weather with steady dignity.

Externally, *Revenge* didn't look like much. Just another generic sport-fishing boat indigenous to the East Coast. At thirty-six feet she was average in size. Her lines were vaguely classic, but that was subtle, and most people wouldn't notice subtle details. Unlike the surrounding boats, no shiny tags or distinctive style indicated any specific builder. On closer scrutiny, it became evident she lacked anything shiny. Railings were unpolished, the hull a drab off-white, and gray canvas covered all glass surfaces. She seemed to blend into the stormy sky. Backed to the dock, her transom was blank; only faded New Jersey registration numbers on the bow provided any identification, however inaccurate, and only because missing registration numbers could draw unwanted attention.

Hammon looked everything over again. Exposure to daylight was bad enough, but separating from his personal sanctuary was worse. Concealed within his trench coat, he forced himself to walk away even as his stomach twisted in protest. Annabel, on the other hand, proceeded without a care in the world and dressed accordingly. She grinned as fat raindrops soaked her cutoffs and tank top in the most appealing way.

Though it was daytime, there was one reason Hammon was able to venture out. The downpour had driven away the summer crowds; they had fled the beaches, docks, and streets and sought refuge indoors, quite literally leaving the coast clear for him to roam. And the satellites peppering the sky, the ones scrutinizing the planet's surface in minute detail, couldn't see through clouds. Rain made Hammon almost as invisible as darkness. He reached into his pocket, switching on the MP3 player tucked in a ziplock bag.

"What aren't you listening to today?" asked Annabel.

Rain streaked his glasses, and he wiped them with his fingers, smearing the lenses. "The usual electromagnetic noise. The Ramones, I think."

The music wasn't important, thus no headphones. Listening wasn't the point. The MP3 player emitted just enough electromagnetic interference to confuse the satellites sorting through the electronic racket rising from the ground, effectively shielding him from detection. He glared up at the sky. "Can you hear me now?"

Not all satellites were evil. Some transmitted benign TV, radio, and Internet signals; some provided GPS coordinates. But then there were the Watchers, the Listeners, and worse yet, the Trackers. Trackers didn't care about clouds or rain or even the Ramones; if they had your digital scent, they could find you no matter what. It was only aboard *Revenge* he truly felt concealed. Hidden beneath the boat's joinery and insulation, every inch of her interior was lined with continuously grounded fine copper mesh, painted over with high-frequency-shielding conductive copper paint. Essentially, he'd created a floating Faraday cage, impenetrable to electromagnetic waves, cell phone signals, CB, TV, AM, FM signals, radio-frequency radiation, and microwaves.

But outside the cabin, his only protection came in the form of his baseball cap and an oversized trench coat, both lined with ultrathin silver/copper-core-thread fabric. It was better than nothing and less conspicuous than aluminum foil. When people see someone dressed like a baked potato, they tend to make negative assumptions.

"Would you relax already?" Annabel stomped her flip-flops in puddles with childlike enthusiasm. "They can't find us."

Maybe they couldn't, but an unsettling feeling rose in Hammon's gut. He'd forgotten something. That wasn't unusual; he forgot things all the time. What now? He rubbed the side of his skull. He couldn't think straight, not with that damned mercury buried deep inside his brain, shorting circuits between neurons.

Think, damnit. What was it?

Then panic hit. Did he lock the boat?

Revenge was already out of view. He remembered leaving the cabin, and he remembered checking the lines but drew a blank on the time in between. He slowed, straining to quell the building dread.

He'd never not locked the boat; all the same, if he couldn't remember, it was possible he'd left his refuge exposed to the world. If there was one area in which Hammon's brain excelled, it was in visualizing disaster. He'd had enough experience to draw on. He froze, sweat trickling down his back.

Annabel paused her puddle-stomping. "What now?"

He blinked. "I can't remember…"

"Go on," she said patiently.

"Did I lock *Revenge*?"

She smiled. "Yes. The boat is locked. I told you."

"You did?" Relief displaced anxiety. If Annabel said the boat was locked, it was. They continued onward. His Converse high-tops were soaked, but the rain was warm, and wet feet only bothered him somewhat. When Annabel wasn't looking, Hammon fished out his wallet and thumbed through the contents. He studied his driver's license as though the plastic card belonged to someone else.

According to the state of New Jersey, he was John O. Hammon, sex: M, hgt: 5-06, eyes: GRY, currently twenty-one years of age and residing in Manasquan, New Jersey. He stared at the miniature photo of his face with aversion. He wasn't so much pale as devoid of color. His skin, what little he revealed, had the unhealthy, washed-out tone of one who avoided daylight and fresh vegetables. The digital fuzziness downplayed his scars. His hair was a dull mousy brown, and his most vibrant feature, his battleship-gray eyes, seemed to absorb rather than reflect surrounding color. His wardrobe of faded black completed the effect. If not for the blue background, the photo could just as well be monochrome. Frowning, he shoved the license back in his pocket.

"You're awfully quiet," Annabel said, skipping past him on the sidewalk. Hammon glanced around. No one but them.

"Just lost in thought," he said as her soaked shirt redirected his brain. She was drenched, her tank top plastered to her well-defined curves. The words "1.6 liters is a soft drink, not an engine" rose and dipped and rose again over her chest. He loved the rain.

"Should I send a search party?" Amusement flickered in her dark eyes. "Or are you still thinking about your dirty pictures?"

His face grew warm. "What pictures?"

"It's cool; you don't have to hide them from me." Annabel grinned and tucked her wet hair behind her ear. "I like them too."

Her playfulness fascinated Hammon. In all the years they'd been together, so much of Annabel remained a mystery, delightful and perplexing. He didn't even know her age; his best guess currently put her somewhere around nineteen. Yet another of her secrets, along with her true name and her past. He'd learned long ago not to ask. If he pried too deep, she'd get upset and go silent for days, and that was hell on earth. Discussion of their lives before they met was off-limits, which worked just fine for him. His brain was like a trailer park after a tornado: some memories lay in twisted, unrecognizable piles, others vanished without a trace. Better to accept things as they were and just go on. It was hard to imagine, but whatever brought Annabel to the ICU was worse than what he'd survived. While his scars were visible, hers lay hidden beneath an unmarred exterior.

Gary swore there was something very wrong with her. Hammon didn't care what Gary said. True, Annabel was far from perfect; Hammon was the first to admit it. She was sarcastic and critical. Without explanation she could turn moody and withdrawn.

And she could be ruthless. She knew him better than anyone; she knew his every fear, his every weakness. Lying to her was impossible. He was a lousy liar, and she saw right through him. But in the end, he and Annabel were both survivors, however damaged. Annabel accepted him as he was and he accepted her, no questions asked. It was that shared, unspoken understanding that bonded them.

13:57 SATURDAY, JUNE 26

39°14'00.46"N/75°01'59.27"W

BIVALVE, NJ

Outside the shop everything had the glaring, washed-out dullness of an overexposed photo, and Hazel squinted as her eyes adjusted. Her potted tomato plants, watered at dawn, were already wilting, and even the more heat-tolerant peppers were showing the strain. The air was thick with a blend of marsh and decaying shellfish, but the sunbaked boatyard hummed with life, none of it human. Terns darted and wheeled, chattering as they picked off flies. A muskrat shuffled into the rushes, and high above an osprey circled, scanning the river for lunch. Hazel crossed the lot and watched as the bird dove, plunging feet first into the water, then rose skyward with an eel struggling in its talons.

Keys out, Hazel stopped beside her Miata. It was a base model older than her, with an odometer that had flipped more than once and a duct-taped convertible roof that leaked so badly it was pointless to close. Still, it had run well, and with white Shelby stripes over the faded blue paint, it almost resembled a 427 Cobra. Almost, especially if she closed her eyes, which wasn't exactly the best way to drive.

But the Miata was history now. Using the Kenworth and a mooring chain, they'd dragged it to shore that morning, leaving a slug-like trail the whole way. Its short stay on the river bottom left the little car coated in mud, and silty water still dripped beneath the doorframe. All that remained of the rear tire was a frayed shred on a rim; she'd driven hard even after it had blown out. But what really concerned her father were the four bullet holes in the rear quarter panel.

Looming protectively over the Miata, the ancient red Kenworth baked in the sun like a dozing dragon. Dull blue flames encircled the front end. The cloudy Lucite wind deflector on the hood read "HAZEL," the painted lettering faded from two decades of highway miles.

Over the years an assortment of creatures had perished beneath the Kenworth's tires; unfortunately, swerving and abruptly braking a loaded semi could result in more fatalities than just the animal in its path. Even considering this distressing need to stay the course, such an inordinate number of poor creatures had shown a fatal affinity for the truck that it had acquired the unsavory nickname *"RoadKill,"* along with iron grates to protect the headlights and grill. Like kills on a WWII fighter, rows of silhouettes covered the door representing numerous deer, squirrels, rabbits, raccoons, possum, skunks, and one Honda Civic.

Even if the Miata hadn't been totaled, Hazel would've preferred *RoadKill* for the task ahead. After twenty years of looking across the hood's expanse, the semi offered a reassuring sense of control and invulnerability. Granted, the door didn't lock, the ignition switch came out with the key, and the heater fan only worked when you didn't need it. Hazel saw this as character; her father argued the Kenworth was overdue for the glue factory.

The windows were already open, but the temperature in the cab still bordered on lethal. Hazel switched on the oscillating fan and pushed the perpetually drooping sun visor up, then adjusted the threadbare seat until she could press the clutch to the floor. She turned the key and pushed the starter, amused when nothing happened. No cranking, no clicking. Like she wouldn't notice her father had disconnected the ignition ground. In less than a minute, Bivalve was swallowed by the dust cloud in her rearview mirror.

Dodging potholes along the rutted dirt road that cut through the marsh, Hazel tried to ignore one detail: she had no idea what she was doing. She only knew she had to do something. But where to start? What would Travis McGee do? He'd track down Micah's friends, acquaintances and co-workers, anyone who might have seen him in the last few days. He'd ask questions, watch reactions, shake trees, and see what fell out.

Hazel leaned forward and lifted the hair off her back, but the hot air blasting into the cab offered little relief. *RoadKill* rattled and hopped; she glanced at the speedometer and eased back. With no load over the fifth wheel, the drive wheels tended to bounce, and airborne wheels didn't brake very well. Driving 450 horses of diesel with limited stopping power required a degree of care. She had to focus.

Just past the Maurice River Bridge, a dark shape plodded across the baking asphalt. Hazel switched on the engine brake and backed off the throttle; *RoadKill* clattered loudly, the diesel's compression strokes slowing the truck. Hazard lights flashing, she blocked the lane so passing sand quarry trucks would have to swing around her, then set the parking brakes with a loud hiss.

The mud turtle eyed her with suspicion as she climbed down, then retracted its head and feet. Hazel scooped it up from the double yellow lines, stepping back against *RoadKill* as a Mack rumbled past.

"You realize this is one reason you guys are endangered." She tilted the turtle, studying its markings and wondering where it was headed with such determination. It blinked out at her as she checked for traffic and trotted across the road.

"Flat pavement equals flat turtle." She placed it in the weeds on the riverbank. "Stay out of the road."

With luck it would forever associate asphalt with bad experiences, avoiding roads in the future. Back in the truck, she flipped on the radio as she double-clutched through the gears, cranking up Shooter Jennings' "4th of July" so loud she couldn't hear herself think or sing, which was just as well on both counts.

First stop was Micah's job: Nelson's Appliance & Electronics in Millville. Hazel had checked there two days back when Micah's absence still fell into the "typical behavior" category, but his friend Keith was on the road and the girls in the office had no useful information to offer.

Millville was a bustling hub of highways, strip malls, fast food franchises, car dealerships, and discount stores twenty minutes north of Bivalve and a half century ahead in time. Of the three Nelson's Appliance stores, the Millville location was the oldest and most neglected. The Trenton site was larger and flashier, and, according to Micah, the new superstore up north in Paramus was the grandest yet.

Hazel swung *RoadKill* through the lot and spotted two vehicles in the employee spaces: a silver Jeep Cherokee with a surf fishing rig mounted to the front bumper and a gleaming navy F350 pickup with a chrome boat propeller hitch cover. Micah's old green Reliant was visibly absent, but her heart jumped when she spotted the white International 4200 delivery truck he usually drove backed to the loading dock, the "SER" peeling, leaving "VICE BUILDS SALES" painted below the Nelson logo. Micah's "HORN BROKE, WATCH FOR FINGER" bumper sticker had been partially covered by one reading: "JOHN 3:16."

Keith Riley stepped around the International as she pulled alongside. Sweat trickled down his neck and molded his T-shirt to his broad, muscular frame. He glanced toward the showroom then strode over, concern in his soft green eyes, a chewed toothpick in the corner of his mouth. Hazel set the brakes, killed the engine, and climbed down.

"Where've you been?" Keith said. "I called last night but you didn't answer. I drove by but I didn't see your car and *Witch* was out. I didn't know what to do."

Keith's calls and visits weren't unusual. They'd dated briefly, and he was having trouble accepting it was over. But he was Micah's friend, so she'd planned to talk to him in the hope he might offer some leads.

She pulled her sticky shirt away from her skin. "You could have left a message." Most times he did: long, rambling ones pleading for her to take him back. Her dad and Joe played them for laughs if she didn't delete them first.

"Not this time." Keith straightened the silver crucifix hanging around his neck. "It's about Micah. Have you seen him?"

"He hasn't called and he doesn't answer his cell." She decided against mentioning *Tuition*'s disappearance, her being shot at and run off the road, or how some sadist had come hunting for Micah last night. "I'm worried he's in trouble."

"So am I." He moved closer and lowered his voice. "But I'm more worried about you. Thank God you're all right."

"Why wouldn't I be?" Her neck prickled. "Do you know what's going on with Micah?"

"I'd rather talk to your father."

"Keith, if you have something to say, say it."

"It's about Atkins." Disgust crossed his face, as though the words alone tasted foul.

Hazel didn't know much about Wayne Atkins, another of the Nelson Appliance drivers; what little she did she'd learned secondhand. He'd never bothered her, seemed to keep to himself. It was no secret he liked to drink and had served time years back for assault. He had an unsettling blood-red streak through one eye, thin, stringy hair, and a noticeable lack of personal or dental hygiene. He reminded Hazel of something left on the side of the road too long, but Micah insisted he wasn't a bad guy once you got to know him. Then again, Micah would say that about Attila the Hun. Micah could see good in the worst people and brought out the best in everyone—except her father.

"What about Atkins?" Hazel asked.

"I warned Micah to stay clear of him, but you know Micah, he'll trust anyone. I told Micah I'd heard Atkins was moving cocaine. I tried to tell Micah he was putting himself in danger, and now he's gone and put you in danger too."

Was this about *drugs*? It couldn't be; Micah had more sense than that. At least she wanted to believe he did. "Who told you this?"

Keith shifted the toothpick and scanned the lot. "People talk, word gets around. Atkins and Kessler were doing business on the side and something went sour."

The pit of Hazel's stomach turned to lead, and she tried not to show it. "Who's Kessler?" After last night she knew the name only too well.

"Some buddy of Nelson's," he said. Nelson was Tom Nelson, Keith's boss. "I've only seen Kessler once or twice. He and Atkins got into it, but I couldn't hear what they said. It was obvious they were both really pissed, looked ready to kill."

Hazel had to fight to keep her voice steady. "What's that got to do with Micah?"

Again Keith checked no one was nearby. "Right after he had that go-around with Kessler, Atkins cornered Micah in the warehouse. He didn't know I was there, and he pushed Micah against the wall, yelling for him to stay out of it, saying if he didn't, he'd see just how fucked up things would get. Those were Atkins's words, not mine. He said, 'Don't make me come after you,' and if Micah didn't listen, Atkins swore he'd break both his legs. When I asked Micah what was going on, he told me to mind my own business."

"What the hell?" Hazel knew Micah liked Atkins, but he also trusted Keith. "When was this?"

"Last Saturday; the last time I saw Micah…and come to think of it, the same day Atkins quit. Then Atkins called me last night, he said he'd heard 'that little dark-haired Moran girl' dumped me and he wanted your phone number. He sounded drunk and he said with Micah gone now and you all alone, you could probably use some company, and he planned on paying you a visit." Keith's powerful hands curled to fists. "He said he had something special he wanted to show you. I called but you didn't answer, and I tried to find you but you weren't around." His voice wavered the way it did whenever he was fighting to stay calm. "Haze, I know you've been avoiding me, but I'm worried about you. There's more going on than you realize. You shouldn't be alone, not now."

"I'm not alone. I've got Dad and Joe."

"I'm just saying…I was hoping we could try again."

Was he seriously trying to use Micah's disappearance to get back together with her? She'd think he was joking, but Keith didn't joke.

"We could start over," he insisted. "Things could be different. I realize I wanted too much too fast and you weren't ready yet. I didn't mean to pressure you. If you need more time I'll wait. I don't mind."

Hazel almost laughed. With anyone else, that probably would have meant exactly what it sounded like. Not Keith. In fact, it was his chivalrous approach to dating that won her over to begin with. He was polite, respectful, and didn't even try to touch her. No, it turned out Keith set his goals for her far higher, and it wasn't until she got to know the real Keith Riley that she'd learned the truth. He was more obsessed with her eternal soul than the body housing it. His sermons on sin and damnation, pressuring her to abandon her godless ways and accept Christ as her savior, quickly grew relentless and scary. She ended it as gently as possible, stopped seeing him, and avoided his calls. Still, Keith refused to accept defeat, and if there was one thing she'd give him, he was determined.

He took her hand. "Listen. If you need me, I'll help you any way I can, no expectations, no strings. Okay?"

Before she could answer, Keith stepped back and glared as Tom Nelson Jr. strode out of the air-conditioned showroom. Gym-toned, with a flawless smile, salon hair, and matching tan, Nelson looked younger than his midforties and dripped with concentrated charm, much of it directed toward getting into the pants of women other than his wife. Micah said Nelson never wasted time on anything over thirty or under a D cup, though, which so far had kept Hazel, with her moderate endowment and intentionally awful fashion sense, happily below his libido radar.

Still, he had a habit of standing too close and touching her arm when he talked. Deliberate or otherwise, it made her skin crawl.

Nelson glared at Keith. "Isn't there something else you should be doing?"

Keith stiffened and spit the toothpick stub to the side. His opinion of his boss was about as secret as Nelson's extramarital pursuits. Keith turned to Hazel. "I'll pray for you. And for Micah."

Nelson chuckled. "Yeah, you do that."

Ignoring Nelson, Hazel offered Keith a grateful smile. She might not share his religious zeal, but she appreciated his concern.

Keith headed back to the loading dock and Nelson stepped closer, gracing Hazel with his finest showroom smile. "I saw the truck and thought it was Micah. But that's not the case, is it?" he said, moving in for the usual "friendly" caress.

Hazel shifted back, leaving his outstretched hand hovering between them. "You haven't seen him?"

"I wish. First Atkins, then Micah." Nelson's smile faded and suddenly he looked his age. "I'm down to one lousy driver, the slowest goddamned one. Keith left the radio on in the cab again last night and killed another truck battery. And today he actually managed to get lost on the Turnpike." Sweat trickled down the side of Nelson's face, darkening his shirt collar. "You see Micah, you tell him he better get the hell back here." He spun on his heel and stalked back to the cool refuge of the showroom.

Before Hazel could get back to *RoadKill*, Keith intercepted her and steered her out of view by her arm. "Haze, I'm serious. I'm really worried."

She pulled her arm free. "So am I—about Micah. Do you know where Atkins lives?"

"You actually think I'd tell you?" Keith studied her, his lips hardening into a thin, whitening line. She knew that face too well: he was growing frustrated with her. "What are you doing out alone anyways? Micah's missing, Atkins threatened him, and now he's looking for you. You're too stubborn to see you need protection. If you won't take it from me, then at least have the sense to stay with your dad!"

Hazel climbed into the cab and started *RoadKill*. "That's where I'm headed," she assured him. "Back to the boatyard, I mean. I was just grabbing soda and hoagies for my dad and Joe." And making one other stop, but she saw no reason to mention that.

I DON'T WANT TO GO THERE

Hammon's pulse rose as they approached the library, and a headache had begun to build. Libraries were public places. Public places meant the public and the public meant strangers. Hammon's well-structured life and mental well-being, both fragile at best, revolved around avoiding face-to-face contact with strangers. But Annabel adored reading, and the library provided Hammon somewhere to leave her safely occupied for a few hours.

"Please behave," he said.

"Who? Me?" Annabel grinned. "I always behave. Unless someone else starts first."

Yeah, this headache was going to be a screamer. He took a deep breath, counting to ten.

"Please, just promise," he said, trying not to sound like he was pleading, which he was.

She offered a saccharine smile. "When do I not?"

He didn't reply. There was no point. Maybe this time he could drop her off without incident. The entrance looked empty. He started in, but Annabel paused in the foyer, dripping on the carpet, scanning the shelves of donated and retired books while Hammon paced. Why did she always do that? She knew he hated standing there, so exposed.

Annabel read off a few titles, pointing out novels by Hiassen and Westlake, which he picked up for her.

Someone was approaching along the sidewalk, head down, umbrella up, dodging puddles.

"Can we go now?" Hammon said, shuffling.

The woman, a stylish thirty-something, stepped in, shaking her umbrella and making a disgusted face at the weather. Then she turned and her eyes stopped on Hammon.

She looked straight at him.

Stared.

His skin prickled. Hammon hunched down and bowed his head, wet hair falling forward, covering his face. Pulling his hat down and collar up, he fumbled with the books, which dropped to the floor. "Let's just go," he whispered, his voice breaking.

In the corner of his eye, Annabel squared her shoulders, tucked her hair back, and Hammon cringed.

"No…" he mumbled. "Please…no…"

"HEY, you!" Annabel locked eyes with the woman. "Yeah, I'm talking to you, you evil primate! Get a good look? Didn't your mother teach you it's rude to stare?"

"No…no…no…" Hammon moaned, face burning, head pounding. "Stop it! Everyone's looking at me."

Stammering, the woman backed into the closed doors, feeling around behind her for the handle. People inside turned to see the commotion as she scurried into the rain.

Triumphant, Annabel said, "See? Confront inconsideration and *voila*, the cowards flee. You don't need to be afraid of them."

"No, you make a scene and *whala*, instant chaos. This is why I can't take you to Gary's."

"No, you won't take me to Gary's because he can't deal with me and you can't deal with that."

The librarian, a petite woman with tidy gray hair, rushed over and helped Hammon collect his books from the floor. She politely avoided looking straight at him.

"Good afternoon, Mr. Hammon. Dropping Annabel off again?"

Hat down, Hammon nodded to his sneakers. "Is that okay?" he asked the carpet. "She's not a problem when I'm gone, is she?"

"If you're so worried, dear, you could take me to Gary's."

The librarian said, "Oh, Annabel is never a problem. She doesn't bother a soul, just keeps to herself and reads. If only all our patrons were as pleasant."

Annabel smirked. "I told him I'm good when he's not around, but he won't believe me."

The librarian smiled. "Don't worry, Mr. Hammon, she'll be fine. We're always delighted to have Annabel visit."

Hazel locked *RoadKill*'s brakes when she spotted the galvanized-steel mailbox marking the narrow gravel drive trailing off the county road, and the massive truck shuddered, slowing enough for Hazel to turn in. The lawn had overgrown the edges, and old tracks of previous tires led back to a weathered gray shingle house. Cats lounged beneath the porch, and assorted food and water bowls dotted freshly painted steps. Several windows had new screens.

Waves of heat radiated off Micah's rusty Reliant, parked beside a set of outside stairs that led to a second-floor entrance. An orange tabby crouched in the shadow of the trunk, below the chrome Darwin Fish and the bumper sticker: "Jesus is coming. Look busy." Grass around the tires grew long and uncrushed.

Hazel shut the engine and climbed down from *RoadKill*. Micah's landlady stepped outside, smiling with what Hazel thought was faint disappointment as she approached, her movements cautious from advanced arthritis. Hazel cut across the lawn, reaching her before she left the shade of the maple draping over the porch.

"Hi, Anita," Hazel began. "I'm sorry to bother you. I'm…"

Anita's smile warmed. "Don't be silly, dear." She held her twisted hand out in greeting. "When I heard the truck, I thought Micah was finally back."

"I guess he isn't here. When did you see him last?"

"A week ago—after midnight, actually, so Sunday morning." Anita leaned against the porch rail for support. "He was driving that new truck of yours. He worried he'd woke me, but I don't sleep much these days, not with this weather. I turned on the driveway light for him and packed him some food."

So Micah had taken *Tuition*. But why? Hazel knelt to pet the orange cat brushing her ankle. "How long did he say he'd be gone?"

"Two days, maybe three. He said he'd mow the grass when he came back." She looked across the lawn wearily. "I used to take care of things after my husband passed on. But Micah's always helping, fixing things without me even asking, fussing over me. And he gave me this silly thing before he left." She chuckled, motioning to the white plastic pendant she wore. "He worried I might have some emergency while he wasn't around, and he wanted to be sure I could get help."

Hazel tried to force a smile but she felt queasy. "Was he driving bobtail, like that?" She motioned to *RoadKill*. "Or was there a trailer?"

"Just the truck." Anita rubbed her swollen knuckles with crooked fingers. "He didn't say where he was going. He seemed hurried and didn't say much at all."

"Are you always home?"

"Oh, almost always. My friend Bea takes me out shopping and to Sunday service."

"Could I see his apartment?"

44

"Of course, dear." Anita stepped back, holding the porch rail. "I haven't been up there myself. I don't chance those stairs."

Escorted by two cats, Anita led the way across the porch. The cats stayed close but out from underfoot, as though they sensed their benefactor's frailty and didn't risk tripping her. Hazel darted around to hold the door, and they entered the slightly cooler stuffiness, where a small fan on the dining room table alternately stirred the curtains and the papers stacked on the mantle. The house was cluttered but tidy, a lifetime of traffic patterns worn into the hardwood floors and the fabric of the corduroy armchair. A faint but ripe odor lingered, and houseflies circled the ceiling.

"Pardon the smell." Anita motioned toward the kitchen dismissively. "Micah usually takes out the trash each morning." She opened the inner drawer of a secretary desk, producing a key.

"Take these inside stairs if you like." Anita nodded to a steep flight at the end of the windowless hall.

Halfway up, Hazel was hit with sickening dread as the odor intensified. Even in the dim light she could see flies speckling the door. Why hadn't she checked there sooner? Her hand was trembling, and she steadied herself, gripping the worn railing as she unlocked the sweltering apartment.

The smell of rotting flesh hit like a wall, and she struggled not to gag or panic. Closets and drawers were emptied into piles, mattresses and cushions slashed and furniture smashed. Hazel swatted flies away, covering her mouth and gagging as she stumbled through the obstacle course. She nearly cried out in relief as she discovered the source of the stench: the refrigerator stood out from the wall, unplugged, the back panel pried off, insulation torn out. The doors hung open, the contents congealed into writhing piles of maggots and mold. Choking back a wave of nausea, she closed the refrigerator and opened windows, gulping in fresh air.

Poor Anita. Who would clean up this mess? Hazel knew she couldn't take the time. She searched through the debris for clues to Micah's whereabouts, though she wondered if whoever was there before had been after more than that. Not one inch of the small apartment remained untouched. Judging by the level of destruction, the previous search must have degraded into a fit of rage. There were fist-sized holes in the walls, and Micah's computer had been smashed to pieces.

Hazel dug under the upturned bed, finding last year's college notebooks, a scattering of smut magazines, and the fossil shark's-tooth necklace she'd given Micah for his seventh birthday. There was nothing to indicate where he'd gone, what he was up to, or who'd trashed the room. If it was Kessler…well, he wouldn't be an issue anymore. But if it was Atkins, their problems were far from over.

A quick check of the phone book confirmed Wayne Atkins was, not surprisingly, unlisted. Hazel took a deep breath, instantly regretting it; she'd never get that smell out of her nose. Her throat tightened as she picked up the shark's tooth, but she reminded herself she had no time to get emotional, she had to keep it together. She closed the door behind her and headed downstairs with the tooth in hand. Anita greeted her with a cold glass of water and a concerned expression.

Hazel slipped Micah's necklace over her head, tucking it down her damp tank top. "Do you have any of his mail?"

"Right here." Anita motioned to a small stack of junk mail on the counter. No bills, nothing of significance. Hazel carried the kitchen trash bags outside and returned to Anita on the porch.

"Call the police. Tell them someone broke in upstairs." Hazel saw the alarm in Anita's expression and tried to reassure her. "By the looks of things, I doubt they'll be back. Still, is there anywhere you can go for a few days, a friend's place?"

"Oh, I couldn't leave my cats. I suppose if anyone cared to bother with me, they would have by now. And besides, I have this." She motioned to the white plastic pendant hung around her neck. "I push this button, they send in the Marines. You be careful, and when you find Micah you'll let me know, won't you?"

I DIDN'T BREAK IT

"What've I told you about working on this boat?"

Gary jumped aboard *Revenge* as Hammon reached the dock. Rain drummed relentlessly on the metal boathouse. While Hammon ducked past him to finish tying up, Gary's dogs raced down to the boat. Charger, a pit-bull/freight-train mix, skidded over to greet him with an exuberant show of high-velocity wagging. Hammon fended him off and scooped up Yodel, tucking the wiggling dachshund under his arm like a football and climbed back aboard.

Gary had opened the small cockpit freezer and was shaking his head in disgust at the melting bags of ice Hammon had packed inside in a desperate attempt to preserve his semithawed Popsicles. Freezer insulation had been torn out and compressor parts dissected beyond repair. Hammon knelt down, petting Charger while avoiding Gary's glare. Aside from Annabel, Gary was the closest Hammon came to a friend and high on the short list of people he interacted with. As black as Hammon was pale, as normal as Hammon was weird, they made for an unlikely combination.

"I asked you a question," Gary said.

"My Popsicles were melting. I just tried to fix it."

"Don't piss on my leg and tell me it's rain. I know you, Zap; you don't fix, you break. Let's try again. What were you really doing?"

"There were bugs in it," Hammon mumbled, not looking up.

"In the freezer."

Hammon scratched at his arm. "I thought there were."

"Which means, as usual, there weren't, and now we're replacing the whole damned freezer. Seriously, why are we even having this discussion?" Gary sighed. "I told you, you think there're bugs, you don't tear the boat apart. You call me, I check it out. Understand? You DO NOT touch the boat. I do. Not that I've ever found a single one."

"They're not really bugs." Hammon scratched under his sleeve.

"Yeah, I know. RFID trackers. Care to explain why anyone would want to track you?"

Hammon smiled sheepishly. "I could but then I'd have to kill you."

"*Riiiight*. From now on, you think something's bugged or whatever, you let me check."

Hammon cringed as Gary opened the cabin and waded in. Yodel burrowed enthusiastically into a pile of laundry, and Charger snuffled his way through plastic bags.

"Christ, Zap." Gary looked around. "You could've built two boats with what you spent restoring this barge, and then—No!" He grabbed Charger, prying a shriveled pizza crust from the dog's mouth. He scanned the disaster area. "Look at this mess." His eyes stopped on the game of Scrabble in progress and two PlayStation controllers. He took a deep breath. "Are you seeing Annabel again?"

"No. She's gone." Gone to the library. It wasn't lying, really, just avoiding another of Gary's lectures on him needing his head examined.

"So you're just playing with yourself again."

Hammon picked at a scab on his arm. "Yep."

Squeezing his eyes shut, Gary rubbed his temples.

"Headache?" Hammon said.

"You could put it that way. What's with the scratching?"

Hammon shoved his hand in his pocket. "Bug bites."

Gary's eyes narrowed.

"Normal bugs. Mosquitoes, no-see-ums. Things that go *squish.*"

Gary studied him and shook his head. Hammon didn't mind Gary's scrutiny. He wasn't looking at the scars but the idiot beneath them. Pete and Freddy climbed aboard, joking around in Spanish as they began removing the freezer. Hammon was cool with Gary's Ecuadorian crew, too; he'd known them so long they were more like family and long past staring. At Gary's shop and boathouse, he was safe. Strangers weren't allowed inside Turner Speed. These were friends. Charger circled the cabin then started retching, and Gary got a queasy look. "You think that mutt'd learn." He picked up a note taped to the console, stating: "FUEL THINGY BROKEN."

"I didn't do it."

"So you keep telling me."

"Sometimes things just break on their own," Hammon insisted.

Charger expelled some half-chewed Cheez-Its onto a dirty towel, and Gary looked ill. "You're cleaning that up," he said, turning away. "I'll have the new fuel sender Wednesday. How're you on fuel?"

Hammon collected up the barf-covered towel, shoving it into a plastic bag. "It still says full, no matter what."

"No shit. I mean, how much have you got left?" Gary picked up Yodel and climbed off with Hammon and Charger close behind. "You should be getting low. Run it down a little more. The less I have to pump out, the better."

Gary walked into the front office, depositing Yodel on the floor and nudging a calico cat off the desk. A large tabby sauntered through the doggie door connecting Gary's apartment to the shop. Hammon lifted a black cat, scratching behind its snipped left ear, the fur soft beneath his fingers. He glanced at the PLEASE DON'T FEED THE STRAYS sign over the door. "This guy's new."

"That's Sirius. I swear I don't know how they find this place."

Hammon placed the cat by the bowls of Friskies lining the counter. "You didn't see the write-up in the cruising guide? Turner Speed, full-service facility. Engine repair, cat chow, litter boxes, Havahart traps, free spay and neuter." Hammon looked at Charger, already settled on the couch, his head dangling over the edge, a one-eyed ginger tabby nested on his back and Yodel using his rump as a pillow. "You'd think the dogs would scare them off."

"Didn't work with you."

"I'm just glad you didn't drag me to the vet to get me snipped and microchipped."

The odds her absence went unnoticed were slim to none, so sneaking back was pointless. Even with the engine brake off, *RoadKill* moved with all the subtlety of an irritable T. rex. The exhaust stacks did little to muffle the downshifting diesel as Hazel rumbled into the boatyard, skidded sideways, and came to a rest in a cloud of dust. She gunned the engine, and crushed oyster shells shot out from beneath the tires, pelting everything for twenty feet as the truck rattled backwards and stopped precisely between her car and the Travelift with inches to spare. *RoadKill* idled as Hazel set the brakes with a loud hiss, then the collection of noise fell silent.

She climbed out with the boat-bag of alibis and peace offerings she'd picked up on the way back—deli sandwiches, cold sodas, chips—and scanned the lot. Joe's Harley was where she last saw it, parked in the shade, and the storage shed remained closed. Her father had taken Joe's old Buick wagon that morning, and it was nowhere to be seen. That was either very good or extremely bad, and lately bad was the rule.

Throughout the drive back, she'd mentally rehearsed what she planned to say. She could already hear her father ripping into her, but she had to tell him what she'd learned, though after the last few nights, she knew it wouldn't go over well.

Hazel reached behind the Miata's seat as she passed it, retrieving the bag containing her previous excuse for driving into town and the one thing her father wouldn't question, argue, or volunteer to pick up: a box of tampons. After thirty-six hours beneath the river, the miniature drowning victims had burst free of their box, bloating into forty soggy bundles with blue string tails. Hazel regarded them, contemplating their premature demise, when the shed door behind her creaked. She jumped and spun around, dropping the tampons.

"Thought you beat me back, eh?"

Her father stepped from the shadows, and by the tightness of his features, she knew he was livid. Joe remained inside, standing between the blue Buick and the biodiesel still, looking uncomfortable with more than just the heat.

"Did I not make myself one hundred percent clear?" His voice carried across the empty yard. "Damnit, Haze, I'm not just saying this to hear myself talk. I didn't want you going out, no less racing around in this rolling violation. I won't even mention what it'd do to our insurance if you got a ticket."

"Actually, you just did." As per his usual rant, as if she'd ever received even a single ticket.

"What do I have to do? Pull the goddamned starter? I can't believe you got this thing running. And you," his wrath shifted to Joe, "didn't even notice. Damnit. I said keep an eye on her while I was gone."

Hazel fiddled with her ring as her father paced, fists clenched. Trapped in his disapproving glare, everything she'd planned to tell him evaporated.

"When I say something it's for a reason," he continued. "What the hell is your problem? Do you deliberately try to be difficult or do you just not think? I figured after last night you'd listen. Didn't you see those bullet holes? That tire," he slammed the side of his fist down on the Miata's silty windshield and the glass crackled, sinking inward, "was *shot* out. *RoadKill* just makes a bigger target." His eyes paused on the shark's tooth around her neck. "You think I don't know what's going on."

"You don't! Micah's missing. He's not answering his phone, and I can't find him anywhere. I think he's in trouble."

"And so are you, as usual, thanks to him."

Hazel stood her ground, ignoring the sun's heat and her father's withering look. "REAL trouble, I mean. Micah took *Tuition*."

"Really? Figured that all by yourself? Nice work, Travis. I'm impressed. But you better consult your little detective guides. The word isn't 'took,' it's 'stole.' Now cut the crap and stop playing private investigator before you get hurt."

Her cheeks burned and she stared down. He didn't get it. He'd never even read those books. Travis wasn't a detective. He was a 'salvage consultant,' which meant he'd recover anything of value from which the rightful owner had been wrongfully deprived and held no hope of recovering, usually for a fee of fifty percent. But Hazel didn't want to be like Travis McGee, not in the literal sense. True, her fictional hero's instincts were sharp, his reflexes sharper. Even when he made mistakes or miscalculations, he always managed to come out on top. But in nearly every story, odds were high someone Travis cared for would meet with a tragic, violent, untimely end, which was precisely what she wanted to avoid. "Someone had to do something, and I knew you wouldn't."

"Is that what you think? Just because I don't tell you everything I'm up to doesn't mean I wasn't out looking for that little shit. Or maybe you hoped you'd find him before I did."

He had her there, and they both knew it. "Well, I found out more about my visitor last night." That stopped him. His voice ominously low, he said, "I'm listening."

She swallowed and forged ahead, explaining all she'd learned regarding Kessler and Atkins. She didn't think her father could get any more pissed than he already was, but apparently she was wrong. He looked like he wanted to rip the hood off the Miata.

"So Micah figured he'd use our truck to make some quick cash," he said, too softly.

"You don't know that."

"It sure looks that way. Typical Micah shit. Last night—"

"Nothing happened," Joe interrupted softly, stepping between them. "If Micah's in trouble, it's his problem. We don't want you winding up hurt, in prison, or both. Trust me, kiddo, I've been there, and it ain't pretty."

"But Micah wouldn't…" she protested, feeling her eyes start to burn.

"Micah wouldn't want anything happening to you either," Joe said. "Let us take care of Micah."

"But…" She turned toward the water, determined not to let them see her cry, and her voice died in her throat. Docked behind *Witch*, a low black powerboat sat like a menacing shadow. It was the sort of thing built purely for speed, though usually those boats were tarted up with colors and graphics louder than their engines. Not this one. It was absolute black. It was the absence of all color. If Darth Vader had a boat, it would look like that. And Darth Vader had no reason to visit Bivalve, New Jersey.

"What's that and why is it here?" Hazel looked from her father and Joe to the strange boat. After the last few days, anything unusual was suspect, and around Bivalve, that boat qualified as highly unusual.

Her father sighed. "That's the one we're hauling north today. The Stevenson boat. He said he'd be here by two."

"Today? We can't do that TODAY."

"I didn't exactly plan for today to be *today* when we scheduled." He rubbed his face. "Let's take care of this, then we'll talk. Stevenson's probably waiting at the office."

"Why do we have to truck it north? It got here under its own power just fine."

"We're not in business to ask why people want their boats moved, just to move them."

"I'm just saying—"

"I know exactly what you're saying. Give it a rest. We have work to do." He looked from *RoadKill* to her, regarding her wrinkled tank top and oversized hand-me-down jeans, belted in at the waist and rolled at the bottom. "And could you for once not look like you dressed from the Salvation Army? We need this job, but we're not that broke."

I FORGOT

"Hey, Zap," Freddy yelled into the office. "July third, Englishtown. You're driving, right?"

Hammon looked up at the Snap-on calendar over Gary's desk in dismay while the well-oiled Miss July smiled back cheerfully as she pretended to torque a carburetor. "Next weekend?"

Turner Speed built fast cars and fast boats, though Gary's true passion was his street-legal drag racers. Gary could build them but hesitated when it came to pushing his masterpieces at the track, which wasn't a winning strategy. When they discovered Hammon had the timing, finesse, and talent, Gary's cars began taking prizes. For Hammon the track fell into the "safe" category: concealed within his helmet and fire suit, he became invisible, visually and electromagnetically. But the true secret to his success, aside from Gary's fine engineering, was simple: he'd already survived burning, asphyxiation, overdosing, drowning, and a bolt of lightning. Hammon didn't fear death in a normal, rational sense. Neurosis, paranoia, and social anxiety dictated much of his existence, but behind the wheel he was invulnerable. Unfortunately Annabel didn't share his optimism, and that in turn generated constant friction between them.

"You forgot, didn't you?" Gary narrowed his eyes. "Yeah, he's driving," he called out to Freddy, "or his Popsicles melt."

"Hell yeah," Hammon mumbled.

"We're running the Fairmont," Gary said, watching for a reaction.

Hammon nodded impassively. "'Kay."

Then he hiccupped.

Gary groaned. "Tell me it's in one piece and running, right? No bug hunts, right?"

"No. It's running great." That much was true.

"Then what?" Gary lowered his voice. "Tell me there're no freakin' surprises I don't want to know about."

Hammon choked back another hiccup.

Looking heavenward, Gary sighed. "I'm being punished for some past-life fuckup, right?" He turned to Hammon. "Put it this way. I expect the Fairmont here Thursday, cleaned up, fueled up, running fine, and smelling like roses, or I'll see to it the only way that floating dump of yours moves is with a towline. Comprende?"

Hammon hiccupped. "Can't we drive something else?"

"No. Let me guess. It's up by he-who-must-not-be-named's place, isn't it? I could give him a call."

The taste of chocolate and Peeps rose in Hammon's throat. "It'll be here."

"Hey, Zap," Pete yelled, "you bringing that hot little girlfriend? We'd all love to see her."

Gary's face twisted and he stormed out to them in the shop with Charger, Yodel, and Hammon on his heels.

"What?" Freddy was snickering. "We like having Annabel around. She makes things in-te-res-ting."

"Cut the crap," Gary warned. "We went over this. We don't discuss *her*."

"She's gone, anyway," Hammon said, trying to cool things before they escalated.

Pete's grin faded and Freddy sobered up.

"Gone?" Freddy asked. "No way."

"Serious?" Pete said. "I thought you two were inseparable."

Hammon nodded, eyes tearing as he choked back a hiccup.

"Damn." Pete shook his head. "She was cool. You two made a good couple."

"Don't encourage him," Gary snapped, glaring at Pete.

"What? The kid was happy. She was good for him. Don't listen to Gary. He's just jealous cause he can't keep a girlfriend."

"Knock it off," Gary growled.

Pete ignored him. "Hey, Zap, isn't she how you met Gary to begin with?"

Gary stalked off in disgust, ignoring the laughter echoing through the shop.

If things weren't bad enough, Dave Pierce was in the office, leaning over the pool table and smirking to himself as Hazel trailed behind Joe and her father. Joe rented the shop in back, but the front office was a public place, open to anyone renting a dock, and that, unfortunately, included Pierce. Hazel didn't know the fellow with him, though judging by his stained Rheingold Beer T-shirt and frayed cutoffs she doubted he owned the black boat, or much else for that matter. While his pal lined up a shot, Pierce appraised Hazel, the corner of his mouth curling lewdly.

At twenty-six, Pierce was fit and undeniably handsome, with an arrogant swagger that came from getting his way too easy and too often. Hazel had hated him ever since she was eight and found him testing the theory that seagulls couldn't burp. On the surface it sounded harmless and amusing, though the truth was far more sinister. He was tossing gulls Alka-Seltzers wrapped in bread with the expectation that they would literally explode, or at least die agonizing, horrible deaths. Fortunately Pierce's potentially sadistic experiment proved that not only could seagulls expel gas, but upon ingestion would foam at the beak and empty the contents of their stomachs midflight. That day Micah explained the concept of Karma to Hazel as Pierce, covered in fizzing fish guts, stood cursing.

Unfortunately Pierce's nature never changed. After the time he tried to rape her, it was her word against his. Beyond her family and Joe, no one believed she'd stabbed him in self-defense; everyone else bought Pierce's claims that she'd inexplicably attacked him. Most people concluded she might be dangerously unstable, which at least kept them at a comfortable distance. Pierce was different though: he seemed to take a perverse pleasure in lingering nearby, almost taunting. He knew better than to push it too far, though; if she didn't kill him, her father or Joe would.

Hazel gave the room a quick scan, and saw no one else but Pierce and his buddy. Stevenson was probably waiting down by the docks.

"This Stevenson guy isn't even here," she said to her father. "Can we go now?"

She turned to leave and walked straight into a large, somewhat heavyset blond-haired man standing in the doorway. He flashed a broad smile, and Hazel backed away, a chilling déjà vu washing over her as his pale gold eyes locked on hers.

Her father looked from Hazel to the stranger. "Stevenson?"

He nodded. "Ian Moran?"

"Yeah." Her father shook his hand and studied him intently. "Why do I feel like I've seen you before?"

Stevenson said nothing but watched Hazel.

"Cape May," she said. "The Topaz delivery last Monday." It was the day after *Tuition* vanished, so instead they drove *RoadKill*. She remembered how the blond stranger watched her maneuver the truck toward the lift, his distinctive eyes studying her in an unsettling way.

"Exactly," Stevenson said, his expression unreadable. "Cape May. The yard manager gave me your name."

Hazel knew it was paranoid, but in light of recent events, she couldn't shake the feeling she was the reason Stevenson was there. She studied him warily while he discussed arrangements with her father. He wanted the boat hauled back and forth to his mechanic, paying extra for the additional days involved. They could stay in his house, only a half hour from Manhattan, he said. They could use the pool and tennis courts. Take in a Broadway show or two, he suggested. He could get them any tickets they wanted.

Hazel leaned toward Joe. "Does he need a boat hauled or is he selling timeshares?"

Her father shot her a dirty look, but Stevenson chuckled. It really wasn't that funny. There was something about him she didn't trust. He spoke with her father but kept studying Hazel with a strange, unnerving expression. He said the engines were stalling under load and he wanted the boat hauled to north Jersey but the shop was in Manasquan. He claimed the problem started in Cape May, but instead of having the boat picked up there, he'd brought it to Bivalve. If he was having problems, why didn't he have them haul it from Cape May?

"Dad." She tugged her father's sleeve. "We need to talk."

"Oh, trust me, we will."

"No. I mean NOW."

Her father turned to Stevenson. "Sorry. Give me a minute."

Stevenson smiled with patient, weary understanding, and Hazel's dislike for him grew. Her father followed her into Joe's shop.

"We can't do it." She lowered her voice as the door closed behind them. "Say *RoadKill's* not running right. Blame me, I don't care. We can't leave, not now."

"You're right. WE can't. YOU can. It's an easy job with no oversize or out-of-state permits. We'll load the boat, and you're taking it north."

"Me? Alone? I thought you didn't want me driving around alone."

"Cut the shit already. You know damned well what I meant: alone around here. And you won't be. You'll have Stevenson for company. He needs a lift."

"You can't be serious!"

"Trust me, I'm dead serious. You've done tougher runs than this alone. I was talking with the manager in Cape May the other day, said he's known Stevenson for years and speaks very highly of him. You won't have any problems. You'll be at the wheel with his expensive toy in tow. If anything, I should warn him to raise his life insurance."

He took a slow breath. "You want to be treated like a business partner, start acting like one. Without *Tuition* around, *RoadKill* is going to need new tires, brakes, and I don't like the way the tranny feels. We need this job now more than ever. You want me to help Micah, fine; Joe and I'll go pay Atkins a visit. But not while you're here. It's not open for debate."

"This totally sucks." Hazel spun around, stalked out of the shop and straight past the audience in the office, slamming the door behind her as she headed down to the docks. The sun glared off the water, amplifying the heat. Hazel lifted her hair up from where it stuck to her back and studied the sky. A cold front was moving in and when it hit, it would hit hard. Restless and aggravated, she walked down the dock to check *Kindling*'s lines were secure.

When they were small, she and Micah played in the ancient runabout, traveling the world without moving from the same mud-bound bank where the boat sat abandoned. At the time she believed *Kindling*, as her father called her treasure, was French for "beautiful boat." With great amounts of Git Rot, caulking, Marine Tex, plundered parts, and determination, they restored *Kindling* to reasonable buoyancy and function. A decade later the little boat remained sound, dry, and reliable. Hazel reset the bilge pump counter and tested the float switch. As she climbed to the dock, a passing gull swooped low, dropping a splattered embellishment across the windshield.

Hazel nodded. "That about sums it up."

She turned on the hose, rinsing away the gull's commentary. The sun baked down, and heat from the dock rose through her sneakers. Water sprayed back from the broken nozzle, soaking her with a hot mist that gradually began to run cool, and she stood for a moment under the refreshing spray, studying Stevenson's boat. The low, narrow, deep-vee hull was clearly built for one purpose: speed. No ports, rails, or hatches broke the streamline flow of the forward deck, from the sharply pointed bow straight back to a low-angled wraparound windscreen. The cockpit was strictly functional, with basic, unupholstered plastic racing seats. Off the stern massive exhausts flanked a pair of equally intimidating surface drives, the razor-sharp five-bladed stainless props mere inches beneath the water. If she didn't know any better, she'd swear it was designed for running drugs, and she recalled Keith's comment about Atkins trafficking cocaine.

The dock shook and Hazel turned, expecting her father. Instead, Stevenson stood between her and *Witch*, lighting a cigarette and studying her with those creepy gold eyes. She would have let her hair fall forward, avoided eye contact, and pretended she hadn't seen him, but it was too late now. Why was he so damned interested in her? She wore no makeup, and Micah's hand-medowns were anything but flattering. Micah claimed she projected a certain vulnerability that triggered a protective instinct in some men and a predatory response in others. Either way, it made her uncomfortable and she looked down, only to realize her tank top was pasted to her as if she were a wet T-shirt finalist. Just great. And she was supposed to drive with that guy in the cab? She dropped the hose and started toward shore. Stevenson shifted, blocking the narrow dock.

"Excuse me," she said, fingernails digging into her palms.

Stevenson only took a slow drag on his cigarette. He looked as though he wanted to say something but instead continued to study her, eyes narrowing as they fixed on her ring. She shoved her hand into her pocket.

"Move," she said, meaning to sound more forceful than nervous.

He took another drag, and his eyes drifted across her. He appeared to be her father's age and roughly an inch or two taller, which set him around six foot three, and he moved with casual, imposing confidence. But up close, Hazel noticed beneath his perfectly tailored clothes he was sweating profusely and carried a layer of padding over an athletic physique gone soft.

Despite her request, he hadn't budged one inch and she was really getting sick of him staring at her. She picked up the hose again, turned the nozzle as if to continue washing *Kindling*, and not-so-accidentally shot an arc of water his direction. Ignoring the burst of spray, he pressed his heel on the length of hose running past him, grinning as her expression dropped with the pressure. He regarded the wet cigarette dangling between his index finger and thumb with amusement.

"That wasn't very nice," he said.

Anger displaced uneasiness. "It wasn't meant to be."

His eyes lit with satisfaction. "The listing in the phone book says 'courteous service.'"

"That's an old ad."

"I see that." The corner of his mouth curled slightly.

This was going to be a long drive. Hazel glanced up at the office again, relieved to see her father heading down. It was about time. She shut the nozzle. "If you'll excuse me, I need to speak with my dad."

With a gracious bow, he stepped aside, and she marched past, ignoring his delighted expression. Vile creep.

"Making new friends?" her father asked as she followed him aboard *Witch*, heading below.

"I don't like him. He's messing with me, and he looks at me weird."

"You *are* weird. And soaked," he pointed out. She glanced down self-consciously, color rising in her face, and he sighed. "Do you want me to find Micah, or is there going to be a problem? Tell me now. Otherwise, get going."

"I'm sleeping in the truck." The truck with no air-conditioning and a door that didn't lock. She stalked into her cabin, changed into dry clothes, and began packing a duffle bag with enough to wear over the coming days. *Witch* rocked and she heard her father talking in the salon, likely going over things with Joe.

"So how long am I staying with creepy?" she called out.

"Could you please act civilized?" her father replied, aggravated. Good; served him right.

"Oh, I'll be on my best behavior," she said with sugary sarcasm. "I was just wondering whether I should pack this…" She stepped out holding up a pair of black lace panties and found herself face-to-face with Stevenson.

He glanced at her father. "Creepy will refrain from responding in the interests of self-preservation."

Face burning, Hazel returned to her cabin, slamming the door on their laughter. Jerks. To hell with them both.

"Hey, Miss Manners," her father called. "You ready to go?"

No, but apparently that didn't make a difference. She sulked out, avoiding eye contact with either of them. Shaking his head, her father locked up *Witch* while Stevenson boarded the black boat and started the engines, which turned over smoothly. Hazel gave her father a loaded look: the engines sounded fine.

"Just bring the trailer around." He walked to the Travelift as Stevenson guided the rumbling boat into the lowered straps. Hazel backed *RoadKill* to the trailer, locked the plate, raised the landing gear, and connected the electric and air lines, then tested the trailer's brakes. Joe snugged the Travelift straps, Stevenson shut the engines, and the boat rose into the air.

Hazel lifted the shark's-tooth pendant and rubbed the smooth fossil. She'd discovered it in the bank of a creek in Belmar. She'd always had a knack for finding things. Unaware that fossilized shark's teeth were common for that area, she believed she'd unearthed a rare treasure and bestowed it upon Micah, who'd promptly lost it. He was forever losing his keys, watch, phone, wallet, his heart, and his way. It was a running joke how many times he'd misplaced the shark's tooth over the years, but Hazel always managed to return it to him. She only hoped it was a sign she'd see him again soon.

A knock on the cab door startled her. She looked down at her father standing beside the truck.

"I was calling you." He studied her. "You okay?"

No. "Just thinking." She tucked the tooth back into her shirt.

"That what I smelled? Good. I was afraid *RoadKill* was overheating."

He waited for the inevitable comeback but she had none. He sighed. "Haze, I'll find him, I promise. Let's get this loaded and rolling." He passed her the shop keys. "Go grab the EZpass; it's in Joe's desk."

This wasn't right. She couldn't just drive away, not now. Hazel climbed down, kicking shells as she trudged across the lot and unlocked the shop. Everything was spiraling beyond her control, and she didn't know what to do. She couldn't shake the terrible feeling that if she left, she'd never return. Behind her footsteps scuffed on the linoleum; she turned to find Pierce blocking the doorway while his friend Rheingold kept watch by the window.

Pierce grinned. "Well, well. Look who we have here, all by her lonesome."

Hazel's stomach sank. Over the years, she learned if she couldn't avoid him, the best way to deal with Pierce was not to acknowledge him. She didn't want to give him the satisfaction of knowing how much the mere sight of him disgusted her or how his presence still triggered a rush of fear she'd never completely overcome. Now he had her cornered, and she couldn't ignore him or her building panic. Instinctively her hand dropped to her pocket and the razor-sharp knife clipped there.

"Don't." Pierce lifted his shirt enough to reveal a handgun he'd tucked into his jeans, right beside the scar she'd given him. "Yeah," he said, seeing the alarm in her eyes. His hand lingered by the undone top button of his fly. "You know you want it."

Rheingold gave him a look. "Cut the crap. That's not why we're here."

Since he seemed to be calling the shots, she asked Pierce's companion, "Why are you?"

"We're looking for Micah."

Of course they were, along with every other lowlife this side of Jersey. What had Micah gotten himself into?

Pierce said, "Yeah, little girl. Where's the blue-haired freak?"

Two of them, one of her. Her father and safety were just outside and across the lot, but she was trapped. She couldn't run, and even if she could find the breath to scream, no one would hear her over the Travelift.

"I don't know." Her voice sounded like someone else's. Someone scared.

"That so?" Pierce lifted the shark's tooth, fingers brushing along her breast, lingering, snickering when she flinched. "I think you know exactly where he is."

She reached to push him away, and his other hand dropped to the gun. Rheingold stepped between them, shoving Pierce back. "I said cut the crap." He gave Hazel a smile meant to be reassuring. "We just want to talk to Micah."

"I don't know where he is." And even if she did, she'd never tell them.

Rheingold's smile evaporated. "We were checking out your car before. I thought we took out a tire, but wasn't sure, the way you kept going. I'll give you, that was some damn impressive driving you did."

Rheingold continued, "I think Pierce is right. You know where Micah is. You let Micah know Kessler wants what he took, and he better return it fast if he doesn't want anything bad happening to you. And I'm sure you don't want anything bad happening to your dad because you're protecting Micah. Understand?"

Hazel looked from Pierce to Rheingold, her throat tight, her mind numb.

Rheingold nodded, satisfied. "She understands." They turned to leave.

"Wait."

Both men turned and Hazel swallowed. "My dad doesn't know where he is. But yeah, I do."

"Is that so?" Rheingold said. "Where?"

"I'll show you." She paused, her mind scrambling. She was running out of options, and once she left with Stevenson's boat, there was no telling what would happen to her father. She had to do something to protect him. She considered the axe soaking in the parts bath, but that would only create a bigger mess than she was already in. What would Travis do? She had one idea, risky as hell, but desperate times called for desperate measures. She'd never seen Rheingold around; it was likely he knew little about the local waters, and Pierce couldn't read a chart to save his life. That might just give her the upper hand. "Wait at the docks. It's easier if you follow by boat."

"See?" Rheingold smiled pleasantly as he left. "Was that so hard?"

Outside, the familiar sound of the Travelift clattered, hauling Stevenson's boat over the trailer. Life as normal. But it wasn't normal, it only looked that way on the surface. Everything was unraveling. She moved to the window, watching as Pierce and Rheingold strolled past the lift. Rheingold turned back toward the office, nodding to Hazel. She backed away from the window and bumped into Stevenson.

He smiled grimly. "We keep running into each other."

When did he come in? She'd never heard the door. Had he been there the whole time? His expression offered no clue, only that unsettling, detached scrutiny. Hazel took a deep breath, gathering herself. "What now?"

"Your father sent me. He needs the truck keys."

"Tell him I'll be right out."

Stevenson leaned against the wall, lit a cigarette, and took a long drag. "I was told not to return without you."

Hazel watched the smoke curl toward the ceiling, and she tried to think. She'd hoped to quietly slip from sight, but clearly that wasn't happening. If this was going to work, the first order of business was a diversion.

"Just a minute." She stepped into the dark shop, re-emerging with a closed cardboard box in her arms. She handed Stevenson *RoadKill's* keys. "Give these to my dad."

He eyed the box suspiciously. "What's that?"

"It's a box full of mind your own business."

He regarded the keys with immense satisfaction, closing his hand around them as though they were some sacred treasure. "My own business." He laughed as he followed her back to *RoadKill.*

Not slowing, Hazel continued past, to the far end of the lot. She checked that no one was watching, then slipped behind the Dumpster and hastily opened the box. She uncapped the two-liter bottle of gasoline she'd lifted from the shop, shoved a bottle-rocket in nose-first, and lit the extended fuse. She dropped the box into the open Dumpster then returned to *RoadKill,* climbed into the cab, and waited.

Roughly two minutes later, the first screeching whistle cut through the humid air, stopping everyone in their tracks. The gasoline ignited with a deep *FHWHOOM,* sending a flaming mushroom cloud upwards, and then the show really started rocking.

"Hazel?" Her father looked around anxiously as white sparks spewed from the Dumpster like a volcano.

"Right here," she called innocently from the truck, admiring the chaos. Contained by the Dumpster, colors frothed from the top in an impressive chain reaction, and a dense cloud of sulfur smoke spread across the lot. It was a shame Micah wasn't there. He would have appreciated the mayhem.

"Stay back!" Her father grabbed *RoadKill's* extinguisher and charged toward the pyrotechnics.

"Okay," Hazel agreed, climbing down from the cab. He didn't define how far back. The docks were back. He should have been more specific, not that it mattered. By the time the confusion sorted itself out, she'd be gone.

Kindling's outboard started with reassuring smoothness. From the boat she watched her father shouting to Joe. The Saturn rockets reached ignition, shrieking as they launched in machine-gun rapid-fire, and everyone jumped back a respectful distance. Hazel spotted Pierce's boat, still docked and puffing blue smoke as she cast off lines; by the looks of it, he was having engine trouble. She could do this, she told herself as she guided *Kindling* into the channel. She had to. Once her father was safe, she'd gladly take whatever grief he'd surely give her. Over the racket from the Dumpster, she could barely hear the rumble of her old two-stroke outboard as she pushed the throttle forward.

Out on the open water with *Kindling* on plane, skimming over the smooth swells, Hazel felt better. Shore was falling away, disappearing into the afternoon haze. Hot wind whipped through her hair, and the shaking in her hands began to settle. She was back in her element, back in control. Kindling's hull was solid and her ancient Mercury 175 hummed at peak performance. Pierce's boat, on the other hand, was forever breaking down, and Hazel knew water had rotted much of the cored hull. Beneath a shiny fiberglass exterior laid a disaster waiting to sink. She figured she'd keep just ahead of them, leading them out toward deeper water, then swing around and ram them with *Kindling's* reinforced bow, shattering their hull like a rotten egg. Then it would be her turn to ask questions while she circled just out of reach. She didn't want to consider the prospect of being shot at, but it was a risk she had to take. And if they did start shooting, she'd keep the bow up, duck low, and hope they couldn't swim and shoot straight.

The next time she looked back, she saw the one thing she hadn't counted on: *Rust*, Joe's old patrol boat, coming up fast. Way faster than *Kindling's* top speed. *Rust* meant Joe, Joe meant her father—and she knew what that meant. She pulled the throttle back, dropping to neutral and awaiting the worst. The boat settled in the water, and the stern wave caught up, lifting *Kindling* as it passed beneath.

She'd plead insanity, she decided; after the last few days, that seemed plausible and far better than explaining she'd been using herself as bait. Rather than watch their approach, she turned to the depth finder, as though it might indicate the trouble she was in. That's what she needed, a deep-shit-o-meter. Or GPS that displayed how far up Shit's Creek she presently was, less the necessary paddle.

As *Rust* drew closer, Hazel looked over, braced for her father's fury, and it took her a moment to process the unthinkable: Pierce was at the helm.

Frantically she pegged the throttle, and *Kindling* leapt forward. It was pointless; there was no outrunning *Rust*, and no ramming her, either: the steel hull would make kindling of *Kindling*. They closed in and Hazel spun the wheel. Pierce overshot and swung around. *Kindling* could turn tighter, but *Rust* could cover more water. Pierce quickly closed the gap between them, and Hazel knew there was only so long she could keep dodging.

The radio barked her name: her father's voice, more terrified than angry, calling for her. She felt a stab of guilt but was too busy to answer. *Rust* came back for another pass, sheets of water slicing away from the bow as it carved through the waves, Pierce grinning like a lunatic. She swung the wheel starboard, but the steerage had been sticking lately and it hung up a second too long. *Rust's* heavy steel bow struck *Kindling* with a ghastly, splintering sound, spinning the small boat around, throwing Hazel from the helm. She scrambled to stand, stumbling on scattered fishing tackle. Cold seawater soaked her sneakers and rose around her ankles as it rushed between the crushed planks.

Pierce idled alongside, using *Rust's* hull to further slow *Kindling* even as the outboard continued to push the damaged boat in circles. "Nice try, Hazel. I knew you were being a bit too agreeable."

Water swirled up to her knees, rising by the second. Hazel scanned the horizon. *Rust* may have been up there in years, but nothing else in the yard could move as fast as the retired patrol boat, and they both knew it.

"Plan on going down with the ship? How 'bout you be a good girl and come with us, we all go see Micah."

Hazel scrambled for the flare gun mounted beside the helm. *Kindling* sank lower, listing to the starboard.

"Get back!" She loaded the orange pistol, debating which way to fire. Despite what she'd seen in movies, signal flares didn't pack much punch. Still, Pierce might not know that, and it would probably hurt like hell. Then again, it could just as likely bounce off the target. She was better off signaling her father.

"Told you she wouldn't cooperate," Pierce said over the revving outboard. "Shoot her before she gets a signal up."

The horror of his words sank in as Rheingold raised a pistol. There was a quiet sound, and stinging burned through Hazel's shoulder. She pulled out a red-tailed plastic dart, staring at the hypodermic needle. An animal tranquilizer, likely stolen from some veterinary clinic.

"How long's it take to kick in?" asked Rheingold.

Pierce secured lines to *Kindling's* cleats, tethering the still-moving boat as it spun them in a slow circle even as it sank lower. "How should I know? Just grab the damned flare gun, we don't need the Coast Guard showing up. And shut that damned motor."

Rheingold jumped aboard the listing *Kindling*. Hazel was cornered, sickening numbness spread through her, but she still had the flare gun. She struggled to fire upward as Rheingold grabbed her hand to wrestle the gun away, and a fireball of brilliant light erupted, blinding and searing hot, striking Rheingold in the face. He flailed backwards, roaring and swatting at his burning face and clothing, then jumped overboard, extinguishing the flames. He paddled next to the sinking boat, cursing and sputtering, scrambling to pull himself aboard. Hazel's legs gave way beneath her. Rheingold was halfway over the gunwale, his singed face contorted in fury, when his grip slid and he fell backwards as the boat continued to turn. The outboard, still revving full throttle, made an awful grating sound as the prop fouled.

Pierce bellowed as he charged aboard and leaned over the transom, but by his expression it was too late. An unnatural heaviness pulled at her, and Hazel tried to stand, but her body wouldn't respond. Her father called again from the VHF, shouting for her over background noise, his voice cut off as rising water shorted *Kindling's* battery and the engine quit. Hazel's brain raced in terror, but her body was paralyzed.

"Fucking bitch," Pierce snarled.

She saw the kick coming; she couldn't even close her eyes, but felt nothing. *Kindling* sank lower and she lay there, unable to hold her breath as water rose and covered her eyes, filling her open mouth. Her vision narrowed into a tunnel of dim light, washing over her in a wave of red.

I'VE GOT TO WATCH WHAT I SAY

With the old freezer out, Gary, Hammon, and crew lowered its replacement into place. At six feet by two by two, it was intended to transport game fish, or, in Hammon's case, enough frozen burritos, White Castle Sliders, waffles, and Popsicles to go long stretches between grocery runs. While he transferred his thawing provisions to the new freezer with space to spare, he silently agonized over the coming week. The car issues were bad enough, but nothing compared to informing Annabel he'd be gone three days. He fished out a frozen Strawberry Shortcake bar, peeling back the wrapper, and offered Gary one.

"Do you eat anything besides junk?"

Hammon contemplated the bar. "It's dairy and fruit."

"Barely. You can't live on Popsicles."

"That's what Annabel—" Hammon coughed, ice cream turning to lead in his stomach. "—used to say." It almost sounded convincing, if not for the hiccup.

Gary's eyes narrowed. "I'm warning you. I hear you're so much as talking to her, I'm calling Stevenson. You might not believe me, but it's for your own good."

TIME, DATE, POSITION UNKNOWN

Hazel stood in cool grass, surrounded by headstones. It was an old cemetery, shady and tranquil, with grave markers of every shape and style bearing elaborate inscriptions; some tilted at random angles, covering the gently sloping ground. Stone angels stood with broken wings and bowed heads, their grief frozen in time. The fragrance of flowers and fresh turned earth filled the air. Parked behind her, *RoadKill* seemed conspicuously inappropriate. Her father waited beside her, concern adding years to his face. Before her lay a new grave. This place and the painful ache in her chest were familiar, but the reason for her presence eluded her. She placed a cluster of wild roses on the damp soil and tried to read the headstone.

"No." Stevenson stepped toward the grave, taking a drag on his cigarette. She studied his grim smile and empty gold eyes.

"Why are you here? You don't belong."

He turned to her father. "Cover her eyes. You don't want her seeing this."

And everything went black.

"You shouldn't be here," her father said, sounding distant. "This isn't your problem."

Stevenson gave a hollow, chilling laugh. "Actually it is. You'd better sit. We need to talk."

She cried out in the darkness but no one answered. She couldn't move, couldn't breathe, and the terrifying realization grew. The grave was hers.

I'M AN ADULT?

By the time Hammon reached the library, the rain had slacked off. He found Annabel quietly perusing a book on mental health. They checked out some mysteries without incident then headed back to *Revenge*. As they walked through the warm drizzle, she kept glancing over.

"What?" she said at last.

"What, what?"

"You're hiccupping. What aren't you telling me?"

Reluctantly he explained the upcoming weekend. It turned out he was the only one who'd forgotten, and Annabel had hoped no one would remind him. "Sure. You go to Englishtown, have your fun, and all I get is this lousy tank top."

"I thought you liked that shirt."

"That's not the point. I get left behind, thanks to Gary's issues, and spend the whole time worried sick. What do you think'll happen to me if I lose you?"

He wanted to say she'd be fine, but they both knew the truth even if they didn't discuss it. Walking down the dock, she let out a long sigh. "You're an adult. I can't stop you."

But she could and he knew it. Hammon pulled in the stern line, and they climbed aboard *Revenge*. Annabel regarded the new freezer unhappily. "Is it me, or does that thing look like a coffin?"

TIME, DATE, POSITION UNKNOWN

Awareness drifted past in fragments. Distant, fading voices, like a bad radio signal, slipped through the blackness. Hazel tried to listen, but the signal was too weak. Or she was. All she could make out was the pitiful whimpering cry of an injured animal.

She opened her eyes, gasping at a sharp pain in her side, and looked around in confusion at a distorted, unfocused world.

"Relax," the unfamiliar voice said.

What was going on? She gazed around at the bewildering shadows and struggled futilely to sit up, her nails digging into smooth fabric.

"Settle down."

There was a steady rocking and soothing rumble of throaty diesels. She smelled frying food and stale cigarette smoke. Exhausted from the dizzying blurs, she closed her eyes. Images flashed in her head. The sputtering flare, paralysis spreading, *Kindling* sinking beneath her—and Pierce.

She bolted upright, backing away. The bunk tilted and she collapsed, crying out.

"Calm down, would you? You've been drugged. It'll wear off but if you fight it, you'll only feel worse. Close your eyes and take some deep breaths."

That wasn't Pierce. Who, then? A man, speaking calm and slow, commanding but not threatening. Her confusion distracted her momentarily from her fear, and she concentrated, trying to think.

"That's it. Try to relax. You're looking a bit more alert. Are you feeling any better?"

A steady voice, deep and firm. She'd heard it before, but where? How long had she been unconscious? Then he sat down beside her, still blurry but close enough for her to recognize the unsettling gold eyes, and she made the connection. She was aboard the black boat. Were they alone? Where was her father? She tried to stand, to back away, and fell helplessly on the bunk.

"Jesus," Stevenson said. "Calm down. You were given ketamine. It's a strong tranquilizer; it'll take time to wear off."

"Where's my father?" Her throat was so dry the words came out a scratchy whisper.

"He's busy right now. You'll see him soon enough."

Her stomach twisted and tears stung in her eyes. What happened to her father and Joe? She'd heard them on the radio, but then what? Everything had gone so horribly wrong, and it was all her fault.

"Where are you taking me?" She coughed, her throat tight.

"You'll be staying with me for a bit."

Stevenson opened the cooler while Hazel scanned the sparse cabin, which contained the lone bunk she occupied and a porta-potty. The remaining space was empty, unfinished, or deliberately left bare. The only way out was past her captor.

"Pardon the lack of amenities." He uncapped a bottle, offering it to her. "This boat wasn't designed for comfort."

She didn't accept the water, and finally Stevenson put it aside. He picked up a small towel, lifting her chin to dry her face, studying her with the same eerie look as in her cemetery nightmare.

Discreetly she slid her hand down to her pocket, relieved to find her knife still there. Eyes locked on Stevenson's, she slipped her fingers through the loop of ribbon on the handle and eased the knife open, clasping it in her fist with the blade tucked flat against the underside of her wrist.

"Please." She swallowed, feeling her lip tremble, and she cautiously lowered her foot over the side of the bunk. "Let me go."

He shook his head. "I don't think so."

She stood unsteadily, staggering toward the companionway. Stevenson moved to stop her, she turned her wrist and swept out at him with the exposed blade. Stevenson jumped back, his hand pressed against his shoulder as blood spread through the fabric of his shirt. In a surprisingly restrained voice he said, "Hazel, put the knife down."

This was bad. She'd panicked and lost the element of surprise. Her coordination was off, Stevenson was twice her size, and he had her cornered in the cabin.

"Listen to me," he said, keeping his distance. "I'm not going to hurt you."

He was lying. "Who else is aboard? Where's Pierce?"

"Dead. It's just us and the autopilot." Palms up, Stevenson moved clear. "I know you're scared. But you're safe now. Understand? Your father asked me to watch you."

She took a shaky step, struggling to keep her balance. "Then where is he?"

"Dropping Pierce in deeper water." Stevenson backed into the cockpit, leaving her space. "They're heading back now. See for yourself."

Warily she followed, spotting *Rust* in the distance, returning. She couldn't tell who was aboard. Stevenson picked up the VHF mike.

"*Rust*, you read me? Over."

"Right here," her father said. "Any problems?"

With a rush of relief, Hazel grabbed for the mike. Stevenson held it back, shaking his head. "Anyone might be listening." He spoke into the mike again. "No, everything's fine. How's the fishing? Over."

"Nothing's biting. We're heading back empty. And you? Over."

Stevenson regarded Hazel. "Just one. Small, but gave me one hell of a fight. Over and out." He hung up the mike. "Now, at least wait a few minutes before you add me to the day's carnage."

Hazel braced herself against the companionway as the boat rolled while Stevenson stood clear, his hand pressed over the slash, inches from his throat. She looked around, noticing strange circles impacted into the windshield.

"Armored glass," Stevenson explained.

Hazel said nothing. *Rust* slowed, drifting alongside. Scrapes covered the white hull: streaks of paint from *Kindling* and black gel-coat. Joe rafted the boats together as her father jumped across and hugged her. Hazel buried herself in his arms. He sat her down and gently opened her fingers around the knife, closing the blade but leaving it in her hand.

Joe chuckled as he turned on the saltwater wash-down pump. "I gather our little Hazel wasn't pleased when she woke," he said. "Lucky for you she was loaded with kitty quaaludes."

"You might've warned me she was armed," Stevenson said, pulling his shirt away and trying to see his wound. It was too close to his throat.

Joe shrugged. "Never occurred to me." He began hosing out *Rust's* cockpit. Blood ran across the gray decks and through the scuppers.

Hazel turned to her father, trembling. "Dad, what's going on?"

"Other than you being grounded till you're thirty? You're safe," he said, giving her a little squeeze.

"Pierce said if I didn't tell them where Micah was, they'd go after you. I couldn't let them…"

Her father stroked her hair back from her forehead. "It's all right."

But it wasn't. Hazel crushed herself against him again, and he held her, saying nothing. Sniffling, she wiped her eyes and glanced toward Stevenson. Her father nodded. "He saw you leaving and figured something wasn't right."

"I thought he was working with Pierce."

"We noticed."

She was sweating, shivering, and nauseous. She swallowed, taking deep breaths, focusing on the horizon.

"You should eat something," Stevenson suggested. "It'll settle your stomach and clear your head."

"What happened to Pierce?" Hazel asked.

Her father said nothing but Joe grinned. "You missed all the fun, kiddo. We dumped Stevenson's boat back in the water, and damn can that thing move. You had to see Pierce's face when we overtook him. He starts firing at us, our friend here takes aim, all cool and calm. Second shot, he takes the side of Pierce's head clean off."

Stevenson didn't seem as pleased. "I wasn't looking to kill him. Corpses don't answer questions."

"They don't ask 'em either," Joe said.

Stevenson gave her father a meaningful look. "We should get moving."

Joe unhitched the boats as her father rose, guiding her into the seat. "We're going back to find Micah. Me and Joe, not you.

You're staying with Stevenson. Even if you were in any condition to help, which you're not, I won't risk you getting hurt."

"But…" Protests raced through her brain faster than she could voice them.

"But nothing. I told you, I want you somewhere safe."

"No!" Hazel looked from her father to Stevenson in horror.

"You'll be fine."

"You can't!"

"You don't know all the facts, and I don't have time to explain. You're going to listen, end of discussion." He gave her a quick hug, then jumped back to *Rust*, pushing the boats apart.

Hazel rushed to follow, panicking as they drifted farther away. "But…"

"Just trust me." Her father nodded to Joe, and *Rust* rose on plane, heading toward Bivalve.

Hazel fought back tears of frustration as she watched the receding shape. Stevenson took the boat out of neutral and pushed the throttles forward, turning east, gaining speed with ease as the diesels rumbled smoothly.

I'M NOT A STALKER

Hammon leaned over the chart table and slipped on a fresh pair of latex gloves. With meticulous care he removed a sheet of letterhead from a folder. Using tweezers he proceeded to glue down random letters cut by a razor from magazines, spelling out:

MY DEaRest BEloVe*d*,

you DoN't kNOw Me, but *I* know you And i LOVE you fro*m* tHe depths oF my heart. When I sEe your *eyes* I know you ARE TRULY looking just at Me, and I aM lost. I wANt you to SPEND The rest of your *LIFE* at My side. I keEP writing, But you NEVER ANswer. That *U*PSETs Me. you NEED to know hoW much you Mean to Me. the thought of you With anyoNe else RIPS Me apart. I wilL not stop untiL you aRe mine Com*p*letely. I Will come for you. I WILL make yOU love me. I a*w*Ait the day I can SEE YOU and touCh *y*our perFect skin and taste your t*e*ars. Then You WILL be Mine FOREVER.

Hammon scanned the letter, pleased. With surgical precision he cut lips and eyes from magazine photos, gluing them down to create a garish border. Annabel wandered over, inspecting his work.

"Disturbing."

"Really?" Hammon beamed. "But is it convincing?"

"That wasn't a compliment. And yes, very convincing. Some of those things you said to me."

"I know. It has to sound real."

"Yeah, well, out of context it just sounds sick. Don't you think that'd be upsetting to read?"

"You seriously think celebrities open their own mail? They've got people they pay to answer fans and track weirdos. I'm keeping someone employed."

"No one'd believe he'd use his own letterhead."

"Maybe. But they'll still investigate." Hammon folded the letter, tucked in a few strands of pale blond hair, eased it into one of Stevenson's letterhead envelopes, and sealed it with glue. "I'll drop this in the mail and we'll get moving."

Annabel sat on the bunk, legs curled beneath her, and sighed. Times like that she seemed much older than him, and far wiser.

"I don't want to hear it," he said.

"I didn't say a thing." She yawned and stretched, getting maximum mileage from every inch of toned skin. She lounged invitingly, her shirt riding up to reveal a slender waist and smooth belly. "Not one thing."

"Uh-huh." Hammon watched her in the corner of his eye as warmth rose in his face and a few other places. "Nice try."

"What?" she asked, the picture of innocence. Exquisite, depraved, tempting innocence.

"Distract me and my letter mysteriously vanishes."

"It would be a worthy distraction, dearest, straight out of your most twisted fantasies."

He grinned. "You've got no idea how twisted my fantasies get."

Annabel laughed. "That's what you think."

17:05 SATURDAY, JUNE 26

38°59'11.36"N/74°40'32.09"W

5.48 NM EAST OF WILDWOOD, NJ

First she tried reasoning. When that failed, Hazel resorted to tears, pleading with Stevenson to turn the boat, skimming effortlessly at thirty knots over the smooth rollers, back to Bivalve. He refused, claiming she was in no condition to help her father, and even if she was, he promised he'd keep her safe.

There was something he wasn't telling her, no matter how much he denied it. Fine. He'd had his chance; she knew what she had to do. She sulked, head down, long hair swirling around in the wind as her fingers slid along the bulkhead, unclipping the fire extinguisher while Stevenson fiddled with electronics. The bracket released, and the five-pound metal cylinder settled into her hand.

Still…he did rescue her. If not for him, she would have woken to Pierce's leering face. She scrutinized Stevenson, uncertain. Was he truly helping or were things going from bad to worse?

Stevenson glanced over. "Don't do it, princess."

"Do what?" she said innocently.

"Whatever you're thinking of doing."

"I wasn't going to do anything."

He stared ahead, a faint smirk curling in the corner of his mouth. Her grip on the extinguisher tightened.

"Right. Well, I'd advise you to hold on with both hands."

He shoved the throttles forward. The boat responded with a thunderous roar, acceleration ripping the extinguisher from her hand and slamming Hazel back into the seat. At that velocity the smooth water felt solid and the hull pounded like a bobsled over lumpy ice. Stevenson turned, eyes narrowed in the wind, his expression challenging. Moving, either to attack or retreat, was impossible. Braced in the narrow seat, she watched the GPS, horrified as their speed climbed over seventy, and she couldn't stop trembling as the world streaked past on fast-forward. Tears streamed from her eyes and whipped off her face. Speaking wasn't an option; the buffeting wind and thundering engines would suck any words away before they were heard.

At last Stevenson pulled the throttles back and shifted to neutral. He let the engines idle a minute, then shut them down. Hazel watched him uneasily as the boat settled into an uncomfortable snapping roll.

"Why'd you stop?" she said finally.

"I wanted to make sure you were all right. You looked terrified."

"Your demonstration of how well this boat runs didn't scare me," she said, her voice wavering. She glanced at the fire extinguisher, thumping across the cockpit deck as they rolled. "I want to go back."

"As I'm well aware. Now, will you be a good little hostage or do I have to tie you up?"

"What did you tell my father to make him leave me with you?"

Again, that unreadable look. He sighed. "I don't blame you for not trusting me. You've been dumped with someone you know nothing about. You suspect I'm part of the present problem and your father's trust is a serious mistake. I can appreciate that. I could try to convince you otherwise, but you'll have to come to your own conclusions."

"What do you *want*?"

Stevenson leaned back, pushing gingerly under his shirt at his wound, still bleeding but much slower now. "What do I want?" He gave a humorless laugh. "In truth, to let you get on with your life and for me to get on with mine."

For the rest of the trip Hazel didn't speak. Stevenson set the boat to a more moderate speed, swinging well offshore to avoid the coastline storms. Hazel locked herself in the cabin and changed into some of Stevenson's clean, dry clothes, which, predictably, left her looking like a shipwreck survivor. She searched for weapons, explosives, or poison, finding nothing. Reluctantly she returned to the cockpit.

By dark they reached the Narrows, then headed up past Manhattan's glittering lights, following the Hudson River north. They passed beneath the George Washington Bridge, lit with strings of white, and along the blackness of the Palisade cliffs towering over the Jersey side. The moon rose over Yonkers, huge and orange. Just past the Piermont pier, jutting a mile into the river, Stevenson slowed the boat, turning toward shore. Hazel straightened up and looked north to the Tappan Zee Bridge. At their low speed, the exhaust back-drafted over the stern with the enticing aroma of French fries—the same smell she'd noticed as she woke from the tranquilizer. "You're running on biodiesel?"

"I heard it's better for the injectors."

Mechanically and environmentally, biodiesel offered many benefits, though the trade-off was a slight decrease in speed, which she would have figured would be a higher priority for someone like Stevenson.

"This thing's pretty quiet, relatively speaking, for all this power," she said. "You realize muffling cuts performance."

"It also limits detection."

"What, for running drugs?"

"Exactly." He stretched, wincing as he moved his shoulder. "Until it was seized, at least. Friend of mine gave me a heads-up when it came up at auction. He claimed it was built to withstand gunfire, not that I thought I'd ever test that. Guess I owe him a drink."

Stevenson pulled on a black windbreaker that had been stowed beneath the console, covering his blood-stained shoulder. They idled past the seawall and up the fairway while he scanned the boats. Hazel stood back, not bothering to ready lines or assist as Stevenson maneuvered into the slip, docking skillfully while she made a point of looking unimpressed. Aboard a thirty-eight-foot Viking, a matched pair of leggy redheads emerged, waving enthusiastically.

"Hi, Jake!" they sang in harmonized unison. A robust older fellow in Topsiders, shorts, and a Hawaiian print shirt followed them above, then strolled down the dock, martini in hand.

"Evening, George," Stevenson said. "Out with the twins today, I see."

George grinned. "The girls wanted to go swimming." Drink halfway to his mouth, he paused, scrutinizing the black boat's hull. "What the hell'd you do, play chicken with a tanker?"

"DUI," Stevenson replied. "Docking Under the Influence."

George poked at the windscreen. "Are those bullet holes?"

"You watch too many police shows, George. I hit a seagull at seventy. Not pretty."

"Sounds like an eventful weekend, my friend." George turned his attention to Hazel, appraising her. She glared across and George chuckled. "Nice specimen," he said, ambling back to his boat. "But you know, when they're that small, by law you gotta throw 'em back."

Stevenson adjusted the dock lines and began closing the boat up. Hazel took a deep breath, gathering her nerve. "Mr. Stevenson, wait."

"Mr. Stevenson? Please, call me Jake."

She nodded. "Look, Jake. I'm sorry. I know I've been kind of difficult, and I realize if not for your help, things might be far worse. I want to apologize for all the trouble I've caused."

He sat back and said nothing, but by the look in his eyes, she knew he wasn't buying it.

"I mean, you've already done more than you needed to; I do appreciate it even if it may not seem that way. I just figured rather than imposing on you any further, I'd stay here on the boat tonight."

"Fine by me. You want to sleep together, who am I to argue?"

"*Together*?"

"There's only one bunk, princess, and I'm sure as hell not leaving you here alone. No, I'd rather wake tomorrow knowing you and my boat are still around." He locked the cabin and stepped off, inspecting the lines. "Now, are you coming?"

Grudgingly she climbed to the dock, marching like a condemned prisoner past rows of pricey boats. Near shore, things scaled down somewhat, ending with a row of daysailers, skiffs, and runabouts, though the parking lot was brimming with high-end cars. Stevenson unlocked a massive black Mercedes S600, opening the door for Hazel. The luxurious interior reeked of cigarette smoke, and the remains of the car radio hung from the dash by a bent bracket and wires.

"Rough neighborhood?" she said.

Stevenson seemed weirdly amused. "Doodle-dee-dah-dee-dah-doe-doe," he chanted softly. "Doodle-dee-dah-dee-dah-doe."

It reminded Hazel of something Micah had on his computer, where animated hamsters danced to an amusingly irritating melody. She couldn't imagine how that tied to the vandalized car and decided against asking. Instead, she stared out silently as Stevenson pulled out of the marina.

Brick buildings converted to cafés and boutiques lined Piermont's narrow main street, retaining their charm in a way that drew the stylish to shop and dine on the warm summer night. Antique sports cars and pricey sedans crowded every available parking space, and strolling couples wandered the sidewalks. Under better circumstances it might have been pleasant; at present it only underscored the feeling that she didn't belong.

A half mile beyond town, Stevenson turned up a winding hill, passed several Victorian houses, and stopped before a pair of massive, rusted iron gates. Bathed in the cool white of the high beams, they opened ominously. Low branches scraped like fingers along the windows as Stevenson guided the Mercedes up a narrow drive.

Ahead, the unlit form of a Federal colonial, dark and forbidding, took shape in the moonlight. Vines snaked across the power lines and engulfed one corner of the house. In the beams of the headlights, weeds sprang from cracks in the drive and a dead tree stood to the side, bark peeling in chunks. Long strips of toilet paper hung from the branches, swaying in the damp breeze like ghostly Spanish moss. The lawn had grown so tall it collapsed on itself in places, and bushes obscured windows, yet even the neglected landscape couldn't diminish the classic architecture.

"You live *here*?" Hazel said.

"Timeshares are still available if you're interested." He pulled into a carriage house, parking beside a black Viper roadster, a tired white Mustang convertible, and a gleaming yellow Chevelle. Hazel scanned the cars, assessing her best means for escape. Sooner or later Stevenson had to sleep, and when he did, she'd be out of there. It was just a matter of time.

Driven by morbid curiosity, she followed him into the dark house, which looked as though it had been vacant for the last century. Moonlight slanted through the windows, stretching in pale rectangles across the entry foyer, and a broad staircase spiraled up three stories. Off the main hall, the surrounding rooms were filled with sheet-draped furniture like something from a gothic horror. Hazel paused before what might have been an ornately framed mirror, only the beveled glass was a void of blackness. Within the hall a cricket chirped softly, echoing through the open space.

"You actually live here? For real?"

Stevenson led her into an ancient but functional kitchen, the first room with any evidence of regular use. "Define live." He switched on the light and dropped his keys and wallet on the counter.

The light shut off. Flickered on. Off. On. Off.

Stevenson grumbled, reaching up, tapping the unresponsive bulb. In darkness he located a fresh bulb from the closet and replaced the dead one. Illumination returned. Shaking the old bulb, he tossed it into the trash, where it landed with an implosive pop.

The room went dark. Then light. Dark. Light. Dark. A cricket chirped.

"Son of a bitch."

He flipped the switch several times in a row, and finally the light remained on. Stevenson retrieved a half-empty bottle of scotch from the cabinet, poured himself a sizeable portion, and lit a cigarette. "Would you like something to eat?"

"I'm not hungry," she lied. "I'd like to sleep." And get the hell out of there, not in that order.

Stevenson leaned against the counter and downed the scotch. "Yeah, it's been a long day." He checked his cell phone. "I'm sure there's a perfectly good reason why your father hasn't called."

Or a really bad one, Hazel decided.

Stevenson guided Hazel up a narrow flight of stairs leading from the kitchen to the bedrooms, of which she had a choice. All were furnished with sheet-draped antiques, from the large, grand rooms to the smaller servant's quarters, and all were unoccupied, save one.

"My room." Stevenson pointed to a door at the far end of the hall, just off the main staircase. "I'll have the TV on. If it's too loud, let me know. I can't sleep when it's quiet, but I'll probably be out cold. You need me, just knock."

"No one else lives here?"

"Just me and the crickets."

I'M HAVING FUN NOW

"According to NOAA Weather," Annabel said, "warm, unstable air over coastal waters will produce scattered thunderstorms and small craft advisories."

Hammon switched the VHF back to Channel 16. "Small craft suggestions." He eased *Revenge* away from the dock. The boat was designed specifically to handle pounding waves and high winds, and Hammon found the conditions entertaining. Annabel manned the helm for the first hour, keeping them on an accurate, steady course. When things really began to kick up, Hammon took over, but Annabel stayed above with him and watched the towering anvil clouds off the west flash spectacularly.

Hammon maintained a love/hate relationship with lightning. On the positive side, it thoroughly screwed up low-grade radio waves, disrupting their invisible messages. However, he knew firsthand that being on the receiving end of a direct hit wasn't amusing, and he'd equipped *Revenge* with the best lightning protection money could buy. Annabel's navigation steered them clear of the thunderheads as they moved north.

01:15 SUNDAY, JUNE 27

41°01'48.76"N/73°55'09.91"W

PIERMONT, NY

For twenty minutes Hazel waited in the darkness, anxiously following the luminous hands on her watch. Her father had twenty
minutes to call and tell her Micah was safe and they were coming
for her. That was all she would wait, not a minute longer. Twenty
unbearable minutes that passed without a word.

Enough was enough; it was time to move. Heart pounding,
she slipped into the hall. Blue light flickered beneath Stevenson's
door, TV voices chattered happily, and a single cricket serenaded,
but Hazel heard no human movement. Cautiously she turned the
knob, easing the door open the slightest bit and peeking inside.
Still dressed, Stevenson lay sprawled across the bed, breathing
steady and slow. A cigarette burned down to a smoldering stub in
the ashtray on the nightstand while a commercial touted exercise
equipment.

"Mr. Stevenson…?" Hazel held her breath, waiting. There was
no response.

Guided by slivers of moonlight, she padded down to the
kitchen, grabbed a flashlight, all the keys, and cash from Stevenson's wallet for fuel and emergencies. She made her way to the car-

riage house and inspected the cars. The Viper was a manual, but too conspicuous. The Mercedes and Chevelle were automatics. The faded Mustang convertible was the odd one out: a bottom-of-the-line six-cylinder base model, but with a manual transmission and the hill, she could roll halfway to town before she'd need to start the engine. She turned the ignition just enough to unlock the steering wheel, lower the roof, and power the gauges, which confirmed a full tank and charged battery. She yanked spark-plug wires from the other three, tossing them into the Mustang. In neutral, she released the brake and pushed the car outward, hopping in as it rolled. She glided into the moonlight with only the sound of the tires crunching over the driveway, building speed as she rounded the house, heading straight toward the iron gates.

The closed iron gates.

She stood on the brakes, skidding to a stop inches from impact.

Stevenson stepped from the shadows. He leaned against the front fender.

"I'm surprised. I figured you'd go for the Viper."

She eased the transmission into reverse, then turned the key. The starter grabbed, the Mustang jolted five feet backwards, and Stevenson fell between the nose and the gate. She slammed into first, revving the engine, creeping forward. Stevenson scrambled clear.

"Cute." He dusted himself off.

"I'm leaving. Open the gate, or I'll open it with this car."

"Like hell you will." In three steps he was beside the door. He reached across, shutting the engine, then grabbed her arm, hauling her up and dragging her from the car, pinning her against the fender. Cursing, she struggled while he held her wrists.

"You are determined," he said coldly, "but not as capable as you want to believe."

"Let me go! You're hurting me!"

"Exactly my point." He released her and she bolted clear of his reach. "You don't trust me, and I can't trust you. It's going to be a long night."

"Fuck you."

"Is that an offer? It would pass the time."

She wanted to hit him, but it would be pointless. She considered running, but that iron fence might enclose the entire property, and she didn't want to give him an excuse to chase her down. How far could she get on foot anyways? She rubbed her wrists. "Go to hell."

Stevenson smiled. "I figured as much."

"What did you say to my father? Why'd he leave me with you? What aren't you telling me?" she said, her voice breaking in frustration.

"Amazing. You won't accept that I'm just trying to help." Stevenson lit a cigarette and leaned on the gate.

"No. I want to know why."

That seemed to amuse him. "How about this. You tell me. Guess right, you win a prize. Actually, you win a prize, right or wrong."

"What's that supposed to mean?"

He turned toward the sky and took a slow drag. "Nothing. Nothing at all."

Hazel watched him, torn between the desire to pick up a rock and bludgeon him or curl up in a ball and cry. Maybe if she wasn't so tired, she could think. She had to do something; she couldn't just stand there in the damp grass all night. Tears slipped down her face, but Hazel didn't move or make a sound as thick clouds covered the moon and blotted out the silvery light. Nearby, she heard a soft, determined buzzing, like a fly trapped in a spider's web.

Stevenson flipped his phone open. "Yeah."

Hazel moved closer, her throat tightening.

Stevenson's expression remained neutral. "Understood. We'll proceed as discussed…Sounds good." He glanced at Hazel. "No, not at all. She's right here…Just fine. No problem whatsoever… Yeah, sure." He offered her the phone.

"Dad?" Her hands were shaking.

"Hi, hon," her father said wearily. "That man's one helluva liar or he's watching the wrong kid. We found your pal, safe and sound. I would've called sooner but my battery died. We just got back to the boat."

"We?"

In the background Micah demanded the phone. Relief flooded through Hazel.

"Can I talk to him?"

"Not now. I've got a—"

"Are you coming to get me?"

"Not yet."

Turning her back to Stevenson, she lowered her voice. "Why'd you leave me with this guy? You don't even know him, but—"

"Are you all right?" he said, clearly unconcerned.

"Yeah, but—"

"Then knock off the melodrama. I have my reasons. Just trust me. You'll be fine. I've got things to take care of on this end, and I want you to sit tight. Do me a favor and stay out of trouble for twenty-four hours."

"In a row?"

I WANT TO, REALLY, BUT…

Hammon didn't move. He didn't want to wake Annabel. She looked so beautiful when she slept, so tranquil and pure. She lay on her side, one bare leg drawn up, covers kicked off. Tangled curls fringed her face and sleeping attire consisted of pink "kitty" print panties and a camisole reading: "Curiosity killed the cat, but for a while I was a suspect."

It was her moan that woke him, a soft and throaty sound. He switched on the dim light over the bunk to check on her.

She was dreaming.

He slipped on his glasses and watched, transfixed.

Her lips parted and she gasped.

He could only imagine what she was dreaming. By her reactions, something good. She bit her lip, moaning again.

With any luck, she'd talk in her sleep. She did that sometimes.

Her hand came up, rubbing her breast, and she made a small, kitten sound.

It was almost unbearable. He desperately wanted to touch her…

"Yes," she whispered.

…hold her…

"Oh, God…"

…feel her…

"Otto," she gasped.

…but he couldn't. He didn't dare break the spell.

Her hand dropped down, across her belly, down…

That was it. Quietly he slipped from his bunk to the head, locking the door. Closing himself into the blackness. Closing his eyes. Losing himself in his own unspeakable dream…

…which didn't include knocking on the door.

"Otto? You in there?"

"N…no…"

She laughed. "Nice try, dear. I heard you get up."

Up was the key word. He groaned.

"…minute…door…locked," he pleaded, invoking the "locked head" rule.

"I know what you're doing in there," she sang.

"Can't…I get…some…privacy?"

"On this boat? Keep dreaming."

That's what he was trying to do. "You're…not…helping…"

She giggled. "I could talk dirty if you want."

08:23 SUNDAY, JUNE 27

41°01'48.76"N/73°55'09.91"W

PIERMONT, NY

Stevenson walked through the back door, cigarette in one hand, *New York Times* and a brown paper bag in the other. He looked drained but smiled as he spotted Hazel standing in the kitchen, freshly showered, long hair still damp, wearing one of his button-down shirts and baggy drawstring shorts.

"You're up." He took a slow drag then crushed his cigarette into the sink and placed the bag on the counter. "I figured you needed your rest so I let you sleep. How are you feeling this morning?"

"Like I want to leave." She regarded the paper bag warily. "What's that?"

"Breakfast."

"You went out?"

"Don't worry, princess. You didn't miss an opportunity for escape. It was delivered."

"Anything of concern in the papers?"

He handed her the *Times*. "See for yourself."

Page by page she scanned the headlines, reading through the synopsis of society's steady decline, relieved to see yesterday's events were not yet known or newsworthy. There was no mention of bodies floating to shore or missing persons. She heard a soft electronic chirp and looked up to the flash of a digital camera. Stevenson inspected the shot on the screen.

"Hostage with newspaper," he explained. "More civilized than the 'severed finger in the mail' method. And less messy."

She wasn't amused. "Here's your finger," she said, offering the appropriate gesture. He snapped another shot, reviewed it with satisfaction, and tucked the camera into his pocket.

"I guess you can take the girl out of the truck stop, but you can't take the truck stop out of the girl." He struck a match and lit the massive stove, which appeared to be as old as the house. "That answers one question."

"What?"

"Whether you had the capacity to be civil. How would you like your eggs?"

"The capacity, yes. The desire, no. And scrambled is fine… thank you very much." Hazel looked around the kitchen. "Do you have any tea?"

Stevenson started the eggs, then opened a pantry closet and pulled a tin off the shelf. "One day, princess, when all is said and done, you and I will have a long talk about life and irony. That is, if you even talk to me by then."

"When all of what is said and done?"

"Nothing. Don't mind me. I get cryptic when I'm overtired."

It was his own fault. She had heard him through the night, wandering the house. "I said I wouldn't try to escape again." It was pointless once he mentioned all the cars had GPS trackers.

"And I believed you. Trust me; if I could've slept, I would have." Stevenson placed a kettle in the sink and turned the faucet. Water shot from the spray nozzle and hit him square in the face. Cursing, he jumped back and shut the water, then inspected the sprayer, removing a broken piece of a Popsicle stick wedged behind the lever. He looked like he wanted to hit something, but then he turned to Hazel and his clenched fist relaxed.

"Is that what it takes?" He wiped his face and filled the kettle. "You almost smiled, for a moment at least. I was starting to wonder if you knew how." He opened the sugar bowl, dipped his finger in and tasted the contents, winced, and dumped them into the garbage. He took a bag of sugar from the cabinet, tasting it first as well, then refilled the sugar bowl. He sliced a bagel into halves and dropped them into the toaster.

"Why am I here, really?"

"Questions, questions." He set plates and coffee cups on the table. "You were in trouble. I couldn't stand back and do nothing." He served the eggs then dropped the ham on the hot skillet. "Not when you're key in my plot for world domination."

"Forget I asked."

Hazel stretched across to the counter, picking up a ten-inch chef's knife. She sat back, spinning the knife around in her hand, tucking the blade flat against the back of her arm, then, with a twist of her wrist, pivoting it around, blade forward and exposed. She repeated the practiced, fluid motion while Stevenson watched, amused.

"Did Joe teach you that?"

"Maybe."

"He's a strange one. He has a military background?"

Hazel shrugged. "Dunno."

"But he served time in prison, right?"

"So I've heard." It was before her time, though from what she understood, he'd still be there if not for some issue over inadmissible evidence. "It's not something he talks about."

"And that doesn't bother you?"

"His past is his own business."

"Yet you trust him, even though you know there's things he's not telling you."

"He's earned it." She swept the knife through the space between them with graceful precision. "What's your point?"

"Nothing, really. Just an observation. Next question."

Hazel switched the knife to her left hand, repeating the fluid motion. Her eyes locked on his. "Why me?"

Stevenson tilted the ham onto the plates as the toaster popped. "An excellent question."

"What's the answer?"

"I never said I'd answer."

"Which answers one of my questions. You live alone because you're a jerk." A small movement on the floor caught her eye. Placing the knife aside, she lunged under the table, then stood, proudly displaying a cricket, live and unharmed, which she released out the back door. "You've got a serious pest problem," she said, returning to the table.

Stevenson chuckled. "You could say that. Next question."

She considered for a moment. "Is this house haunted?"

He seemed amused. "What do you mean?"

"The lights, the water, and why'd you paint all the mirrors black? I think there's a ghost here, and it wants you gone."

"You have no idea. Do the mirrors upset you?"

"Appearances are overrated."

Stevenson beamed. "You and Annabel have a lot in common."

If he expected she'd ask who Annabel was, he had a long wait ahead. "She doesn't like you either."

"That's putting it mildly." He brought her tea to the table, his eyes pausing on the shadow between her breasts. Hazel glared up, tugging the shirt closed.

"Why do you keep staring at me?"

"A rhetorical question, considering you've already jumped to your own conclusion. Actually I was looking at that shark's tooth you keep touching like some sacred amulet. And despite what you believe, I've no intention of getting into those little black panties, even if your father hadn't threatened me with dismemberment. Don't get me wrong, you have many delightful qualities. Just not for me."

"Is that it?" Hazel started eating. "You don't like girls? That's cool."

"No. I prefer women. Trust me, you're appealing, but temperamental, immature, a little too skinny, and way too young. Next question?"

Heat rose in her face. "Don't you have someone your own age to play with?"

"My own age?" He chuckled. "How old do you think I am?"

"I don't know. Older than my dad."

"Thanks a lot." He turned back to the stove as the water started to boil. "Try thirty-two."

"So it's true. Smoking makes you look older. *Way* older. Don't you have somewhere else to be, like a job or something?"

"First of all, it's Sunday. And I set my own hours."

"Doing what?"

"I'm a developer. Drug running's just a hobby."

No wonder she disliked him. He was one of *them*. There was probably a fleet of bulldozers with his name on the sides. And that also explained the neglected house; he didn't see the beauty beneath the disrepair; he'd likely bought it only to knock it down.

Stevenson grinned the least bit. "I take it you don't approve of property development."

"Knocking down perfectly good homes to stack starter mansions on top of each other? Endless beachfront condos and highways lined with bigger, shinier malls? No."

"You don't think Bivalve could benefit from a nice condo complex and some strip malls? Look at all that unutilized waterfront."

Was he serious? "Paving the planet isn't progress. Bivalve is being utilized just fine, but I guess there's no profit in that."

"That's an inspiring sentiment. Tell me more. I'll get you a soapbox if you'd like." He picked up his cigarettes and lighter. "I'd love to hear this."

"Never mind." It was pointless. Greed-mongering land speculators like him didn't care, and no amount of persuasion would change that. "This may be your house, but you light that thing, and one of us is going outside. Personally, I'd prefer it be you."

"You're saying I can't smoke in here?"

"Precisely."

"Say please."

She glared at him as she rose, picking up her plate and mug.

"Okay." He grinned. "Sit down. You win."

He headed out to the yard, quietly laughing the whole way.

I'M KEEPING THINGS IN BALANCE

Hammon waited until Annabel was in the shower before he turned on the computer and pulled up the "Contact Us" page for Jehovah's Witnesses. He was pleased to know that even in this troubled world, happiness, accurate Bible knowledge, and God and His Kingdom were mere keystrokes away. As he washed Ring Dings down with Mountain Dew, Hammon filled out the form requesting further information.

Then he realized it was quiet. Too quiet. He didn't hear water running. Annabel stood behind him, wrapped in a towel, reading the contact information he'd entered.

"Otto, dear, we discussed this."

He blinked, frowning. "We did?"

"Don't even try the selective memory act with me. We talked and you know it. I thought you were going to stop."

"I never said that. And besides, this is spiritual guidance. It's something he could use."

"Oh, just like the popcorn on his car manifold. And calling his obituary in to the papers. I'm sure he needed his mail redirected to Wisconsin. Or supergluing all the buttons on his car stereo at full volume with the Hampsterdance song on repeat."

Hammon grinned. He'd used 3M 5200 marine adhesive, glued the car's fuses as well, and disabled the hood release so Stevenson couldn't disconnect the battery. He wished he'd seen that one. Or the time the police showed up to investigate the marijuana growing behind the carriage house that some "concerned" citizen reported. Or the annual IRS audits. Or the anonymous tip to airport security that Stevenson was traveling with a forged passport, carrying weapons and explosives stashed in hidden compartments of his luggage. Hammon made sure the bomb-sniffing dogs earned their kibble that day.

Annabel sighed. "One day Stevenson's going to get fed up and do something awful."

"He already did!" He took a deep breath, willing himself calm. It wasn't Annabel he was mad at. "I'm keeping things in balance."

"Releasing three hundred crickets into his house?"

"Reminders that I'm still here. It's my job to make sure he never forgets what he did."

"Which was what, precisely?"

Hammon blinked, tracing the scars running along his face. Like a fault line, the surface revealed only a fraction of the full damage. It ran deep within his brain, leaving gaps between cells and neurons. He could feel the mercury trapped in his gray matter like fruit inside Jell-O, imbedded so deep that any attempts to remove it would cause more harm than good.

"This mess…" He held his skull like a specimen on display. "Stevenson did this, and he knows it." He let his head go and rubbed his arm, digging at a tiny scar. "There's something I know that he wants. I just can't remember what."

Hazel's frustration grew as the day wore on and her position remained unchanged. Stevenson alternated between irritating her with pointless conversation and retreating behind closed doors for phone calls too hushed to overhear. Her father hadn't called or showed, leaving her essentially a hostage, unable to escape. Under the premise of cricket hunting, she searched the house from basement to attic, finding several passages hidden between the walls, fourteen crickets, a few surprising details about her host, and more questions she knew he'd never answer. The crickets crawled around an empty Hellman's jar with holes in the lid, and the questions retreated to the back of her mind, growing and multiplying. Bored and restless, she devised more creative ways to amuse herself.

First, she determined Stevenson never went more than a half hour without checking on her and rarely made it past forty-five minutes without a nicotine fix. That provided sufficient time to set up. Then, with captive crickets as a centerpiece on the kitchen table, she sat down, put her feet up, and began reading the *Times*. Right on schedule, Stevenson strolled in. He paused, studying her.

"Should I worry?"

"About what?" she asked innocently.

"You almost smiled when you saw me. You're up to something. The question is: What?"

Hazel shrugged. "Funny. Isn't that what I asked you?" She gathered her hair, weaving it into a loose braid. "How about this? You tell me yours, I'll tell you mine."

"Nice try." Stevenson scanned the counter, spotting his cigarettes at the far end. He regarded Hazel's legs, blocking passage like a tollgate.

"Is there a problem?" she asked, not bothering to move.

"Not at all."

"Smoking's an awful habit and very bad for you."

"Your concern for my health is heartwarming." He circled the table the long way.

She shrugged. "Your funeral."

"Interesting choice of words."

As Stevenson stepped toward the cigarette box, his ankle snagged a length of hundred-pound test monofilament fish line, which tugged free a fork strategically wedged beneath the edge of the door frame to the basement stairs. From there the line descended to the basement and looped over a beam. Earlier Hazel had stacked several weights from a dusty weight bench on a table beneath that beam, secured the line to them, then carefully eased the table away, leaving them suspended. Stevenson knew none of this; he only felt the tension of the fish line for a split-second before it snapped tight, jerking him off his feet and landing him flat on his ass.

"Yes!" Hazel laughed. "Ten points!"

The equation was simple. Distance of drop equaled distance of pull, and it worked precisely as calculated. Stevenson sat up, inspecting the monofilament loop around his ankles.

"Is there a point to this?"

"It amused me. With the right wire, tension, and travel, a simple snare like that could be deadly."

"I'll have to remember that." He freed his legs. "Joe certainly taught you some fascinating tricks."

"Survival skills." Which included animal snares; but when she and Micah were little, neither wanted to hurt innocent animals, so instead they stalked one another. The game was Safari and the rules were simple. One point if the quarry took the bait but escaped, five for snagging the prey, ten for getting them off their feet. "The key to successful fishing is location and bait. I told you cigarettes are bad for your health."

Stevenson stood, straightening his shirt. "No, princess. *You're* bad for my health. So, are you getting hungry? I figured we'd go out for a while."

I HAVE MY REASONS

It was approaching high tide when *Revenge* emerged from the fading twilight and idled up to the Piermont docks. Hammon smiled a sharp, dangerous smile. Darkness energized him. No one noticed his arrival, and Stevenson's black boat sat abandoned. Perfect.

Beside him, Annabel sighed loudly. "Tell me again, why are we here?"

"I've got stuff to take care of."

She offered no assistance as he tied up, grumbling to herself how this was a mistake. Hammon returned to the bridge, shut the engine, and sat beside her.

"Annabel, please. No headaches. We've been over this."

"What if Stevenson catches you? Then what?"

"He hasn't yet, he's not gonna now."

"He'll put you back in the hospital. If you end up there...you know they won't let us stay together," she insisted, an uncharacteristic trace of fear edging into her voice. "You know what they'll do to me!"

"I won't let it happen, angel. I promise. You know I love you."

"How much?"

Hammon grinned, all fangs. "This much." He held his thumb and forefinger apart as far as the scars would allow.

Annabel regarded the distance. "That's not a lot."

He beamed. "No, look! It's to scale." He placed his hand along the chart index. "It's over four nautical miles. Now, relax, everything'll be fine."

Hammon performed his usual predeparture rituals and jiggled the knob to confirm it was indeed locked.

"The boat is locked," Annabel assured him.

Hammon nodded, satisfied, and they headed toward the lot. Annabel paused beside Stevenson's boat, studying the damage. "Damn!"

Hammon continued past. "I didn't do it."

"I know. Were those bullet holes?"

"We can hope." Hammon unlocked the padlocked shed he rented to store the Fairmont, shining his flashlight around and underneath the car, confirming it hadn't been touched in his absence. While the 1978 Fairmont was somewhat conspicuous by virtue of advanced age, it retained a certain utilitarian blandness that rendered it otherwise unmemorable, especially at night. It looked stock, though Gary thoughtfully concealed an obscene amount of horsepower beneath the hood. Most important, it predated any automotive computers, electronics, or other digital refinements. For Hammon's purposes it was essentially invisible.

He unlocked the car and stepped back as he opened the door. Even with the forest of pine-tree fresheners dangling from the mirror, it was ripe inside. He rolled down the windows, and within a few minutes on the road, the stench began to subside. Annabel said nothing as he followed 9W south, crossing the state line into New Jersey, then weaving into the more isolated roads. After a mile of passing no traffic, he eased onto the shoulder and looked around.

"We're alone," Annabel said. "Go ahead, I'll keep watch."

She sat on the hood while Hammon trudged back, took a deep breath, and unlocked the trunk. The dim bulb reflected off the blue poly tarp from which an unspeakable odor rose, and Hammon fought not to gag. He pulled on stiff, blood-stained gloves, grabbed the shovel, then closed the trunk and headed down the slope, beyond view of the road.

"Make sure you dig deep enough," Annabel called.

19:29 SUNDAY, JUNE 27

41°05'22.21"N/73°54'54.83"W

NYACK, NY

Hazel scowled at the plate of soft-shell crabs, and she could almost hear her father. Knock off the drama, he'd say. Drop the hostage act. It wasn't as though Stevenson was mistreating her or giving her the least reason to complain and she knew it. That in itself aggravated her even more, sitting there at a small table in the private courtyard of a quietly elegant but clearly expensive waterfront restaurant, wearing a pretty sundress Stevenson had had delivered to the house. It was wrong.

"Couldn't you have just ordered pizza? Isn't that standard hostage-feeding procedure?"

Stevenson smiled that insufferable smile of his. "Personally, I prefer the more civilized approach. Provide your hostage space, nice clothes, and the best soft-shell crab in town. And you didn't seem to mind driving the Viper."

Stevenson insisted she drive, claiming he was too sore from his kitchen tumble. Now, *that* was melodrama. And she'd never admit it, but the car's power was intoxicating, and she'd had to suppress a grin as she accelerated out of turns, pressed into the seat. The Viper was quick and responsive, ready to devour as much road as she'd give it. It demanded complete attention, and while she blurred through sunlight and shadows, eyes narrowed against the wind, every thought beyond the next curve evaporated. He directed her into a long loop of back roads and highways, smiling with satisfaction as she slipped between gaps in the traffic, watching patterns and judging distances and speed. She was having fun; she was showing off and she knew it but she didn't care. It wasn't every day she had the chance to drive a car like that.

"We could've driven to a White Castle. I'm not even hungry. And these clothes weren't necessary. Mine were dry, I could have worn them."

"Then I'll be returning you in better condition than I found you. Just humor me. You do clean up nicely, though."

"Bite me."

"Well, visually at least. Out of curiosity, on the Parkway, you looked upset when we reached the state border. Why was that?"

So he did notice when she slowed at mile 171, passing the large yellow sign on the grassy shoulder that stated simply: "LAST EXIT IN NEW JERSEY."

"Anyone ever mention you pry too much?"

"You didn't answer my question."

"It's none of your business. How's that for an answer?"

"Not very civilized."

"You think I care? I'll elaborate. I don't want to talk about it, AND it's none of your business."

"I'm not sure whether to be insulted or impressed by your determination to distrust me. Then again, you don't trust many people, do you?" Stevenson leaned back, sipping his scotch. "You should be careful. You go through life pushing people away, one day you might push away the wrong one."

She wasn't about to ask what he meant, he'd only give some equally cryptic answer. Maybe it had something to do with the blue-eyed beauty whose picture graced the background on the computer in his study. Perhaps she was the mysterious Annabel he'd spoken of, though Hazel had no intention of asking. She wanted to avoid all possible conversation, especially subjects of a personal nature. Instead, she glared at her plate, the mouthwatering aroma tormenting her. She'd intended to stage a small-scale hunger strike in protest of her captivity, but her grumbling stomach betrayed her.

Stevenson laughed. "I thought you weren't hungry. You lied."

"Then we're even."

"How so?" Stevenson savored a mouthful of crab, the image of casual indifference, though behind his relaxed smile something subtle had shifted. Hazel let the silence linger. Stevenson stared back, eyes locked on hers. Waiting.

"I saw your study," she said at last. Framed articles from architectural and environmental magazines spotlighting Stevenson's work covered the walls. A headline proclaimed: "ONE MAN'S CRUSADE; FIGHTING SPRAWL ONE FACTORY AT A TIME." The photo showed Stevenson standing tall before an old textile mill, his expression somber. The article highlighted his work converting outdated manufacturing properties into office and residential space utilizing geothermal climate control systems and solar energy. The interview described him as "driven" and "private to the point of reclusive." Another article focused on his geothermal climate controls applied to historical structures, including his own award-winning and once immaculately manicured home.

"Why'd you say you were a developer?"

"Because I am. It's amusing to watch you make your own assumptions. You already decided you disliked me; far be it for me to alter your opinion with facts. Again, you should be careful; not everything in life is as it first appears."

"Sure, Yoda. Whatever you say."

It was senseless letting good crabs die in vain. Hazel stabbed a leg with her fork. Stevenson grinned victoriously.

"Tomorrow, you drive the Chevelle. That relic from my muscle-car phase sits too much these days."

"Whatever."

"Tell me, princess, what makes you so wary of people?"

"You mean not blindly trusting? I don't know. Blame it on homeschooling and an overprotective father. The sheltered, unconventional environment I grew up in. A lack of peers. Take your pick."

"Your father raised you alone, right? What about your mother?"

"She's gone."

Hazel ripped off another crab leg, slowly chewing. The discussion was over, not that there was anything to discuss, really. Her parents met freshman year of college and Hazel was the unintended result of their passion. Much in love and determined to provide for his new family, her father quit school, bought the old Kenworth, and they moved onto *Witch*. Her mother soon concluded she wanted more than life aboard a leaky hand-me-down boat with a newborn and a truck-driving dropout. She needed space—space that included returning to school, graduating, and ultimately marrying well and settling in Westchester. When she was small, Hazel accepted the simple answers her father offered. As she grew older, she came to hate her mother for abandoning them, but by that time it was an opinion she kept to herself rather than upset her father. Eventually her attitude shifted from resentment to pity. Her mother chose wealth over love, or maybe she never was truly in love. She'd moved on and eventually built a respectable life with her husband and new children while Hazel's existence remained the skeleton in her tidy suburban closet. Currently, Hazel had a half brother and half sister she'd never met. For Hazel, growing up with her father aboard *Witch* and crisscrossing the country in *RoadKill*, there was never a doubt she'd gotten the better part of the deal.

Stevenson waited until she finally swallowed her food and sipped her water. "Your father said he practically raised Micah."

"He did."

"Care to elaborate?"

Hazel meticulously dismembered her crab. "No. Why do you want to know?"

"I'm just curious why you're so close."

"And I'm curious why you're so curious. You already seem to know a lot for the little time you spent with my dad."

"You risked your life for Micah. You tried to kill me to go back for him. No one has to tell me you're close. And I'm just making conversation; it's what people do. No need to be so defensive. All right, different subject. What's the story with the diamond ring? You're engaged?"

Hazel glanced at her left hand. "Maybe." Actually, it was a facetted Cape May diamond: a piece of quartz common along southern New Jersey beaches. She figured someone like Stevenson could tell the difference.

"May I see it?"

She studied the ring and shrugged, slipping it off. Maybe if he thought she had a boyfriend, he might back off. Stevenson held it up, inspecting the stone. He tilted it and chuckled as he read the engraving inside.

"*Hazel&Jeremy4ever*. That's sweet. An optimist, this Jeremy. Forever is a long time."

Hazel snatched the ring back, looking away as she slipped it back on.

"Did I say something wrong?"

"No." It was none of his business. None of her life was, and least of all the shy boy with bright blue eyes and easy laugh whom, only two weeks after he'd given gave her that ring, she'd watched lowered into the ground in his casket. She shouldn't have shown Stevenson the ring. Why was she even talking to him? "Why are you so determined to pry?"

"You are intriguing. It's fascinating how often you deflect my questions with your own."

"As often as you avoid answering mine."

The corner of his mouth twitched up. "You do make it frustratingly tempting. I may just say the hell with it all and keep you for myself."

His tone was joking, but there was chilling seriousness in his eyes. Hazel backed her chair away from the table. "You know what I've noticed? You're always smiling, but you're not happy, are you? You've got money and all those fancy toys, but no one to play with. You live alone in that big, empty house. Is that a 'fear of commitment' thing, or just that you're such a jerk you drive everyone away?"

Stevenson sipped his scotch, his expression distant and unreadable. Finally he rose, cigarettes in hand. "I know how smoking upsets you, so you'll excuse me if I step away for a minute."

He didn't return until after she'd finished eating, and he didn't touch the rest of his meal. While it was a relief that he made no more attempts at conversation, Hazel had the uneasy feeling she'd crossed some line. He was right about one thing, though. The crabs were delicious.

I'M ONLY DOING THIS FOR ANNABEL

Rocks. Dig a hole anywhere in north Jersey, you hit rocks. Hammon continued, trying not to think, just get done and fast. Two feet of rocks and roots, and his muscles were screaming. He returned to the car, carefully removing the lumpy tarp, keeping the ends up. This one wasn't too messy, but…his stomach wrenched at the memory of the last time…the cold soup of piss and blood and God knows what else soaking into his clothes, the smell so thick he could taste it. He'd puked so hard his ribs hurt for days.

Annabel looked on somberly. Hammon hoped she understood he did this for her. He dragged the tarp to the hole, positioned so he wouldn't have to look as it unrolled. He couldn't. It was too…He didn't want to think about the bloody, mangled remains.

No, it was better not to look. Looking meant nightmares. Pull the tarp aside, pick up the shovel, refill the hole, cover it with leaves and branches. Return the tarp, folded messy side in, the shovel and gloves back in the trunk, and leave. Miles rolled past, neither of them speaking.

"Poor thing," he said finally. Someone had to say something. "At least it got a decent burial."

"Do you think it was someone's pet?"

"No. Probably a stray," Hammon said, unsure whether that would make her feel better or worse.

"But…Someone hit that dog and left it in the road to die like that. Do you think it suffered?"

Hammon shook his head, swallowing. "Killed instantly, I think," he lied. Annabel had some serious issues when it came to death and burial, and seeing her cry tore into him. If performing these unsavory rituals brought her some small comfort, that was reason enough. He looked across.

"You okay?"

She nodded weakly, then shook her head.

"Not really. Can we go back to the boat and leave?"

Hammon sighed. "Sorry, angel. I've got one more stop."

"The house of evil? No thanks. Drop me by *Revenge*, I'll wait for you there."

Even after they left the restaurant, the silence continued. Apparently his injuries no longer bothered him and Stevenson drove, following the Hudson shoreline while Hazel stared at the Tappan Zee Bridge glittering across the dark water and tried to ignore the undeniable tension. She wondered what nerve she'd hit; it might be useful for future reference, but if she asked he'd likely read too much into her interest.

Stevenson pulled into the marina, scanning the docks. His grip tightened on the wheel. "Son of a bitch." He climbed out, looking from the boats to Hazel and back, cursing under his breath and pacing around the car, his jaw rigid.

"You," he ordered, "follow."

She was torn between the opportunity to be difficult and interest in what had him so agitated. Curiosity won and she tagged along as he stalked out, straight past his black boat and up to a drab white sport-fishing boat.

"Wait here." He climbed aboard and pounded on the salon door. When no one appeared, he looked around, took his keys, and unlocked the cabin. He kicked a bucket out of the way, stepped inside, and slammed the door, leaving Hazel alone and baffled on the dock.

It was a plain, nameless sport-fisher. Very plain, Hazel realized, almost neglected-looking, though without any traces of actual neglect. The waterline was clean, dock lines unchafed and neatly tied. No scrapes from hard dockings, no signs of overdue maintenance, nothing. It didn't look like any production model Hazel knew, and there was a subtle grace to the boat. Stevenson emerged, his expression grim. He climbed off, heading back to the lot. "Let's go."

"Nobody home?" Hazel trotted to keep up. "Interesting boat. Whose is she?"

"Mine."

"You never said you had another boat. She wasn't here yesterday."

"You never asked, and it wasn't here because someone else was using it."

"Is she a custom build?"

"Very. Just get in the car," he ordered. "Remember, the more cooperative the hostage, the sooner you get released."

His expression made it clear there'd be no more questions. She sank into the passenger seat and looked back. From that distance the boat seemed to fade, ghostlike, into the darkness. Stevenson shot out of the lot, screeching down the narrow road, and it was all Hazel could do to suppress a grin when red and blue lights flashed behind them, siren blipping. Stevenson pulled over and fished out his wallet as the officer ambled up.

"Evening, Jake. A bit heavy on the gas, don't you think?"

Stevenson grimly offered his license.

"Put it away." The cop gave Hazel a friendly smile. "I figured you should know your car's been reported stolen. Again. By you, as usual."

Stevenson gave a short laugh. "Which one this time?"

"All of them. You know, you could press charges. Filing false police reports is a criminal offense."

"Just let it go, okay?"

The cop didn't look pleased, but he didn't look surprised either. He glanced at Hazel. "She as young as she looks?" he asked, voice lowered.

Hazel tilted her head and peered up shyly. "I'm seventeen."

Stevenson nodded in agreement. "Mentally."

She shot him a dirty look. "He's kidnapped me, taken me across state lines, and he's keeping me hostage."

"Adorable, isn't she?" Stevenson chuckled. "My friend's kid. I got stuck babysitting."

The cop cracked a smile. "You sure you don't want to press charges with the cars?"

"Positive."

"Your call," he said as he returned to his patrol car. "Don't be surprised when you keep getting pulled over."

Stevenson rolled away at a good clip, heading back to the house. He shot through the opening gates with inches to spare, raced up the driveway past the carriage house, straight across the lawn, and parked beside the kitchen door. Hazel followed him inside.

"Mind telling me what's up?"

"A little, yeah." He pulled out a chair. "Do me a favor. Be a good girl, sit here and don't move." He stalked down the hall.

Be a good girl? Was he serious? The hell with that. "I'm going to take a nap," she called to his back. "I'll be upstairs if you decide to tell me what crawled up your—"

There was a soft chirp.

She paused.

It went silent, then started again, chirping in cycles.

It was behind the wall in a narrow passage she'd found earlier, leading from the kitchen to the dining room. It wasn't unusual in a house of that period, dating back to a time when servants were expected to perform their duties unseen. Hazel pushed the panel beside the pantry inward and slipped into the space, waiting silently. Cricket stalking was an art.

Heavy footsteps approached and she eased the door closed. Stevenson's shadow passed along the floor. Hazel held her breath and watched through a small gap as he checked the halls, up the stairs, and down the basement. Likely looking for her, but she wasn't about to announce she was between the walls chasing bugs. He took a manila folder down from above the kitchen cabinets and dialed his cell phone.

"Yeah, I know. I saw the goddamned boat. Is he still seeing Annabel? You're sure?…I was wondering how she's wearing her hair these days." He flipped through the file, listening. "Let's just say I have a little surprise." He grinned. "You'll see."

He ended the call and keyed in another number.

"We have a problem…No, *her* I can handle. That other issue we discussed has come up sooner than expected. Exactly. We could do without that complication right now."

Stevenson paced as he listened, repeatedly looking out at the driveway as though someone might pull up at any moment. Hazel's uneasiness grew; something was up, serious enough to concern Stevenson.

"We'll move now. I'll call when we get there…Her? I expect she'll be difficult, but she'll cooperate. She'll have no choice."

Hazel's mouth went dry and she sank backwards. The cricket sang, reverberating through the wall. Stevenson paused, turning, and Hazel stiffened, terrified he would hear her anxious breathing.

"Everything's set on this end. I have it. You watch; when word gets out I've got that Freightliner and cargo, we'll see who makes the highest offer."

Hazel covered her mouth, fighting to stay quiet. She knew they couldn't trust Stevenson! Why wouldn't her father believe her? Stevenson looked up the hallway again, his expression chilling.

"No. Get rid of *Witch*. I'll deal with Hazel." Stevenson nodded grimly. "You think she'll be that much of a problem?…That's your call. I'll let you handle the messy part when the time comes…Call me once the boat is gone. I'm going to collect my little friend and get moving. Don't worry." He laughed. "She gives me any problems, I'll just dart her."

Stevenson snapped the phone closed, shoved the file above the cabinet, and charged upstairs. Hazel's pulse rushed in her ears, and she felt paralyzed but she knew she couldn't just hide there; when Stevenson didn't find her he'd expand his search, and he'd realize she'd overheard. She wanted to ambush and interrogate him, but that was too risky; too much could go wrong. No, the better choice was escape while she had the chance and warn her father. Grab all the keys and remote for the gate along with that folder and whatever it contained, steal a car, and get the hell out of there.

Taking a deep breath, she slipped out, knife in hand. She slid a chair to the counter and climbed up to grab the folder, peeking inside.

Her face grew hot as she recognized police reports and her psychiatric profiles from her run-in years earlier with Pierce, with the words "extremely introverted" and "exhibits sociopathic tendencies" highlighted. Telephoto pictures showed her climbing out of the Miata, dated three days before it sank; photos of her father and Joe going about their daily lives, all taken from a distance. *Witch, Kindling, RoadKill,* even Joe's Buick. More photos, the Miata again, muddy now, a close-up of the bullet holes. *Tuition* beside a brick building; another of the door with that morning's edition of the *NY Times* in clear focus against the Moran Marine Transport logo and star. Photos of minifridges and A/C units inside the trailer. And finally, her reading that same *Times* edition, flipping Stevenson the finger.

Footsteps pounded through the hall, approaching fast.

"Hazel? Damnit, I don't have time for this."

She rushed to get down, misstepped, and the chair slid out from under her. All at once she was on the floor, dazed. Stevenson entered the kitchen, rushing up to her. She pulled away as he tried to sit her up.

"Are you okay? What were you…"

Then he spotted the folder in her left hand. She lunged, grazing his scalp as he ducked and grabbed her wrist in a crushing grip. He yanked her to her feet as he rose, holding her suspended and pinning her against the counter. Carefully he unwrapped her fingers and flung the knife, clattering across the tiles.

"You are predictable to a fault." He wiped the blood from his face.

"Son of a bitch," she cursed, twisting to get free.

"I know. Vindicating, isn't it? You kept telling your father not to trust me, but he wouldn't listen." He lowered her enough that her toes brushed the floor, then released her hand. "Now, are you going to settle down and behave?"

"Go to hell."

"I figured as much." He kept her pinned against the counter. "I guess it's time you and I had a little talk."

Twisting, she reached backwards, struggling to escape.

"If you'd just listen for a minute," he said, his voice bordering on aggravation.

She grasped for the bottle of scotch, but it slid clear.

"I heard enough." The sugar bowl smashed to the floor.

"Good God. Knock it off already." He grabbed her hands, wrapping his arms around her and pinning her wrists together behind her back. "Settle down."

He was too strong, too close, holding her too tight, his chest pressed to her face. In a panic she turned, sinking her teeth into his arm. The taste of blood mixed with the smell of stale smoke on his sleeve, and he roared as he jerked back, slipping on the sugar. His head smacked against the edge of the counter as he went down. Furious, he started to rise as Hazel backed away. She grabbed the metal tea kettle from the stove and swung hard, with both hands, and again until he stopped moving.

I'M OFF TO THE HOUSE OF DOOM

Hammon dropped Annabel off at the marina, then stopped off at the Gas-on-the-Go/Quickeemart up the road to stock up on non-Annabel-approved food, Krazy Glue, toilet paper, and snacks for the crickets. Best he'd determined, crickets thrived on Frosted Flakes. Then he headed back to Piermont, as usual getting stuck at the town's lone traffic light. He glanced at the vacant passenger seat and tapped his fingers to the clicking of his right turn signal. He was anxious to be done and back with Annabel aboard *Revenge*. The reflection on the dashboard went from red to green and Hammon looked up, lifting the clutch—

—and stalled, nearly getting rear-ended by a white Lincoln as he watched Annabel pull up to the red light in Stevenson's Viper, waiting to turn left. The Lincoln's horn blasted behind him and Annabel spun, anxiously checking the empty road behind her. The horn sounded again and she turned, following the sound, her eyes meeting Hammon's while a stream of obscenities rose from the Lincoln pulling around him to go straight.

Surprised as he was, Hammon couldn't help but smile at the sight of her even as his brain began to process that something was seriously wrong with that picture. What was she doing there? Had she gone to Stevenson's house before him, and why? Why was she driving Stevenson's car? Hammon's light went yellow, then red, and hers turned green. Behind her, headlights approached. She looked back at the lights, then turned to Hammon, turmoil in her dark eyes, damp with tears. Tires screaming, the Viper fishtailed and shot past him, disappearing around the bend.

Hammon's smile faded and he sat, utterly confused. What was Annabel doing and why did she look so upset? Was she in some sort of trouble, and if so, why hadn't she told him? Something was very wrong, and if it involved Stevenson, it was the worst kind of bad.

Headlights off, Hammon pulled through the open wrought-iron gates, anxiety building. Stevenson never left those gates open. He killed the engine and coasted to a stop under cover of the overgrown hedges, then fumbled around his backpack, digging past squished cellophane-wrapped Ring Dings, his Game Boy, wadded napkins, and crushed chips, at last feeling the shape of a small gun. He knew no one would take a DayGlo orange-and-green water pistol seriously, but in the darkness it might be mistaken for the real thing.

As with the gate, the kitchen door was ajar, and Hammon struggled to focus over the clamoring alarms within his brain. Inside the house, on the other hand, all was quiet aside from random crickets. He spotted Stevenson's bloodied shape next to the overturned chair. Hammon leaned closer, lime Slurpee rising in his throat.

Stevenson was still breathing shallowly.

Hammon couldn't decide whether he was disappointed or not, but he knew Annabel couldn't have done that; she just wasn't capable. Someone else did it; someone else wanted Stevenson dead. Or did they? Were that the case, finishing him off would have been easy. Whatever happened, murder wasn't the goal. He pushed Stevenson with his sneaker.

"Hey, Jake, wake up. Who did this?"

No reply.

"I guess I oughta get help, eh?"

Still no reply.

"You pissed someone off real good. Again. As usual."

Was whoever'd done this still there? The back of his neck prickled, and Hammon scanned the shadows anxiously. "Hey, Jake, don't move. I wanna look around."

Right. If he didn't barf first. Gun drawn, he searched the dark house, hearing only scattered crickets. At least his pets were happy. Whoever did this was long gone. Stevenson's desk had been ransacked, but the hidden space beneath the bottom drawer, where Stevenson always stashed an envelope of cash, remained untouched, and once again Hammon cleaned it out.

He returned to the kitchen, picked up the cordless phone with a paper towel, and dialed 911. A neutral voice asked the nature of his emergency.

"Uh, yeah. Someone's attacked me. I'm bleeding! HELP!" He dropped the receiver next to Stevenson. That ought to do it. He deserved a freakin' merit badge. Within the receiver a small voice repeated questions Stevenson was unable to answer. Stay calm, it assured him, help is on the way.

On that note it was time to depart, more confused than when he'd arrived. There was only one thing Hammon knew for sure: something in his fragile little universe had shifted out of orbit. It was time to retreat to *Revenge* and the safety of dark, open water...and he desperately needed to talk with Annabel.

But Annabel and *Revenge* were gone.

It was unimaginable, but undeniable. They had vanished. Why would Annabel have left him?

She must have figured out what he'd kept from her, what he'd kept from himself. Maybe it was something he said in his sleep, or something she found. Something in the damned snow. Something Stevenson wanted. Whatever the case, she'd figured it out, and…and what? If she knew, she was in danger. He had to go after her. He had to find her.

She couldn't be far, not yet, not with *Revenge*. With Stevenson's black boat he could catch her.

Only it wouldn't start. The key he'd lifted from Gary's shop fit the ignition, and he knew about the fuel kill override, but the boat refused to cooperate. With each passing second, the distance between him and Annabel grew. He unwrapped the foil around his phone, connected the battery, and hit the speed dial. Pete answered over a radio thumping obnoxiously in the background. Hammon tried to speak, managing a choked hiccup.

"Just a sec," Pete replied. "GAR—it's Zap!"

Shuffling and mumbling.

"Yeah? Hey, Zap. Speak up! Will you guys kill that goddamn noise!" Gary shouted graphic suggestions regarding the radio and someone's anatomy, and then there was silence.

Hammon hiccupped.

Gary sighed. "What now?"

"How do I start Stevenson's drug boat?"

"NO! Whatever you're doing, the answer is no."

"It's an emergency."

"Define emergency."

"*Revenge* is gone."

"Just chill. You forgot where you docked again. Think back. Where—"

"No. She's gone." Hammon swallowed a hiccup. "For real."

"For real? You're sure about that." Then Gary laughed. "I'll be damned; that's what Stevenson meant. He said he had a little surprise for you. Serves you right. I told you that airport stunt would bite you in the ass. I mean seriously, they strip-searched the bastard! I warned you there'd be payback; it was just a matter of time."

"It wasn't him! When I left Stevenson he was unconscious, tied up, and bleeding."

Gary sobered up. "What?"

"I didn't do it! I found him that way! I even called an ambulance!"

Silence.

"I said I didn't do it! Now why won't this boat start?" Hammon lifted the engine cover, with no idea what he was looking for. The compartment light switched on, and immediately he spotted the problem. "Uh, yeah, never mind."

"What do you mean, never mind?"

"I didn't do it."

"Do what?" Gary groaned. "Look, stay where you are. I'm coming; we'll find your damned boat."

Hammon stared down at the slashed hoses and shattered fuel-water separator bowls. Was that Annabel's doing? Was she trying to stop him from following, or was she running from someone else? Hammon tried to speak, but his voice was gone. His brain, on the other hand, wouldn't stop screaming.

22:32 SUNDAY, JUNE 27

41°00'01.35"N/73°53'26.73"W

HUDSON RIVER, SOUTHEAST OF

SNEDEN LANDING, NY

Beneath the shadow of the Palisades, Hazel tried to focus, fighting her growing panic. She couldn't reach her father and Micah, not at her father's number or Joe's.

Was she too late? Who had Stevenson been talking to? The file offered no clues. Hazel scrolled through the menus on Stevenson's cell. The Received Calls history was empty, and Calls Dialed listed only her attempts to reach home; Stevenson must have deleted his records.

Hazel surveyed the helm, scanning the backlit gauges. The anonymous white boat had seemed the best choice for escape; better than driving a car already reported stolen, better than Stevenson's black boat, which was low on fuel and highly conspicuous. By all appearances the white boat looked to be a fast, modern sport-fisherman and a wise choice for a quick getaway.

The key turned, lighting the gauges and confirming full fuel tanks. Once she'd located the fuel cutoff override, posing as a bait pump switch, the engine softly rumbled to life. It wasn't until she was underway that she discovered the boat moved at the sedate, fuel-efficient speed of a displacement cruiser, with a hull that would never break nine knots. On a good day, *Witch* could go faster, but by that point there was no turning back; she was better off slowly pressing on.

The flybridge console was a mess of empty 7-Eleven coffee cups, soda cans, Twinkies, and Good Humor wrappers. One area not buried was an illuminated Plexiglas chart table overflowing with paper charts of the region: well-used and worn, cluttered with scribbled notes of headings, with corrections for magnetic variation and compass deviation. Her temperature was dropping in the damp night air so Hazel slipped on the old sweatshirt hanging from the pilot's seat. She tucked her hands into the pockets, finding a tiny flashlight, Sweet Tarts, receipts, and mint Chapstick.

Closer to the city, the waters were twilight bright, and Hazel strained to distinguish which of the endless lights of the harbor were floating, underway, or shoreside red and green traffic signals. She'd be glad once she cleared lower Manhattan.

She hit redial on the phone again, and fresh tears welled up when no one answered. Something had gone wrong, she was sure of it. There was no way to help. She'd given up on leaving messages for her father to call back: they were pointless and the phone's battery was down to one bar.

I'VE LOST IT

"Who would beat Stevenson senseless and take *Revenge*?" Gary asked as he headed *Temperance*, his twenty-eight-foot Seabright Skiff, down the dark Hudson River. He studied Hammon, whom he'd located in Piermont futilely attempting to hot-wire a twenty-three-foot Searay.

Hammon didn't have an answer. Annabel did, and he searched his memory, trying to understand why she'd left him. Did his brain delete something critical? That happened sometimes; there'd be gaps and blanks where he couldn't recall things he'd said or done; they'd been occurring more and more lately.

"And you're sure you didn't fuel up," Gary said.

"Positive," Hammon said, though the more he thought about it, the less certain he became.

"So the gauge reads full, but their range is limited. We're moving at twice *Revenge*'s top speed. We'll catch up in no time."

Shadowed step for step by Yodel, Hammon paced the cockpit, stepping over Charger every fourth step. Lights from buoys, ships, roads, vehicles, traffic signals, and waterfront buildings glowed like a multicolored galaxy. And somewhere within that galaxy, aboard one little boat, was Annabel. He had to find her.

At the helm, Gary turned. "Sit down already, damnit!"

Hammon dropped into the other seat, and Yodel, tail tucked under, curled at his feet.

Gary said, "They sabotaged Stevenson's boat, so they figured they might be followed and didn't want to be." He studied the laptop's screen, which displayed a digital image of the water and shoreline. A slow-moving red dot progressed past Jersey City.

Hammon said, "That's off by miles."

"Just look for your boat."

"It shows us by Ellis Island; we're nowhere near there."

"The settings must be off. Just watch for *Revenge*."

Hammon looked across at the Spuyten Duyvil swing bridge spanning the entrance to the Harlem River. "Why are we going this way?"

Gary scanned the laptop display. "Odds are they're heading to open water."

"She could've taken the Harlem River? She could be headed toward the Sound. What if…"

"She?"

Hammon hiccupped. "*Revenge*."

Gary regarded him suspiciously then fiddled with the laptop, adjusting *Temperance*'s course slightly. He seemed more preoccupied with the screen than the water around them. Hammon leaned over, examining the display. He had enough problems; the last thing he needed was Gary trusting a defective navigational program.

"You really should use paper charts," Hammon said.

"I thought I told you to look for your boat."

Hammon glared at the computer. "I don't trust electronics."

"So I've heard."

"What program is that? Maybe I can fix it."

"Zap, you couldn't fix your way out of a paper bag. Just watch for your damned boat."

It didn't look like any navigational programs Hammon knew. He recognized the features of the harbor, but there were no depths or navigational aids. Gary never used the laptop for navigation, he usually went by the radar display beside it, which offered an accurate picture of their present position. The dot on the laptop generated a constantly moving GPS position, far ahead of them but progressing slower than *Temperance*'s current speed, more like—

Hammon jumped up, pointing at the screen with a shaking hand. "That's...that's..."

Gary slumped back wearily.

It was...it had to be...that dot was..."It's *Revenge*."

Gary nodded in defeat.

That was *Revenge*, and...

Horror washed over Hammon as the cluster of pixels progressed across the digital harbor. "That...that...that's..."

"Your worst nightmare."

"You've been *tracking* me? YOU? *TRACKING* ME?"

"Making sure you stayed out of trouble. And monitoring engine temperature, rpm, everything. Sorta a digital babysitter."

"You...had...a tracker in *Revenge*...all this time...You swore..."

"I lied. You gave me the idea to begin with, always ranting about everything they do. Point is, there's your damned boat. Have a meltdown after we get it back."

Hammon gazed numbly at the screen. Upset as he was, he was also that much closer to finding Annabel and some answers.

"What I still don't get," Gary said, "is who'd want to beat the shit out of Stevenson?"

Hammon leveled a skeptical look at him.

"Besides you. And why would anyone bother stealing that barge?"

Hammon stared out at the dark water. "Dunno." He hiccupped.

Gary's eyes narrowed. "What?"

He couldn't say it. Gary would go ballistic.

"Spit it out!"

Hammon shook his head.

"Okay, then." Gary pulled back on the throttle. *Temperance* drifted to a stop, settled in the water, and rocked with the outgoing tide. "I guess you don't want your boat back."

Hammon's stomach lurched with each roll. If he told Gary, he knew what would happen. But the longer he remained silent, the greater the distance between him and *Revenge* grew. He swallowed hard and forced his dinner to stay put.

"Annabel did it."

01:03 MONDAY, JUNE 28

40°46'00.23"N/74°00'32.95"W

HUDSON RIVER, WEST OF PIER 86, NYC

Hazel noted the time on the chart as she approached the shoreside Lincoln Tunnel ventilator shafts. To port, marking West Forty-sixth Street, the *USS Intrepid* was strung with white lights like a well-armed house at the holidays. The Empire State Building and Chrysler Building gleamed, jewels in a postcard-perfect skyline. It was amazing how beautiful the world could be even as it disintegrated.

Green buoy 31 leaned with the outgoing tide, gonging softly as Hazel passed Ellis Island. She marked her time and position. Ahead, the Statue of Liberty beckoned and green 29 flashed. Beyond that, the upper bay opened up and the Verrazano Narrows Bridge arched across the water forming a glittering gateway. She kept herself distracted by plotting her course and calculating the boat's lack of speed as she reached each mark.

Aside from radar, depth finder, and a VHF radio, the boat was oddly electronics-free. The entire trip north, Stevenson navigated solely by a high-end GPS chart-plotter, and panic hit as Hazel realized her slow motion escape had one massive flaw. Like his cars, the boat may have been equipped with a locator beacon;

Stevenson could have been following her position all along. Hazel studied the chart and the surrounding waters, eased the throttle back, and moved out of the main channel. The depth finder showed the bottom rising to thirty, then twenty, then eighteen feet. To her relief no one nearby changed course. She slowed to a stop, reversed, and let the windlass feed out the anchor line, pausing to feel it bottom out and set, then laying out a modest scope. She wouldn't be staying long.

With the boat in neutral, she left the engine idling. Diesels operate on the principle that highly compressed fuel self-detonates. No distributor, no spark plugs. Even with the batteries disconnected, so long as the fuel pump was mechanical, the engine would run until either fuel or oxygen was cut off. She'd have no running lights, instruments, or gauges, but she had the compass, a flashlight, and a chart. That was all she needed.

First things first. She went forward and confirmed the anchor line was just that: line, not chain. Chain would be difficult to haul up once the windlass had no power. Line, on the other hand, she could cut and run, sacrificing the anchor for a quick exit.

She returned to the cockpit and tried the door.

"The boat is locked," said a soft voice within the cabin.

I CAN'T DEAL WITH THIS

"Let me be sure I got this right," Gary said. "You think Annabel beat the shit out of Stevenson and stole your boat."

Hammon nodded. "Uh-huh."

Gary slumped back in his seat. "Dear God. Why me?" He looked at Hammon, shaking his head. "We've talked about this. Shit, kid." He rubbed his face. "You stopped taking your damned medication again, didn't you?"

Hammon blinked, saying nothing. The pills didn't help. They only made things worse.

"You haven't been taking your meds," Gary said.

"Does NoDoz count?"

Gary looked at the laptop and sighed. "Look, it's not like I got something against you being happy, and I really hate to rattle your coping mechanisms, but there is *no* Annabel."

"No! You're wrong!" Hammon insisted, his voice breaking. This was why he couldn't talk to Gary about Annabel. Gary didn't understand.

"For your sake I wish I was. She doesn't exist. You understand that, don't you? Annabel isn't a real person, she's just something you created in your head, a delusion or whatever."

"No!" Hammon clapped his hands over his ears, turning away.

"Christ, Zap, are you seriously that messed up? I hate to say it, but like it or not, that's the truth. Annabel doesn't exist."

Gary was wrong; she *was* real. She had to be. "What about her clothes…and her…her…stuff. Her books, her music, her magazines, her toothbrush, her…"

"All bought by you, right?" Gary stared ahead with a pained expression. "Why in all the years I've known you, have I never seen her?"

"She pilots *Revenge*…She keeps a better course than me."

"It's called an autopilot," Gary said flatly.

"So then who messed up Stevenson? I saw Annabel; she drove right past me."

"You think you saw her. Like you think your nonexistent little girlfriend beat a two-hundred-fifty-pound man unconscious, stole his car and then your boat." Gary sighed. "Or maybe you snapped, went postal, and now you can't deal so you're blocking it out and letting your imaginary friend take the blame."

"That'd be pretty fucked up." Hammon paced the cockpit, scouring his brain. "Am I really that screwed up?"

"That, my friend, is and always has been the big question."

"Then what about *Revenge*?"

"Don't know. Coincidence?" Gary put *Temperance* into gear. "I'll tell you one thing. We'll overtake them soon enough. It'll be real interesting to see who's aboard."

Heart pounding, Hazel stood, knife raised to the darkness, listening. Only the engine's soft idle replied, exhaust gurgling as water slapped the transom. Buoy 31 gonged in a tug's wake.

She'd assumed the boat was empty, but Stevenson said a friend had borrowed it, and a horrifying realization hit: whoever was aboard may very well have been the other half of Stevenson's phone conversation.

There was nowhere to go; Hazel knew she had to face whatever lay beyond that door. Throat tight, fighting not to panic, she said, "We have to talk."

Nothing. The boat rolled and Hazel shivered as dew collected on the decks.

Damnit. This wasn't good. She couldn't stand there all night like that.

"Please…I had to get away and…"

Still no answer. She tried again to open the door.

"The boat is locked," said the soft feminine voice within the cabin.

"I got that, yeah."

She took a deep breath, trying to stay calm as her shaking fingers brushed the handle. The instant she did, the same voice repeated, "The boat is locked."

She pulled back, paused, and tried again.

"The boat is locked."

Each time her fingers contacted the cool metal, the reply was identical. Fear eroded into disbelief. She touched the knob.

"The boat is locked."

It was a recording, activated by touch. How and why was something else altogether. And sure enough the boat was, as it insisted, locked. Leaving the engine running, Hazel separated the keys and unlocked the cabin. The boat had nothing to say about that.

IT APPEARS I'M INSANE

It was pointless trying to reason with Gary. Hammon understood what he was saying about Annabel, deep down inside he sort of half knew. But he also knew he'd seen her driving the Viper. Or had he?

"What are we doing?" he asked, his voice cracking.

"Looking for your boat," Gary replied with strained patience.

"So *Revenge* is real. I was just checking." He studied Gary. "How do I know you are?"

Gary smacked him across the back of the head.

"Ow!" Hammon whined. "It was a valid question!"

"And that's my answer. Put it this way. In all these years, did you ever actually touch Annabel?"

Only when he was dreaming or dead. Hammon squeezed his pounding skull. His brain hurt from trying to sort out what was and wasn't real. He liked it better just accepting everything at face value. It was easier and way more fun. If Annabel wasn't real, then neither was what had been, up to that point, a workable existence. She was his guidance, his happiness, his love, and if she didn't exist, neither did any of that. He turned to Gary in desperation.

"So *Revenge* is gone, right? What if I docked somewhere else and forgot? I've done that, but when I did, Annabel..." His voice trailed off. Annabel told him where he left the boat. And where he parked. And where he left his keys, and his glasses, and…"How did Annabel always know things I forgot?"

"Maybe that's the part of your subconscious that remembers whatever your conscious brain blocks."

That sort of made sense. But he had bigger problems, and now Annabel wasn't there to help sort things out. "Someone took *Revenge*, for real. Somebody who knew about Stevenson and about me. That's really not good."

Gary rubbed his face. "Really?"

"Really what?"

"Never mind. Forget I said anything. You're good at that."

"Good at what?"

Gary shook his head. "Nothing."

02:45 MONDAY, JUNE 28

40°33'56.94"N/74°01'50.39"W

AMBROSE CHANNEL, RARITAN BAY, NJ

Hazel counted four seconds between the green flashes in the darkness and listened for the melodic gong of G19, marking Ambrose Channel. At nine knots on a heading of 200 degrees it was eight minutes to G17. She checked her watch, noted the time, and swung to a heading of 206 degrees. A pale glow appeared beside the chart, softly buzzing: Stevenson's phone with an incoming call from Joe's shop. She grabbed it and flipped it open.

"Dad?"

"Haze?" her father said, his voice hoarse.

"Dad! Is everyone okay? I've been calling all night! Stevenson has *Tuition*!"

Her father didn't reply. In the background, Micah shouted something to Joe.

"Did you hear me? Stevenson has *Tuition*; he was talking on the phone, telling them to get rid of *Witch*! I'm not making this up! You have to believe me! He had a file on all of us from before he hired us, with pictures of *Tuition* taken yesterday. He said he was going to take me somewhere and he'd drug me if I gave him any problems, but I got away."

"Oh, Christ. Hon, where are you?"

"Headed to Lou's place." Her father would know that meant Forelli's boatyard, and they both knew the Forelli family would keep her safe, no questions asked.

"Haze, what did you do to Stevenson?"

"I didn't kill him. I wanted to, but I didn't."

"Hon, listen to me. I'll come get you, but you've got to stay out of sight until then. Understand?"

"Yeah, but you and Micah…"

"We'll be fine. Just do as I say. Stay put, wait for me. And don't 'yes' me. I'm serious this time."

"I promise, Dad. I will."

I'M INSANE AND I'M BOATLESS

Hammon watched the slow-motion video game play out on the displays. There was the little boat shape on the chart plotter, that was *Temperance*, and there was the red dot on the laptop, that was *Revenge*. Hammon stared at the screens, sick to his stomach. Ironically, the concept of a tracker aboard *Revenge*, which should have been freaking him out, was the least of his concerns. It was the last link to the only part of his existence that actually existed.

"This tracker," Hammon said. "How long's it been there?"

"Since we first launched that barge, what's that, three years? In case you got into trouble, I'd know where to find you. You had some serious problems back then."

He still did. He'd just gotten better at hiding them. "Anyone else got access to this?"

"You mean like Stevenson?" Gary shook his head. "No. Just me. It's buried in the engine room, disguised as an inverter, with a rechargeable backup battery. We find the boat, I'll show you. How do you think I found you whenever you went missing?"

"You always said I called you. I didn't?"

"Nope. What's that tell you?"

Hammon nodded. "So now what?"

"I figure we get close, hang back, and do some fishing while we see where they're headed, then wait till they run out of fuel or tie up, whichever comes first."

"And then?" Hammon swallowed. He hadn't been seasick in years, but the urge to stick his head over the side was overwhelming. His world had been okay up to that point. It might have been built on illusions and delusions but it worked. Now it was shattered, his sanctuary violated and stolen from him. There was nowhere safe anymore, not even inside his brain. The only thing he had left was that tiny digital blip on the…

Hammon hiccupped.

Gary turned. "What?"

Hammon pointed at the screen. A pop-up stated: SIGNAL LOST.

"I didn't do it."

Gary leaned over, examining the display. "It's…wha'd you touch?" He hit refresh. A window came up reading: NO SIGNAL RECEIVED.

"I didn't do it!"

04:14 MONDAY, JUNE 28

40°27'55.27"N/74°15'24.97"W

CHEESEQUAKE CREEK, PARLIN, NJ

Dead ahead, flashing red and green buoys flanked the entrance to Cheesequake Creek. Hazel guided the boat through the inlet, taking care to keep the submerged portions of the east breakwater at a respectable distance. Three bridges lay ahead. The first, with a clearance of twenty-five feet, wasn't a concern. The second, a railroad bridge, had a clearance of three feet, but as far as Hazel recalled, it remained open unless a train was due. And the third, where the Garden State Parkway crossed the creek, marked the end of the navigable waters. But she wasn't going any further; to starboard the fuel dock at Forelli's Boatyard came into sight, a single light shining on the closed dock house. A slim shape bounded from the shadows, blue curls blowing across his face as he waved.

"Micah?" Hazel blinked back tears of relief. She edged the boat along the dock and he jumped aboard, climbed to the bridge, and lifted her off the deck in a bone-cracking hug. His hair and clothes smelled like a campfire.

"Hey, brat," he said. "Took you long enough getting here. I was starting to worry."

She buried her face against his shoulder. It seemed as though they'd been apart for years, and she'd started to feel like she'd never see him again. She looked to shore. "Where's Dad?"

"Head into the pit." Micah pointed toward the Travelift, rumbling to life. "We want to haul this thing before anyone's up and around."

Hazel spotted Tony Forelli at the controls, his stocky, barrel-chested shape a welcome sight. He waved a hairy arm, directing her in.

"Drop the straps low," she called over the lift's engine, pointing down and moving her hand in a horizontal circle: the standard signal for lower. "She's deeper than she looks."

Tony nodded and the motor whined, dropping the slings.

"We'll stick it in the east shed," Tony's father, Lou, directed. Still in his bathrobe, he looked around, scowling. "Tony, where the hell's your brother? I want Nicky out here now!"

Guided by Tony's signals, Hazel eased the boat into the lift, gave a quick goose in reverse, then dropped into neutral, bringing it to a stop. Nicky jogged barefoot and bare-chested from the clapboard cape overlooking the yard. He pulled on a sweatshirt as he ran, waving to Hazel. At fourteen, he shared the family tendency toward a broad build and thick black hair, though so far it remained isolated to his head and not covering the rest of him like a sweater.

"Nicky, get the shed open," Lou snapped. "And get some shoes on, damnit."

"Where's Dad?" Hazel said.

Micah studied her soberly. "You're okay?" He lifted her chin. "What'd that guy do? Your dad wouldn't tell me anything."

Hazel shut down the boat's engine. "Don't worry; you don't have to avenge my honor if that's what you mean. Where's Dad?"

"I broke your record for unlock and hotwire," Micah said proudly as he and Tony positioned the straps. "You'd think people would learn not to park in front of the lift. There's enough signs warning them not to block it."

Motors whined and slings tightened, hoisting the boat from the water. It swayed, suspended in the creaking straps, and the lift began to motor across the yard. Lou certainly wasn't wasting a second moving the boat out of sight, and still Hazel didn't see her father anywhere. She turned to Micah, uneasiness growing.

"Micah, where the hell is my dad?"

By his sheepish expression she knew she wouldn't like his answer. "He figured we'd be safe here and I could keep an eye on you." He paused, his dark eyes clouding. "Him and Joe went to see what's left of Stevenson."

"No! Damnit!" she cried in frustration. "He told someone to get rid of *Witch*! Why won't anyone ever listen to me? They have to move her!"

"Haze, it's just a boat," Micah said, his voice wavering.

Hazel stared at him, stunned. How could he say that? *Witch* was her home. That boat had been in the family for generations. She was irreplaceable! Micah turned away, and through her shock Hazel realized he was wiping his eyes.

"Micah?"

"I'm so sorry," he whispered. "I really fucked up."

Her grip on the wheel tightened as uneasiness gave way to dread. "Micah, what happened?"

He pulled a piece of damp, singed fabric from his pocket; Hazel unfolded it, her chest tightening as she studied the "NO WAKE ZONE" needlepoint that had hung outside her cabin door.

"We were pulling into the yard when we saw the flames. Your dad took an axe to the hull and sank her before she burned to the waterline. She's in one piece on the bottom until we can raise her. I dove down to…check…I…" His voice trailed off. "I…I'm so sorry."

Hazel blinked back tears and stared down at her hands, not knowing what to say.

"No one got hurt?" she mumbled finally.

"You mean your dad? Him hurt? Seriously?"

That was the most important thing, everyone was safe. Hazel didn't want to think beyond that. She realized she was unconsciously piloting the boat, turning the wheel as they approached the entrance to the shed at the far end of the yard.

The lift stopped and Tony lowered the boat until the keel settled on blocks Nicky had scrambled to set in place. He and Tony propped stands beneath the dripping hull, releasing the straps, then Tony pulled the Travelift back out to the yard while Nicky rolled the shed doors closed. Still Hazel sat there at the helm, frozen.

Micah put his hand on hers. "C'mon, hon. Ride's over."

"Where do we go now?" She looked around the brightly lit, windowless shed, feeling trapped. "It was safer out there…in the dark."

"We're safe here."

"Are we?"

Micah gave a weak smile. "Look at it this way. I lost *Tuition*, your car's history, *Kindling*'s gone, and *Witch*…well, she's gonna need some major work…and let's not mention your offerings to the Atlantic. The way I see it, things can't get much worse."

"Don't say that. Fate has a sick sense of humor."

Lou propped a ladder against the transom and they climbed down.

"Weird." Micah looked the boat over in the light. In contrast to the sleek, modern lines above the waterline, it carried a deep, ballasted keel, full skeg, and massive rudder.

Nicky bounded over, gazing at Hazel speechlessly while Lou knelt, inspecting the huge prop. He thumped on the hull. "Wood?" He flipped his Motorola open. "Tony? Call your uncle; tell Sal to send over an empty truck...not a Dumpster. A compactor. And tell him grab a dozen bagels on the way." He snapped the phone shut. "Nicky, quit mooning at Hazel and go make some coffee."

Color rose in Nicky's face, and he scrambled out the side door. Micah winked at Hazel. "Guess who hit puberty."

Lou stepped back, staring up, rubbing his chin. "Your dad says you two're in deep shit, and the less I know, the better. He said keep you out of sight until he gets here. This," he motioned toward the boat, arms spread, "is a problem."

Hazel studied the gracefully curved hull. "I had to get away. I figured I'd beach her somewhere. There might be some sort of tracker aboard, so I disconnected the batteries."

Lou's phone beep-beeped.

"There's no coffee filters in the break room," Nicky said.

"Then use a paint strainer." Lou turned to Hazel. "Your dad's instructions were very clear. He said make however you got here disappear. We strip anything of value; tomorrow night we tow what's left out and sink it."

Hazel looked up at the boat in dismay. "Couldn't we just hide her?"

Lou shook his head. "This thing's custom. We're talking big money. Sooner or later someone's gonna come looking for it. It's got to go. It was never here, no one ever saw it, no one knows nothing."

I TRIED

The first time Hammon saw Annabel, he was nothing but burned flesh and shattered bones. He was dying, or maybe already dead, the overwhelming pain receding, releasing him. And she appeared, a child no older than him, dark eyes filled with knowing sympathy, this angel in black, slender and delicate, long curls surrounding her like a veil. Then the doctors pulled him back, hooked him up to life support, stuffed the remaining brains into his shattered skull, and stitched what they could back together. He was alive, barely. But his angel was gone.

Until he slit his wrists. Unsure which way to cut, he played tic-tac-toe across his raw flesh. It was easy, numb with painkillers from his latest session of skin graft torture. He would've succeeded if no one had noticed. But as his heart stopped beating, she appeared.

Round three: a long drive in a small garage. He'd hoarded painkillers just for the occasion. He knew how it worked now: she wasn't real, but that didn't matter. When he was dead, or nearly there, she would come. Soothing numbness spread until he was too weak to cough back the suffocating fumes. He closed his eyes, drifting off, waiting. The music, Oingo Boingo's *Dead Man's Party*, became distant. Then he felt a kiss, light and gentle. He turned to see his little angel.

She looked disappointed. "Why are you doing this?"

That seemed pretty obvious. "I wanna be dead."

"You're not supposed to be."

"Do you know how much it hurts to live?"

That same solemn look. "I do."

"You're not gonna stop me."

In reply she only smiled.

He grinned. "I don't think I remember ever seeing you smile."

"Until now, you never said anything funny." She leaned over, kissing his forehead. "I'm sorry."

He later recalled overhearing doctors arguing, baffled by how he'd driven the car through the garage door, across the driveway, the street, and into the neighbor's lawn; by the levels of drugs in his system and carbon monoxide in his bloodstream, he should have been dead.

He was, for a moment at least. He felt Annabel's kiss.

The fourth time he made sure she couldn't stop him. It was March, and there was still snow on the ground. Again, the overdose of painkillers, enough to numb the shock of hypothermia when he pulled back the pool cover and slid into the deep end, straight to the bottom with barely a ripple. It was a new record for him, he'd flat-lined for over twenty minutes before they found him. There was no reasoning with Annabel, she was furious. But before water filled his lungs, his body temperature had plummeted. The sudden, rapid brain freeze and tranquilizers in his bloodstream had slowed his metabolism. It was rare, but not unheard of, surviving prolonged cold-water submersion. Annabel swore if he so much as tried to kill himself again she'd leave forever. He struck a bargain: if she'd stick around while he had a pulse, so would he.

The fifth time he died wasn't intentional. He was standing on *Revenge*'s bridge, gazing up in fascination. Over the freshly launched and christened boat, the sky had turned an ominous gray, clouds churning like boiling lead.

"Are you looking to get zapped or something?" Gary shouted from shore. "Get down below."

Hammon laughed as raindrops pelted him. "Lightning won't hit this. It'll hit a sailboat, they're higher."

It tickled as his hair stood on end, and he remembered a strange odor. Then he was flat on his back staring up as Gary knelt over him, cursing, pounding Hammon's chest. He heard cracking: his ribs, it turned out, and he wondered how Gary had gotten to the bridge when he was on shore a blink earlier. Annabel stood behind Gary, her expression grim.

"Get up," she said.

"Huh?"

Gary jumped back, looking at him as though he'd risen from the dead.

"You did," Annabel explained. "You were gone for a few minutes. Again."

"I don't remember." He didn't feel anything; that would come later.

"Your eyes," Gary mumbled.

They'd gone from blue to gray.

04:46 MONDAY, JUNE 28

40°27'24.61"N/74°16'09.29"W

PARLIN, NJ

"First things first." Tony propped a ladder against the boat and climbed up to the cockpit. "Disconnecting the batteries was smart, but those trackers usually have backup power. Let's take a look."

"Good luck finding anything." Hazel gathered her hair and tied it back. "The cabin's a mess."

"We can deal." Tony motioned to the garbage truck beeping its way backwards into the shed.

Nicky climbed aboard as Hazel opened the cabin. Micah peered in, aiming a flashlight around. He turned to Tony. "You're gonna need a bigger truck."

"What died in here?" Tony shined his flashlight through the salon. "Good God; it's worse than Nicky's bedroom."

Laundry, open bags of chips, empty burrito wrappers, Styrofoam cups, and half-empty soda bottles carpeted the floor. Pizza boxes, papers, and magazines buried a small sofa. A PlayStation and two controllers hooked into a TV set with an old radiation shield duct-taped over the screen. A milk crate brimmed with *Maxim*, *Weird NJ*, and *Hot Rod* magazines. A baseball cap rested on the compass, Cheez Doodles nestled beneath the depth finder, junk mail blanketed the console, and no two curtains matched. Tony opened one, only to find the window bricked closed. Not actually bricked, but covered in brick-patterned contact paper. The next was a poster of a tropical shoreline. Other windows featured the Manhattan waterfront, Stonington, Maine, and Seaside Heights, New Jersey.

Micah crunched through the salon. "You sure you stole the right boat?"

"I wondered at first, but the keys fit, and," Hazel held a stack of junk mail up to the light. "Jake Stevenson. J. Stevenson. Stevenson…"

Beneath the debris, the boat was solid wood, constructed with fine joinery. Three steps led down to a dinette covered by dirty non-skid plates and coffee cups. To starboard, a head and a biological warfare experiment shaped like a galley. Up forward, more debris buried the V-berths.

"Your pal Stevenson is one very disturbed individual." Micah passed her a *Maxim* magazine. Nearly every photo of a woman had the eyes and lips cut away. Page after page of mutilated faces gaped back with sightless jack-o'-lantern grins. Hazel closed the magazine, shuddering.

Tony studied the black rectangle over the head sink. "That's a unique decorating statement." He dug around then backed out with a small stack of pictures and a stunned expression. "This is seriously creepy."

"Creepier than those magazines?" Hazel turned. "What now?"

"Porn."

That got Micah's attention. "Really? Lemme see."

Tony's face glowed red. "You don't want to."

Micah grabbed the pile, flipping through them. "Whoa… Uh…That's just wrong." Clearing his throat, he handed them back to Tony. "I can't look at these."

"Since when were you squeamish over porn?" Hazel teased. "I've seen your apartment."

"Trust me. I don't have anything like this."

Hazel grabbed for the pictures, but Tony rolled them behind his back. "Just trust us. You don't want to see them."

Nicky snatched the pictures, dodging clear of his brother. He stared from them to Hazel. Crimson rose in his face.

Hazel seized the pictures. In truth they were fairly tame, more erotica than porn; vintage black-and-white photos of a young woman with dark curls bobbed in a 1920s style, intimately though not graphically exploring herself. That wasn't the disturbing part. It was the girl.

"Cut your hair," Micah said, "that could be you. *Is* you."

Hazel looked through the pictures, trying to convince herself there was no resemblance when undeniably there was. She shoved them into a grocery bag, burying them beneath Styrofoam cups and snack bags. "Weren't we looking for a tracker?"

She showed Tony the circuit breakers, parallel battery switch, and master switch she'd shut down. "Nicky, get some power up here."

Nicky nodded, discreetly lifting the grocery bag as he exited, returning minutes later with extension cords and droplights, further illuminating the disaster area.

"You think everything else was weird? Check this out." Hazel moved debris to open the hatch, lowering a droplight into the engine room as Tony and Micah stared in awe. An immaculate Lehman diesel gleamed like a jewel, surrounded by the best fuel systems money could buy.

Tony climbed down, inspecting the neat, color-coded wiring, looking around the spotless compartment. "This boat's got serious grounding and a fortune in soundproofing. If there's anything alarming, I don't see it. I'd say our best bet's to get the chainsaws and break it up. I'm sure I can find this beauty," he patted the diesel affectionately, "a good home, but the sooner this boat's chopped up and carted away, the sooner there's nothing to find."

Hazel looked around and felt ill. The boat was supposed to be a means of escape, not a casualty; why should it pay for her crime? If it were Stevenson's black boat, she'd be the first one with the axe. But this was an endangered species: a wooden boat. To imagine it had survived all these years only to meet this unfortunate end by her actions was unthinkable. She turned to Micah, desperate. "But…she…we can't!"

"She?" Micah gave her that same pained look her father did whenever she went off on him for suggesting it was time to sell *RoadKill*.

"We need a boat. *Kindling*'s gone, and *Witch*…" Her voice trailed off. She couldn't even say it. "Stevenson owes us a boat."

Tony shook his head and repeated what his dad had said: "Someone sank a chunk of cash into this thing. You can bet they'll be looking for it."

"Yeah," Micah said, "But all my uncle said was, 'make it disappear.' I noticed when I got here, that old Wheeler in the boneyard's moved from repair row to death row."

Hope rose in Hazel. "*Mardi*?" That boat had been magnificent once, but abandoned for decades and long past restoration. She knew just what Micah was thinking.

Tony said. "The hull's shot on that."

I PROBABLY NEED MY HEAD EXAMINED

"Shit." Hammon mumbled. "Shit-shit-shit-shit-shit." He whacked the side of the display with no improvement. He whacked his head against the display, but that didn't help either. Gary grabbed him by the hair before he could try again. His already precariously balanced brain was pushing overload. If he accepted Annabel's nonexistence, would she cease to exist? Was that how it worked? Had he lost his boat, his dearest companion, and his mind all in the course of one night?

"Quit it," Gary said.

"But...I thought it wasn't supposed to do that."

"It isn't." Gary slumped against the companionway and stared blankly at the chart, where Hammon had compulsively scribbled the progressing positions of both boats, at least until *Revenge's* position had vanished.

"I'll be damned." Gary leaned closer. "See the course before the signal died, moving from mark to mark." He traced his finger along the chart. "They took Chapel Hill South Channel. If they were heading east of Sandy Hook, they'd take the Narrows to Ambrose Channel. The signal stopped here, heading two hundred, forty-seven degrees, which puts you here." His finger stopped at Green 11A, north of Keansburg. "I'd bet they weren't planning on going much further. Think about it; they left Stevenson for dead, then took *Revenge*, not Stevenson's boat. They probably wanted to keep a low profile but expected more speed than they got. And…" He circled Keyport and the Raritan River. "I were them, I'd tie up and split before it gets light. I'd bet up one of these creeks, we'll find your boat."

But they didn't.

Yard by yard, marina by marina, they searched. Great Kills, through Arthur Kill, up and down the Raritan River, no boat. The farther they went, the closer Hammon crept toward total breakdown. Hope turned to despair as the sky grew lighter. If *Revenge* wasn't already abandoned, it wasn't going to be. It could be hidden under a tarp, in a boat shed, anywhere.

"My entire life is in that boat."

Gary sighed. They'd reached the navigable end of Cheesequake Creek. Overhead, tires hummed along the Garden State Parkway.

"That barge of yours couldn't just disappear into thin air." Gary turned *Temperance* around. He'd been defensive ever since Hammon suggested the rechargeable backup battery may have passed its useable life span. Hammon wasn't blaming him, just suggesting a possibility, but Gary took any overlooked detail personally. So Hammon sat scratching Charger's head and staring out at the passing, *Revenge*-less scenery.

And then he saw Annabel.

Wrapped in his favorite sweatshirt, standing on the riverbank in the light of the rising sun, she gazed across the water, her expression distant. Time froze and Hammon watched, captivated, afraid to blink as the light breeze brushed the curls in front of her eyes. How could something that seemed so real not be real? Was his brain that screwed up?

They rounded the bend, and he lost sight of her, breaking the spell, snapping him back to reality. "Gary, go back."

"You saw *Revenge*?" Gary swung *Temperance* around. The dogs, sensing the sudden change, rose expectantly.

"That way." Hammon pointed toward the yard they just passed. "Over there." If Gary could see her, it was proof he wasn't completely insane.

But she was gone. On the east side, a Travelift cautiously lifted the hulk of an ancient sport-fisherman, the weathered hull so sprung the low sun shined through in places.

"That, my friend, is *not* your boat. I think it's time we call it a night."

Hammon blinked. Annabel *had* been there; he'd seen her.

Then again, maybe he hadn't.

23:48 MONDAY, JUNE 28

40°27'24.61"N/74°16'09.29"W

PARLIN, NJ

"Just in case," Hazel said, rigging a snare beneath the freshly rechristened *Mardi*, still high and dry inside the south shed. "Moderate tension. Catch and hold, not kill. I warned Tony."

Micah hauled the ladder up and laid it in the cockpit. "You are a twisted child. You know that, right?"

"So say the pysch reports. 'Exhibits potentially sociopathic tendencies.'"

It had been a long, exhausting day, and though it was late, neither of them was ready to sleep. There was too much to discuss, and for the first time since Hazel arrived, they were finally alone. They'd spent the day within the shed with Tony, Nicky, and Lou, cannibalizing the derelict Wheeler. Pieces were pried and Sawz-alled off the old boat, then just as crudely grafted onto the stolen boat using bolts, wood screws, epoxy, and 5200. Work was quick and sloppy, with leftover house paint slapped over everything, and by day's end the sleek boat was transformed into a forlorn, neglected-looking wreck. And while not as spacious as Tony's efficiency apartment, the "new" *Mardi* offered individual bunks and privacy to talk. So after pizza and showers, they left Tony out cold on the couch in front of late-night TV and returned to the boat.

"Cute," Micah said, referring to Hazel's kitty-cat top and pajama pants. "That was kind of Stevenson, leaving clothes aboard for you."

"I think they're for some girl he knows. But they were never worn, they fit, and I'm too tired to care."

They spread borrowed sleeping bags across the V-berths. Hazel claimed the starboard side and Micah posted the charred "NO WAKE ZONE" needlepoint on the port bulkhead. Power remained disconnected, and an oil lamp cast warm light through the cabin. Micah contemplated the galaxy of luminescent dots scattered overhead, glowing in a perfect representation of the winter sky, his expression troubled and tense.

"So let's hear it," Hazel said at last. "Why'd you take *Tuition,* and what the hell is going on?"

"I fucked up," Micah admitted. "Kessler said he'd pay me five grand cash if I did a delivery for him. Haul a load of broken mini-fridges to a warehouse in Florida, swap them for repaired ones, and deliver to some other stores, all off the books. He didn't want mileage showing on the company trucks. I figured I'd use *Road-Kill,* but he said use the new rig or no deal; he didn't want me breaking down or getting pulled over."

He paused, as though expecting Hazel to say something. She already had a list of questions, but she wanted to let him talk, which once he got rolling he usually did. Seeing that she was still waiting, finally he continued.

"It seemed so simple. You and your dad were sailing a delivery down to Maryland, and I figured I'd have *Tuition* back before you returned. I'd tell your dad I hauled a boat for someone, give him some of the cash, and so long as I didn't get a scratch on the truck, he couldn't be too pissed."

"And did you even wonder what you were really hauling?" Hazel said, realizing how reproachful that sounded. "Keith said he'd heard Kessler was moving drugs."

Micah rubbed his face and closed his eyes. "Kessler said it was appliances, and that was fine by me. I didn't know; I didn't want to know. All I knew was it was cash, I've got a fortune in school loans, and my daddy didn't save up a truckload of money to send me to college."

It was the one sore subject between them, one they rarely touched upon. Her father was a first-class hard-ass at times, but he'd always put Hazel ahead of everything including himself, and sometimes she took that for granted. She reached across and gave Micah's hand a squeeze.

"I'm sorry, hon," he said. "It's just…yeah, trust me, I know… in hindsight it was a stupid move. Real stupid. I knew it at the time. I didn't let myself think about it; I just drove. Each place I delivered, they had at least one or two broken units for me to take back. I made the last delivery in Elizabeth then pulled off at Vince Lombardi to fuel up. I figured I'd better return *Tuition* topped off. I run in to take a leak and grab a coffee, not five minutes, and I *know* I locked the truck." Micah dug in his pocket, producing the keys. "I come out and *Tuition's* gone. The only things left were a bunch of busted freezers in the trailer and A/Cs, and my phone in the cab. I called Kessler from a pay phone, and he went ballistic, screaming how if I didn't have that cargo back, I was good as dead. I was screwed; if Kessler didn't kill me, your dad would for sure. Joe wasn't answering, so I called Atkins then spent the night hiding on the side of the Turnpike until he got there."

"Why Atkins?" Hazel sat up. "Keith said Atkins threatened to break your legs."

Micah grinned. "Yeah, I guess that sounds bad out of context. He'd been driving for Kessler, doing the same run once a month using his own rig. He actually thought he was moving appliances, nothing more, and he wasn't getting paid all that much. The last time Atkins drove, Kessler paid him from a duffle bag filled with bundled hundred-dollar bills, and when he saw all the cash, Kessler actually tossed him an extra grand, 'a bonus,' to forget what he saw. Atkins decided he didn't want to get pulled over and find out what he was really hauling. He told Kessler no thanks, keep your money, find someone else. When Kessler came to me, Atkins tried to steer me clear. But I didn't want to hear it; all I could think of was paying down my student loans."

"How do you know Atkins wasn't setting you up?"

"Because he wouldn't. He's a good person."

"Who called Keith, saying he knew I was all alone and could probably use some company? He wanted to pay me a visit and show me something."

Micah burst out laughing. "I knew that'd freak you out! I couldn't just call you, that was too risky. I figured Kessler was watching you, and I knew you'd start looking for me, but if Keith relayed that message, we both know your dad would sure as hell drop by to have a word with Atkins."

Hazel didn't quite share Micah's unquestioning faith in Atkins, but voicing her opinion wouldn't change anything. "These shipments, who else knew about them?"

"Anyone along the route, I guess. Or maybe someone just wanted a nice new truck."

"Not just anyone," Hazel announced at last, sitting up. She brought out the manila file, hidden beneath the bunk mattress, and passed it to Micah. "Stevenson has *Tuition*."

He inspected the photos of *Tuition* and the cargo. "Yep. That looks like all of it. Why didn't you mention this sooner?"

"I wanted to hear your side first. There's something I learned from Travis McGee; he called it 'Meyer's injunction,' from his friend Meyer. It goes, 'Don't mix up what you really know with what you think you know.' I figured it was better to see what you could tell me."

Micah held up the photo of her reading the *Times*. "Excellent composition. I like the way the sunlight catches your hair. Nice touch with the finger. This come in wallet size?"

"It's not a joke. I still don't get where Stevenson fits in."

"Atkins thinks Kessler was just middle management."

"Speculation."

"No. He said the routes weren't in Kessler's handwriting. Maybe Kessler and Stevenson were partners."

"Then why intercept his own shipment? And who was he talking to on the phone?"

"Dunno. What else you got there?"

"His wallet." She passed it over. "And his phone, but he deleted everything in it."

Micah examined Stevenson's driver's license. "No way! JAKE Stevenson?"

"You know him?"

"Not personally, but I've heard of him. This guy, he's like a legend in green engineering. My thesis on the economics of global warming, half my information came from his articles and work. We talk about him all the time in the engineering department. No way he's dealing drugs."

"You don't know that; maybe the economics just work on paper." Hazel stared up, picking out constellations and brooding. Something didn't fit, but she couldn't put her finger on what. Then it hit her. She sat up, sniffing. "Do you smell smoke?"

Micah sniffed. "Wet paint, mildew, stale Fritos. My clothes smelled like schooner flambé, but I left them in the cockpit."

"I mean cigarette smoke. All Stevenson's things smelled like an ashtray." She looked up at the stars on the ceiling. "But not this. Whoever borrowed the boat had it for a while, which means this mess isn't Stevenson's…and neither is the porn or the weird covered windows." She chewed her lip, thinking. "But all the mirrors in his house were painted over the same way. Odd. What if whoever borrowed the boat is who Stevenson was talking to?"

Micah lay back and contemplated the painted galaxy. "Well, we know it sure as hell wasn't Kessler."

"I'd love to pay Stevenson a visit and ask him some questions."

"I don't think he'll be answering anything for a while." Micah mock-punched her in the shoulder. "You really need to work on your self-control."

Hazel wasn't amused. "I didn't hit him that hard; just enough to keep him down."

A midday call from her father confirmed she indeed had not killed Stevenson, but come "damn-near close." He was in critical condition, more or less comatose, and the police were seeking information regarding a girl he'd been seen with earlier that day. It was vital she and Micah stay out of sight. They assured her father they were locked in the old building and going nowhere.

Hazel said. "We can't just sit here like this, doing nothing."

"You heard your dad. We're supposed to wait for him here."

"And suddenly you're listening to my dad? Seriously, he left you in charge of me! *You.* I mean, no offense, but that's like leaving the inmates in charge of the prison, and we both know it."

"That's what Joe said. Your dad called it the lesser of two evils."

"What's the greater?"

"He wouldn't tell me. Plausible deniability, he said. If I didn't know, then you couldn't beat it out of me."

I'M JUST LISTENING TO
THE VOICE IN MY HEAD

More alone than he could remember in years, Hammon pulled into the boatyard he'd seen that morning. In the glare of the Fairmont's headlights, he read a plywood sign propped against a fifty-gallon drum:

Welcome to Forelli's Boatyard.
We are moving boats. Cars must be left UNLOCKED with keys IN IGNITION or they WILL be forklifted into the creek. Thank you.

He drove through the dark lot, surrounded by shadows of blocked-up boats, and a quick look over the slips confirmed *Revenge* wasn't in the water. A few runabouts and cuddy cabins sat on the hard dirt along with a cluster of weary sailboats, a stocky old Cheoy Lee trawler, and several shrink-wrap-cocooned shapes. Two were close enough in size to be possibilities. The Travelift stood to the south beside a tired wooden shed large enough to conceal *Revenge* four times over. Hammon parked in the darkest corner and slipped out of the Fairmont, grabbing his backpack and locking the car. From the shadows he watched to see if anyone noticed or cared.

Apparently no one did. The docks were devoid of all life. Lights shined from a small Cape Cod on the north side of the yard, the shades drawn. The blue glow of a TV flickered from behind a second-story window over the south shed, but no one looked out. It was a shopping-cart yard.

There were yacht clubs: gated, manicured establishments with pools, tennis courts, and private memberships; and there were marinas: friendly family places open to anyone who paid for a slip, with clean showers, maybe a clubhouse and pool and "dock carts" for moving gear. And then there were boatyards: gravel and dirt paved, overgrown, undergroomed places dealing in the messy business of keeping boats running, with an eclectic assortment of shopping carts pilfered from local supermarkets and home improvement superstores. In general, shopping-cart yards were somewhat lax regarding security other than perhaps a mellow dog or cat. Hammon saw no signs of any four-footed patrols. But a lone video camera rotated atop the shed, covering the span of the property.

Hammon stepped between two boats, where the camera couldn't follow. He removed his backpack and pulled out a small, highly accurate paintball gun with a night scope. He timed the camera, steadied his breathing, took aim, and fired. The camera lens continued its sweep, now sporting a fresh splat of water-soluble white paint. Local gulls would take the blame and the next good downpour would rinse it away. Hammon moved on, inspecting covered boats, none of which were *Revenge*, when a slender shape emerged from the shadows.

"You are here," he mumbled.

She smiled. "I was never gone, dear."

Hammon fought the urge to reach forward, to touch her dark curls, feel her satiny skin. He knew better. "But you're not real. I know that now."

"You always did, in your heart at least; but you never wanted to face reality. Far be it for me to complain. Why shatter a perfect illusion with messy facts?"

"Like the fact that I'm nuts?"

"A technicality. Does it change anything?"

She had a point. He could let it bother him or he could simply accept it and move on. He was more concerned with finding *Revenge*. Once he found the boat, he could search for his lost mind. He turned his attention to the locked shed, which raised the stakes from temporary vandalism to breaking and entering. He rummaged through his backpack for the appropriate tools, pressed his shoulder to the door frame, and set to work. Aided by a few picks and some gentle persuasion, he convinced the lock to cooperate, then opened the door a quarter inch, listening for alarm sounds but hearing nothing alarming.

He slipped through, shining his flashlight up at the darkened superstructure of a weathered black Wheeler that had seen better decades. It sat neglected and forlorn: the centerpiece in an arrangement of oil drums, paint cans, old fenders, tarps, delaminated plywood, and other random junk piled high against the hull. The boat looked familiar, but bore no resemblance to *Revenge*'s sleek lines. The bridge was shorter and higher. Wide overhangs surrounded the salon. Heavy, work-scarred rub rails ran from bow to stern, and rows of lobster-boat-type strakes covered the hull. A long pulpit jutted from the metal-sheathed plumb bow. And rising from the cockpit, a short mast projected upward, rigged to a boom with heavy block and tackle, ideal for raising lobster pots or massive sharks…

"That's it!" Annabel laughed, delighted. "It's the boat from *Jaws*."

Hammon swept the beam across the stern, where faded, stained block letters read "*Mardi*." He sighed. *Revenge* was probably hundreds of miles away.

"That's something I've always admired in you," Annabel said. "Your optimism."

Hammon trudged out of the shed. "Realism. Why you think I hate reality? Guess it's time for Plan B," he said, with no Plan B in mind. It just sounded like the thing to say.

"I'm already on it," Annabel said, skipping toward the docks.

"On what?"

"Plan B. I bought another boat."

Hammon squeezed his eyes shut for a moment. "You... Wha...How...?"

"Online. Think about it. You saw 'me' here this morning, but that wasn't me, just like it wasn't me in the Viper last night. When I looked up information on this place—"

"Looked up when? How?"

"I told you. Online, at Gary's. You wouldn't remember, you thought you were asleep. Anyways, the yard had some boats for sale. I figured I'd buy one so we'd have some privacy, somewhere to rest, a good excuse for being here, and a way to keep watch. I transferred the money online."

"Annabel...which boat?" A bad feeling grew as he scanned the docks, spotting his worst nightmare.

"That's her!" Annabel beamed. "Isn't she neat?"

"That thing?" He'd never seen the boat before, yet he recognized it. "Good God, angel, it's a dinghy!"

"Oh, seriously. She's not that small."

"You've gotta be kidding. It's…it's…" He was at a loss for words. Bow to stern, it couldn't have been more than twenty feet.

"Her name's *Nepenthe.* How cool is that? She has an inboard diesel, standing headroom in the cabin—"

"What…where…how? And what's with all those ropes and the big pole in the middle?"

"She's a sailboat. Gaff rig, in fact."

"And that means what to me? In case you forgot, I can't sail."

"Trust me, I know what I'm doing. Have I ever guided you wrong? It made sense: we're yard customers now, not trespassers. It's perfect."

"Wha…no. 'Perfect' is twice that big and has zero sails."

"It's somewhere to sleep, and it's bigger than Gary's couch."

"Barely."

Annabel planted her hands on her hips, and her eyes narrowed.

"Let's get something clear right now. Everything from your brainstem up, I own. Understand? You're just the tenant. I get the right side of your brain, as in I'm always right, and you get the left, as in you get what's left. I control the majority, and I'm not staying at Gary's place. I do the thinking and I need rest. Like it or not, I bought that boat. The paperwork and keys are under the starboard seat cushion."

23:58 TUESDAY, JUNE 29

40°27'56.56"N/74°17'17.25"W

MILE 123, GARDEN STATE PARKWAY, NJ

Just before midnight a white 1986 Volvo wagon heading up from Great Adventure pulled off the Garden State Parkway and into the Cheesequake service area, parking in the southeast lot. Four college-age males with a weed-induced case of the munchies spilled out, unaware that they were under surveillance. Joking and shoving, they piled into the building, oblivious to the figure slipping from the shadows to follow them. They gazed up at the glowing menu over the twenty-four-hour Burger King, debating how to best spend their remaining cash, when a pretty, dark-eyed girl with bobbed curls approached, asking how to find Seaside Heights.

Their eager, stoned attempts to give her skimpy tank top directions were almost comical. Though north and south were alien concepts, the group was determined to help, offering to drive, lead, follow, and in one case, marry her. When at last they agreed on an incorrect route, she nodded tentatively, then tried to repeat it back, even more confused than them. Pouting, she sighed. "Could you tell me again?"

A lanky, clean-cut young man strolled up, smiling. "It's cool, sis." He held up a map. "I got it."

The girl thanked her disappointed new friends, then she and her companion exited the west end of the building.

"See," Micah said as they headed toward the white 1986 Volvo wagon parked in the northwest lot. "I said the short hair works for you."

Hazel ran her fingers along the back of her head. It felt light and tickled. "I hate to break it to you, but they weren't looking at my hair."

"Exactly. Now they can see the rest of the package."

"Yeah, well, how about next time I hot-wire the car and you distract the horny stoners."

"I don't think I'm their type." Micah combed his fingers through his trimmed, nonblue hair. "And even if I was, I look like a total dork."

"You look adorable."

"I look like I'm twelve."

Aside from the shark's tooth tucked beneath his T-shirt, all his body jewelry was gone. It was Hazel's idea. If they planned to embrace a life of crime, they needed to be less recognizable. She cut her long hair into a loose bob, quite similar, Micah noted, to vintage-porno girl. Trimming his hair was almost paint-by-numbers, cutting off four inches of blue, leaving an inch of brown.

"The way I see it, we're doing them a favor, stealing their car." Micah opened the door for her. "They were in no condition to drive. Even if they remember where they parked, I doubt they'll call the police, at least for a while."

"We're not stealing." Hazel started the engine. "We're borrowing. By dawn, it'll be right back where they left it."

WHERE THE HELL IS BIVALVE, NJ?

Much as Hammon hated to admit it, Annabel was right: the little boat she'd bought provided them a sheltered bunk in which to grab a few hours of much-needed rest. Within the cavelike cabin, he slept through much of the day and into the evening, waking just after dusk. Under the guise of sending flowers, he'd called the hospital, only to learn that Stevenson had checked himself out. So Hammon pulled into the state park bordering Stevenson's property then skulked through the woods to get closer and watch the house with a night scope.

"Looks like he's alone," Annabel said.

Hammon scaled the wall near the carriage house, lowered himself into the yard, and attached the tracker he'd acquired from Gary's shop to the Mercedes. Soon after, the Evil One emerged, moving stiffly, and drove off.

Hammon tailed him down Route 46 to an industrial park in Little Ferry and a brick warehouse beside the Hackensack River. Lights out, Hammon stopped short of the lot and waited on the shoulder, noticing as a rusted blue Buick wagon pulled up. Hammon ducked behind rows of trailers then circled to the back. The Buick shut down and a large man emerged, approaching Stevenson.

"Who's that?" Annabel whispered.

"Someone I wouldn't want to meet in a dark alley." He watched them shake hands, joking, it appeared, about Stevenson's injuries. Then they opened a warehouse door to reveal a red tractor-trailer truck.

"They seem pleased," Annabel said.

Hammon crept closer, pulled the envelope from his pocket, and scribbled down the Buick's description and plates. The semi lacked plates, but the door read "Moran Marine Transport," with a phone number and address, which Hammon copied.

"Bivalve, New Jersey?" Annabel said. "Is that even a real place?"

Stevenson and the stranger inspected the trailer's contents, closed the warehouse, and returned to their cars. By the time Hammon reached the Fairmont, they were both long gone. He wasn't sure whether to track Stevenson or look for the Buick, but Annabel decided they check out the address on the truck instead.

00:15 WEDNESDAY, JUNE 30

40°27'20.89"N/74°17'45.77"W

ROUTE 9 NORTH, SOUTH AMBOY, NJ

Hazel pulled into the White Castle drive-through. "Are you sure this is a good idea?"

"Hell yeah. I think better on a full stomach." Micah scanned the menu sign. "Get a sack of ten Sliders. With cheese. And four orders of fries. And onion rings. And clam strips. And those fish whatevers."

"I meant talking to Atkins. You trust him?"

"Completely. He risked his neck to help me when he didn't have to."

"Why? What's in it for him?"

Hazel ordered, paid, and passed Micah the food. The aroma of White Castle filled the Volvo, but she had no appetite.

"Believe it or not, Haze, not everyone has a motive. Some people do the right thing because it's the thing to do." Micah shot his straw wrapper at her, missing. "Pull into that gas station up ahead, I'll call him from there."

Reluctantly Hazel swung in and parked. Micah jogged over to the phone, but Hazel couldn't hear his conversation over the passing cars. He returned, shaking his head. "Nope. He's never heard of Stevenson."

"So now what?"

"We drop in on Keith, see what he knows." Micah slid a square burger from its box, popping it in his mouth. He offered her one. "Eat. You'll feel better."

"Why not just call?"

"Face-to-face he says more."

"I guess. He doesn't think highly of your friend Atkins."

Micah grinned. "Most people don't."

"You sure he'll be home? We should call first," she said, still hoping to avoid the visit if possible.

"It's a weeknight; Keith *never* goes out on weeknights. Saturday he goes fishing, and Sunday's the Lord's day; you should know that." He squeezed the ketchup packet into his mouth and chased it with a handful of fries, smiling blissfully. "C'mon, hon, you're making me feel guilty. It's not fair, I can't enjoy this if you don't."

Hazel ate to pacify him while Micah continued to talk, mostly about school, girls he wanted to ask out, and other neutral subjects as the dark miles rolled by. The sparse traffic thinned. Finally Micah said, "So I hear you dumped Keith. What happened?"

"We didn't have much in common. Why'd you fix me up with him?"

"He kept asking. Keith seemed decent, and I thought it'd be good for you. He asked if you were seeing anyone, and I said you'd vowed to never give your heart again after the tragic death of your one true love."

Hazel glared at him. "That's not funny."

"But it's true. Seriously, you were what, fourteen? I think it's time to let it go, and I figured Keith'd be a good place to start. He's so polite it's obnoxious. He actually asked permission to date you and vowed he'd treat you with the highest respect."

"Oh, he was perfectly respectful. He wasn't after my body... just my soul."

"I don't follow."

"He wanted me to find God."

"God's lost?" Micah chuckled. "Oh, right. I saw something on the back of a milk carton. It said, 'Have you seen this deity?'"

"I'm serious. He'd start going on about Jesus, salvation, and how we must 'fight temptations of the flesh.' I mean, Jesus had the right idea with that 'do unto others' thing, but sermons on sin and eternal damnation aren't my idea of a fun date. It got old fast, and real creepy. That, and how what he liked most about me was that I was, how'd he put it, 'pure and undefiled.'"

Micah raised an eyebrow. "He said that? For real?"

"Yeah, for real. He told me he was a terrible sinner before the Lord saved him, and I should open my heart to Jesus. The more I wouldn't denounce my heathen ways and convert, the more determined he got."

"You never told me this."

"He's your friend; I figured you knew."

"Not really. I remember him saying how Christ's true believers would float into the sky and there'd be empty cars and planes crashing all over the place. I just thought he was stoned."

"Nope, no drinking or drugs for Keith. That's the Rapture, and he says it will happen. I figure if it doesn't hurt anyone, what the hell, believe what you want. But it was scary how insistent he was that I believe it too."

Micah looked around as Hazel pulled up to the stop sign. "Take a right...your other right. Starboard. Go past the pizza shop, four doors up, and here we are." Micah pointed to a small house; Hazel continued past and parked two doors down.

She'd never been to Keith's apartment; she'd kept their dates on neutral ground. The shades and curtains were closed and light glowed from a lone window. She recognized Keith's Jeep by the surf-fishing rod holder and the stickers. There was a parking permit for fishing at Sandy Hook along with "Got Jesus?," "CHOOSE LIFE," and "In case of Rapture, this vehicle will be unmanned." They left the car unlocked and headed toward the house, skirting around to the back door, not visible from the street.

"He means well, right? He's just looking out for your soul."

"Screaming at me that I'd burn in hell."

Micah seemed stunned. "I've never seen Keith even raise his voice."

"He takes his faith very seriously. He said it was my fault, I made him lose his temper because I wouldn't be saved. And since then, he keeps calling, trying to convince me to come back. Thanks but no thanks."

Micah knocked and they waited, listening for movement. He knocked again, harder, while Hazel backed up. She didn't want to be there; deep down she was sure it was a mistake. Micah offered her a quick smile, squeezing her hand. "I hear him in there. Yo! Keith! C'mon, dude, open up!"

The kitchen window shade shifted. "Micah?" Keith peered out. "Hazel!" He was barefoot, wearing faded Levis and no shirt, as if he'd dressed in a hurry. It was possible they woke him, though Hazel didn't detect any traces of sleep in his eyes.

"Hazel…you're all right!" He reached for her hand but she stood clear. He glanced around at the dark yard then ushered them inside, locking the door and switching on the light. The florescent bulb buzzed and flickered, casting drab illumination over the kitchen. The counters and floors were clean, but the room was dull and colorless. On the wall a single print in a plastic frame, titled "Footsteps in the Sand," showed just that.

"I've been worried sick." Keith stared at Hazel with an odd mix of enthrallment and anxiety. "After your boat sank and I saw your car…I felt like I was being punished. I've searched everywhere for you. I kept praying you were safe somewhere and the Lord would bring you back to me. But then I heard you were dead," he said, his voice breaking. "Both of you."

"Really?" Micah grinned. "Says who?"

"Kim in the front office. She said her cousin's boyfriend's brother heard that the Coast Guard found your old runabout sunk three miles south of Thompsons Beach with a body aboard. The crabs didn't leave much to identify."

"Her cousin's boyfriend's brother? Cool." Micah beamed at Hazel. "We're urban legend!"

"The police came by work asking questions." Keith stared at Hazel. "They're looking for Atkins. The warehouse guys think Atkins dumped Hazel's body somewhere in the pinelands." Keith cleared his throat and wiped sweat from his forehead. "There's a pool going for where and when they'll find her."

Micah chuckled. "What's your money on?"

Keith dug a small metal case out of his pocket, opened it, and tucked a toothpick in his mouth. "Gambling goes against the scriptures," he said hostilely, then turned to Hazel, his expression softening. "I'm just grateful you're safe."

Micah nodded. "If you were a betting man, who'd you say wants us dead?"

Keith chewed at the toothpick, worrying. "Atkins. I tried to warn you, both of you. You can't trust him."

"Anyone else?"

The toothpick twitched. Keith glanced away and gave his head an odd, rigid shake. "No. No one. Why would anyone else want you dead?"

Hazel heard a small sound down the hall, quiet but definite, and Keith stiffened. His eyes met Hazel's and then dropped to the floor. He stepped over to the chipped enamel sink, noisily restacking the dishes drying on the rack.

Hazel eased her knife out and the blade locked open with a soft click. Micah's fingers closed over her wrist. "This is a mistake." She tried to pull her hand free. "He's hiding something." A tall shadow moved in the hall. "And he's not alone."

I'M IN THE MIDDLE OF NOWHERE,
AKA BIVALVE, N.J.

"Annabel, I don't think we're in Jersey anymore."

They had long since left everything familiar behind. The road dissolved into ground fog, and the scenery turned into mile upon mile of scrub pines occasionally opening to lush acres of produce, almost as if to validate that the "Garden State" was indeed just that. The night air was rich with fertilizer and growing vegetation. It was alien to Hammon: beautiful, desolate, and unsettling. Eventually the highway ended, and they wove through smaller roads.

"Maybe this Bivalve place doesn't even exist," Hammon said as they passed a "Muskrat Crossing" sign and the pavement turned to crushed white shells.

"Maybe not. But we're there."

Hammon shut the engine and coasted into the lot. He looked up at the "Go Away" sign. "I'm guessing there's no security camera." He scanned the desolation, not seeing *Revenge*. Or much else, for that matter.

Annabel took in all that was Bivalve at two a.m. "I think I saw this place in a horror movie."

Hammon wandered past a row of dying tomato plants and over to the docks. The smell of damp smoke lingered, and a few of the pilings were charred on one side. Tilted masts emerged from the water, rising from the ghostly shape of what had been a magnificent boat.

"Spooky," commented Annabel.

Hammon swept the flashlight along the submerged wreck. Oddly, it resembled a scorched, sunken double-masted version of Annabel's little sailboat. Burnt rigging lines swayed with the current, and oil still leaked to the surface.

"No slime or barnacles. This was recent," Annabel said.

Hammon shuddered and backed away. He pulled the envelope from his pocket and made some notes. Parked beside a decrepit Travelift and a mud-encrusted Miata stood an ancient tractor trailer, bearing the same logo as the semi Stevenson had.

"HAZEL." Annabel read the faded air dam. "Why do I feel like I should know that name?"

Hammon ran his hand across the grill cover to confirm the massive truck was, indeed, real, then added that information to his notes and stuffed the envelope back into his coat pocket.

From the darkness at the end of the hall, a woman stepped forward, offering Hazel and Micah an embarrassed smile. "I'm sorry. I didn't mean to frighten you. When I heard someone pounding on the door, I was afraid it was my husband."

She was tall and graceful, and despite wearing no more than Keith's T-shirt, every inch of her, from her honey-blonde hair and diamond solitaire earrings to her neatly pedicured toes, projected elegant refinement. Hazel had no idea who she was, but Micah seemed to.

"Uh, hi, Mrs. Nelson."

She laughed uncomfortably. "Please, Micah. It's Valerie. And this shy thing must be the lovely Hazel that Keith's told me so much about. You're correct, Miss Moran. Keith is hiding something. He's trying to protect my good name and his own. It wouldn't reflect well on either of us if word of this spread."

Valerie Nelson, Hazel realized. Mrs. Tom-the-Appliance-King-Nelson. Hazel glanced at Keith, who suddenly couldn't meet her eyes. In fact, all his color was gone and he looked like he wanted to melt into the floor. This put a whole new spin on his sermons about sins of the flesh.

Micah shrugged. "You won't hear us telling anyone."

"My husband…" she began.

Micah said, "What you do is your own business. We didn't see you, you never saw us."

Valerie smiled gratefully. She studied Hazel, concerned. "I couldn't help overhearing you're in trouble. What happened?"

"We'd rather not to go into details," Micah said. "Just that your husband's buddy Kessler thinks I have something I don't."

Valerie said, "The other day I overheard Tom on the phone, saying Kessler disappeared. He seemed a bit…aggravated."

"Yeah." Keith nodded. "No one's seen Kessler in days, not that anyone seems too broken up about that. I wouldn't be surprised if Atkins did kill him."

"Have you heard anything else around work?" Micah asked. "Anyone talking, anything unusual?"

Keith said, "Only Tom complaining about being shorthanded."

Valerie said, "When Tom's home, which is rare, he never discusses business. Or much else for that matter."

"Either of you ever heard of a guy named Stevenson?" Micah asked.

Keith shifted the toothpick to the other side of his mouth. "The name doesn't ring any bells. What's he look like?"

"Big," Hazel said. "Tall, kind of heavy, blond hair. Creepy."

Valerie shook her head, and Keith said, "No. You think he's connected with Kessler and Atkins?"

"We don't know," Micah said.

"I'm sorry." Keith spit chewed splinters into the open trash pail. "I wish I could be more help. I hear anything, I'll let you know."

Valerie looked to Hazel again, worry in her soft blue eyes. "Are you two okay? Do you need anything? Money or somewhere to stay? My girlfriend has a beach house in Long Island, very private; I go there whenever I need some time alone. You could stay there; you'd be safe."

Micah shook his head. "We're good for now, we just want to know what's going on." Hazel leaned against him, and he squeezed her hand.

Valerie watched Hazel as though she were an injured bird. "If you reconsider, the offer stands."

"I'll pray for you. We both will." Keith looked from Micah to Hazel. "You should open your hearts to Jesus. He can save you."

Micah nodded. "We'll take that under consideration."

Halfway down the driveway, Micah began to snicker.

"The look on Keith's face." Micah stretched, yawning. "Priceless. I'm telling you, if there is a God, clearly He's got a sense of humor. There you are on Keith's doorstep, the answer to his prayers, and you catch him with his pants down." He yawned again as they walked up to the Volvo.

"You're okay to drive?"

"I'm good." He opened the door for her. "But you need rest. Get some sleep; around Trenton we'll pull off and switch."

She didn't want to sleep. "So that's Tom Nelson's wife."

"Yeah, that caught me by surprise. Not like I blame her. I mean, I never got why Tom would bother cheating, married to that. At thirty-three she's hotter than most girls our age. She used to be one of those Hooters girls; she was even in their calendar."

Hazel yawned. "This whole trip was a waste of time."

"Keith and Mrs. Nelson. How weird is that? Or maybe not." Micah rolled down his window. "A few weeks back, I'm at the bar with some friends and she comes in, looking real upset. She's drinking alone, so I go talk to her. Turns out she just realized Tom was cheating on her. I don't get how she didn't know sooner— I mean, everyone else did. She was already pretty drunk, so I offered to drive her home. We get there, the house is dark, Tom's car's gone, she says lately he's over at Hooters every night. She loses it and starts crying. I'm trying to make her feel better, telling her how hot she is and what a jerk Tom is not to appreciate what he's got. Next thing I know she's got her hand down my jeans."

Hazel opened her window, hoping the fresh air would wake her up. "Too much information. I really don't need to hear this."

"I didn't do anything. Well, I did; I panicked. I was like, whoa! I started saying all these dumb, noble things on how we should wait, go slow, get to know each other. Pretty stupid, huh? I'm acting like we're on a first date when all she wanted was to get even with Tom."

Hazel watched the passing lights; even at that late hour that stretch of road was busy, but she was so tired her vision was starting to blur. She leaned back and closed her eyes, just for a moment.

"C'mon, hon. Get up."

"Huh?" Hazel yawned, looking around at the empty highway, bordered with darkness and trees, trying to understand how everything had changed so abruptly. "Where are we?"

"Cheesequake. I let you sleep. You needed it. I'll drop you at the yard and return the rental."

"And walk back alone? Think again."

"It's not even a mile."

"I don't care. I'm not letting you out of my sight again. Ever."

"That'll be real awkward on dates." He pulled into the nearly vacant rest stop and returned the car to its original space as Hazel gathered White Castle boxes.

"Leave those. It'll give the stoners something else to ponder."

At four a.m., traffic was sparse as they walked along the northbound shoulder of the Parkway. Hazel said nothing. This was her favorite time of day: quiet and peaceful. Most night owls had turned in, and the early birds were yet to rise.

"Haze," Micah began. "If Atkins hadn't helped me, I could've gotten hurt, or worse. You understand that, right?"

Her throat tightened and she didn't answer. She understood all too well. She slipped her hand into his the way she had when they were small.

As they hiked up the low hill that bordered the west edge of the boatyard, a car slowed and pulled to the right lane. Hazel watched the old Fairmont rumble past, turn signal flashing as it approached the upcoming exit.

"Weird," she said.

"What?"

"I saw a Fairmont just like that the night I left Stevenson's."

Micah shrugged. "Coincidence."

"I guess," she said, recalling the boy in Piermont's haunting smile.

The boatyard was still dark, but a faint hint of color tinted the eastern sky. Skirting the lit areas, they walked back to the shed.

"Wait." Hazel grabbed Micah, pulling him to a stop.

Parked in the shadows beside the shed, the Fairmont clicked and ticked as the engine cooled. They looked around but there was no one in sight. Hazel switched on her flashlight and swept it across the car, noticing the wide rear tires mounted on steel rims. Dual exhausts were barely visible. Hazel shined the light into the car. The backseat was loaded with boat bags, fenders, and lines.

"Damn," Micah said. "Five speed and a full roll cage. You can bet there's something evil lurking under the hood. Man, I'd love to borrow this one."

Hazel stared into the darkness and listened to Micah's steady breathing. How could he just shut off like that? They were no closer to knowing how Stevenson fit in this mess or where her father was and what he was up to. And now there was that blue Fairmont sitting just outside like an enigma. Was the driver that boy she'd seen the night she'd torn away from Stevenson's place in the Viper? Part of her almost hoped it was; she recalled his eyes, in that brief moment he looked at her, as though he knew her completely, and more important, he understood, absolutely and unquestioningly. She knew it was only her imagination taking that passing instant of his smile and building it into something more. Or maybe it was that same boy, but there was something entirely terrible about his proximity.

She only knew she couldn't sleep, and the harder she tried the more it eluded her. She rolled over and fluffed her pillow, unable to get comfortable, finally giving up in frustration. Quietly she dressed, pulling on an oversized black sweatshirt and tucking her cropped hair beneath a baseball cap. She slipped off *Mardi* and out of the shed. She didn't go far, just far enough to see the Fairmont still parked off to the corner, locked, silent, and troubling.

Hazel wandered down the vacant docks, past the weekend toys: open fishing platforms, ski boats, and cuddy cabins.

Farther out were a few cruisers, trawlers, and livable sailboats. Was the Fairmont's owner aboard one of them? The old Chris Craft Commander was a possibility, except the wide stretches of glass lacked curtains. To live on a boat was to live in a fishbowl: with no privacy from the traffic on the dock, curtains were a necessity. The Grand Banks looked lived-in, but she'd seen a retired couple aboard. She passed the Luhrs, Formula, and Mainship, filing them under "maybe." A few sailboats joined the list, including an old Flicka she'd personally hauled there two years back, though none appeared occupied.

She was on the finger dock in the shadow of the Blackfin when she heard footsteps and turned as a shadow headed toward shore. He must have exited one of the boats she'd already passed. Hazel followed, walking softly, her pulse rising as the figure moved with the slightest limp toward the Fairmont. Unfortunately he never turned enough for her to see his face as he climbed into the car, started it, and headed out.

I'M RUBBING OFF ON ANNABEL

Annabel looked back as they drove out of the boatyard.

"I'd swear someone was following us."

Hammon checked the rearview mirror. "I don't see anyone."

"If I think we're being followed, does that make me a paranoid delusion?"

"Just because you're paranoid doesn't mean they aren't really after us."

19:19 WEDNESDAY, JUNE 30

40°27'24.61"N/74°16'09.29"W

PARLIN, NJ

"Behind every dark cloud is an even darker cloud," Micah announced.

"I thought we were making progress." Hazel tied a trash bag closed. "It's not so bad with the biohazards gone."

"It's another T-shirt." Micah held up a wrinkled black shirt stating that very sentiment. He sorted the debris, separating the piles of laundry from books, magazines, CDs, and anything else of interest. The batteries remained disconnected, but orange extension cords snaked onboard, providing volts for lights and a Shop-Vac. Armed with kitchen gloves, bleach, disinfectant, and scouring pads, they'd passed the day scrubbing their way through the cabin. They removed cardboard covering the salon windows and scraped black paint from the mirrors. The unspeakable ice-box was beaten into submission. The microwave was declared beyond hope and tossed, and a fresh tank of propane connected to the lines for the ancient four-burner galley stove. For Hazel, the worst part was the bleach vapors, triggering flashes of her last night aboard *Witch*.

"There's quite a collection. Let's see." Micah rummaged through the T-shirts. "'I haven't lost my mind…it's backed up on a disk somewhere.' 'Everything I need to know I learned from the people trapped in my basement.' 'When the pepper spray runs out, can I have your number?' 'I'm just one big f#&*ing ray of sunshine, aren't I?' 'Sleep is overrated.' And my personal favorite, 'I do very bad things and I do them very well.'"

"How about the notes? 'Eat something healthy.' 'Check for bugs.' 'Meteor showers, 1:45 7/1.' And I keep finding this one." She held up a Post-it. "'It's in the snow.'"

"Meteor showers tonight? Cool. What time's it now?"

Hazel checked her watch. "Almost seven-thirty."

"A.m. or p.m.?" Micah dragged a heavy black trash bag to the cockpit. Hazel shuddered momentarily, recalling Kessler's disposal.

"Does it matter?" Within the windowless shed, there was no day or night, just industrial floodlights. Absolute light or absolute dark. Hours dragged out, unmeasured and undefined, leaving Hazel too much time to think. She wouldn't have minded if that thinking yielded answers, but so far she'd come up empty.

"These cleaners are giving me a headache." She peeled off the rubber gloves, dropping them in the galley sink. "I need some air."

Micah joined her as she exited the cabin and climbed to the bridge. She stared over the wheel at the compass. "We've been on the same heading for days, and the horizon hasn't changed. It's like ocean cruising without the ocean."

"At least we haven't hit any bad weather," Micah said, returning to his stack of *Maxims*.

"Yet." She picked up the Westlake novel she'd found aboard and stared idly at the page. Was the Fairmont still out there?

Should she go check? Maybe the owner would be near, and then at least she could know one way or another whether it was the boy she'd seen in Piermont.

Micah lowered his magazine. "What now?"

Hazel looked up. "What?"

"You're sighing. A lot."

Hazel traced her finger along the wheel. "Ever meet someone…I mean, just see them on the street, not even talk to them, and the moment your eyes meet you feel like you've known them your whole life? Is that weird?"

"Nope. Happens to me all the time. Like a few weeks back I saw this girl in Dunkin' Donuts, and the minute I looked at her, I knew we were meant to spend the rest of our lives together. She smiled back at me, and I knew she knew it too."

"So what did you do?"

"Nothing. She had a boyfriend the size of a Mack truck and he wasn't smiling."

A loud crash sounded from below, and a symphony of graphic, physically unachievable remarks rose from Tony. Micah glanced overboard then leveled a critical eye at Hazel. "Didn't I say no more snares?"

"You're no fun." She climbed down to Tony, lying flat on his back, and offered him an apologetic smile as she helped untangle fish line from his ankles. "Sorry about the security system."

Tony sat up. "Security for what, exactly?"

Micah climbed off the ladder and helped Tony to his feet. "Haze thinks we're being followed. You know who owns that old blue Fairlane?"

"Fairmont," Hazel corrected.

"Same difference."

Hazel rolled her eyes. "Is not. Ford stopped building Fairlanes in North America in 1971. It's a Fairmont."

"Lane, Mont, whatever." Micah turned to Tony. "Who owns the old blue Ford POS?"

"That thing? That's the guy who bought *Nepenthe*. You remember, the Flicka Hazel hauled here two years back."

"What's he look like?" Hazel asked, trying not to sound too curious.

Tony shrugged. "Hard to say. I never really seen him during the day. Young. Kind of short, glasses, brown hair. Kind of weird. Talks to himself. Why?" Then Tony's eyes narrowed. "Wait, never mind why. Your dad called. He said he'd be coming soon and he wanted to be sure you weren't doing any 'salvage consultant shit,' whatever that means."

Hazel brightened. "Soon when?"

"Didn't say. Just soon." Tony regarded the tangle of fishing line. "So please refrain from snaring customers. Especially the ones who pay up front."

I'M NOT SURE ANYMORE

Hammon passed the day sweltering aboard Annabel's so-called boat, fans running, lying on the bunk and sweating, trapped by the sun beating down on the decks above. Much as he hated to admit it, he was grateful for the place to hide, and impressed by the surprisingly sturdy little bath toy.

"Told you so," Annabel said. "It's a Flicka. These things can cross oceans."

"So can plastic soda bottles. And they're about the same size."

And yet the boat contained all the necessary comforts in a neat little package, as well as privacy Gary's couch lacked. Tucked up forward were V bunks. To port stretched six feet of stove/sink/chart table, with ample storage and standing headroom to spare. Starboard, a short settee and the world's smallest enclosed head/shower. Wedged beneath the cockpit was a miniature diesel. All in all, just enough space for one person. Barely.

"One?" Annabel said.

"So much for privacy."

"You could lock yourself in the head," she teased.

Hammon didn't reply. It was pointless arguing with himself and he was exhausted. He'd improvised curtains over the ports using a cut-up old sail bag and duct tape and made extra space earlier in the day by moving the spare sails into the Fairmont. The boat came from an estate sale, fully provisioned with everything from charts to cutlery, pots, pans, plates, life vests, and expired flares. Sometimes he wondered what he'd do without Annabel.

"I shudder to imagine."

Still, it freaked him out that she'd bought the boat without his knowledge or consent, and it left him to wonder how much control he truly had over his own actions.

"Don't concern yourself, dear. It's only in your best interests."

02:02 THURSDAY, JULY 1

40°27'24.61"N/74°16'09.29"W

PARLIN, NJ

Tired as she was, Hazel couldn't sleep. Yet another day had come and gone, with them no closer to any answers. A storm was approaching, she was sure of it. The question was, when would it hit and what damage would it leave behind?

She sighed, watching Micah contentedly sprawled across the port bunk. She sighed even louder; still he didn't move.

"Micah?"

Nothing. Not a flicker of consciousness. He'd always been a deep sleeper, able to doze through the roughest weather. She fought the urge to smack him with a pillow.

"Fine. You sleep. I'm going for a nice, long walk. Alone."

It just wasn't fair that he could sleep so sound. She was too restless. Hazel slid off the bunk, dressed in the dark, then lit the hurricane lamp in the galley, lowering the wick until only a sliver of blue flame remained.

The yard was silent and empty beneath a clear night sky. The moon was approaching last quarter and random fireflies blinked over the Phragmites reeds. The space where the Fairmont usually parked was vacant, and Hazel wasn't sure whether she was relieved or annoyed, or why it even mattered.

A flash of light shot across the sky, then another, reminding her of the note she'd found earlier. This was a perfect excuse to wake Micah. More meteors followed, nearly one a minute, and she was halfway back to the shed when an approaching rumble broke the stillness and headlights rounded the boatyard entrance. Hazel flattened herself behind a blocked-up boat, her adrenaline rising as the Fairmont rolled past. The car braked, backed into the far corner, and shut down. No interior lights came on, the door just opened and a shadow emerged. It might have been the boy from Piermont; it was too dark to be sure. He stood, back to her, staring upward. Then, rather than heading to the docks, he wandered through the brush and out to the riverbank.

Hazel waited, frozen. She could get Micah, but by time they returned her target might be gone. And it wasn't like she was going to do anything; she simply wanted to see who it was while she had the chance. What harm was there in that? If he was, as Tony said, *Nepenthe's* owner, that pretty much ruled out the possibility that he was any danger to her. All the same she opened her knife, slipped her hand into the ribbon loop, and tucked the blade against her arm. Ahead, a faint outline marked the boundary between land and water, with a figure sitting slump-shouldered at the edge. Hazel watched, waiting, but he did nothing.

It was time for a closer look.

I'M SORRY

Hammon stared up as streaks of light cut the darkness: pieces of the universe crashing and burning. It was beautiful in a depressing way, and he was compelled to watch, empathizing with those bits of cosmos. Did they realize they were getting too close to the gravity that would pull them in and destroy them? Did they deliberately hurl themselves into the irresistible force of a spinning planet like moths to a flame, bent on their own destruction? Or were they innocent bystanders, merely passing through the galaxy, only to be drawn into inevitable doom? Whatever the case, it verified one of Hammon's theories: gravity was a myth; the earth sucked.

He shouldn't have snapped at Annabel. She'd only been trying to help, but he'd lashed out at her in frustration, reminding her that she really didn't exist and her opinions didn't count for much, being they were actually his. And, considering he was out of his freakin' mind, arguing with his hallucination, his opinions were utterly worthless. Finally she'd disappeared, leaving him to contemplate how lonely existence was without the voice in his head for company. Was he being drawn toward his own destruction or initiating it?

"I'm sorry," he apologized to the darkness. "I really am. I know you're there and I know you can hear me. It's just easier to talk when I can see you."

Nothing. Only blackness around him and self-destructive stars overhead.

She was giving him the silent treatment. It served him right.

But then a faint glow appeared, brightening to the warm flame of a hurricane lantern. Annabel stood motionless before him, her expression wary. He offered a weak smile.

"Please stay," he said, his voice breaking. "I don't want to be alone."

He watched, transfixed, as the breeze played through her curls. The lantern she carried was a nice touch, casting a soft circle of light. She wore a loose pair of cargo pants and his favorite old sweatshirt. The details were amazing, so vivid and convincing. Another symptom of his eroding grasp on reality. She stood, not speaking, only waiting.

"You win," he conceded. "If reality means you don't exist and madness means you do, then I surrender to insanity."

Still she said nothing, only studied him, looking uncertain.

Hammon sighed, blinking his left eye. "I really am sorry," he said plaintively, blinking his right eye. "I know you're not really here, but I don't care. I just don't want to be alone anymore."

She moved back the slightest bit then paused. "I'm not here?"

"No. You, sweet angel, are no more than a delightful hallucination. Exhibit A in the gallery of how scrambled my gray matter is. I looked it up: auditory and visual hallucinations are 'particularly associated with psychotic disorders such as schizophrenia.' They tried putting everything back, but they didn't get all the mercury. Wires got crossed, brain cells got lost." He rubbed his head, sighing wistfully. "Brain cells…too many gone. Miss 'em sometimes."

02:12 THURSDAY, JULY 1

40°27'23.67"N/74°16'06.12"W

PARLIN, NJ

Hazel stood motionless, uncertain how to proceed. She wasn't sure what she'd expected, but it certainly wasn't this. He was indeed the same boy she'd seen in Piermont. Glasses, baseball cap, straight, mousy brown hair falling across his eyes, skin so fair it seemed almost translucent. Her age, maybe a bit older. In the dim light she could see faint scars covered the right side of his face, partially concealed by his hair. Hazel knew she shouldn't have been there to begin with, and maybe it was time to just leave. He'd already admitted he wasn't right in the head. But the defeat in his eyes held her. He seemed utterly harmless, more than that, wounded. And if he owned *Nepenthe,* then his presence in Piermont, one tide's sail away, was most likely simple coincidence.

He gazed up with haunting eyes and smiled sadly, sharp fangs gleaming in the lamplight. That caught her off guard, yet she found herself more intrigued than alarmed.

"It's all gone," he said. "My life, my mind." Desperation filled his face, and he winked his left eye. "You're not gonna disappear again, are you? I'm afraid to blink, but my eyeballs are getting dry."

"No." But she remained beyond reach, the reassuring shape of her knife in hand. "I won't disappear."

Blinking, he smiled an innocent, childlike smile…with fangs.

"Why do you think I'm a hallucination?"

"I said I was sorry," he insisted, looking even more hurt. "And I am. Really."

"I know. All the same, how do you know I'm not real?"

He giggled and her fingers tightened around the knife.

"That's funny?"

He nodded, hair falling in his eyes. "Hysterical. Terrifying. Okay; now you ask why. All right. I'll play along, even though I'm really just talking to myself. How do I know? Simple: if you were real, there's no way in hell you'd talk to a messed-up, burned-up little freak like me."

The night was cooler than usual, and Hazel crossed her arms, fighting not to shiver. Keeping space between them and the knife concealed, she knelt down, set the lantern aside, and scraped a small pit with a clamshell. She placed some dry seaweed and driftwood in a pile then struck a match. The flame caught, growing, while her companion looked on uneasily. She added more wood, and the fire crackled, radiating warmth.

"So you have some scars. Big deal. Actually, I think you're kind of cute."

"More proof you don't exist. You see past the damage; it doesn't matter to you. That's what makes you beautiful, most of all. But no real girl—especially one that happens to look exactly like my fantasies, and what's the odds of that—would stay and talk to a burned-up, screwed-up, delusional, certifiably imbalanced…"

"Dangerous?"

"Huh?"

"Unbalanced I get. Personally I think sanity is a relative thing." She knew only too well what it was like having others analyze her mental state, and how easy it was to start to believe them. "Look close enough, deep down most people are all a little crazy. Some just hide it better. But are you dangerous? Could you hurt me?"

The horror in his eyes was unmistakable. "I'd never...you know I couldn't..." He actually looked ill. "It'd be impossible, there's no way...I swear, I'd die for you before I ever...I love you."

"Love?"

He nodded, smiling with a gentle intensity that held her locked in his gaze. It was that same look that had been haunting her since Piermont, as unnerving as it was sincere.

"Of course. It makes sense; I imagined you. You're my idea of perfect, and not just physically, which you definitely are. It's who you are and how you are. From the start you saw me, not this mess of scars and loose screws. Then again, it's easier to be in love with something you created in your head. Reality can't screw it up."

Hazel sat back, considering. Any reasonable person would have been long gone; though she'd never been what most people consider reasonable, and somehow his words made perfect sense to her. It seemed a bit of a stretch to think that he was following her and this was some elaborate, convincing act. The more logical explanation was that he'd seen her that night in the Viper and decided he'd only imagined it. It was sweet in a strange way.

She picked up a pebble, tossing it idly toward the creek. There was a soft *plunk* in the darkness. The fire hissed and snapped, spreading a circle of heat. Hazel studied the boy, blinking back at her through thick glasses. "Maybe I've been real all along and you only imagined you imagined me."

"Right. You're real set on this existence thing today, which means I am, which means I'm right back where I started, sick of being alone. Life sucks. You want a reality check? You're as real as that." He pointed at the crackling fire, casting dancing shadows around them. "I can touch it, and I won't feel a thing." Then, to prove his point, he reached his hand straight into the flames, deliberately holding it there.

"No!" Hazel jumped toward him, grabbing his arm, pulling it back.

He gazed at his hand in pain and wonderment. "That HURT," he mumbled, genuinely confused.

"Of course it did." She turned his sweaty hand over, inspecting the scarred skin. Two fingers had no nails and his pinky was partially amputated, but those were old injuries. His sleeve was singed, but he seemed otherwise unharmed. "What'd you expect?"

"You…you're…you're…"

The space between them and the reassuring safety it had provided were gone. Holding his trembling hand in hers, she realized she'd moved dangerously close. She still had her knife, lethally sharp and ready, tucked in her other hand, while he gazed at her, eyes wide. She smiled hesitantly. "Real."

I'M SO CONFUSED

Hammon couldn't speak. He couldn't move. He couldn't breathe. His skin stung from the flames, and he could feel the soft warmth of her fingers against his.

It was impossible.

"Why'd you do that?" She looked down at their hands, seemingly as amazed as him that they were touching.

He stared back at her, paralyzed, while his heart tore at his ribs. She held her right hand, encircled in ribbon, in an odd way as she cautiously lifted his chin. Her left hand released his; she pushed his hair back from his eyes, exposing more damage, and he flinched as her fingers brushed across his cheek.

"You were hurt terribly," she said, her voice gentle. "You must be used to pain."

He blinked, his brain searing as the mercury shifted. "You never get used to pain," he choked.

"You're shaking."

Annabel was *real*, there beside him in the damp sand, *touching* him! This wasn't actually happening; it couldn't be. It was impossible. It made no sense. Not that he was complaining. He was thrilled. And terrified. And confused. Very confused. "Am I dead?"

She paused, looking puzzled. "No."

"You're...*REAL*."

"I think we've established that."

"You're real and you didn't leave."

"Should I?"

"No! Please...stay..." he said. "Forever."

Annabel was real. How was that even possible? It didn't make sense. She turned, looking up as a meteor cut across the sky.

"This *is* pretty weird," Annabel said. "Even for you. And it's about to get a whole lot weirder."

"What?" he mumbled.

She looked back at him. "What, what?"

A second Annabel strolled from the darkness behind him, curiously studying the one beside the fire. The standing Annabel turned to Hammon. "Steady," she said.

Hammon looked from the real Annabel sitting beside him to the other...the one standing...the...

"Annabel, version one," she said, her satiny voice sliding through his skull. It was like seeing double, except this Annabel wore low jeans and her "I quit the band, now I just play with myself" T-shirt. She looked the other Annabel over. "Despite the resemblance, she's not me, and I have no idea who she is."

Hammon stared from one to the other. Why didn't either of them say something sooner?

"She has no idea, dear, and I didn't want to spoil the fun." Annabel grinned. "This was way more amusing. I figured I'd keep quiet and see where it went. So, it appears I exist."

No, the girl beside him existed. Annabel was still...

"Same thing," Annabel replied.

"I'm not so sure..." he said.

"Not sure about what?" the girl asked tentatively.

"Talk to her, not me," Annabel said. "Tell her you're not sure what to say."

Hammon nodded, hiccupping. "What to say. Who are you? Where did you come from? What are you doing out here alone? Will you stay with me forever?"

Annabel said, "I think that last part was pushing it a bit."

The girl studied him, uncertain. "I couldn't sleep. I was watching the meteor showers." She glanced up at the sky as a streak of light appeared and faded. "And you?"

Hammon hiccupped. "Same thing. Insomnia. Watching stars crash into the sea."

"Listen carefully and don't say a word," Annabel said. "She's the girl we saw in the Viper leaving Stevenson's. She's wearing the sweatshirt you left on *Revenge*. Odds are she knows what happened to Stevenson and where *Revenge* is. But here's the thing: if only you can see me, how is it we look identical?"

There was only one possibility: Stevenson had microchips inside his head and stole his thoughts.

Annabel giggled. "Or maybe he saw your porn and found a good match."

Okay. That worked too. Either way, the resemblance was undeniable. Which meant Stevenson was using this girl to get to him. Hammon watched her watching the stars and wondered if she knew who he was.

Annabel said, "I don't think so. And I wouldn't say anything or you might scare her away. I'm amazed you haven't already."

She had a point. This girl was like Gary's feral cats, curious but wary. If he sat still, did nothing threatening, and made no sudden moves, they might approach, ever ready to bolt. Hammon rubbed his burned hand. "Not that I'm complaining, but do you always talk to strange weirdos, alone, at two in the morning?"

She gave a hesitant smile. "Most times I don't talk to anyone, weird or otherwise."

"You talked to me, even though I'm messed up, and I got these." He curled his lips, trying to look fearsome.

She laughed. "I'm sorry. Should I be afraid?"

"You're not?"

"You don't strike me as dangerous. A little unbalanced, perhaps, but not terribly scary."

Maybe. But if Stevenson was using her to get to him, she was in danger whether she knew it or not. He had to protect her, whatever it took. Suddenly it was blindingly clear what he had to do.

"Your intentions are good," Annabel said, "but that's a terrible idea."

It was for her own good. If she'd talk to him, God only knew who else she'd trust. She didn't see the danger in that, and that in itself was dangerous. He'd be breaking his promise, but he had to; it was the only way to be sure she'd be safe.

Annabel's features tightened, and she tucked her hair back. "I said NO."

There was no one around. No one to see. He'd have to move quick, catch her by surprise. She'd probably struggle, and he didn't want to hurt her. He'd have to restrain her and keep her from screaming. Once they were aboard *Nepenthe*, far from shore, then he'd explain.

"I'm warning you. Don't." Annabel stepped between him and the girl. Like that could stop him. She was starting to be a real pain in the brain.

Annabel's eyes narrowed. "Don't test me, or I'll show you pain."

He shifted slowly, calculating the distance between them, when the mercury inside his head turned molten. The world tilted, everything blurred, and a vortex of nausea rose within him. He collapsed to the ground; eyes squeezed shut, damp palms pressed to his forehead.

"Are you okay?" his tangible companion asked.

"I warned you," said the intangible one. "Remember, inside your skull I call the shots. Stay still, you'll be fine. Make one move toward her, you'll see double for a week."

Hammon looked through tearing eyes from Annabel to her concerned twin. He was already seeing double.

"Headache," he gasped, sinking into the cool sand.

02:21 THURSDAY, JULY 1

40°27'23.67"N/74°16'06.12"W

PARLIN, NJ

Hazel studied the boy lying helpless before her, pain etched in his face. He had no idea she'd followed him there or, if threatened, precisely what she was capable of. Discreetly she closed her knife, clipping it inside her pocket, a mere reach away.

"Lay still," she said softly. "And close your eyes."

"I can't," he answered, wincing. "You'll disappear."

"I won't; I promise. Now, close your eyes." She moved closer, leaning over him, her pulse rising. "My dad gets bad headaches sometimes. He says I'm a carrier, but this seems to help." She brushed the hair back from his forehead, pressing her fingertips lightly to his temples, rubbing in slow circles.

"Can I keep you?" he asked, his voice faint.

"What do you mean?"

He gazed up with a wide-eyed, childlike expression. "Stay with me. Forever. I don't want to be alone anymore. Run away with me. Please. Right now. Tonight." His hand came up, touching hers, pressing it to his scarred cheek.

"Maybe." She smiled gently. "But I know nothing about you."

Beneath the pain, his face lit up. "Okay, right! Yeah, uhm, then let's start over. Hi, I'm Otto Hammon, I'm twenty-one, and my blood type's A-positive." He glanced away for a second. "Or you can call me Zap. My friend Gary—he's real, like you—he calls me Zap from when I had a run-in with some high voltage and sorta grounded out a lightning bolt." The tips of his fangs glinted as he smiled. "Sort of like shock treatment on a cosmic level." He tried to sit up, shuddered from the pain and fell back again. His gaze shifted and he nodded slightly. "Okay…Okay!"

"You sure you're all right?"

"No. Yeah. Depends what you're asking. I'm fine, long as I don't move. You can keep doing that rubbing thing; that feels nice."

She leaned over, brushing the hair from his scarred forehead. "You know, we might have met much sooner." Hazel prodded the embers with a stick and sparks floated up, fading out. "I'm the one who moved your boat."

"My boat?" Hammon bolted upright. "You mean *Re—*" He gasped and fell across her legs, squeezing his eyes shut, whimpering.

Hazel stroked his forehead. "*Nepenthe.*" She tossed more wood on the dying fire. The flames rose for a moment, sputtered, and faded, yielding little warmth. "I trucked her here two years back, but you weren't around that day. I would have remembered you."

His eyes flickered and he scowled into the darkness as though an apparition had made an aggravating comment. But then he half nodded, looking back to Hazel. "Right. *Nepenthe.*" His forehead creased as he concentrated. "You move boats? By truck? Moran Marine Transport, right?" He brightened. "You're Hazel!"

She rubbed her arms. "That's me."

"Are you cold?" He wriggled out of his trench coat, offering it to her. "Here."

"What about you?"

He fidgeted, glancing anxiously toward the sky. "I'm good. Take it, please."

She slipped into the coat. It was soft and warm, with the faintest scent of baby powder.

Hammon studied her, looking troubled. "How do you know I might not want to hurt you?"

"I don't, really. But you said you weren't dangerous."

"Still, what if I grabbed you and tried to drag you somewhere dark and isolated…"

"Like right here?" Maybe it shouldn't have amused her, but it did.

"That's not the point. What I'm saying is, what if I tried to do something awful?"

"Like what?"

He blinked.

"Awful is rather vague," she said. "More detail would help. Awful like gruesome murder and dismemberment, or awful like kinky perverted. You need to be more specific." Even by the dim firelight, she could see color rise in his face. "Thought so," she said, idly rubbing his temples.

"The point is, you don't know," he insisted, his voice breaking.

"And neither do you. For all you know, I'm an axe murderer."

He sighed and sank back across her lap like an offering, gazing up with rapt devotion. "I wouldn't mind as long as you never leave me."

Hazel traced her fingers along his, amazed by her own behavior. It was strange but she felt so safe, so comfortable, as though she could trust him. His eyes were mesmerizing, and her heart raced, her pulse so loud in her ears it sounded like someone running.

No. That *was* someone running!

"Get down," Hammon hissed, pulling her to the ground as a beam of light bounced through the lot, arcing back and forth.

"Hazel?" Micah called in hushed panic. The light swept past the smoldering fire and back, then locked on them, approaching fast as Hammon lay frozen, unblinking.

"What the…oh, God, Haze…" Micah leaned close, tentatively poking Hammon. "Is he dead?"

Hammon hiccupped.

"Guess not." Micah glared at her. "You scared the crap out of me; I wake up and you're gone." He aimed the beam at Hammon's face. "Who's your friend?"

Hammon's trembling grip on her arm tightened. Hazel snatched the flashlight, switching it off. "This is Otto." She pulled her arm free and gave Hammon's hand a reassuring squeeze. "Otto, this is my dear, annoying cousin Micah. Otto owns *Nepenthe*. You remember, the boat I delivered here two years back. Small world, isn't it?"

"Microscopic," Micah said flatly. "Why's he lying there like that?"

"He doesn't feel good."

Hammon nodded in agreement. "Headache."

Micah shot Hazel a look that could have come straight from her father. "You scared the hell out of me, disappearing like that. You know you shouldn't be out alone like this with some weird guy." He glanced at Hammon. "No offense."

"None taken. I tried to tell her the same thing. She could get in trouble…or worse."

"See? Even the weird guy agrees. I think we should be getting back," Micah said, holding his hand out.

Hazel didn't move. "Why?"

Micah's eyes narrowed. "Because I said so."

"Wow. For a second, you sounded just like Dad. We're just sitting here talking."

"Yeah, well, I'm not leaving you alone with some strange guy I don't know. Let's go."

"No, wait!" Hammon stared off at nothing for a moment. "Yeah, okay. That might work." He looked from Hazel to Micah. "Anna...uh...I was thinking, we could maybe all go get something to eat and hang out a while. You know, just talk. All of us, I mean."

"We could do that," Hazel agreed. "No one'll know. And I'm hungry."

"It's two thirty in the morning," Micah countered. "What's open?"

Hazel laughed, sensing victory. "Half the diners in New Jersey."

"And White Castle." Hammon struggled to sit up, digging keys out of his jeans. "There's one right down the road. If either of you can drive stick, we could take my car."

I'M GOING TO COMBUST

"You're welcome," Annabel said smugly. "And from now on, when I say something, don't argue."

She was right, as usual. If not for Annabel's actions, none of this would have happened. He wouldn't have been at that boatyard to begin with, owning a boat that seemed to lend him instant credibility with his wary new friends. And he wouldn't be heading up Route 9, riding shotgun in his own car, with Hazel at the wheel, grinning and shifting expertly while Micah shared the backseat with some spare sails, lines, and Hammon's hallucination.

"Talk to them," Annabel said. "See what we can learn. Like where they're from."

Hammon nodded. "You two live around here?"

Hazel looked back at Micah.

"We're visiting friends," he said.

"Deliberately vague," Annabel said.

Hammon said, "For how long?"

Micah glanced at Hazel in the rearview. She shook her head ever so slightly. "Hard to say," Micah answered, examining the roll cage. "This car is too cool. I'm driving on the way back." He met Hammon's eyes in the mirror. "You race professionally? That how you got all messed up, in some epic wreck?"

Hazel twisted back and whacked Micah on the shoulder. "Sorry," she told Hammon. "Micah has the tact of a five-year-old."

Hammon shrugged. "It's okay. And yeah, pretty much, crash, burn, crispy to well done. Lots of fun reconstructive surgery, grafts, metal rods, and plates and all."

"And the fangs?" Micah asked.

Hammon nodded. "Yeah, I know, it's kind of weird, right? They're implants. I was pretty messed up after that whole wreck. Physically and mentally, I mean. I was actually dead for a time. And for a while I really wished I'd stayed that way."

"You were dead?" Micah leaned forward between the seats. "Like flatline, no pulse, no breathing, for real? That is *so* cool. What was it like?"

Hazel gave him a smack in the arm.

"I'm just asking!"

"It's okay," Hammon said. "It was peaceful; that's all I remember, at least until I got pulled back. Then there was pain. Drains in my skull, skin grafts, endless surgeries; like I was some twisted torture experiment. My face was real busted up and most of my teeth were history and the doctor said I'd need implants. I was feeling pretty morbid, hung up on the whole 'undead' thing, so I insisted on the fangs. But my one doc was cool, he said they might be good for my mental state, and I could always change them back. But now I've got this thing about going near hospitals and pretty much anyone in a white coat, so I never got around to it. It's hard to explain; when I did it, I had my reasons. Most times it's not an issue. I usually just avoid daylight. And people. And smiling."

Micah grinned at Hazel. "You think your dad freaked when I dyed my hair blue? He'll *love* this! Hey! You got satellite radio. Sweet!" He leaned up farther and poked at the presets, set to alternative rock, big band, and classical. He elbowed Hazel. "No country."

"You like country?" Hammon asked.

"Hell no," Micah said. "I hear fiddles and banjos, I get nervous. But her dad has satellite radio in his rig, and all he'll listen to is commercial-free, cussin', cheatin', drinkin', honky-tonkin' music."

"He's serious," Hazel said. "A while back my dad hauled a boat for someone who sells high-end sound systems, and in exchange the guy installed a real nice setup. But don't dare change the station and you're supposed to turn the volume to zero and shut the radio before you shut the truck, or you get a twenty-minute lecture on how that degrades the sound quality on the speakers."

"Like you can even tell with that music." Micah grinned at Hammon. "Know what you get when you play country music backwards? You get your dog back, your house back, your pickup back, and your wife back."

"It's not all bad," Hazel said. "There's some good alternative stuff, like Cross Canadian Ragweed, Wilco, and Cowboy Mouth."

Micah grimaced. "Watch it, Haze. Your Down Jersey roots are showing."

"And what's wrong with Down Jersey?" she challenged.

"What's Down Jersey?" Hammon asked.

"The Jersey Everglades," Micah said. "The southwest end of the state. Miles of desolate, barren, godforsaken salt marsh, sand, pines, and bugs so big they'd carry off a Buick."

"Bivalve," Annabel said.

Hazel smiled. "Heaven."

"Yeah," Micah said. "If you're the thirteenth Leeds child."

Hammon nodded like he knew what that meant.

"The Jersey Devil," Annabel explained.

Ahead, a red tractor trailer swung wide into the oncoming lane. Hazel and Micah swiveled in unison as they passed.

"Wrong stacks," Micah grumbled quietly.

Hazel nodded, scowling. "Wrong running lights."

"I'd put money on it the truck Stevenson's got has a real nice stereo," Annabel said, "But what's Stevenson doing with their truck?"

They pulled into the Route 9 White Castle, nestled beneath radio and water towers. Hazel parked and climbed out, holding the seat forward for Micah. Hammon stared at the building, radiating terrifyingly white light.

"You coming?" Hazel said, waiting.

"I figured we'd use the drive-through." That was why he'd suggested White Castle to begin with. He couldn't go inside. There was light inside. LOTS of light. What if she was repulsed? What if—

"Seriously?" Hands on her hips, Annabel glared at him. "You vowed you'd die for her, and you can't even go into a freakin' White Castle?"

She had a point. He took a deep breath and climbed out, following Hazel through the glass doors and into florescent-lit doom. The lights scorched down, though no one seemed to notice him or care.

"And you didn't burst into flame," Annabel said. "Go figure."

"Give me a minute," Hazel told him, ducking into the bathroom. Hammon backed behind the polished stainless-soda dispensers. Without his coat he felt naked and exposed, and he pulled his shirt closed, trying his best to will himself invisible.

Micah strolled over. "You okay?"

Looking down, Hammon nodded.

"You sure? You look like you're gonna pass out. Relax. I think she likes you. That little rag boat of yours scored some high points. And besides, she digs scars."

"See," Annabel said. "There you go."

"And that's why we need to talk."

And here it comes. The "get lost" speech. Micah stepped to the counter, ordered half the menu, then turned to Hammon. "You got to understand: Haze, she's grown up kind of sheltered. She doesn't usually let people get close. I don't want to see her get hurt. She gets upset, that could be real hazardous to your health. You follow?"

"Are you telling me to leave?"

Micah's eyes narrowed. "Would you?"

Hammon swallowed, straightening. "No."

"Even under threats of violence."

He shook his head. "No."

Micah nodded. "Thought so. You seem decent. Weird, but with her that's a plus. I'm just saying, be careful. Real careful." He lowered his voice. "Don't upset her, don't make any sudden moves or try anything stupid without her permission, you'll be fine."

Annabel said, "I have a bad feeling Stevenson upset her."

Hammon's stomach twisted; he could still picture Hazel passing him in the Viper, her eyes glistening with tears. He didn't want to imagine what Stevenson had done; the possibilities were too awful to consider. All he knew was first chance he got he'd be paying that evil bastard a visit.

"Steady," Annabel said. "Don't get all worked up until we know more. Stevenson may be a scumbag, but I don't see him doing anything to hurt a kid like her."

Hazel returned as Micah paid and she studied Hammon, looking from him to Micah with concern. "What?"

Hammon couldn't speak. Micah only grinned. "I told him how you're into weird guys in trench coats." Micah turned to Hammon as he collected the food and moved to a table. "She's even got a poster of Silent Bob on her cabin door."

"CABIN," Annabel pointed out. "Not bedroom. I'll bet that sunken boat in Bivalve was theirs."

Hazel glared at Micah in mock aggravation, shooting her straw wrapper at him as she took a seat. She looked up at Hammon, still standing, and she slid over, making space beside her and smiling reassuringly. Micah spread the feast across the table and they dug in, eagerly grabbing fries and clam strips.

More than anything Hammon really wanted to pretend all was good and they were just three kids out late having fun, but he suspected Hazel and Micah were in more trouble than they realized. For their sakes, he needed to learn what he could about their connections to Stevenson and *Revenge*'s disappearance.

Coached by Annabel, he delicately fished for information. His new friends spoke of random things—music, food, movies, and pets—but behind the smiles and laughter, their answers were cautious, avoiding anything too specific, especially names and places. They worked as a team, casually skirting and deflecting his questions, redirecting the conversation. Every so often Hazel seemed to relax a bit, or perhaps she was getting tired. Her guard would drop, and Micah would shoot her a meaningful glance, a gentle kick under the table, or he'd interrupt her altogether.

There was one thing Hammon did confirm, though, much to his profound amazement: Hazel seemed genuinely interested in him. Even as he stumbled over his own words, she understood exactly what he meant. She didn't appear concerned by his weirdness; in fact, as Micah had said, it seemed to set her at ease in some inexplicable way. She listened intently as he spoke of Gary's shop, cars, dogs, and cats. Annabel steered him clear of mentioning *Revenge*, hidden trucks, sunken schooners, or evil beyond all measure, even as questions piled up in his brain.

By the time Micah announced that they should start heading back, Hammon concluded he knew next to nothing about Hazel, only that she'd somehow stolen his boat and his heart and he couldn't live another day without her. Her path had crossed Stevenson's; he didn't know how or why, but clearly things had gone badly. She was trusting, innocent, and vulnerable, and she was in more danger than she could comprehend. It was up to him to protect her.

The first hint of day was creeping over the horizon as they parked at the boatyard. When they'd all gotten out, Micah said, "Sorry, kiddies. Fun's over. The sun'll be up soon, which means our friend here needs to return to his coffin, and our hosts might not appreciate us being out all night."

Hazel nodded, color rising in her cheeks. "Can we have a minute?"

Micah rolled his eyes but strolled on toward the shed. Hazel turned to Hammon. She nibbled her lip, apprehension in her eyes.

"Kiss her," Annabel whispered.

Hammon froze. He couldn't breathe. He was going to pass out. The sky was growing brighter by the second. He had to do something, anything, beside stand there paralyzed. Hazel stepped forward, touched his hand, and he jumped. This was insane. Why couldn't he have just kidnapped her? Then things would have been under control.

"Doubtful," Annabel said.

He'd try again and this time he wouldn't let Annabel stop him. He needed some rope, strong and secure, but soft enough not to hurt.

"No," Annabel snapped. "You need to kiss her, tell her you'll see her later, then go pay Stevenson a visit."

"There you go again." Hazel pushed the hair back from his eyes. "Off somewhere in your head."

"I'm afraid it'll all fall apart. That's the story of my life. You're gonna snap out of your trance and run screaming. Things like you don't happen to me."

"You worry too much."

Hammon hiccupped. "Force of habit. Survival of the paranoid."

What about chloroform? Did it really work, or was that just in the movies? Where would he even get it, and was it safe? He wouldn't use it if there was any risk. He didn't want to hurt her, only to protect her. Once he kidnapped her, they'd be alone together, miles from shore, safe from the world, then he could explain everything.

Annabel sighed impatiently. "What part of *no* don't you get?"

Hazel fidgeted, waiting. There was duct tape aboard *Nepenthe*. That would work. He moved closer, breathing in the scent of her skin, and he started to lean to kiss her, then panicked, ducking to the side.

"I'm sorry," he mumbled, backing up.

Her arms slipped around his waist, pulling him close, and she smiled. "It's okay." Her lips touched his, and tentatively she kissed him.

"Awwww," Micah said behind them. He'd walked back for her. "How nauseatingly sweet. Now break it up, young lady, before you get cooties."

"Yeah," Annabel snickered. "And you need to lock yourself in the head for a while."

"I'll see you tonight?" Hazel asked.

He'd find Stevenson, find out what happened that night, then he'd be back. He'd get everything he needed. Rope, duct tape…He was sure he was forgetting something important. But what?

"To knock it off and tell her yes," Annabel said. "And give her your number."

"Definitely. Here." He dug a paper from his pocket, scribbling on it. "My number. I've got some things to do, but I'll be back, definitely. About nine, okay? You like soft cones? We'll go to the Dairy Queen."

"Okay." She smiled. "Oh, wait. Your coat—" Hazel started slipping it off.

"Keep it. Then you have to see me again."

And this time, he'd be ready.

04:39 THURSDAY, JULY 1

40°27'24.61"N/74°16'09.29"W

PARLIN, NJ

Micah unlocked the shed and held the door open. "Getting a bit bold, don't you think?"

"Go ahead; let's hear it. He's weird. He's strange. He's got fangs."

"Definitely not playing with a full deck. One minute he's talking to you, next he's staring at nothing." Micah locked the door behind them.

Hazel smiled to herself. "He's sweet."

Micah chuckled. "You make the perfect couple: you're homicidal and he's insane. He ask you to the prom yet?"

"No. Just to run away and stay with him forever."

"Why do I think you'd actually consid—" Micah paused as Tony charged down the stairs.

"Where the hell were you two? I've been looking half the night for you."

"Don't tell Nicky, but Hazel's got a boyfriend." Micah said, elbowing Hazel and snickering. He studied Tony's expression and his grin faded. Hazel's throat tightened. She knew that look: it was the look of bad news.

239

"What's wrong?"

"Joe called," Tony took a deep breath. "There was an accident on Route Eighty. Your dad's in the hospital."

Hazel spotted Joe's old Harley off to the side of the Emergency Room lot as Micah parked Tony's pickup. Inside they were given visitor's badges and directions to the Trauma Unit, where they found Joe staring stoically out the window. He gave them a grim nod then picked up a phone on a table in the corner.

"Ian Moran's daughter is here…yeah…okay." He hung up and turned to them. "The doctor'll be out in a minute."

"What was he doing, Joe?" Hazel demanded. "Why was he up here, and where were you?"

His face clouded, but before he could answer, a tall woman with close-cropped sandy hair and a weary expression approached.

"Miss Moran? I'm Dr. Ramos. I've been treating your father." She guided them to an area where a sofa and armchairs were clustered in an attempt to give the sterile setting a sense of intimacy and warmth. "Please, have a seat."

Hazel stood firm. "I want to see my father."

"In a moment. We have your father stabilized. When he was first brought in, we believed his injuries were all from the automobile accident. He'd suffered multiple fractures and internal injuries and had lost a great deal of blood. In the ER they discovered three gunshot wounds. He was very fortunate, relatively speaking: the shot to his neck and chest missed major arteries. But it did cause internal bleeding, and his left lung was punctured and it collapsed."

Hazel felt like she was going to be sick. "But you said he's stabilized."

The doctor nodded. "At this time our primary concern is shock. He lost a fair amount of blood, and as I said, one of his lungs collapsed. He's been conscious at times, but we're keeping him sedated now to manage his stability."

Dr. Ramos rose. "He's strong, that's in his favor. He's got a decent chance of pulling through. You can see him, but I must warn you, he looks pretty bad. He'll be unresponsive, and we have him on a ventilator."

They followed the doctor to the door through which she'd entered. She tapped a code into a keypad and proceeded as the door automatically swung open. Holding Micah's hand in a vise-like grip, Hazel started to follow, but the doctor stopped and shook her head.

"I'm very sorry, but only immediate family are allowed in the Critical Care Setting. How are you related to the patient?" she asked Micah.

Micah started to pull his hand free, but Hazel wouldn't release it. "He's my brother," she said, prepared to argue the point. The doctor merely nodded.

They followed her down a short hall, which opened to a large area. In the center was the nurses' station, where several nurses went about their business as monitors beeped and phones rang. Rooms circled the outer wall, each with floor-to-ceiling sliding-glass doors. In some, curtains concealed the interior while others were open, revealing patients in their beds and yet more nurses. It wasn't until the doctor approached one of these rooms that Hazel realized in horror that the unconscious, terribly battered figure lying within was in fact her father.

His long hair had been shaven away; his face was swollen and barely recognizable. Thick tubes snaked from his mouth to a machine that provided steady mechanical respiration and made an unsettling noise each time his chest forcibly rose and fell. Narrow lines fed solutions into his bloodstream. Gauze dressings covered his neck, and a blanket lay across his chest, concealing the lumpy shapes of more bandages. On the opposite side of the bed, a redhaired woman in colorful scrubs keyed numbers into a pad on a large square machine; with each change it gave an audible beep. Hazel reached forward, cautiously touching her father's hand.

"He feels so cold," she said, her voice small.

"It's normal," said the woman in scrubs. "It's a symptom of shock and a side effect of some of the drugs we're using. Hi, my name is Chris; I'm Mr. Moran's nurse," she said with a gentle smile as Dr. Ramos quietly left the room. "I can answer any of your questions."

Hazel studied Chris, reading over the hospital ID tag on a retractable line pinned high up on her scrubs. In the ID photo, she smiled cheerily yet projected a certain "take no prisoners" attitude.

"He doesn't know we're here?" Micah said.

"We never assume a patient can't hear or experience what's going on around them. You'd be surprised what some people remember even when they're in comas. We're sedating him, replacing blood loss, and monitoring everything closely."

LCD monitors diligently tracked his vital signs. They reminded Hazel of a marine chart-plotter-radar display, but the readings left her no bearings to his position. There were so many things around him she didn't understand: red buckets and tubes running to them, red and white plugs, switches and lights. Hot tears welled up in her eyes, and she took her father's hand, holding it gently.

Her father's fingers tightened around hers.

"Dad?" she cried.

His eyes partially opened. She wanted to hug him, but feared she'd hurt him.

"Oh, he's fighting the sedatives again," Chris said matter-of-factly. She turned to a machine controlling the flow from a glass bottle of white liquid, fired off a few quick keystrokes, then turned back and laid her hand on Hazel's father's arm.

"Mr. Moran, relax now." Her voice was soothing. "Relax, everything is going to be okay, but we need you to help us by not fighting this." Alarms blared on the ventilator, and lights lit up all over its board. More alarms dinged on the heart monitors, but Chris remained calm and focused. Hazel watched helplessly as her father's eyes flew open and his mouth moved, but the tube made it impossible to see what he was trying to say. Hazel cried out, certain he was choking. Didn't his nurse see this? A woman in solid green scrubs entered the room. She gave a few touches on the ventilator and the machine quieted.

"What's up?" she asked Chris.

"He woke up. I upped the Diprivan, give it a sec to work."

The alarms stopped clamoring; his grip went slack, and his hand fell away. Hazel lifted her hand to her mouth, stifling a cry. Micah pulled her back, hugging her.

"He's one tough cookie, I'll give him that," Chris said. "That'll work in his favor. But right now he has to stay sedated to protect him from himself, so to speak."

"He was trying to say something!" Hazel cried.

She nodded. "The ventilator tube prevents that. He'll be able to speak normally when he's extubated." She came around the bed and walked them back toward the hall. "In a few days he'll be much improved. For now...I'm sorry, but sometimes family can agitate a patient more than is good for them. That's why we limit visitors to immediate family and only for fifteen minutes at a time."

Micah steered Hazel to the side, hugging her as she cried. "You heard the nurse," he said, his voice breaking. "He'll be okay. He's a tough bastard. Even horse tranquilizers can't keep him out."

I'M BACK AT THE GATES OF HELL

"Three bullets and he's still kicking." Stevenson's footsteps pounded as he paced the kitchen, phone in hand. "That's one tough son of a bitch. You think he'd be able to ID anyone?"

Crouched in the twilight shadows of bushes outside the screen door, fighting not to hiccup, Hammon shuddered. He'd planned to march in there and confront Stevenson about Hazel, but this conversation stopped him in his tracks.

"Did he shoot someone?" Annabel said.

Hammon knew Stevenson was ruthless, but this raised the bar several notches.

"That's your choice," Stevenson said. "Either way I'm going ahead with this." The kitchen light switched off and Stevenson stalked out, straight past the dense bushes concealing Hammon and over to the carriage house, tearing away in the Mercedes.

"Follow him," Annabel ordered.

No. He was going back to the boatyard and Hazel. It was already past eight. It'd take him an hour to get back there. She'd be waiting like they planned. Waiting, so vulnerable. He grabbed his backpack, feeling the rope and duct tape inside.

"I said follow Stevenson."

No. He'd stick with Plan A: Kidnap Hazel. Then he could keep her safe from Stevenson and everything else. And he'd have her alone, all to himself.

Annabel glared at him. "You want another migraine, or will a stern warning suffice? Who got shot? Who's next? What's Stevenson doing with that truck? Why does Hazel look identical to me? The best way to help her is learn what Stevenson's up to and stop him."

The hours stretched on as Hazel listened to the hush of air circulating through the ducts, muffled voices behind closed doors, and intercoms paging in codes. Beyond view she could hear activity, and she kept sitting up, expecting someone would appear with news. Intermittent updates came, along with brief visits to her father, whom the doctors deliberately kept unconscious. They claimed he was improving, though Hazel only saw machines breathing for him and feeding him fluids. Each time Micah ushered her out, she broke down, sobbing into exhaustion.

At one point the police came by to speak with her, Micah, and Joe regarding the shooting, questioning them about possible suspects and motives. Hazel didn't mention anything regarding Stevenson; as far as she knew, he wasn't in any condition to swat a fly. Another possibility was whoever Stevenson had been speaking with that night, but again she kept that to herself.

After they left, Hazel finally drifted into a fitful sleep on the waiting room couch, curled up in Micah's arms with Hammon's coat over her like a blanket. She woke in a cold sweat and looked in confusion at the darkness outside the window.

"How long was I asleep?"

"Not long enough," Micah said. "I didn't want to wake you, but you were crying."

She sat up, staring numbly at the framed print on the wall. The halls and rooms were full of them, soothing impressionist landscapes of rolling hills, trees, and ponds. The one above her resembled an overgrown cemetery, less the graves and markers, bringing back details of that reoccurring nightmare. Stevenson was there again, and Hammon as well, smiling in that sad way, blocking her from reading the inscription on the carved granite. She needed to see for herself, to know if it said what she feared it would.

"The headstone...it was..." Her voice trailed away as her awareness shifted from the horror of her nightmare to the one surrounding her. Micah studied her with concern while Joe dozed, his tattooed bulk slumped across an armchair. He'd been the first to learn of the accident when the police back home came by looking for Hazel. She had questions for him, but there were always others nearby, or he'd slip off before she could corner him.

"Why don't we get some food?" Micah straightened his arm, stretching as he rose. "You haven't eaten since White Castle."

She stared blankly at the fabric lining Hammon's coat. It shimmered slightly, as though threads of fine metal were woven throughout. "I'm not hungry."

He held out his hand. "C'mon."

She didn't move. They all should have been out on the water, far from this awful place, with nothing but the wind and the rise of the waves, hundreds of miles from anywhere.

"Do I have to carry you?" Micah scanned the hall. "Or maybe there's a spare wheelchair around."

Joe opened one eye, very awake, regarding them both. "How about this. She doesn't eat, I take her back to Forelli's myself."

Hazel sat up. "Where were you, Joe? Why weren't you with my dad?"

Joe let out a long sigh. "He didn't want me involved. He said if things went bad, one of us had to stay out of prison to keep watch over you two, and I shouldn't get locked up over something that wasn't my fight. Plausible deniability, he said."

"What was he doing?" Micah said.

Joe shook his head. "I don't know, but I plan to find out." He rose, straightening himself stiffly. "I've got some calls to make. Go eat something. I learn anything, I'll let you know."

Reluctantly Hazel followed Micah through the halls, past stations of chatting employees, past rolling beds, some with occupants, their mouths slack, past rooms of ailing and dying, staring vacantly at TVs or nothing at all.

"Dad never said where they took Stevenson." If he was in a coma, he might be only rooms away from her father.

"I doubt he's here," Micah said. "First off, there's hospitals closer to where he was. And even if he is here, what can he do? He tries anything, those alarms would start sounding and Nurse Ratchet'll put him right back in a coma."

The cafeteria décor might almost have managed to mask the institutional surroundings if not for all the patrons in scrubs and white jackets. Hazel stared at her dining choices, realizing she still didn't have any appetite. Micah gathered up some food and led her to a table, urging Hazel to sip her tea while she picked at a corn muffin. He checked his watch.

"You really should give your boyfriend a call. The poor guy's probably waiting at the boatyard, thinking you had second thoughts."

Hazel pinched crumbs into tiny clumps. "And say what?" She couldn't explain how, while they were together under the stars, her father was fighting for his life.

"Family emergency."

She'd been wrong to think she could ignore the danger surrounding her family, even for one night. She thought of her father lying there, helpless and broken, and more tears came, burning hot. "I should tell Otto to forget he ever met me. He'd be better off."

She wiped her eyes with the back of her hand and dug through Hammon's overstuffed coat pockets for the White Castle napkins she'd shoved in there hours earlier, pulling out an MP3 player in a ziplock bag and a thick envelope.

Micah leaned over. "What's that?"

"It was in Otto's coat pocket."

The return address, printed in an elegant, understated font, was Stevenson's. Sloppy notes scribbled across the envelope read:

RUSTED BLUE BUICK WAGON/ FAKE WOOD ON SIDES NJPLATES: UHE-631

RED FREIGHTLINER—MORAN MARINE TRANSPORT BIVALVE NJ

OLD SAILBOAT BURNED/SUNK

RED KENWORTH MORAN TRANS PLATE AVA-8744

HAZEL

With shaking hands, Hazel opened the envelope and counted seven banded bundles of hundred-dollar bills, loose hundreds, fifties, and smaller bills. Trembling, she removed a printout confirming transfer of fifteen thousand dollars from S&T Enterprises to Forelli's Boatyard on June 28 for the purchase of one 1986 Flicka sailboat.

"Crap. This is bad," Micah said.

Hazel searched the other pockets. Bazooka wrappers. A novelty floaty pen. A glow-in-the-dark yo-yo. Linty gummy bears. More napkins.

"Do you think he shot Dad?" Was that where he'd come from when he'd pulled into the boatyard? Had she been watching meteor showers with the very person who'd just tried to kill her father?

Micah tilted the pen and watched a tiny sailing ship inside traverse the distance. "He didn't strike me as the mercenary type, but anything's possible. So now what?"

Hazel stared at the cash and notes, furious with herself. She'd been foolish to let her guard down. He seemed so sweet, so harmless, and the whole time it was only a convincing, effective act, one she'd fallen for completely. And what was the point of it? Stevenson must have told him to get close and gain her trust. She wiped away her tears and forced a smile. "I believe he's taking me to Dairy Queen."

"Huh?" It took Micah a moment to shift gears. "Hell no! You are not playing Travis McGee with that nut job. Absolutely not!"

"What's your plan? Wait around until someone else gets shot? So long as he doesn't realize we know he's involved, we have the advantage."

"No. Plain and simple, no. It's too risky, whatever you're thinking, you know your dad wouldn't want you doing it."

"Yeah, well, he's not in a position to argue right now, is he?"

"No, but I am. Anyone's going to deal with Hammon, it'll be me."

"Us. We do anything, we do it together. And we don't—"

She paused as she spotted Joe running down the hall. Joe *never* ran. Hazel rose anxiously, stuffing everything into the coat's pockets as he charged in.

"Your dad's awake," Joe said, out of breath. "He wants you."

They raced back to the room to find Chris ordering her father to calm down and trying to keep him from sitting up while alarms beeped incessantly. Shreds of torn paper lay on top of his blanket.

"Mr. Moran, settle down NOW or I'm going to sedate you again and then you won't be able to write to Hazel. Understand?" She looked at Hazel. "I told him I'd give him a few minutes to communicate with you and your brother, and now he's making me regret that decision." She glared at Hazel's father, and he grudgingly sank down on the pillows. Chris sighed and hit buttons on the screens and machines, quieting them. "You have ten minutes. He's not going to get better like this. He'll bust stitches."

Her father's expression softened briefly when he turned to Hazel, then just as quickly shifted to anger. He scribbled forcefully on the pad.

WHY AR YOU HERE

"Joe got us," she said.

He ripped the sheet off. The pencil tore through the paper as he wrote:

WHY STILL HERE!

Hazel stood speechless and Micah's eyes narrowed.
"Because we give a shit about you!"
His right eye fell partially closed.

IL LIVE. STA WITH LOU.

His face slacked, drained.

"He needs to settle down," Chris told Micah. "He needs his rest. He's doing himself more harm than good; he's maxing out on the sedatives."

Micah glared down at him. "Try a bigger hammer."

He wrote again, holding out the pad to Hazel.

LOVE YOU. GO.

Tears streamed down her face as she leaned over, carefully kissing him on his cheek. Micah guided her outside, and she broke down in his arms.

"See? He's getting better." Micah stroked her hair. "He's already back to being an asshole."

Chris stepped out, offering a weary smile.

"Whew! Clearly he's improving. I was about to take him to the CT Scan department, but he was so agitated to see you first."

Hazel swallowed and wiped her eyes. Her father didn't want to see her; he wanted to see her *gone*. If only she'd known what he'd been doing, maybe she could have helped him, and maybe he wouldn't be in this awful place now. "How long will he have to be here?"

"I can't really say. His lung still has a suction tube in it to keep it inflated while it heals. His other wounds are draining, but there's no further active bleeding that we can see. We've given him blood, and his blood counts are improving. So far, no signs of infection, but it's too early for them as yet. To heal, what he really needs is rest."

Hazel nodded, sniffling. "He doesn't want us here."

"Let me write down your contact numbers; I have Joe's but not yours. There's normally a policy that one family member be the spokesperson…so that's you, Hazel?"

Hazel's phone had gone down with *Kindling*, and Micah's was still missing. "I don't have a phone right now. I'll get one and call you with the number."

"And we need a password for phone conversations. I know it seems silly, but the Federal Government requires us to make sure we know who we're talking to over the phone. It's not always me you'll be speaking to, but I am his primary nurse, so he's my patient whenever I'm on shift."

"A password?" Any of their boat or truck names wouldn't be hard to guess, not that Hazel knew who else might call or why. "Busted Flush," she said. It was Travis McGee's boat, named after the pivotal poker hand that won it for him.

"Busted Flush," Chris confirmed. "Should I ask?" She wrote it down and then studied Hazel. "I know you want to be here for your father, but I'm sure you're exhausted as well. There's no point living in a waiting room; it can't be very comfortable for you, and it won't accomplish anything, especially since it appears your father won't relax until I assure him you've left. I promise I'll call if anything changes."

Hazel hesitated. "He was shot. Someone tried…someone shot him."

Chris nodded. "And he's safe here. No one can get in those doors unless they bust through with AK-forty-sevens. Trust me," she laughed, her bright blue eyes sharp and serious, "NO ONE gets past me if they don't belong. Not even your tattooed friend camping in the waiting room. I'm only letting your 'brother' slide because it's obvious he's holding you together."

"We should let Joe know we're going," Hazel said as they left the ICU. But he was nowhere in sight.

"He's probably outside on his phone. We'll call him and explain. We need to get a phone and call Nurse Chris with the number." They returned to the lot but didn't see Joe. Micah unlocked Tony's pickup and opened the passenger door for Hazel. "Then we decide what we're doing about your boyfriend."

She slapped the envelope down on the dashboard. "He's not my boyfriend." Her face burned and she was grateful for the darkness.

"Sorry, hon." Micah reached over, squeezing her hand. "Just kidding."

She knew he was, but she was still furious with herself, falling for Hammon's act so completely. Micah started the truck while Hazel stared back at the hospital, and it took a moment to register as she watched a tall, heavyset figure with pale hair climb into a massive black Mercedes.

"Get down!" She grabbed Micah's collar, pulling him below the dashboard with her.

Head sideways, he looked over. "What are we doing?"

"I think I saw Stevenson. It was dark, but it looked like him." She sat up slowly, peering out. The car was gone. "Where do you think he went?"

"Hard to say with my head wedged under the steering wheel." Micah sat up. "I thought Stevenson was in critical condition."

"He didn't look critical to me."

"Maybe your dad heard wrong. Or he heard what Stevenson wanted him to hear."

A horrible realization hit Hazel. "You think he followed us, or is he after Dad?" She shuddered at the thought of her father lying there, so helpless. "We have to go back."

"Wait," Micah caught her wrist as she reached to unclip her belt. "Stevenson was leaving, right? And Chris was taking your dad for a CT scan. I'm sure he's safe." He put the truck in gear, pulling out of the space. "You know what I think? I think it's time for a safari."

"Just so long as we're not the prey."

Hazel was thrown against her seatbelt as Micah slammed on the brakes. He stared toward the Dumpsters in the far corner of the lot, shaking his head. "No fucking way."

"What?"

Then she saw it, parked in the shadows. A dark blue Fairmont.

I'M OUT OF HERE

The Trauma Center was the last place Hammon wanted to find himself again, even as a visitor. Annabel flat out refused to enter the building. But if Stevenson was there, intent on finishing what three bullets started, it was up to Hammon to stop him. If only he could get that far. At every turn harsh whiteness and sharp right angles closed in; voices echoed all around and carried through the halls, suffocating him. The building seemed to pulse with unseen birth and death, sickness and pain, sucking him under. His worst nightmares lived within these walls, and the farther he went, the harder it became to move, as though gravity was increasing. Horrifying memories assaulted him and he stared down, terrified that anyone might look too close. There were too many people who might recognize his face. They should. It was their creation.

This was a mistake. He couldn't find his way, and he couldn't find Stevenson, not that he knew what he'd do if he did. Without Annabel's calming guidance, he stumbled along, disoriented and anxious, whipping his head around at every noise, certain someone would peg him as a lost psych patient and drag him back to treatment. Then he'd never escape. He'd never be able to see or help Hazel. Terrified, gasping for air, Hammon finally found his way back to the soothing darkness of the parking lot.

Stevenson's car was gone. He could track it, but he'd made up his mind. He'd stick with Plan A: get Hazel alone aboard *Nepenthe* and take her far from Stevenson and whatever dangers he presented. He had one problem, though; Annabel would try to stop him. There had to be a way around her interference and the blinding headaches that went with it. Maybe those medications; they were supposed to make the voices go away. There was a time he couldn't imagine living without Annabel. That's why he'd thrown them out. But now...

Annabel emerged from the shadows as he unlocked the Fairmont, and Hammon's heart sank. She knew what he was planning. She always knew. She stood, hands tucked demurely behind her, staring with solemn intensity. A single tear ran down her cheek.

"It's not that I want to get rid of you," he mumbled apologetically. "You got to understand, it's what I have to do."

"I do understand," she said, her voice breaking. "Nothing's coincidence..."

"Huh?"

"Haze, no!" Micah shouted, rushing over as she swung a tire iron, hitting Hammon square across the right knee with a sickening crack. He dropped like a sack of bricks onto the pavement beside the Fairmont and stared up through crooked glasses, seeing double as pain rippled through his body.

Annabel strolled past Hazel and glared down with zero sympathy. "Serves you right, after all I've done for you."

Hazel stood over him, tire iron raised for another strike. "Don't move," she warned. "Or I swing again. Understand?"

Hammon nodded numbly, blinking to clear his vision, noticing with detachment how his right leg twisted in a disturbing angle. By the look of things, it was unlikely he'd be able to stand. Hazel wiped her cheek against her shoulder as Micah stepped between them.

"Hon, I thought we agreed I'd handle this," he said, his voice gentle. "You know how you get."

"I think I'm being remarkably restrained, considering."

"You are." He tried to take the iron. She wouldn't release it. "But someone might hear him screaming."

"He isn't screaming," she pointed out. "Yet."

"Oh, that's not good," Annabel said. "What'd you do to piss her off?"

"I don't know…" Hammon choked.

"Don't know what?" Micah studied the unnatural angle of Hammon's leg and cringed. "Damn, he's got some amazing tolerance to pain."

Hazel placed the iron against his damaged knee. "Let's see how much," she said, each word razor-sharp, her eyes focusing hatred like sunlight through a magnifying glass.

Hammon gazed up, helpless and confused. "Why?"

"That's what I'd like to know," Hazel said. "I guess Stevenson figured I'd fall for the sweet, shy act, and I guess he was right. You really had me fooled."

Micah held out the envelope with all his notes and cash. "I warned you not to upset her."

Annabel groaned. "You left that in your coat?"

He was going to be sick. "That's not what it looks like."

"It looks to me like Stevenson paid you a stack of cash to steal our truck, burn our boat, and…" She pressed down on the iron. "My father's in that hospital and it looks *exactly* like someone tried to kill him."

Hammon moaned aloud. THAT was who Stevenson shot? This was even worse than the worst he could imagine. "I didn't do it!"

"We saw Stevenson leave," Micah said, his voice low. "Why was he here? What does he want?"

Hammon shook his head. "I don't know."

The pressure on his knee increased, and he choked back a sob, more from frustration than pain.

"Where's our truck?" Hazel demanded. "And what's Stevenson doing with it?"

Hope rose in Hammon. He could prove he wanted to help! He knew where Stevenson stashed the red Freightliner; he could show them! He was about to speak when a jolt of agony ripped through his brain and he shuddered, gasping incoherently.

"No," Annabel warned. "You do that, you could lead them straight to Stevenson."

She was right, but pain choked his words. Annabel said, "Tell her you don't know."

"Don't…know…" he whimpered obediently.

"Who is he working with?" Hazel demanded, again pressing down.

"I don't know!"

Micah sighed in disgust. "Give it up, Haze. He doesn't know anything."

She didn't look convinced. "Then what's Stevenson paying him for? I saw him in Piermont; he must've turned around and followed me straight to Forelli's."

"No," Hammon stammered. He wished she'd just hit him again; that hurt less than the way she was looking at him, like she could see straight through him and hated what she saw.

"Tell her the truth," Annabel said.

The truth? He didn't know it himself. He only knew she and Micah were in trouble, and they were running from Stevenson. "I didn't tell Stevenson anything. He doesn't know I found you."

"Not that!" Annabel said.

"And I didn't shoot your father."

Hazel's eyes narrowed. "I never said he was shot."

"Stevenson did…"

"Stop saying Stevenson," Annabel snapped. "You're digging your own grave."

"I swear…I…uh…oh…God…" he choked, his voice edging toward hysteria. He banged his head against the pavement, fighting back a giggle. This wasn't funny. Headlights swept through the lot, casting long shadows beneath the Fairmont. The car stopped, lights shut, doors slammed, and voices receded. He could call out, but if help came, Hazel and Micah would leave and he might never find them again. He had to make them understand he wanted to help. Through one lens of his glasses, he watched Micah open his backpack.

"Rope. Duct tape. A paintball gun." Micah dug out the compact neon-pink-and-green "toy" Glock, inspecting it, feeling the weight. "Holy shit! This thing's real."

Hazel took it from Micah and leveled it at Hammon. "You painted a real gun to look like a toy?"

Micah reclaimed the gun. "It hasn't been fired in a while."

"He could have cleaned it."

"Then it'd be clean. It's hard to fire with a petrified gummy bear wedged behind the trigger." Micah flipped through Hammon's wallet. "Driver's license says he's John O. Hammon, from Manasquan, New Jersey. Fairmont registration in Stevenson's name. Jersey boat registration, thirty-six foot, wood, diesel, also Stevenson. One library card."

Hammon heard the *thunk* of the trunk releasing. "Oh shit," he mumbled.

Annabel looked back. "Oh shit."

Micah surveyed the contents. "Oh shit."

"What now?" Hazel walked over. Micah blocked her. She pushed past then turned back to Hammon. "A shovel and a tarp?"

"For burying things," he admitted.

"Things?" Hazel said.

Annabel shook her head. "Your communication skills suck."

He couldn't remember the word. Think…damnit…"Dead things." Hammon winced from the pain in Hazel's eyes. "I know last night…I talked about hurting you…I meant that…" he struggled, breaking into nervous giggles. "I was only gonna kidnap you, then…"

"Otto, just shut up already!" snapped Annabel.

"Haze, give me the tire iron," Micah said.

Hammon's brain itched as the stitches inside came undone. He moaned, rubbing his skull against the pavement. "I WON'T HURT YOU!"

Micah looked around. "He's getting loud. Someone might notice."

No! If anyone came over, they'd leave and he would never see Hazel again. He couldn't let that happen.

"I'll be quiet," he insisted, desperately looking as cooperative as possible, lying next to the tire like…"Roadkill!" he said brightly, at last recalling the elusive term. Somehow, it only seemed to further infuriate Hazel.

"Hon, let's go," Micah said. "He's just hired help. He doesn't know anything useful."

She looked down at Hammon. "We can't leave this here."

He'd been reduced to "this." "Hazel…" he pleaded.

She knelt down, looking at him with those beautiful dark eyes, hating him.

"Tell her the truth," Annabel said.

"I was just looking for *Revenge*. I…I'm…" Hammon choked, searching for the words.

"Sick. You're sick."

He knew that. "I'll follow you. I promise."

"No." Micah wrapped a strip of duct tape across his mouth. "You won't." Another length bound his arms behind his back.

Hazel wiped her face against her shoulder and turned to Micah. "We have to get rid of…"

Hammon flopped around like a landed fish, and he struggled to speak against the tape, desperate to get their attention. Micah glanced down and Hammon stared up. Please don't kill me, he pleaded silently. Micah turned away, talking to Hazel too quiet for Hammon to hear.

"That's not encouraging," Annabel said.

They turned back to him. Micah grabbed his shoulders, and Hazel took his ankles, lifting him and rolling him into the trunk, onto the muddy, stinking tarp. The shovel dug into his spine.

"His leg isn't broken." Hazel shoved the twisted right limb into the trunk. "It's a prosthetic. That's why he didn't scream." She snapped open a vicious little knife and lowered the blade to his throat.

"Haze," Micah said gently. "Don't."

"Why not?" Her troubled eyes met Hammon's for a second that lasted an eternity. "He found us once, he'll find us again. And you saw what he's got with him."

He tried futilely to explain through the duct tape. Annabel leaned against the car. "I think you're doing better not talking."

Hazel was in danger, and once he was dead, he couldn't help. He'd failed. The blade pressed to his flesh as Hammon gazed up, helpless. He'd given up on struggling. It was pointless. He couldn't stop her. He was doomed.

"We kill him," Micah said, "Stevenson just sends someone else."

"We'll worry about that when it happens."

Hammon studied Hazel, so beautiful even as she was about to kill him. Her eyes, so innocent and deadly, looked straight through his broken soul, and his heart wrenched the same way it did that first time her gentle fingers caressed his scarred cheek. He leaned his face against her arm, savoring the bittersweet sensation of his damaged skin pressed to her smooth perfection; it felt so good, but it was the last time they'd ever touch. A single tear caught beneath her trembling lip.

"No." Micah closed his hand around hers, lifting the blade, pulling her away. "I won't let you do this."

It didn't matter. His heart would seize first from the horrible, crushing anguish.

"Go back to the truck," Micah said. "I'll deal with Hammon."

"But…" she protested. "You…*you* can't."

Micah handed her the backpack. "Go."

Hammon heard a door open, then close. He twisted sideways, trying to catch the edge of the tape, hoping to scrape it off. He struggled to figure a way out of the tape, out of the trunk, and out of a terrible misunderstanding rapidly approaching an unpleasant conclusion.

"You look uncomfortable," Micah said.

Hammon bobbed his head frantically, wondering why that would matter. Micah rolled him forward, pulled the shovel out from under him, and straightened his glasses.

"I warned you not to hurt her. She actually trusted you, and you broke that trust."

Micah looked around, then raised the shovel over his head like an axe.

21:57 THURSDAY, JULY 1

40°53'02.67"N/74°03'28.47"W

HACKENSACK, NJ

Hazel watched, barely able to breathe. Just one swing, then Micah surveyed the results with grim satisfaction. He returned the shovel to the trunk, slammed it closed, and tossed the tire iron into the bed of the yard truck.

"Well, that's that." He climbed in and started the engine, pulling out.

For several miles neither spoke. Hazel wanted to break down but she couldn't. Not yet, maybe not ever. She curled up, knees to her chest, arms wrapped around her legs.

Micah sighed, breaking the silence. "On the bright side, things can't get much worse."

"You keep saying that, but they do."

"I'm just trying to cheer you up. Your dad's got Nurse Chris watching over him so he's probably safer than any of us. He'll be back to his mean old self in no time. *Witch*'ll get fixed…"

"And now you're killing people."

He switched on the radio and flipped through stations, stopping on a Chili Peppers tune. "Your point?"

Her throat was tight and she felt sick. This was what they'd come to? "You're not a killer."

"I guess all the video-game violence must've desensitized me. You shouldn't let it bother you; you're just tired. And I don't know about you, but I'm getting hungry."

Hazel stared at Micah, stunned. "How can you eat after…?"

"Hammon?" He shrugged. "I did what I had to. You wanted him dead, right?"

"I don't know. I guess."

"Don't blame yourself. I never would've figured him for a hired thug. He seemed like a nice kid."

"With an emergency roadside burial kit." Had that been meant for them? She shuddered at the thought. Why did she let Hammon get so close? It was a careless, dangerous mistake. She'd lowered her guard, put their lives at risk, and turned Micah into a murderer as a result. "Can we not talk about this right now?"

"I'll give you, that stuff in the trunk was pretty creepy. Still, something doesn't fit. Like, why didn't he call for help instead of just staring at you like a lost puppy?"

"I don't know and I really don't want to discuss it."

"It's like he didn't even try to defend himself. I don't get it."

"You mind telling me what you're driving at?"

"That diner there." Micah pointed toward the lights up ahead. "I'm just trying to figure it out. You trusted him, and that's not like you."

Was he deliberately trying to upset her? "You don't get the concept of 'drop it,' do you?"

Micah pulled into the diner's nearly vacant parking lot. "You actually liked him, didn't you?"

"Will that shut you up? Yeah, fine. I fell for the shy little boy-scout act. But he's dead and so is the horse. Stop beating it." Hazel stared out at the neon lit windows. "And I said I'm not hungry."

Micah chuckled. "Relax, hon, I didn't kill your boyfriend."

"What? I saw you."

"Scare the piss out of him. I hit the spare tire. I said I'd take care of things. You were angry, not like I blame you. But it messed up your judgment. First off, I don't think he shot your father and neither do you, or that swing you took would've been at his skull. Alive, he's leverage and potential information. We've got his phone. Let's see who he's dealing with and what they know. Second, I might know where *Tuition* is. And lastly, I've got a feeling Hammon's part of something he doesn't understand any more than us. Let's eat. We've got a busy night ahead."

Micah killed the headlights and pulled onto the shoulder, just down the road from Turner Speed. Floodlights shined across the lot surrounding the drab cinder block building. Massive roll-up doors covered a pair of service bays. On the second floor, the blue flicker of a television danced.

"Tell me that's not a perfect place to stash a rig," Micah said.

Hazel nodded. "Unfortunately it looks like someone's home."

"Watch and learn." Micah set Hammon's cell phone to speaker and pushed the speed dial for "Gary."

"Zap? Where the hell are you?" grumbled an aggravated voice.

In an official tone Micah said, "We're sorry. Hammon can't come to the phone right now, he's a bit tied up at the moment. And gagged, so he wouldn't have much to say anyways."

"Who is this? You're the one who beat up Stevenson and took his goddamned boat. Where's Hammon? What'd you do to him?"

"He's okay, for the time being at least. You tell him, next time he crosses us he won't be so lucky."

"Tell him how? Where is he?"

"At the hospital. Go to Hackensack. When you get there, call me back."

"Look, you got issues with Stevenson, that's your business. Leave the kid out of it. He's fucked up enough already, he doesn't need this. I don't need this."

"Neither do we."

Micah shut the phone. Hazel said, "And that accomplished what?"

The TV blinked off and a figure rushed outside, climbing into a black Dakota pickup. "I'm guessing that's Gary."

"Ever seen him before?" Hazel asked as the Dakota screeched out.

"No, but now we've got roughly two hours, and we've got keys."

They waited as the taillights moved down the road, heading toward the Parkway, then they stalked closer. Aside from a cat with part of its left ear missing, no one took notice. A second cat, also sporting a tipped ear, appeared as they approached the boat racks.

"Damn," Micah commented as he looked over the storage racks, occupied by an assortment of sleek fiberglass speedboats, each gaudier than the next, with tacky graphics and names like *Liquid Assets* and *The Dominator*. There was one exception: a stodgy battleship-gray twenty-eight-foot plumb-bowed cruiser with a flush deck and round bronze ports, resting on a custom cradle.

Micah said, "What's this relic doing here?"

Hazel read the name, *Temperance,* and smiled. "She's a Sea Bright skiff. Tough, stable, and very popular with rum runners during Prohibition. They could launch and land in beach surf and outrun the Coast Guard cutters. I'll bet this thing's got some serious balls."

They moved toward the buildings, hanging in the shadows. Three more cats appeared.

"Guard cats?" Micah mused. "Weird…they're *all* missing part of their left ear."

"They're feral. Otto said his friend Gary feeds the local strays. The tipped ears mean they're part of a maintained colony and they've already been captured, neutered, and released."

"Clearly we're dealing with some bad-ass hardened criminals."

A sign outside the door warned the premises were protected by Smith & Wesson, though the length of heavy chain and an oversized, slobber-stained water bowl were far more ominous. Inside, they could hear nails clicking on cement and noses snuffling at the door.

"Otto told me Gary's dogs are mushes." Hazel held up crackers she'd brought and jingled Hammon's keys as she unlocked the door, hoping to elicit a friendly response. A massive mutt sized her up and eagerly accepted her offerings as they entered. "The big one's Charger, and the little one was some kind of snack food…Twinkie or Ring Ding…"

"Yodel!" Micah petted the black-and-white dachshund. The whole dog wagged enthusiastically, then rushed to grab a grungy tennis ball. From then on searching presented no problem so long as they tossed squeaky toys and tennis balls as fast as the dogs brought them. Under observation of several cats, they entered the rear shop, which housed assorted automotive and marine projects in various states of completion.

"Nice toys." Hazel inspected an '89 Mustang Coupe, hood off to reveal a spotless 351. "But no *Tuition.*"

Escorted by the dogs, they opened the office. Invoices and bills blanketed the desk, and a quick jiggle of the mouse woke the computer from its screensaver. Micah double-clicked the QuickBooks icon and grinned when he saw it set to "Remember password" box. A quick search under "Stevenson" revealed large deposits starting five years earlier, funding the property purchase and business incorporation. Tools and equipment, jobs in progress and completed, inventory, payroll, insurances, utilities; all standard business expenses, nothing suspicious or alarming. They headed upstairs with the dogs right behind. Hazel liked having them along: they'd be the first to know if anyone was returning.

Aside from the stacks of car magazines and catalogs, the apartment was tidy. Laundry in the hamper, clothes folded in drawers. No weird drugs. A reasonably clean kitchen. Dishes in the dishwasher, some beer, milk, and leftovers in the fridge. Hazel dug through the cabinets, and the dogs perked up, hoping for handouts.

Micah checked inside the hall closet, stepping on a squeaky alligator. "Hammon uses this address, but I'd venture he doesn't live here. It's too neat." He flung the toy and Yodel bounded after it. Charger picked up the alligator with a ferociously growling Yodel still dangling.

Hazel looked as Micah searched around the TV. "You see anything?"

"*Star Trek, Terminator,* a whole bunch of Marvel movies. If they weren't the bad guys, they'd be cool to hang with."

Micah bounced a soggy tennis ball down the stairs, wiping his hands on his pants as Yodel raced after it. Charger had it figured out; he'd let Yodel do all the hyper scrambling then claim the toy after Yodel retrieved it.

"This was a waste of time." Hazel sat on the floor and scratched Charger's head. Yodel pushed in and climbed onto her lap.

"No. We just established one more place *Tuition* isn't."

I'M PRETTY SURE I'M DEAD

From the velvety blackness, blinding light appeared. This was it. Hammon knew the drill. Go to the light.

Only this time he wasn't going anywhere. He was still lying on that stinking tarp in the trunk of his car, and he still felt like shit. That wasn't right.

The light moved closer, burning his eyes.

"Zap? Oh shit."

"That sounds like Gary," Annabel said.

The flashlight beam swept across him, but Hammon couldn't move. "Jeez." Gary poked his shoulder, then slumped back, shaking his head. "Christ, kid."

Hammon blinked.

"JESUS!" Gary jumped backwards. He leaned over cautiously. "I thought you were dead. You look dead." He yanked the tape off Hammon's mouth, along with some hair and skin. "You smell dead."

Hammon sucked in fresh air, coughing.

Gary peeled the tape off Hammon's hands. "What the hell happened to you?"

"Reality."

Agonizingly Hammon propped himself up on his elbows, feeling like a voodoo doll as stabs of pain shot through his stiff body. With Gary's help he hauled himself out, balancing against the bumper and repositioning his damaged leg. Gary cringed and looked toward the glowing emergency room entrance. "At least you're in the right place."

"It's just broken. I'm not going in there. What're you doing here?"

"Some kid called. He said to tell you the next time you cross 'them' you won't be so lucky."

Hammon brightened. They didn't want him dead…at least Micah didn't.

Gary said, "And ten minutes ago, the signal went live again. Care to explain?"

"You mean THE signal? *Revenge*?" Hammon grinned. Hazel and Micah were on the move again, and he could track them. "You have to show me!" He started toward the driver's door, his leg buckled, and he landed in a twisted pile.

Gary looked ill. "You seriously need a doctor."

"I'm fine. Just give me a hand, I'm sure I can jury-rig it." Hammon pulled himself upright, balancing on one leg. Holding the Fairmont, he hobbled around to the door, dragging his damaged limb. His backpack was gone but they'd left the duct tape. He eased himself into the car and grabbed his leg, propping it straight.

Gary winced. "You need that looked at, and you need to explain what the fuck's going on."

"We need to get moving, dear," Annabel said. "Now."

Hammon nodded. "I know, but I can't drive like this."

Gary's eyes narrowed. "I didn't say drive."

"I was talking to Annabel."

"Annabel?" Gary rubbed his face.

"Just cause she's not real doesn't mean she's gone. That's not important. I've got to follow that signal."

It took a round of show-and-tell to convince Gary he didn't require medical attention, at least not for his leg. His head was another matter. Finally Gary gave up, locking his truck and heading the Fairmont toward the Turnpike. "So you don't remember why you were at the hospital or how you wound up in your trunk."

Hammon shook his head. "Nope. Not a clue. My brain must be shorting out again."

"And you don't know who called me."

"Nope." Hammon hiccupped.

"And you're not gonna tell me why you're lying through your pointy teeth."

"Nope."

He was operating on Annabel's advice. Don't explain, not that he could even if he wanted to. He had no idea what was going on.

Gary glanced into the backseat at the gear from *Nepenthe*. "Should I even ask why you got a carload of sailboat shit?"

"Nope."

"And the fact that the signal came on in the middle of this all, just coincidence?"

Hazel's words still echoed in his head. "She said nothing is coincidence."

"Annabel?"

Hammon nodded. "Yeah, Annabel."

"No," she snapped. "I said, 'Shut up, already.'"

Gary watched the monitor on his laptop. *Revenge* was underway, heading south. The plan was to switch over to *Temperance* and follow by water.

"How far you think they're going?" Annabel said.

"Damned if I know." Hammon rolled his pants leg up, assessing the damage, past and present. The prosthetic began midthigh; Hazel's shot was lower, mangling the knee joint. He rigged a splint with sail battens and duct tape. It would hold, but he'd walk with a nasty limp until he got it fixed. A horn sounded and Gary swerved back into his lane.

"Watch the road," Hammon said. For years he'd been obsessively self-conscious of his physical condition. Time in the trunk gave him a new perspective about what really mattered.

"You never mentioned…that."

"Never came up." Hammon wrapped more tape around his repair. "I'll need a hand with this. The foot and socket look okay but the knee's history. That sucks; I just got this one three months ago. German engineered, state-of-the-art microprocessor controls, but I got a feeling assault by tire iron isn't under warranty. Good thing she hit this side."

"Brilliant," Annabel grumbled.

Gary's eyes narrowed. "She?"

Hammon blinked. "Who?"

"You said…" Gary tapped his fingers on the wheel. "I wish I had a better idea what I'm dealing with."

"That makes two of us."

"I meant you. Five years, I got no more idea who or what you are than when I found you holed up on that freakin' boat."

"I figured you were happier not asking. I know I was." Hammon tested his leg, wrapping it a few more times. Satisfied, he pulled the pants leg down.

Gary stared ahead. "And I'm not supposed to ask what the hell's going on."

He had to find her. She needed him. He'd make her see. The tracking system showed them running along the outer shore, passing Rumson. "You wouldn't understand."

"You've got that right." Gary swung onto the shoulder and snapped the laptop shut. "I've put up with lots of weird shit over the years, and I've tried to roll with it. Either you start talking or you can kiss finding your boat good-bye."

"But…" *Revenge* was his last link to Hazel. Reluctantly Hammon related everything up to the present, the whole while glancing anxiously at the computer. "She's in trouble," he insisted.

"You sure she didn't take a swing or two at your head? Wake the fuck up. She's not in trouble, you are. You've been set up. The question is, why?"

"She couldn't kill me."

"She only tried to cripple you. How touching."

"Someone's after them and they think it's me. But they don't understand, whoever's after them is using them to get to me."

"Let me guess: the people with the tracking microchips." Gary eyed him skeptically. "If I hadn't got that call and found you like I did, I'd think you lost it completely. Seriously, what's anyone want with you?"

Hammon stared out the window. "I know things."

"What things?"

Hammon sighed. "That's the problem. I don't remember."

05:07 FRIDAY, JULY 2

40°10'49.98"N/74°01'47.35"W

BELMAR, NJ

July 2 dawned with vivid shades of red, pink, and orange shimmering off the water.

"Damn, that's freakin' breathtaking." Micah gazed up as they docked the freshly fueled-up *Mardi* among the fleets of charters and fishing boats in transient slips at the Belmar Municipal Boat Basin. "Almost leaves you without words."

Hazel regarded the sky as she tightened the spring line. "A depression's moving in."

"Can't you just once say, 'Oooh. Pretty sunrise.'"

Hazel looked up. "Ooooh. Pretty. My dad's been shot, my life's falling apart, people are trying to kill us, and the weather's going to get ugly."

Micah grinned. "But on the bright side…"

She glared at him. "Don't say it."

They passed the day catching up on sleep aboard the boat. Through a late-day call from nurse Chris, Hazel learned her father was making a strong recovery, and making himself a pain in the process. If everything continued smoothly over the coming hours, he'd be headed into surgery with an orthopedic specialist to pin together his ankle, fibula, and tibia, all shattered when the Buick's engine crushed into the firewall. They checked in again as darkness fell to learn surgery was scheduled for Saturday morning. The next call, made from a pay phone blocks away, left Micah pale.

"Keith couldn't find anything on Stevenson, but he said last night Atkins's trailer burned to a shell. The cops didn't find Atkins, but they're still sifting through it."

"He might not have been there," Hazel said, without much conviction. The way things had been going, her optimism had worn thin.

Micah dialed Atkins's number. Hazel leaned closer, trying to listen in as he scribbled down "NY, SDH-896" then hung up.

"What's that?" Hazel said. "A license plate?"

"This," he pointed to the paper, "is code for a time and place. We set this up back when things first hit the fan, just in case. Atkins is a bit on the paranoid side. Then again, he's been right so far. Here," he showed her. "Add all the numbers, you get twenty-three. So twenty-three minutes after each hour, give or take." He underlined *NY*. "That means the Turnpike. 'NJ' is the Parkway. Take the last letter," he circled the *H*. "That's the eighth letter in the alphabet. So subtract eight from the eight-nine-six, then divide by eight," he explained, figuring it as he did. "And that's where we meet: at the rest stop by that milepost at that time at the furthest end of that lot. No one shows, leave and come back in an hour."

"Mile one eleven." She knew Micah trusted Atkins completely, but she couldn't help but wonder if they'd been sent the coordinates for a trap. "The Alexander Hamilton rest stop in Secaucus."

"And we need a car."

The vehicle of choice was a Chevy Blazer from which a mildly intoxicated couple emerged, laughing as they stumbled into the pub across the street. There was no debate or discussion; Hazel pointed, Micah nodded, and minutes later they were rolling, Micah at the wheel.

The sky darkened and light rain began to fall, and the dismal wiper blades only smeared the view of the taillights ahead. Micah remained uncharacteristically quiet, which made Hazel more uneasy than she already was.

At Newark she watched cargo planes taxiing around terminals and runways. A Fed-Ex jet roared as it raced Turnpike traffic then rose into the night sky. Rows of boxcars lined up on rail tracks, hauling cargo to and from the container ships docked along the Elizabeth waterfront. Massive cranes ceaselessly transferred loads between ships, trains, and trucks in a well-orchestrated ballet. Further ahead oil refinery lights twinkled. There was a certain beauty to the industrial landscape, alive and shimmering in the rainy night.

"You know what the problem is?" Micah stared out. "People fly into Newark, see this, and figure the whole state's the same thing."

Hazel glanced across, noticing his tight grip on the wheel.

"It's not just that," she joined in. "Half the country, they've never even been here, they watched some TV show or movie and they assume Jersey's a toxic wasteland populated with mobsters."

Micah nodded grimly. "Everyone says they air's lousy, but nobody points out where most of that pollution comes from: out west. The jet stream carries all the smog from coal-burning power plants and dumps it here. I'm sick of Jersey-bashing. Atkins says the state slogan should be, 'Welcome to New Jersey, now go home.'"

Hazel counted the numbers on the mile markers, her anxiety rising as they increased. What were they headed into? Try as she might, she couldn't shake the awful feeling this trip was a mistake.

"It's too bad we took Hammon's phone," Micah said.

"How so?"

"We've got no way of calling him."

"And why would we want to do that?"

"Because you're no fun when you're morose. Around Hammon, at least you were smiling."

"Yeah, until I learned Stevenson sent him."

All the warning signs were there, but she'd chosen to ignore them. She'd been careless and completely misjudged Hammon, endangering them both. She was turning out to be a poor excuse for a salvage consultant.

They passed through the Meadowlands, reaching the Alexander Hamilton service area on schedule, and Micah parked beside a dingy red Corolla. Hazel watched warily as the greasy-haired driver unfolded himself from the car, greeting Micah with a round of friendly profanities.

"Didn't even recognize you when you pulled up." Atkins looked Micah over. "Good move losing the blue hair and crap on your face. Finally showing some sense."

Hazel remained beside the Blazer, scanning the lot for threats, and backed up slightly as Atkins approached.

"You nervous, girl?" His discolored eye locked on her in an unblinking stare. "Smart. Micah said you got a good head on you." He nodded toward their surroundings. "The last hour I been watching, no one's came and parked over here. I warned Micah this shit was coming. Your boat, my trailer. Word is your dad's had a bad accident, only I'm betting it wasn't an accident."

"No," Hazel said. "Someone shot him."

Atkins nodded. "I was afraid of that. This's getting ugly. Some-one out there's rattled and wants us all gone. They shot up my trailer while it burned. Good thing I was out. Come dark I swung by your place looking for Joe. He wasn't 'round, but I found this stuck to your old Kenworth." He pulled a sloppily folded paper from his pocket, smoothed it, and passed it to Hazel.

Micah leaned his chin over her shoulder to see. It read: "FOUND" with the photos of *Tuition*, the trailer's interior, and Hazel, *Times* in hand, finger raised. At the bottom was a 201 area-code number.

"That's Stevenson's number," Hazel said.

Atkins leaned back against the Corolla. "This's just the thing I tried warning you about. I don't know what's become of Kessler, but he weren't working alone. You got this Stevenson on one end, Kessler's partner on the other, and us dumb schmucks stuck in the crossfire. I figured I call, play along, see what they say. Maybe we can turn it to our advantage, but I wanted to run it by you kids first."

"Why?" Hazel said suspiciously. Micah shot her a look but Atkins only nodded.

"When I quit, Kessler said it weren't that easy. I know his operations. So do you all, at least as far as they figure. Likely there's bullets out there with our names on 'em. We work together, watch each other's backs, maybe we make it out whole."

"So, what's the plan?" Micah asked.

"I thought about that the whole ways here." Atkins's unset-tling gaze fixed on Hazel, an awful smile filling his face. "From all Micah's told me 'bout you, I figure you'll appreciate this."

First step was arranging the meeting.

Atkins called from the pay phones while Hazel and Micah stood lookout. The conversation was brief, and Atkins scribbled down notes. He hung up and they returned to the relative privacy of the cars.

"My contact, he didn't give me any name, but he's one smooth-talking son of a bitch. He says I got an interesting little operation. He said he could keep everything for himself, but without the right marketing connections, it don't do him much good. He says in exchange for twenty-five percent of the profits, he'll return it and become a silent partner. He says anything unfortunate happens to him, he got documented information goes out to the DEA and all."

Atkins wiped his face. "He said Kessler got sloppy, and he's got someone more reliable to replace him. And he said there were some loose ends. I'm guessing that'd be us. But he said he's already got that being taken care of."

"Somehow," Micah said, "I don't think that means limos and room service."

"Not likely. We're meeting by the truck at midnight to shake on our new partnership."

I'M SOGGY

Hammon watched the raindrops trail down the Fairmont's windshield, reflecting the lights of the Emergency Room, and he waited for one more chance to see Hazel. He didn't know what else to do. He wasn't able to find *Revenge*; the tracker signal had dissolved into the offshore fog long before he was anywhere close. She and Micah hadn't returned to Forelli's boatyard, and no one knew where they'd gone. The hospital was his last hope; Hammon was sure Hazel would return to see her father, and when she did he'd talk to her. He'd explain everything. Maybe he could regain her trust and she'd stay with him forever. Yeah, right. Who was he kidding?

"She's hurting," Annabel said. "And she thinks you betrayed her."

"She thinks I'm a psycho and I'm after her."

"You are. Just talk to her."

"And say what?"

An alert chirped on his new replacement phone: Stevenson's Mercedes was proceeding south on 9W, heading toward the hospital. That decided it; Hammon would confront Stevenson and demand to know what he wanted with Hazel. But the signal exited on 80 toward Little Ferry. Abandoning his vigil, Hammon followed, back to the warehouse and the Moran Marine truck.

Hammon parked a block away. Using the night scope liberated from *Temperance*, he circled the building's unlit south wall. Gary's repairs on the damaged prosthesis left him somewhat stiffly mobile, and he moved with caution and a slight squeak. Roughly fifty yards from the warehouse, he settled into the Phragmites along the riverbank, ignoring the clammy mud oozing into his sneakers. A light drizzle continued to fall, and the wet pavement glistened orange beneath the glow of the sodium vapor lights. Beside the building, Stevenson leaned against the black Mercedes. Waiting.

"For what?" Annabel asked.

A few possibilities crossed Hammon's mind, none of them good. All he could do was wait and see. Overhead, landing lights cut through the rain as a small jet swept in on approach to Teterboro Airport. A tail strobe flashed, and running lights cast an eerie glow as the plane dropped so low it seemed as if the landing gear might graze the trees. Stevenson turned toward Hammon, his face illuminated momentarily as he lit a cigarette, and Hammon panicked, thinking he'd been spotted. Stevenson gave the slightest nod to a row of flatbed trailers to his right. The night scope revealed a prone shape behind one trailer not twenty feet from where Hammon crouched, pistol positioned like a sniper, and the shape gave a low thumb's-up in return.

"Damn," Annabel said. "A little further and you would've tripped right over him."

Another jet dropped through the clouds, lights glaring, engines whining as it slowed to land. Hammon lowered the scope, shielding his eyes, guarding his night vision just in time: down the road a car turned, its blinding high beams sweeping the riverbank weeds. Hammon looked up again to see a Chevy Blazer pulled up near Stevenson. Behind the flatbed, the gunman shifted, targeting the stooped figure that emerged. Stevenson unlocked the warehouse and rolled up the door to reveal the truck.

When Hammon turned his head and strained to hear their hushed discussion, he saw what none of them could: two slender figures approaching from the opposite end, slipping from shadow to shadow along the flatbed trailers.

"They don't see the gunman!" Annabel said.

They didn't, but if they continued, the gunman would undoubtedly spot them. Hammon tried to shout to them, but words choked in his throat. He had to do something, anything, even the wrong thing.

He bolted toward the flatbed at a frantic, clumsy hobble, armed with the only pathetic weapon he could scrounge up that day: a sock full of fishing weights. The gunman whipped around and Hammon swung down, striking the gunman's shaved head with a satisfying *thwock*. The gunman went down, and Hammon looked back as one slender shadow yanked the other down. The gunman groaned and raised a thick, tentacle-tattooed arm, grabbing the trailer and struggling to stand. Hammon swung again and this time he stayed down.

"Is he dead?" Annabel asked.

Hammon watched the rise and fall of his breathing; he was just out cold. Hammon retrieved the pistol he'd dropped, feeling the weapon's weight and balance, and he grinned. That and the box of ammunition were just what the doctor ordered.

Annabel screamed as the tire beside them blew out. Shots struck the pavement as Hammon rolled beneath the trailer. Between the tires, Stevenson and his companion crouched low, shouting accusations at one another as they both scrambled for cover.

At entrance by the north end of the lot, a muzzle flashed and four more shots cracked through the air. Stevenson went down as his companion dropped beneath the semi. An engine started and tires screeched into the night. Then silence.

"What the hell just happened?"

"I don't know." Annabel peeked out. "But I think Stevenson's dead."

22:52 FRIDAY, JULY 2

40°50'26.86"N/74°01'57.41"W

LITTLE FERRY, NJ

"Would someone please tell me what the fuck just happened?" whispered Micah.

Huddled in the dirt behind a Dumpster, Hazel pressed against him. "Someone shot Stevenson and it wasn't us. I think they're gone."

Micah rose, cautiously scanning the darkness. "I think I need fresh underwear."

Hazel's spine tingled and she held her breath, anxiously watching the shadows as they skirted the lot, braced for the next round of gunfire. None came. She'd heard someone leave in a hurry, but who?

Atkins crawled out from under the Freightliner and regarded the crumbled figure sprawled facedown in a dark puddle beside the Mercedes. "I got a feelin' one of them bullets was meant for me."

Hazel studied Stevenson, bewildered. It was unsettling seeing him so diminished, one arm twisted awkwardly behind, his jacket hiked up across his back. He wasn't supposed to be dead. That wasn't the plan. He still had too many questions to answer. She reached to roll him over, and Atkins pulled her back.

"Don't touch him. Don't touch anything. We better clear out before the cops show up. Let them deal with this guy and whatever's in the truck."

Hazel looked up from Stevenson's body to the Freightliner towering above him, studying the Moran Marine Transport logo and numbers. Something wasn't right. Micah took her hand, tugging her toward the Blazer. "Let's go."

She didn't move. "That's not *Tuition*."

"Yeah it is," Micah said, his voice slightly pained. He squeezed her hand gently. "C'mon, hon, we've got to go."

"Amber clearance lights." *Tuition*'s were port and starboard running lights, like *RoadKill*'s. It was a minor detail that anyone who didn't know the truck might have overlooked. "And there's no dent in the fuel tank from where Dad dropped the toolbox that time, and no satellite antennae."

"Shit..." Micah mumbled. "She's right."

Atkins looked dourly from the truck to Stevenson's body. "Either that dead bastard was trying to double-cross someone or someone was trying to double-cross him. Either way, that ain't good."

Hammon charged out from behind the trailers, pistol raised, eyes wild, breathing in rushed gasps as he grabbed Hazel.

"There's...there's..." he stammered, looking from Hazel to Micah. Abruptly he stiffened, his grip crushing tight, pain contorting his face, then collapsed in a twitching pile. Over Hammon, Atkins stood, stun gun in hand.

"Let's go," he said. "By time he comes round the cops'll be here; they'll find this nut, the gun, and Stevenson."

I'M NOT SURE

A slow, misty drizzle fell, and for a moment or an hour, Hammon couldn't tell which, he considered maybe he'd been struck by lightning again. There was that same agonizing burning ache from every muscle simultaneously contracting, though he couldn't recall the flash or the smell. Gradual control returned to his limbs, and he rolled over to find himself staring at Stevenson lying facedown in a dark puddle. He looked at the warehouse and the semi looming over them, and it all started coming back. Except Hazel. Hazel was gone. Again. He dragged himself to Stevenson's body, rolling it over, regarding the gaping hole in the front of his sodden shirt.

Annabel knelt down. "That's a change. You're alive, he's dead."

Stevenson coughed.

Hammon jumped, splashing in the puddle of blood as he recoiled. No, not blood, just water. "What the fuck?"

He poked at Stevenson, realizing some of his bulk was a Kevlar vest beneath his shirt.

"Son of a bitch," Hammon mumbled. "Freakin' brilliant."

Stevenson groaned, one eye half-open, staring up blankly. In the distance, sirens wailed.

"Time to go, dear," Annabel whispered.

"No argument here." He staggered back to the hidden Fairmont. His clothes were soaked and heavy, his brain was screaming, and his heart felt like it had been run through a shredder. He checked his phone. All was quiet in tracking signal land.

Annabel sighed. "I think I've misjudged the situation. This may require a less subtle approach."

08:14 SATURDAY, JULY 3

40°10'49.98"N/74°1'47.35"W

BELMAR, NJ

The morning news radio cheerfully rattled off a summary of the tristate area's madness, mayhem, politics, and sports, followed by traffic and weather, but made no mention of Stevenson or a shooting in Little Ferry. Micah wanted to check the newspapers; Hazel wanted to speak with Chris about her father's progress. And they needed to stock up on provisions. So they locked up *Mardi*, still docked in Belmar, and headed out.

The report from her father's nurse was positive: he was scheduled for surgery later that morning, and they didn't anticipate any problems. Chris told Hazel to check back in the afternoon. Next came Joe, who sounded exhausted and had nothing to report. They assured him they were keeping low, staying out of trouble, and absolutely not up to any private investigator bullshit. Then a quick call to Tony at Forelli's Boatyard, again offering the same lies. The call to Atkins's cell went unanswered. They left the 7-Eleven, groceries in hand; as they crossed the street back to the docks, Hazel froze, halting Micah in his tracks. Tied up down the dock from *Mardi* sat *Temperance,* the boat they'd seen at Gary's shop, like a little gray cloud in the blue sky.

"Maybe it's just coincidence."

Hazel gave him a skeptical look.

"You think Hammon knows we're here?"

"Likely." Her pulse rose at the thought of seeing him again. It was just adrenaline, nothing more. He was working for Stevenson, clearly he was following her; running into him was the last thing they needed. She scanned the area. Was he already aboard *Mardi*?

"That bastard just keeps coming. How did he find us?" Micah said. "We left him out cold."

She didn't say it, but Hazel knew the answer: there was a tracker hidden somewhere deep within *Mardi*. "Head toward the tackle shop. If he's in there, at least it's public. If he's not, we can keep watch."

Inside was cool, dark, and vacant other than a weathered old salt behind the counter who greeted Hazel with a broad grin and a wink. She smiled politely and glanced out while Micah pretended to inspect fishing gear. He said, "We'll never outrun *Temperance* with *Mardi*. I think it's time we ditch the boat."

"We have to go back first." Hazel watched the dock. "Stevenson's file's aboard."

Across the lot, two men hauling an ice chest between them slowed as they passed *Mardi*, motioning and joking. A barking melee erupted from *Temperance*'s cockpit, and they scrambled back in synchronized surprise. Realizing the dogs weren't jumping ashore, the men laughed off their fright and ambled off to load their gear into a dusty minivan.

"Gary's dogs," Hazel said. "Which means Hammon probably isn't alone. But no one checked why they were barking or came out to settle them, so I don't think they're nearby, at least not aboard *Temperance* or *Mardi*. But they left the dogs, so they'll be back." She hastily gathered fishing gear, stacking it at the register. "I've got an idea, but we'll have to work fast."

Hazel paid, passing Micah their purchases, and they returned to the docks. The dogs spotted them, circling the cockpit, tails wagging. Hazel dug sliced turkey from the grocery bag.

"Keep watch," she told Micah as she climbed aboard to an ecstatic greeting. "Hey, boys! Miss me?" She passed cold cuts to her new best friends, then unlatched the engine cover, pulling it forward. The dogs looked on, unconcerned as she set to work. Satisfied, she slid the cowl back in place, scribbled a quick note on the back of her shopping list, and propped it on the throttles.

"Now we wait and watch," she said as they returned to *Mardi*.

Before long the first victim appeared, coffee in one hand, brown paper bag in the other. The dogs, basking in the morning sun, lifted their heads as he climbed aboard. Hidden on *Mardi*'s bridge, Hazel and Micah monitored his movements by emergency signal mirror.

"It's Gary." Hazel angled the mirror. "He's alone and he looks pretty steamed."

"Where's Hammon?"

"Don't know. I think Gary's wondering the same thing. He just checked the cabin, and now he's even more pissed. He's checking up and down the docks, and…" She went silent for a moment. "He looked straight past and didn't give *Mardi* a second glance. I don't think he recognizes her."

Hazel watched as Gary thumped into the helm seat, opening a coffee and unwrapping a bagel. He looked down at the dogs eyeing him expectantly.

"Are you guys begging?" Gary's voice carried over the water. "You know better."

Tails flogged the deck.

"No. Go lay down."

Charger flopped down obediently. Yodel yawned, joining him. Gary stared absently ahead then paused, coffee halfway to his mouth.

"He spotted the note," Hazel whispered. "He's reading the shopping list…wait. He just flipped it."

"And?"

"SON'VABITCH!" Gary yanked back the engine cover. "SON OF A BITCH! MY ENGINE!"

Micah chuckled. "You do such beautiful work."

"It represents a desire for security and solitude contrasted against an inner turmoil arising from the fear of nonbeing."

"Meaning you break shit so people will leave you alone."

"Precisely."

Gary knelt beside the destruction and groaned. Heads lowered, the dogs hung back as he glared at them.

"You two! You're supposed to be guard dogs. This," he pointed at the vandalized engine, "is what you're supposed to guard."

Charger slinked up, licking his face.

"Don't even talk to me." He stared at the engine dejectedly, shaking his head and rubbing Charger's ears.

"Fuck it all," he told the dogs.

Micah leaned over. "Now what's he doing?"

"Digging through a locker…wait…he's climbing into the bilge with a roll of duct tape." Hazel turned the mirror, scanning the lot and the docks. "I still don't see Hammon. But this might work even better."

Contorted to reach the bottom of the hose, running off four-letter words in various combinations, Gary didn't even look up as *Temperance* swayed. Charger and Yodel rushed to Hazel, tails wagging.

"Don't talk to them," Gary snapped as he knelt in the bilge water. "They're as useless as you. No, at least they stayed aboard. There was a time direct sunlight would keep you huddled in the cabin; I guess love cured you of that. While you were gone, your little angel shut the thru-hulls and sliced the raw water hoses to ribbons. And the goddamned bilge-pump hoses too. She says she wants you to stop following her." He ripped off another length of tape, wrapping the hose. "What I don't get is why she left a warning not to run the engine."

"Irreversible destruction is an act of desperation," Hazel said. "Not to mention it's a nice boat. I may want to steal it."

Gary spun and stared up in shock. Charger leaned against her, and Yodel lay at her feet. Micah stood on the dock holding Hammon's colorful "water pistol." "I'll be damned. You're real."

"As are you." Hazel said. "With Hammon, it's hard to be sure. Gary, right?"

He nodded, studying her outfit uneasily. Over her tank top and cut-offs, she wore baggy hip waders and rubber work gloves. Her gloved hand held a thirty-amp shore power cord, the end stripped to bare wires. Micah grinned, plugging the other end into the dock receptacle. Gary looked down at the salty bilge water around his ankles and Hazel slowly smiled.

I'LL BE DAMNED!

Hammon limped along the docks, indifferent to the blue sky. Without his coat to shield him from the bombarding radio frequencies, he was completely exposed, but he was too numb to care. After the last few days, satellites were the least of his worries. He was missing something obvious. The signal had flickered briefly, right there in Belmar, but by the time they'd arrived, *Revenge* was nowhere in sight. And considering last night's events, he could only imagine the worst. His quest to help Hazel was an epic fail.

He watched with detachment as three sunburned friends cheerfully jammed thirty feet worth of gear onto nineteen feet of precariously overloaded Bayliner.

"You're gonna need a bigger boat," joked the fellow loading tackle boxes and coolers even as the boat settled lower in the water, threatening to sink at the dock.

"Yeah right," replied the one at the stern. "The wife nearly divorced me for buying this one."

"No. Check it out." He pointed toward the black boat docked behind them. It looked like it had been painted with house paint, and not very neatly at that. A mast and boom towered high over the cockpit, and weathered rope work covered railings from bow to stern, creeping like ivy up the ladder to the bridge. "It's the boat from *Jaws*. It's got that lookout tower and everything."

"Can't be. The boat in *Jaws* sank in the end. For real, not just in the movie. Not like that piece of crap doesn't look far behind. And where's the shark barrels?"

The debate continued as the fishing buddies ambled down the dock, checking for shark jaws mounted on the bridge, unaware of the invisible vision following them, equally intrigued by the weary old boat.

"No way!" Annabel cheered, bouncing with delight.

"What?"

"You don't recognize her?"

Hammon studied it. "Yeah. It was in the shed at Forelli's. Amazing what you can accomplish with enough Git Rot and Marine Tex."

"It's scary how dense the brain I occupy is at times. That's *Revenge.*"

"And you say I'm nuts."

Annabel huffed. "Look past the colors and the sloppy paint. Ignore the bridge, that's been changed. So were the rails. And they added the mast, strakes, and the pulpit. They even plumbed the bow, but look at the shape of the transom. I'm telling you, that's *Revenge.*"

"Impossible."

Then Hammon noticed the cockpit freezer, now painted black. The cockpit door, hatches, and drains were identical to *Revenge*'s, and there was his bucket, the one he always propped against the cabin door.

"I'll be damned…"

08:32 SATURDAY, JULY 3

40°10′49.98″N/74°01′47.35″W

BELMAR, NJ

Gary crept backwards, trying to climb clear of the wet bilge.

"Stay where you are, and we'll both be happier. I don't want to kill anyone, but I'll do what I have to." She held up the power cord. "Fascinating how lethal standard alternating current is. Muscles contract and freeze, you can't scream or move, and your heart just stops. Cardiac arrest, then death. Quiet, neat, and simple."

"Yeah, aside from the burn marks and the sizzling flesh," Micah added helpfully.

"What do you want?" Gary mumbled.

Hazel swung the cord in a lazy arc. "Answers. Starting with: where's Hammon?"

"I don't know." Gary glanced from his wet feet to the cord in her insulated hand. "He disappeared. He does that a lot."

"What was Stevenson trying to pull last night?" Micah asked.

Gary looked from Hazel to Micah and back. "What happened last night?"

Hazel sighed. "Hammon didn't tell you? Stevenson claimed he had our truck, but it was just a look-alike."

"What truck?" Gary's eyes followed the exposed wires. "Don't take this wrong, but I don't know what the hell you're talking about."

Micah leaned forward. "Look, we know Stevenson sent Hammon after us. Why?"

Gary shook his head. "Hammon hasn't spoken to Stevenson in years."

"Really? Then explain this." Hazel pulled the envelope from her pocket, holding it out for him to read. "There's over seven grand in here."

"Yeah," Micah said. "And according to your computer, Stevenson's put a lot of cash into your business."

"You were in my office?" He glared at the dogs. "Why do I even feed you two?"

"So what's your dealings with Stevenson?" Micah said.

"He's a customer...with lots of money to spend."

"And what about Hammon?" Hazel asked.

Gary slumped back, looking uncomfortable with the question. "It's a long story, and it doesn't make any sense."

Hazel glanced at Micah, who looked around and nodded. "We're listening."

Gary shrugged and shook his head in defeat. "Five years back I'm working at this boatyard, and I find the kid holed up aboard a derelict boat. He's a mess, all scarred up, afraid to let anyone look at him, he won't even come into the light. I figured he's some runaway. I tell him he can't stay there but he won't leave. He says if he buys the boat, then could he stay. I tell him the boat's wrecked, it's too far gone to bother fixing. I give him half my lunch and try to find out who he is.

"Next morning he's still there, but now he's got papers showing fifty grand wired into my bank account. Payment in advance, he says, for fixing the boat. Says if I need more, he'll get it. I don't know how the hell he got my bank account, but he knew everything about me. Then I get a call from someone named Stevenson. You know what he says? Fix the boat. He says if I need more money, just call him, but whatever I do, don't tell the kid. Hammon says the money's his, Stevenson stole it, and he's just stealing it back. No explanation, no clarification. Ask him, he shuts up for days."

Gary sat back across the engine, rubbing his forehead. "You got to understand, the kid's not all there. He thinks people are tracking him with microchips. He hears voices, he sees…" Gary looked at Hazel. "He's got this hallucination he calls Annabel. That's why he was on the boat to begin with. He'd never been on a boat in his life; he can't even swim, but Annabel told him 'go to the boats.' He does whatever Annabel tells him. He says you're identical to her, and that's another part of the conspiracy."

"He may be more right than he realizes," Hazel said. "Stevenson said something about someone named Annabel. I had no idea what he was talking about and I didn't ask." And suddenly her first conversation with Hammon, when he refused to believe she was real, made so much more sense.

"He says you're in danger and he wants to help you."

"He said he wants revenge," Hazel said.

Gary almost laughed. "That's his goddamned boat. The one I found him on. The boat you stole. That's *Revenge*."

Micah said, "And the tarp and shovel in his trunk?"

"That's Annabel again. She can't deal with dead animals in the road, says they deserve proper burial. Look, I know the kid's got some serious mental problems, but he's not violent or dangerous."

"He killed Stevenson last night," Hazel said.

Gary looked like he'd been struck; it was obviously news to him. A boat motored past and small waves slapped the hull while Hazel waited for a reply. It came in the form of a soft hiccup.

"One, I didn't do it, and B, he's not dead." Hammon gave Micah a quick salute as he limped toward the boat.

Hazel started to speak but found herself without words. The last twenty-four hours had taken a heavy toll on Hammon. In direct daylight he looked less like a boy scout and more like an escaped psychopath. His clothes were wrinkled and stained, his hair wild and tangled, his breathing quick and shallow. But beneath the strain, Hazel could still see sadness in his gray eyes.

"Last night," he began, swallowing nervously as he stood beside the boat. "I…uh…I didn't…I wanted to tell you…" He blinked, eyes wide as he struggled for the right words. "I had to…" He stared at her helplessly. "I…I'll…"

He squeezed his eyes shut and took a slow, deep breath, pressing his palm to his forehead.

"Last night," he said again, each word slow and deliberate. His eyes opened, locking on Hazel with unnerving intensity, and he pushed his hair back, tucking it behind a disfigured ear. "I didn't shoot him and he isn't dead. Even if he wasn't wearing Kevlar, he'd need a heart to hit in the first place." He sat on *Temperance*'s gunwale, swinging his bad leg over as he climbed aboard. The corner of his mouth curled upward as he approached Hazel.

"I missed you," he told her, his voice low and steady. He stopped, inches between them, eyes practically aglow. His hand came up, fingers gently tracing across her cheek, sending a strange thrill surging through her. "I can't tell you how worried I've been. I had to see you again."

"Uh…Zap," Gary said. "You might want to stay back. She's sort of armed."

Hammon regarded the power cord and grinned. "She's bluffing. She wouldn't do it."

Hazel glared at him, color rising in her face. "Don't test me."

"I'm not. You wouldn't risk hurting the dogs." His fingers moved down to her throat. "You know, my dear, last time I saw you, I didn't get to say a proper good-bye." His other hand slid back around her waist, pulling her against him. "You're trembling," he whispered, his hand lingering along the small of her back.

"So are you."

"You do that to me." His hand slipped beneath the waders. "By the way, now you're grounded."

Her eyes narrowed defiantly. "You like living dangerously."

"You have no idea." His fingers followed the curve of her throat. "And besides, the circuit's off."

Heat rose in her face. "What makes you so sure?"

"The plug glows when there's current. I like what you did with my boat. She was right there in that shed, and I never even realized. I found *Revenge* and I found you. I missed you so much, Hazel. Did you miss me?"

Hazel dropped the electric cord in disgust. "Go to hell." Gary scrambled clear as Hammon reached down, picked up the end and brushed the bare wires against his palm.

"You did! I saw it in your eyes when you hit me and when you stuffed me in my trunk! You were hurt. You wouldn't be hurt if you didn't like me. Like now…you're only upset because you can't decide if you want to hit me or let me kiss you."

"You really believe that?" she snapped, her voice faltering.

He nodded brightly, hair falling in his eyes. He pushed it back, exposing his scarred temple. "More than ever."

"You're insane."

"One way to be sure." He slid his hand behind her neck and pulled her close, gently kissing her. Her lips parted, initially in protest, but her words were smothered. She felt his breathing, his pulse, and she felt herself kiss him even as she pressed her knife to his throat. He paused as she increased the pressure, laughed for a moment, then his kiss turned serious: hard, deep, and passionate, sending disturbing shivers of pleasure through her. She knew she shouldn't have been responding the way she was; she knew she could have stopped him, but instead she melted against him.

"So I'm right," he said, his lips brushing hers as he spoke. "As usual."

Gary coughed. "Uhmm, Zap. You do know she's got a knife to your throat..."

"You bet I do." Hammon grinned. "Talk about a turn-on."

Hazel stepped away in frustration; Hammon hooked his fingers in the wader straps, pulling her right back. "I like the outfit: kinky. Good thing you're wearing these. It might be dangerous, you getting..." He paused, a mischievous sparkle in his eyes. "Wet." He kissed her again, even more powerfully. "Or is it already too late?"

Behind her Micah cleared his throat and cracked his knuckles the way her father did whenever he was reaching his limit. Hazel's mind went blank; she was still back on that kiss; she could hear her pulse rushing in her ears, and she couldn't decide how she felt or why. But she had to stay focused. She staggered slightly as the deck swayed beneath her.

"Otto, why are you following us? It's more than just the boat, isn't it?"

Pain washed across his face. He blinked, staring at her in confusion. Color rose in his cheeks. "What...no!" He coughed and swallowed. "Uh...no, I mean, yeah." He rubbed his forehead, taking several deep breaths. "There's way more to it than you real-ize, and Stevenson isn't dead. Pure evil doesn't die that easy. But I didn't shoot him, and neither did the guy behind the flatbed. There was someone else."

"What guy behind the flatbed?" Micah said. "And *who* else?"

"I don't know; I didn't see them, just the one guy. Big. Mean looking. He had…" Hammon turned to the emptiness. "What's the word?" He held his arms out dramatically. "He had a sea monster…"

Gary groaned and Micah shook his head.

"I'm serious!" Hammon insisted, his voice breaking.

"And we're leaving." Micah reached across and guided Hazel to the dock. He released *Temperance*'s bow line. "Hon, get *Mardi* started."

She stood, hesitant, wanting to say something, anything, but unable to. Hammon stumbled after her, but Micah stepped between them.

"Back off, Hammon." Micah unhitched the stern line and gave *Temperance* a firm shove away from the dock. A breeze caught the disabled boat, and it drifted toward the channel.

Hazel boarded *Mardi*, still somewhat dazed. She turned the battery switch and started the engine as Micah brought in all the lines. Hazel tweaked the throttle as they motored past *Temper-ance*, keeping them parallel to the disabled skiff.

"You might want to drop anchor," Micah suggested while Gary studied *Mardi* in disbelief and Hammon gazed at Hazel. "I'm sure someone'll tow you back in."

Hazel pushed the throttle forward and they left *Temperance* bobbing in their wake.

"Another low-speed getaway," Micah said. "I'm telling you, if this was a movie, it'd be real boring." Then he chuckled. "You see

Gary's face? You had him scared shitless, at least till your boy-friend got there."

"He's not my boyfriend."

"Could've fooled me. Sucks that he's the bad guy. You make such a cute couple. Strange, the way he looks at you. Somewhere between the purest, most innocent love and the darkest obsession."

Hazel nibbled on the edge of her nail. "I should have…" Her voice trailed off. She wasn't sure what she should have done. "Someone else was there last night besides Hammon?"

"Other than the guy with the sea monster?" Micah sighed. "Bat-shit crazy, that's what he is. What I don't get is how he keeps showing up. We've been through every inch of this boat. If something's sending a signal, it's hiding real good. Not that it matters anymore. They've seen her. They know our speed. She was invisible so long as they were looking for something else. We might as well paint her florescent orange." Micah put his arm around her shoulder. "Sorry, kiddo. I know you like this thing, but it's time we take some of Hammon's cash and get something white, plastic, and anonymous."

One hour later they docked in Point Pleasant. Hazel received a call from Chris, who reported that her father came through surgery smoothly, with a grocery list of pins, screws, and bolts securing bones in place. Micah placed the next call to Joe and swore he was doing a fine job of keeping Hazel clear of all unacceptable activities; she mouthed "liar" in the background. He glared at her and dialed Atkins. Listening intently, he scribbled down "NJ, KLE-865" then hung up, working out the equation.

Hazel looked at the final number. "One seventy-two. The last exit in New Jersey."

"What did I say about you getting morose? Cheer up." Micah grinned. "We need a car again, and I know just the one I want."

I CAN'T DO IT

Hammon stared at the wildflowers in his hand, and lunch rose in his throat. Flowers. Seriously. Who was he kidding? He shouldn't have even been there. He was putting Hazel in danger.

"No, you're protecting her."

"From you, I mean." He was still furious with Annabel's little stunt back in Belmar.

"You were about to pass out; someone had to do something. And besides, she didn't seem to mind." Annabel grinned. "Or is that what's upsetting you, dear?"

"This is so wrong. I'll just talk to her. I'll explain. I'll make her understand."

"Otto, your explaining skills are right up there with her understanding skills. There's no way she's abandoning Micah to run away with a schizophrenic stalker. Like it or not, you know what you have to do."

No. He didn't want to think about it.

"It was your idea in the first place. Either you do it or I will."

That was what scared him.

"You said it yourself. It's for her own good. This just proves it. You don't want someone else hurting her."

Annabel was right and he knew it. Hammon climbed out of the car, fighting to appear calm as he hobbled toward *Revenge*, docked in a small Point Pleasant marina. Hazel looked relieved but nervous as she rushed over to him.

"You're here." She bit her lip and backed against the thick overgrowth bordering the lot. "I was afraid you wouldn't come, after everything that's happened."

"I promised." He was going to be sick. Taking a deep breath, he offered her the flowers, which she accepted with a hesitant smile. "Micah actually left you alone?"

She nodded apprehensively. "We needed a car, and he went to steal one. He told me not to call you, but I had to."

Hammon relaxed the slightest bit. He'd been dreading the idea of dealing with Micah first. This was much better.

"Just like the night you met," Annabel said. "Micah's a nice kid and he means well, but his carelessness puts her at risk."

Hazel walked along the yard's edge, past several abandoned boats.

"But why did you call me?" he asked.

"I wanted to see you." She searched his eyes. "I had to know, why are you following me?"

He'd planned out everything he wanted to tell her, but as she watched him, waiting expectantly, his mind went blank. "You took *Revenge*," he mumbled, knowing that was the wrong answer even as the words left his mouth. "I was looking for my boat."

She held out her hand, offering the keys for *Revenge*. "If that's all you want, you can have her back."

His hand closed around hers. "You think it's that simple. You return the boat and this just ends?"

"What, then? Why did you have that money and all? What is this really about?"

She'd never understand. "You're too trusting, coming here alone. What if I wanted to hurt you?"

"Do you?" Hazel asked, her innocence ripping through his heart like a stake. Annabel was right. She was too vulnerable. He knew what he had to do, much as he hated the idea.

"You're stalling. Just do it," Annabel ordered. "Now."

Everything in the dark turmoil of her eyes and the full flush of her lips begged him to kiss her. She started to speak again, and he pulled her close, kissing her. At first she resisted, then she began to soften, to melt against him, hesitantly returning his kiss as he eased the pistol from beneath his shirt.

Annabel said, "Pull the trigger and it'll be over. You have to. It's for the best."

He felt sick as he raised the gun behind her and broke the kiss, gasping for air. His hand was shaking.

"I'm sorry," Hazel whispered.

That confused him. He was the one about to do something unimaginably horrible…why was *she* apologizing? For a moment he almost asked, but decided he didn't want to know. "So am I." His throat tightened. "Please, angel, forgive me."

He squeezed the trigger. There was an abrupt, muffled sound, Hazel's eyes widened, and she gave a small cry, stiffening. She struggled, weakening, until she slumped against him. He rocked her gently as she trembled and shuddered, and he whispered soothing sounds, tenderly stroking her hair. She looked up, wide-eyed, and a tear ran down her cheek.

"Why?" she said, just a whisper.

"I told you. You're mine. Forever." He kissed her again, the gentlest kiss, tasting her warmth as she faded. He lowered her to the ground, tracing his fingers along her cheek, wishing it hadn't come to this, when the world exploded in a flash of blinding pain.

TIME, DATE, POSITION UNKNOWN

Hazel opened her eyes to find herself curled in the passenger seat, her head resting on the center console, cushioned by Hammon's coat. She looked around the Fairmont in confusion. At the wheel, Hammon glanced over, smiling grimly. She struggled to sit up, staring out at the narrow road unwinding in the headlights as foggy darkness closed in around them.

"What happened?" she asked, her voice small.

"You fainted."

"No...I...it was..." Hazel murmured, straining to remember. "Something else..." Something unclear. Something terrible.

Hammon slowed the car, turning off the road and between massive iron gates, weaving beneath overgrown trees and down a low hill. Through the gloom they passed a mausoleum. Ahead, the ghostly shape of an angel stood, wings broken, head bowed in frozen grief. Hazel knew this place well, but why had Hammon taken her there?

He shut the headlights and engine, then turned to her.

"This should be far enough."

"For what?"

He grinned crookedly, a single fang catching the faint dashboard light, and Hazel shivered, turning away. Darkness surrounded them in every direction. She could hide in the darkness. She tugged at the door handle. It wouldn't release.

"You think you can keep running from me?" His eyes gleamed as he moved closer. "I told you I'd find you." His fingers touched her cheek. "I'll keep you safe, so no one can ever hurt you," he whispered, his lips brushing hers. "Ever."

His mouth caressed hers, his teeth grazing her lip. Hazel gasped, trying to push him back. He kissed her slowly, with a building intensity that threatened to pull her under. She eased her knife from her pocket, opening the blade as his kiss sent heat racing through her and his hand slid up beneath her shirt, pressing warm against her belly.

"I told you, I'll follow you forever." He gazed at her, his wide, colorless eyes filled with childlike adoration, his fangs glistening. Her grip tightened around the knife. His throat was bare and exposed. It would be easy to drive the blade deep into his white flesh. She knew exactly where and how to make it fatal; he wouldn't even be able to scream. She squeezed her eyes shut as his lips brushed her damp eyelashes.

"You can fight or you can surrender." He eased her down across the seat. "It doesn't matter. Either way, you're mine, forever."

She tried to speak, but words died in her throat. She stared up, blinking back tears. His eyes burned into hers and she turned away, staring across at the soft glow of the dashboard as he moved over her. Just one slash, she told herself. So simple. Just do it. Just kill him.

"Are you okay?"

She couldn't. She felt paralyzed, drowning, helpless.

"Hon, you okay? Talk to me."

This wasn't happening. Her head spun, her blood burned, and she moaned in desperation.

"That's enough," she heard Micah say. "You're seriously freaking me out now."

She blinked, staring around the Fairmont. Micah was at the wheel, and she was huddled in the passenger seat. He took the car out of gear and rolled onto the Parkway shoulder. Hazel struggled to sit up, blinking in bewilderment. It was just the two of them. A disorienting blur of headlights flashed by in the darkness. "What happened?"

"You don't remember our plan to ambush Hammon? Well, it worked. And don't feel guilty; I know you were kissing him to stop me from whacking him, but trust me, he needed whacking."

It was coming back in fragments. Micah nodded.

"You were doing a first-class job of distracting him. I figured I'd give you a minute, let you have your fun; you seemed to be getting into it. Then I hear this weird little *pop* noise, and I'm wondering what it was, then I see you struggling, and you slump in his arms. He's holding this." He passed her a pistol. "I swear my heart stopped. I knocked him out, then pulled that," he pointed to a dart with a red tail, stuck like a pushpin in the dashboard, "out of your backside. If I wasn't so pissed, I'd laugh. Your boyfriend shot you in the ass with a tranquilizer dart."

Hazel stared at the gun and felt sick.

"This is the same gun Pierce shot me with when *Kindling* sank. The gun Stevenson was going to use..."

She rushed to roll down the window as a wave of nausea threatened to overtake the dizziness, gulping the damp night air and letting the breeze blow the cold sweat on her face dry. It wasn't hard to figure where Hammon got the gun.

Micah looked grim as he wove through slower-moving traffic. "When will people learn the hammer lane isn't meant for old Saturns, minivans, and people on cell phones?" He turned to Hazel. "You okay?"

"Yeah. A little sore, a lot wiser, but okay."

Micah's grip on the wheel was tighter than driving conditions warranted. "That could have been a bullet instead of a dart. I never should've assumed Hammon was harmless. I put you in danger just so we could drive something with horsepower and a good stereo."

"It was my idea too, and we were both wrong." She'd wanted to see Hammon again, to talk to him, to see him smile and hear him say it was all some innocent, bizarre misunderstanding. "I couldn't accept he's really working for Stevenson." She should have known better. She turned and looked backwards. "He's in the trunk?"

That was the plan, to grab Hammon along with his car, to keep him hostage and question him at their leisure.

"Sorry, hon. I was more worried about you. I left your boyfriend in the bushes."

Hazel nodded. Considering the circumstances, she would have done the same. "He's not much use, anyway. Unless we're looking for sea monsters, that is."

"Uh, yeah, about that. I think I know what he was trying to tell us, and you're not going to like it."

Reluctantly he handed her a piece of paper covered in Hammon's scribbled handwriting. Hazel read:

> Hazel & Mika took Revenge Why? Did they beat up stvnsn? *Likely. Why were they there?* Looking for tractor-trailer? *Maybe—Why does Stevenson have Moran truck?*

Stvnsn met scary guy by truck in littlfery / *Who was that??* Stvnsn signaled guy (shaved head, squid/tentacle seamonster tattoo) was tattoo guy there to shoot whitetrash guy who tazered me? *Did tattoo guy shoot Hazel's father?* Who shot Stevenson?

Hazel stared at the note. "*Joe?*"

"It sure looks that way."

"Joe's working with Stevenson?" She read it over again, stunned. "Joe? Why?"

"God only knows. Money, I guess."

"You think *Joe* shot Dad?" Her trust in Joe had always been absolute. He was family.

Micah rubbed his face. "I don't know what to think anymore. There's a whole lot we don't know about Joe, other than that he'd still be in prison if not for some bullshit technicality."

Hazel scanned the traffic stretching behind them then shifted around anxiously. "You think Dad's safe? Should we call the hospital and tell them?"

"So long as your dad's in the ICU, Joe can't get anywhere near him. Your dad's as safe as he's going to be, probably safer than us. And maybe it's not what it looks like. I mean, we're talking about Hammon."

"But if he saw Joe meet with Stevenson..."

"I don't know. All I know is we've got seven darts, and I want some answers." Micah downshifted and shot past a BMW with Florida plates, the oblivious driver focused on his cell phone. "And I don't get Hammon. I mean, what's the deal with him? It's almost like the poor bastard was trying to warn us. But then, why'd he shoot you? I can't figure where that guy fits."

Hazel watched out the back window. "I've given up trying."

I'M BACK ON GARY'S SHIT-LIST AGAIN

Hammon lay in the dirt and stared up at the overcast sky, sifting through the dull throbbing in his brain, trying to remember where he was and why. Annabel leaned over and looked down with concern.

"Point Pleasant. You kissed Hazel and shot her with a tranq-dart, then someone ambushed you."

He sat up in panic, collapsing as his balance lagged. Taking a deep breath, he tried again, slowly looking around.

At Gary, his eyes filled with scathing fury. "Welcome back, you little shit."

"Hazel?"

"Gone...this time with your car."

"We have to find her!"

"WE don't have to do anything. WE are taking you to the hospital to get your head examined. You shot me with a goddamned tranquilizer dart! Have you lost what little mind you've got?"

Annabel stifled a giggle. "Told you he'd be pissed."

Hammon glared at her. "You're the one that shot him, not me!"

"Do *not* blame the voices in your head," Gary snapped.

"Voice. Singular." Hammon rubbed the aching lump on his skull. "But someone ambushed me..."

"You don't get it. Hazel lured you here to take your car. You won't be happy till she kills you." Gary dragged Hammon to his feet, escorted him to the passenger side of the Dakota, shoving the open laptop aside. Hammon pulled it onto his lap.

Annabel scanned the screen over his shoulder. "I think I see how he found you. He's got a tracker in the Fairmont. It's twenty miles up on the Parkway."

Hammon watched the signal creeping north.

"I really don't need this shit." Gary started driving in no particular hurry, heading southbound. "I'm not even supposed to be here today. I should be at Raceway Park, surrounded by horsepower and scantily clad beauties who don't want to electrocute me. Not risking my ass saving yours, which, for the record, won't happen again. I'm through with helping you chase after that little sociopath. The next time you fuck up, you're on your own."

Annabel said, "Knowing them, they're heading straight into trouble."

And Gary was going the wrong way. "We have to help them," Hammon insisted.

"No we don't," Gary muttered.

"Hazel's in danger. She needs help."

"In so many ways. That girl's psychotic. And you seriously need meds."

Hammon's brain pounded and he felt nauseous. He leaned forward, head between his knees, and Annabel whispered an idea inside his skull.

"Uh, Gary…"

"What, damnit?"

"I don't feel so good. I think I'm gonna barf."

He slammed into the dash as Gary swerved onto the shoulder, screeching to a stop. Hammon opened the door and leaned out, head down, sucking in deep breaths. Gary climbed out, backing away from the idling truck, pacing and shaking his head in disgust. "You puke in my truck, you're walking home."

"I'll try not to," Hammon said feebly. Gary had a notoriously low tolerance toward visual examples of an upset stomach; the mere sight of someone losing their lunch was enough to make him toss his own cookies. Hammon rocked slowly, dropped his head again, and made a ghastly retching sound.

"For chrissakes, get out of the truck and puke somewhere else!" Gary grumbled, turning away.

"Now!" Annabel shouted.

Hammon sat up and scrambled to close and lock both doors as he climbed across to the driver's seat. With his damaged leg it was clumsy but he managed, throwing the truck into gear and spinning a 180, leaving Gary on the shoulder, screaming obscenities into a cloud of dust.

20:40 SATURDAY, JULY 3

40°57'54.90"N/74°03'53.34"W

GARDEN STATE PARKWAY NORTH, PARAMUS, NJ

By the time they reached Paramus the sun had set. Micah fiddled with the satellite radio, turning up the Clash. In Hillsdale, deer stared out from the grassy median, eyes glowing eerily as they stood beneath a sign for the upcoming service area. At Exit 171, Hazel spotted a fox stalking dinner. Micah pulled into the left lane, glancing silently at the yellow "LAST EXIT IN NEW JERSEY" sign as he circled through the Montvale service area.

"Last exit," Hazel said as they passed the main building. "It sounds so final."

The first wave of Fourth of July travelers had passed through on Friday, but traffic was still heavy, and minivans, sport-utilities, and station wagons loaded with kids, dogs, luggage, beach chairs, and bicycles filled every available parking space. Occupants of the southbound cars were, for the most part, pale and restless, the northbound crowd sunburned, weary, and subdued.

"Over there." Micah pulled up beside a rusted red Corolla parked off toward the commuter spaces. The sight of Atkins was as repellant as it was relieving. Hazel had come to question her trust in everyone, but she sensed Micah was right: beneath the skeevy exterior, Atkins was a genuinely good person.

He nodded a greeting. "You kids okay? I was getting worried."

"Yeah, we're fine." Micah smirked. "But getting a car was a pain in the ass for Hazel."

"Ignore him," Hazel said. "What's up?"

Atkins flashed the few teeth he had in a revolting grin. "I was down at the police station back home chatting with our nice law officers, discussing my barbequed trailer, an' I overhear your dad's rig turned up down the road from here. I came up and took a look for myself. Door's painted over, no plates, but it's a match."

"Welcome to the retail center of the universe." Micah said as they followed the Corolla down Route 17 south and Hazel studied the passing scenery of shopping centers and strip malls. "I was studying this place in Economics. Even with some of the most restrictive blue laws in the U.S. closing the entire town on Sundays, this little town still ranks first nationwide for retail business. You know, *Paramus* is the Indian word for 'shopping center.'"

"Seriously?" Hazel looked across the vastness that was the Garden State Plaza, teeming with traffic and people. It was the largest mall in the state and one of four major malls within Paramus.

"Actually, it means 'place of the fertile soil.'"

Hazel scanned the traffic; threats could lurk anywhere in the endless ebb and flow of vehicles, and they'd never know it. A black Mercedes cruised toward them, and she tensed until she saw the driver was a blonde woman, chatting merrily on a headset. Micah glanced over.

"Hon, relax. We'll be fine. You've just got to watch your ass."

Hazel glowered at the dart in the dashboard, knowing she'd have to ride out Micah's jokes until he got bored or found something better to tease her about. She couldn't blame him; it was somewhere between funny and absurd, and it made no sense. Hammon made no sense. Everything he did contradicted every fact she knew. She didn't say anything, but she really wished Micah had stayed with the plan and stuck Hammon in the trunk. It shouldn't have mattered, but she wondered how he was. Had Micah hit him too hard? Was he still lying unconscious or dead in the bushes? Maybe they should have called Gary to check on him and make sure he was okay.

"Quit sighing," Micah said. "Cheer up. I've got a feeling things are going to start happening."

"Things *have* been happening. We could do with a few less things."

"Good things, I mean," Micah said as they crept past the mall. "Would you believe this used to look like Down Jersey?" He wove through the dense traffic fighting to squeeze into the acres of overflowing parking lots. "I read this was once all celery fields. People think these malls always existed, like George Washington shopped there and they planned the American Revolution in the food court."

Hazel knew he was only trying to keep her preoccupied by pretending he wasn't as nervous as she was. She shifted, checking behind them.

"Sore butt?"

She shot Micah a dirty look. "How do you know someone didn't follow us?"

"Not someone. Hammon. You figured he would, and you're disappointed he hasn't."

"If I never see Hammon again, it'll be too soon."

"Bull." Micah chuckled. "You get within ten feet of each other, sparks fly. You two go together like alcohol and firearms."

"He shot me!"

"With a tranquilizer gun. I think he wanted you alive, unharmed."

"That's reassuring."

Micah followed Atkins's Corolla around the perimeter service road, pulling up behind the Freightliner. Despite spray paint covering all identification, there was no mistaking the truck, from the mirrors and grill to the port and starboard clearance lights and the satellite radio antenna. The trailer hung open and empty.

Hazel scanned the area. There was too much traffic, too much activity. The back of her neck prickled as she climbed out. Maybe it was how easily she'd been shot, but her radar was on high, and she couldn't shake the feeling they were in the crosshairs of a gun sight. Atkins stood watch while Micah unlocked the truck. The cab light flickered on. He climbed in, opening the passenger door for Hazel. She inspected the tidy cab as Micah slid behind the wheel.

"I can't reach the pedals. Whoever drove last has the seat way back."

"Don't move it." Hazel leaned over and looked at his feet. "You're back about four inches. Who do we know that's around six foot two and can drive a rig?"

"Joe," Micah said hatefully.

"Maybe." Hazel spotted something under the edge of the driver's side floor mat; she picked up the small sliver of bleached wood, smooth in her fingers, with the faintest scent of mint. "Maybe not." She passed it to Micah, who made a sour face as he held the toothpick splinter up to the cab light. He slipped the key into the ignition, turning it enough to power up the accessories. Music burst from the speakers, proclaiming with rapturous enthusiasm, "And Jesus said, I will make you fishers of men." The Christian hits station: praise set to a pop beat.

"Someone didn't shut the radio," Micah observed.

Hazel switched it off before the next chorus of hallelujah. She thought of her father with tubes running into his arms and down his throat, and some very un-Christian thoughts crossed her mind. Micah squeezed her hand.

"Got anything?" Atkins called up.

Hazel's eyes met Micah's. Micah said, "Nothing."

They'd discussed it on the drive north. Atkins had already helped enough. He'd been shot at, and his home was destroyed; they didn't want to put him through further risk. They climbed down from the truck.

"Think we should take *Tuition*?" Micah said.

Hazel looked from the Fairmont to the truck, considering. "Not yet."

Atkins nodded. "I'd say you two come with me, but that'd make the lot of us a bigger target. I'm what you call conspicuous, and no haircut's gonna help much. You got my cell. You kids get any ideas, you call. I'd give my left nut to strangle whoever the fuck's behind this all. You," Atkins gave Micah a punch on the arm. "Cut the jokes and take care of that little girl."

"Stevenson, Joe, and Keith," Micah said, back at the wheel and heading south. "Who'd've figured?"

"We can't keep running. It's time we start setting things straight."

"Yeah. But how?"

"We want to stay out of range. I've got an idea, but we'll need to set things up. And we need a boat."

"I'm almost afraid to ask."

Hazel broke into a cold smile. "We're going to listen to Jesus. We're going fishing."

Micah grinned. "Can I get a hallelujah?"

I'M GAINING ON THEM!

Hammon caught up to the Fairmont on the trip north, moving close enough as the Garden State Parkway cut through the middle of the Holy Sepulcher Cemetery to see two heads in the car.

He was relieved to see Hazel conscious, and, he imagined, quite pissed. He pictured the anger in her eyes and he grinned. Next time they met things would definitely be interesting.

"You have issues," Annabel said, studying the endless rows of headstones lining both sides of the Parkway.

"You should know."

He lowered his speed. The tracker allowed him the luxury of following a mile back. They wouldn't spot him, and fortunately as a rule, Gary never let the fuel drop below a half tank. Unfortunately he also kept the little pickup spotless, leaving nothing edible to forage. Hammon didn't dare stop, not for chips, soda, or some much-needed aspirin. He watched Hazel and Micah meet with the Corolla and inspect yet another red semi. Hammon parked behind a van, far enough back to watch without being seen. All identification had been painted over or removed. A thick haze of dust coated it and it looked abandoned, but where did it fit in the grand scheme of things? His heart skipped as Hazel talked with the skeevy dude in the Corolla.

Annabel said, "Captain Whitetrash is definitely the same guy we saw the night Stevenson got shot. I think he's on their side."

Hammon settled in his seat, feeling dejected. He was on their side too. They just didn't know it.

"Otto, look." Annabel pointed across the lot at a glossy dark blue quadcab Ford F350 with dual rear tires. "That truck was at the rest stop."

"Shit…" He had a feeling she was right.

"Of course I am. It's got the same stupid boat prop hitch cover."

Inside the Ford someone sat motionless. Maybe they were just having a beer or smoking a joint. Hazel and Micah locked the semi, speaking for another moment with Capt. Whitetrash and then returning to the Fairmont, with Micah driving. The Corolla pulled away, then the Fairmont, followed seconds later by the Ford. Hammon followed as they all pulled onto the Parkway south.

The Corolla exited to Route 80, but the 350 stayed on the Parkway, hanging ten cars back, the chrome boat prop a spinning blur. Hammon pulled close, memorizing the license plate. He had no phone and no way of warning Hazel or Micah, even if they would listen. He could speed ahead and signal them, but after shooting Hazel, he imagined his credibility was lacking. His best bet was to hang back and watch, ready to assist. How, he had no idea. He was unarmed, barely able to walk, and driving a truck half the size of the one he tailed.

The road ahead lit up as thick clouds flashed pink from within. The sky opened up, thunder shook the truck, and the line of taillights before them became obscured. Inside the Dakota the mood matched the weather, and neither Annabel or Hammon spoke as the wipers pounded away on high.

Miles passed, the rain passed, traffic thinned, and the Dakota's fuel gauge crept toward "E." The Fairmont had to be on fumes by then as well. Ahead, crisp white lights at the service area shone like a beacon, summoning drivers to the petroleum oasis, and Hammon knew he'd have to stop or he'd be pushing the truck.

He breathed a sigh of relief as the Fairmont exited, gliding up to the first open pump beneath the shelter, then panicked as the 350 pulled off, circled like a shark, and stopped on the far side of the farthest island of pumps.

Neither Hazel or Micah noticed either of the pickups, and whatever the 350 intended likely didn't involve a public setting. Hammon parked directly behind the 350, swiping Gary's credit card and shoving the gas nozzle in, not waiting for the attendant.

A clean-shaven man in his forties stepped out of the Ford, filling the truck himself as well. Neat and well-groomed, dressed in slacks and a casual button-down shirt, he wasn't what Hammon expected, but there was no question he was following the kids, watching them intently. He'd left the driver's-side door open, and as Hammon hobbled past and picked up a window squeegee, he spotted the keys still dangling in the ignition. He paused beside the man, holding the squeegee out so it dribbled dirty water between them, and leaned against the Ford's open door for balance.

"Cute girl." Hammon grinned, all fangs. His elbow discreetly pressed the door lock down. "A little young for you, though. Or are you checking out the boy?"

Mr. 350 glanced at Hammon, assessing him, and turned away in disgust. Hammon shrugged, "accidentally" bumping the 350's door closed as he limped clumsily back to the Dakota, squeegee in hand.

"What the hell?" the man called after him, but Hammon ignored him. Hammon was finishing a hurried, half-assed job on the Dakota's windows when the familiar sound of the Fairmont's engine rumbling to life carried through the damp night air.

Across the way, Hazel had taken the wheel, Micah riding shotgun. Hammon tossed the squeegee aside and leapt into the Dakota as the Fairmont pulled away. A stream of obscenities rose from Mr. 350; he grabbed the fire extinguisher beside the fuel pump and smashed the truck's window, unlocked the door, and jumped in. Mumbling a quick apology to Gary and the Dakota, Hammon accelerated around the 350, cut across, and braked abruptly as the big truck tore away from the pumps. The Ford's front end smashed into the Dakota's passenger side, wedging the trucks together. The F350's enraged driver fought to clear the deflating airbag from the wheel, gunned his engine, and rammed the Dakota aside as he accelerated away.

A family in a minivan stopped, kids pressed to the windows and gaping out in awe. Mom in the passenger seat called over, "Are you okay?"

Hammon nodded blankly. "Fine…" He struggled clumsily to get the Dakota in gear.

"You want me to call the police?"

"Yeah. Police. Yeah." He scribbled down the plate number, passing it across. "Tell them that guy's chasing the girl in the Fairmont."

23:39 SATURDAY, JULY 3

40°11'47.33"N/74°06'00.78"W

GARDEN STATE PARKWAY SOUTHBOUND,

NEPTUNE, NJ

"That's the fifth time in the last mile you checked the mirrors." Micah glanced out the rear window.

"That damned Suburban rides our tail whenever the road's straight, then falls back for curves. I doubt he's following us: he's just a lousy driver."

The rain passed, but in the distance the clouds flashed ominously. Hazel sped up slightly. She wanted more air between them and the Suburban, and she wanted to reach the boat and be underway before the next storm. It was possible Hammon was still where they'd left him or maybe waiting aboard *Mardi*. She checked the mirror, filled with grill of Chevy.

"The hammer lane's wide open. He could pass any time, but no, he's using us as a pace car." She tapped the brakes, and the Suburban fell back.

"How do these things work?"

"What things?" She glanced over to see Micah playing with the darts. "Leave them alone. We need them."

"They're cool." He held one up in the beam of the Suburban's headlights, studying it. "They have pressurized air to push the plunger. The needle hits, this little sleeve here pushes back, and..."

A fine mist sprayed her arm.

"Oops."

"Get it off me!" Hazel dug around the messy car for a napkin. "What if it's absorbed through the skin? You had to play with it, didn't you? Now we're down to six."

He wiped her arm with a waded-up flannel shirt then packed the darts away. "Sheesh. Don't go all PMS-y just cause your prom date didn't show."

"Give it a rest already. It's not funny."

"But it's true." He flipped the radio back to alternative. The Talking Heads cheerfully proclaimed they were on the Road to Nowhere, and Micah sang along. Hazel liked the song but switched back to the country station for spite. Micah flipped back to Talking Heads.

"Admit it. If Hammon wasn't after us, you'd be after him."

She wasn't admitting anything.

"I think he really likes you."

"And nothing says that like a tranquilizer dart." Hazel fought back a yawn. It had been a long night, and it wasn't over yet. She flipped on the turn signal and exited the Parkway. "Home stretch."

"Maybe Stevenson hired Hammon but he's so charmed by you he changed his mind. It could happen."

"In the movies maybe."

"No. It's a time-tested truth, guys do the stupidest, most irrational things just to get laid...including fall in love. We can't help it; it's the way we're wired. I'm telling you, the poor deluded bastard's hopelessly in love with you. And whether you want to admit it or not, it's mutual. I just wish I'd meet someone who looks at me the way you look at him."

"Can we change the subject?" And the station; from Rancid to the Mavericks, soulfully covering "Blue Moon."

Micah groaned and rolled his eyes. "Okay. New subject. What if *Mardi*'s gone?"

Hazel considered. "We need her for this. We find her and borrow her back."

"And if your boyfriend's aboard?"

Hazel glanced in the rearview mirror. "He isn't…aboard, I mean. And he is NOT my boyfriend."

"What makes you so sure? That he's not aboard, I mean."

Hazel fought a smile. "He's *right* behind us."

Micah looked back at the crumbled grill and single misaligned headlight closing in on them, high-beam flashing. "Isn't that Gary's little pickup? I don't remember it all smashed up like that."

The Dakota pulled alongside, window down, Hammon blasting the horn, shouting and waving.

Micah said, "I think he wants us to stop."

Hazel glanced over, the corner of her mouth curling up as her eyes met Hammon's. "Like hell. First one to the boat wins." She downshifted, flooring it, and the Fairmont shot away.

I HOPE THIS WORKS

Hammon watched with relief as the Fairmont's taillights shrank.

For miles he'd hung back, headlights off, hoping the maniac in the 350 wouldn't notice him. Where were the police when you needed them? But as Hazel exited the Parkway, vanishing into the looping curve leading toward Route 34 South, and the 350, half a dozen cars back, followed and began to close in, Hammon knew it was time for more drastic measures.

The 350 outweighed the Dakota roughly two to one. Still, Hammon knew if he caught the Ford just right he could swing it out of control. He'd pulled that maneuver off successfully in demolition derbies but never at that speed, and he wasn't sure he wouldn't lose control in the process.

He timed it as they moved through the exit; he downshifted and cut inside the curve, ramming into the 350 behind the right rear tire. The Ford careened sideways, spinning off the wet road into the bushes as Hammon fought to keep Gary's Dakota pointed forward.

"YES!" Annabel cheered.

Seconds dragged by in freeze-frame as the Dakota lost traction, threatening to tumble off the road and join the Ford. Finally, inches from leaving the pavement, the tires grabbed, allowing him to head off in pursuit of the Fairmont.

He was counting on Hazel to react as she did when she saw him. It was late and the roads were clear. His hit to the 350 would slow it down, but it wasn't a crippling blow. His only hope was to chase her far enough ahead. With any luck she and Micah would get *Revenge* underway before he or anyone else caught up.

00:14 SUNDAY, JULY 4

40°7'58.51"N/74°05'19.87"W

NJ-34 SOUTH, MANASQUAN, NJ

"You better hope we don't pass a cop." Micah looked out the back window. "He's gaining again."

"Not for long." Hazel floored it and the Fairmont responded with seemingly limitless acceleration. She refused to glance at the speedometer as scenery blurred past, certain that knowing their actual velocity would unnerve her. "I'll lose him in the turns for sure."

There was little traffic on the road at that hour, and she easily slipped around the other cars, blasting through a yellow light. Behind her, Hammon ran the red.

"I can't believe we're having a high-speed chase and you're listening to 'Blue Moon.' This is so *not* car chase music!"

"Micah, shut up."

"Next chase, I'm driving."

"Would you be quiet?"

He did, at least until the next song came on. Hazel winced.

"Yes!" Micah raised the volume and held up an imaginary CB. "Breaker Six-Nine, this here's Rubber Chicken. You copy? Mercy snakes alive, I think we got us a con-voy." He looked back at the Dakota. "By the way, how many vehicles do we need to qualify for 'convoy' status?"

The light ahead was red. With no cross-traffic in sight, Hazel shot through as lightning crackled overhead, illuminating the wet road. In her mirror, Hammon never even slowed. "In case you haven't noticed, I'm trying to drive."

"And doing a fine job. Keep up the good work." Micah held his hand to his mouth, making static sounds. "Was a new moon, on the third of July, in a Kenworth, haulin' boats. 'Bout a mile outta the Parkway, we're about to put the hammer on down. 'Cause we gotta little ol' convoy, rockin' through the night, yeah we gotta little ol' convoy, ain't she a real fine sight? C'mon join our convoy, ain't nothin' goin' our way…We're gonna roll this freakin' convoy, cross the Garden State. Con-voy…Con-voy…"

Hazel tried not to grin. Micah didn't need any encouragement. "Did I ever mention you're real annoying?"

"All the time. Hey, Bandit, you wanna give me a ten-nine on that POS Dakota?"

Another flash of lightning split the darkness, followed by a loud crack that shook the car.

"Still on our back door. I've got some distance, but he'll catch up fast when we stop."

"Well, put the pedal to the metal. Heh-heh…they just said something about getting laid at the Jersey Shore…" Micah resumed his off-key singing. "An I sez, this here's the Rubber Chicken an I got my EZpass. So we'll blow through the high-speed lane…and keep the darts off our ass!"

"I'm going to waste one on your ass in a minute."

"That song's messed up. They say there's a toll to get into Jersey. That's wrong. Everyone knows you get into Jersey for free. You got to pay to leave."

Thick raindrops smacked the windshield. "It's just a song."

"And a movie, right?"

"Yeah. And in the end the hero drove off the bridge in flames."

"But he lived, right? Everyone thought he was dead but he wasn't. So who's the hero? Us, or Hammon?"

Ahead, the road crossed the Manasquan River. Micah beamed.

"Dang it, Cousin Daisy, I think the bridge's out. You're gonna hafta jump it."

Hazel concentrated on the road ahead and the misaligned headlight behind, ignoring Micah. At the rise of the bridge, the car lifted, momentarily catching air.

"Yeeeee-haaaww!!!" Micah said.

Hazel downshifted, drifting through the turns, leaving Hammon further behind. "You better hope the boat's still there, or we'll see who's laughing. Grab our stuff."

Micah collected the backpack from the floor. "Shit!" He began searching frantically around the seat.

"What?"

"My lucky shark's tooth…I can't find it!"

Ahead, Hazel spotted *Mardi*, illuminated as an arc of blue-white light shot across the darkness.

"We don't have time!" Hazel shouted as thunder rumbled through. She skidded to a stop beside the boat.

The wind was building, holding *Mardi* against the dock, fretting in the rising chop. Warm drops pelted them as Hazel dropped the stern line and climbed to the bridge, starting the engine. Micah dropped the bow lines, jumping aboard. Hazel pushed the throttle forward, guiding the boat clear as the Dakota screeched to a stop and Hammon spilled out.

"Go!" He screamed across the water. Lightning cut the sky, and he ducked in terror as thunder cracked. "Get out of here!"

For a moment Hazel froze, confused. In the flash of lightning, she watched Hammon dodge between parked cars as the 350 skidded in, ramming the Dakota.

"That's not good." Micah climbed to the bridge as they moved toward the inlet.

Lighting cracked overhead and the figure from the 350 lunged, knocking Hammon to the ground.

"Why do I get a horrible feeling he was trying to warn us," Micah said as Hammon curled into a ball, attempting to shield himself from the assault.

"He doesn't even have his gun."

Micah pulled the colorful gun from the backpack. "But I do. Go back."

I'M SCREWED

Hammon struggled to stand, but the wind was still knocked out of him. He had to get up, he had to stop this maniac, but the ground refused to stay level, and he collapsed back to the pavement. Mr. 350 dragged him to his feet by his hair, supporting him with the hard pressure of a gun muzzle to his throat, smiling a flawless white smile as Hammon gasped and coughed and Annabel looked on helplessly.

"The freak from the rest stop," said 350, still smiling.

He dropped Hammon and kicked him in the chest, patting him down as he retched. Breathing was excruciating, and his vision swam with tears of pain and frustration. Lightning flashed and the ground shook with the thunderclap. Fury burned inside him, fueling Hammon past the agony, and he launched himself at the infuriating smile.

Mr. 350 spun, his expression never wavering, and kicked him back down. Hammon wrapped his arms over his head, trying to block the assault. Through the pelting rain, he saw *Revenge* emerge from the darkness, bearing down on the dock at full throttle. No! Why weren't they leaving? He tried to stand, failing.

"Stop!" Micah slammed into 350, knocking him backwards. Lightning flashed and thunder cracked like gunfire. Through the steady hiss of rain, Hammon heard a truck speeding away. He tried to move but couldn't.

"Otto?" Hazel leaned over him, her face soaked and hair dripping.

"Go…" Hammon said, his voice lost in the storm. "Leave now…"

00:27 SUNDAY, JULY 4

40°06'07.91"N/74°02'43.27"W

POINT PLEASANT, NJ

Micah climbed back aboard *Mardi*, slumping against the freezer as the rain pelted down.

"HA!" He beamed, out of breath. "Take that, you son of a bitch!" He reached around, lifted the lid, and pulled a Popsicle from the freezer, unwrapping it. "Tom fuckin' Nelson! We should've known." He took a bite. "And I shot that bastard!"

Lightning flashed overhead and Hazel saw a dark smear on Micah's rain-soaked shirt. She knelt beside him as he lay back across the deck, gazing at the flashing clouds.

"Some storm." He grinned. "We should get going. You think we should bring Hammon?"

There was a small hole in his shirt, just above his belt. Gently Hazel lifted the edge, her chest tight. "You've been shot!"

Micah sat up, poking his finger through the fabric. He lifted it, regarding the pea-sized hole beneath. "I'll be damned. Shit, I didn't even feel it." He looked at Hazel and laughed. "Hon, relax. It's just a little hole...see? I've had worse paper cuts. It doesn't even hurt. You should go back and check on your boyfriend. Poor guy got the crap beat out of him. He's got to be way worse than me."

Lightning flashed overhead, illuminating the cockpit for a frozen moment. Hazel slid her hands under Micah's back, trying to lift him.

"Micah, get up...let's get to the car."

He grinned and squeezed her hand. "Relax. I'm fine, just tired."

"No, now," she insisted, tugging his hand. "Micah, please."

"Haze, go check on Hammon first. I'm okay. Really. Just do me a favor. Tomorrow, let me sleep late."

I'M HURTING

Hammon opened his eyes to excruciating, blurry misery. Every breath was laced with shattered glass. Every old fracture, every pin, every screw inside him screamed with fresh agony. Even blinking hurt.

He tried to call out, coughing as needles stabbed through him, but no answer came. Glasses missing, soaked, he stared up at nothing. Even if he managed to get up and walk, he'd likely step straight off the wharf. He'd drown and no one would know or care.

Best he could determine he was still in one piece. Nothing major seemed broken, but he was blind, stranded in the middle of nowhere, with no idea what happened to Hazel and Micah and no prospect of finding out. He'd just lie on that pavement until he rotted.

"That's your plan?" Annabel asked.

Hammon shrugged, regretting it as waves of pain rippled through him. "Got any better ideas?"

"Not really."

"Did we win?"

"Wish I knew."

Hammon only wished he knew how Hazel was. She wasn't there beside him. He hoped that was a good sign.

"That, or a really bad one."

Not only did she have him and Stevenson after her, but now she had 350 as well. Could things get any worse?

A deep rumble carried through the air, approaching fast.

"If that's a GTO, I'd say yes," Annabel said.

He heard a door open then slam.

"What the fuck'd you do to my truck?"

"You're in trouble now," chanted Annabel.

"Gary?" Hammon moaned. "I can't see."

"And apparently you drove that way." A shadow moved in the fog. "I should leave you like this. You might live longer."

Hammon didn't move. What was the point? He couldn't blame Gary. "Why're you even here?"

"Hazel called me. She said you did something stupid, she wouldn't say what, only that you got beat up pretty bad. She told me where you are and asked me to make sure you're okay. She said to tell you she ever sees you again, she'll kill you herself. Then she asked me to keep an eye on you. She was afraid you might 'hurt' yourself. She actually said please. Explain to me, if she's so set on getting rid of you, why does she give a damn?"

03:56 SUNDAY, JULY 4

40°07'40.54"N/73°59'06.70"W

NORTH ATLANTIC, 2 NM EAST OF SEA GIRT, NJ

Soaked to the skin, shivering, Hazel sat at the helm, cell phone to her ear, waiting.

The storm had cleared, pushed through by a cold front. Brilliant stars dotted the sky above *Mardi,* chugging steadily along, alone and safe in the darkness. She and Micah had already discussed what she would say. On the eighth ring, Keith answered.

"Hello, Keith."

"Hazel? Is everything all right? Where are you?"

She took a deep breath, fighting the tightness in her throat, letting the silence hang. She had to sound calm, and she wanted him to sweat.

"Hazel?"

"The time for repentance is at hand," she said softly.

"What?"

"Micah and I know what you did, Keith. So here's the deal. Fifty percent, we disappear. You don't comply, our next call is to Tom Nelson. This isn't open to negotiation. Understand?"

"I don't...I..." He began to stammer and cough. Micah was right. Threatening him with Nelson was more effective than her original idea, saying they'd call the police.

"Fine, Keith. That's how you want it, we call Nelson right now. I'm sure for a fifty percent recovery fee he'd love to learn who screwed him over. Care to gamble? Oh, right, you don't believe in gambling. The Good Lord wouldn't approve. Yet you stole our truck, sat back, and watched the fallout from a safe distance. That's okay with Jesus?"

"It wasn't supposed to happen this way. It was supposed to be Atkins driving that night."

"And that makes it right? Maybe I'll just save us the trouble, call Tom now, and let you two sort things out."

"I'll get your money," he said, his voice weak.

"I thought so. Listen carefully. I hear the stripers are running at Sandy Hook, off North Beach, up past the old Nike missile base. Grab your surf caster, get yourself a little GPS, and learn how to use it. You got a pen and paper?"

For a moment he didn't answer, and Hazel wondered if she'd lost the connection. Then she heard shuffling. "Uh, yeah..."

"Take down these coordinates," she instructed. "Forty degrees twenty-eight minutes nine seconds north, seventy-three degrees fifty-nine minutes forty-three seconds west. You got that?"

"Uh, yeah. Forty, twenty-eight, nine north, seventy-three, fifty-nine, forty-three west," he recited back, his voice faltering. "But you know I don't understand that boat stuff. Can't we just meet somewhere and we'll talk?"

"We are meeting and we will talk, but you'll do it on our terms. Follow those coordinates. There'll be a beach chair and a flashlight in a bucket. Have the money in a backpack, and wear the backpack. No briefcases, no grocery bags. Nothing around you. We don't want you carrying anything but that rod. Nine forty-five tonight, you walk out, sit down, pick up the flashlight, and shine it on your face. Nine forty-five. No earlier, no later, no exceptions. Come alone or the deal is off. Sit nice and polite on that chair with the light on your face, or the deal is off. You sit and you wait, and when Micah and I feel safe, then we talk. We're only doing this once, and if anything makes us think you're trying to be clever, which you aren't, you'll never even see us, but we'll be phoning the appliance king. Understand?"

"Yeah," he said, his voice faint.

"How's it feel, Keith? Tell you what…we'll cut you ten percent discount just for a picture of your face at this very moment."

I DON'T HAVE A CLUE

July 4 dawned crisp and bright. The previous night's rain had scrubbed the world clean, leaving a sharp, high-contrast morning, and the water sparkled like scattered diamonds. The humidity was gone, replaced by a light west wind and excellent visibility. Along the Jersey shore, the waters teemed with boats of every shape and size, making it easy for Gary, Hammon, and the canine crew to blend with the masses as they followed *Revenge* in a borrowed twenty-four-foot Sea Ray. They hung back a mile, guided by the signal, which, for a change, remained constant.

"Why?" Gary said. "I can only figure they'd been disconnecting the batteries. Why not this time?"

"Maybe it's a trap," Annabel suggested.

Hammon lifted binoculars to watch Hazel, who sat alone on the bridge. Every so often she scanned the water, likely for *Temperance*. He hadn't seen Micah all morning and that worried him.

Gary said, "Why don't you talk to Stevenson? See what he knows."

"Yeah. Sure." Hammon dug around the boat, discovering half a bag of stale Cheetos in the cuddy cabin. "When hell freezes over." The dogs sat up, watching expectantly as he popped a cheese curl in his mouth. It was rubbery but edible.

"Maybe you could 'talk' to him with a baseball bat," Annabel said.

Hammon chewed his Cheetos. "Tempting but risky. It's better he doesn't know I know she exists."

Gary raised a disapproving eyebrow. "Annabel?"

She smiled brightly. "Yes?"

Hammon squeezed his eyes shut. "Yup."

"You mean, even with that one," Gary pointed toward the horizon, "clubbing you like a baby seal, you're still seeing Annabel?"

Hammon shrugged, sipping cold coffee. "Pretty much." He tossed each dog a Cheeto. Charger caught his in midair while Yodel scrambled after the orange curl. Charger chewed for a moment, then dropped it to the deck. Yodel wouldn't even pick his up.

"Christ, Zap. Even the dogs won't eat that. No wonder you look like shit. When's the last time you got any rest?"

"Counting unconsciousness?" Hammon stared ahead at *Revenge*. "I'm fine."

"Seriously? You've been popping NoDoz like they're Tic-Tacs. You look like you've been run over. You need sleep."

"He's right," Annabel said.

"I said I'm fine."

Just before nine Hazel docked in Belmar. She tied up then disappeared into the cabin, reappearing with Hammon's backpack over her shoulder. She stood for a moment, looking strangely uncertain, then locked up and headed ashore. Gary circled back and docked farther down the fairway while Hammon watched

Hazel enter the chandlery. As Gary shut the Sea Ray, Hammon rose, starting for the dock. Gary grabbed his shirt.

"You don't learn, do you? You won't be happy till she kills you."

"I'm going to *Revenge*; I got to talk to Micah. I got a feeling he got hurt last night or he'd be with her. You see anyone bother her or she starts back, call me."

Gary drained his coffee. "You know what you're doing?"

"Nope."

"And I'm not going to talk you out of this, am I?"

"Nope." Hammon fished through his pockets. He knew he had the boat keys; they were with his car keys, which Hazel had left dangling in the Fairmont's ignition.

"You know you're insane."

Hammon shrugged. "Was that ever in question?"

"I'd say it's been nice knowing you," Gary called as Hammon hobbled toward *Revenge* with Annabel by his side. "But I'd be lying."

Revenge sat peaceful and serene, sunlight reflecting blazes of light across the dark hull. Hammon hesitated, feeling strangely uncomfortable.

"She's still our boat," Annabel said. "It's not like you're stealing her or anything."

Still, it felt like he was trespassing as he climbed aboard and knocked on the salon door. "Hey, Micah. It's me, Otto. Look, man, we got to talk."

The freezer compressor kicked on. He knocked again, burping coffee, Cheetos, and Munchkins as his stomach churned.

"That's it. I'm coming in." He reached for the door.

"The boat is locked," *Revenge* announced, and Hammon smiled. Beneath the cosmetic alterations, the mechanical systems, including the locks, remained unchanged. He glanced back, took a deep breath, unlocked the cabin, and stepped inside, braced for a blow to the head or a bullet to the chest.

Or not.

"You sure we're on the right boat?" Annabel said.

Hammon looked around the salon, baffled. Daylight filtered through curtains, softly lighting the tidy cabin. Polished wood and bronze gleamed. Hammon's throat tightened and he slid the door closed.

"Micah? Look, I just want to talk."

Other than the hum of the cockpit freezer compressor and water gently lapping against the hull, there was silence. A latch held the head door open. The mildew smell was gone, and the mildew as well. The sink shined and a new seashell-print shower curtain was neatly tucked aside. In place of the black rectangle, his reflection stared back, perplexed. He reached up, touching his face, his scarred fingers tracing across his scarred cheek. Was *that* what he really looked like?

"Step away from the mirror," Annabel ordered. "Now's not the time."

Hammon backed out to the spotless galley. His microwave had vanished, leaving the counter clear aside from two coffee mugs and two plates drying on a dishtowel. On the dinette, his non-skid travel mug contained an arrangement of daylilies, shriv-eled dandelions, and wilted loosestrife: the flowers he'd given Hazel right before he shot her. The forward cabin, like everything else, was clean, with clothing folded in small stacks.

"So where's Micah?" Annabel said.

Hammon didn't have an answer, only a bad feeling. His phone buzzed, the screen reading "haze rtng get out."

No. He'd stay, and he'd talk to her.

"Gary's right," Annabel said. "You'll never learn. This isn't the place or the time."

"You got a better idea?"

"Of course I do."

12:49 SUNDAY, JULY 4

40°13'25.85"N/73°54'35.34"W

NORTH ATLANTIC, 4 NM EAST OF

ASBURY PARK, NJ

With the gear stowed, Hazel headed out, watching for *Temperance*. Close to shore an armada of boats of crowded the waters, but none looked familiar or troubling. She decided to run further offshore where there was less traffic and anyone approaching would be clearly visible long in advance. The air was clear and the water smooth; under different circumstances it would have been a perfect day, and Hazel wished Micah was beside her on *Revenge*'s bridge. For a moment she smiled darkly. Despite the name across the transom, the boat's true name seemed more fitting, especially for the work ahead.

At slack low tide, she reached Sandy Hook, positioning *Revenge* and dropping anchor. She was surprised and slightly concerned that Hammon hadn't materialized. Maybe Micah was right; Hammon had been hurt worse than she realized when she left him lying in that lot. Or maybe he'd finally gotten the message, if not from her then Gary, and taken her warning to heart. Her chest tightened at the thought of never seeing him again, but it was for the best, for his sake as well as hers. The farther he was from her the better off he'd be, and she had to stay focused, blocking all else out. It was the only way she'd get through.

I'M BALLAST

Years before when Hammon rebuilt *Revenge,* he'd designed a narrow passage connecting the lazaret to the engine room. A hidden lock released the watertight hatch, concealed behind the acoustic insulation, which allowed him to slither through to the cave-dark space below the cockpit.

Hammon had settled on a lumpy nest of old dock lines and spare fenders lying between the massive fuel tanks. Surrounded by the warm, musty scent of bilge and the working parts of his boat, he listened to the thrum of the prop and water rushing around the hull. By Gary's choppy texts, he knew they were heading north. Tucked inside the secure, confining darkness, gently rocking with the rhythm of the engine and Annabel singing softly to herself, Hammon drifted into much-needed sleep. He woke hours later as the RPM dropped to an idle, momentarily reversing. His phone buzzed and he read "anchrng sndy hk."

The engine went silent and *Revenge* rolled. Footsteps descended from the bridge and Hammon panicked, fearing Hazel might open the lazaret to find him trapped and cornered. He listened as she paced the deck.

"Hi, Chris…How is he today?" She gave a strained laugh. "Really? And he wonders where I get it. Tell him he better start behaving or I'll park *RoadKill* outside the hospital and camp in the sleeper until he cuts the bullshit."

She was silent for a moment. Then: "Thanks, Chris, I really appreciate everything you're doing. Tell him he has to get better. He's…" Her voice trailed off. "Tell him I love him."

Hammon listened through a pause of unbearable silence, then:

"Mr. Atkins? It's me. If you're there, pick up…Hey. No, I'm fine, but…no, he can't talk right now…Look, I hate to ask, but we need a favor and you're the only one we trust. We need you to pick up *RoadKill*. The door doesn't lock, and the key's under the upper bunk. Just please, watch your back, and don't let anyone see you, and I mean *anyone*…be real careful no one follows you. Get a trailer that locks up tight…Do a walk-around, check the brakes, lights, you know the deal.…Not far, but I don't want to be stopped with the load I'll be hauling. Go to the state marina in Leonardo, back up to the bulkhead where I can bring a boat alongside. Drop the truck by eight tonight, and leave."

Another pause. "I don't know! Take a bus, walk. I don't want you there."

She paced the cockpit. "Please…All right, I'll explain when I get there. Watch your mirrors, keep it shiny side up, greasy side down." She gave a tense laugh. "Yeah, I guess *RoadKill* doesn't have a shiny side. You know what I mean…be careful."

More pacing, more silence.

"Hey, Micah…How's it going?" Her voice wavered. "This totally screws our plans, you getting shot like that. But I was right; you did need a doctor."

The air around Hammon became suffocating. Micah got shot helping him.

"It's not fair," she said. "You're supposed to…we're a team, right?"

Another pause, a strained laugh. "Hey. Guess what Chris told me? She says Dad tried to check himself out today. He got moved from the ICU, she said he didn't have to stay there anymore, which is good I guess. Still, I wish they'd kept him there; he's safer and I like knowing Chris's keeping in eye on him. They put him on a portable heart monitor, and he decided he could leave. He didn't get far but he tried. He's only going to hurt himself trying stunts like that."

Hammon heard her sniffle for a moment. "I didn't say anything about you. You know he'll just get upset." Another sniffle. "Don't worry about me. I'll be fine, I promise. We've got a good plan; I can handle it." There was a long silence, broken only by water slapping the transom.

"I'll be okay, really. I can take care of myself," she said, her voice breaking. "I love you."

15:34 SUNDAY, JULY 4

40°28'17.43"N/73°59'34.76"W

SANDY HOOK, NJ

Hazel knew Micah would give her such grief if she didn't eat something, but a bowl of cereal was all she could manage, chewing mechanically and forcing herself to swallow. Then she washed up, climbed into the starboard bunk, and set the alarm. She had a long night ahead, and she needed her rest.

Sleep, however, didn't come easy. She rolled and shifted, unable to get comfortable. Closing her eyes, she tried to clear her head, which only made matters worse. She listened to waves lapping the hull, occasional passing boats, even planes overhead. Time dragged and her mind filled with troubled thoughts. She could still see Micah's grin as he laughed off being shot, and even while it was obvious he wasn't in pain, tears started to flow at the memory. She was too tired to stop them, too tired to hold back, and finally she quietly cried her way into an uneasy sleep and the cemetery with the fresh grave.

Part of her remained conscious enough to know it was a nightmare, but that awareness couldn't pull her away from the dreadful headstone she was compelled to read. Yet again Stevenson awaited her, sipping scotch, this time with a gaping, bloodless hole in his chest. He stood laughing with Micah, comparing bullet wounds. Hazel reached for Micah, but Hammon stepped between them, half grinning.

"See. Told ya." He motioned toward Stevenson. "No heart."

Stevenson nodded grimly, lighting a cigarette. "Why don't you let go?"

She looked down. In one blood-covered hand, she held a cluster of wild roses, the thorns piercing her skin.

Micah smiled sadly. "She hates letting go, even when it hurts to hold on. Let go, hon. It's okay."

She knelt, placing the roses across the turned mound of soil.

"The other hand too."

Blood seeped between her fingers, clutched around something slippery and gelatinous. She uncurled her fist to reveal a pair of glazed orbs. She dropped them, shuddering, and they gazed up for a moment, setting down roots and sending out vine-like tendrils of veins. Buds appeared, opening into more eyeballs. Blue ones, brown ones, gray ones, gold ones. Hazel stepped back as the vine spread, curling around the headstone, staring back at her. She was sure every blossom was someone she knew, and she was afraid to look up. She couldn't; she didn't want to see the hollow, eyeless stares. She knew if she looked she'd see they were dead.

"Hazel…" Hammon took her hand. "Wake up. You're having a bad dream."

And abruptly she was back aboard *Revenge*, curled in the bunk, Hammon leaning over her in the faint light of the oil lamp, studying her with gentle concern. His glasses were bent and scratched, his face was bruised, his hair tangled, and still the sight of him made her heart race.

"You were dreaming," he said.

"I still am."

He brushed the hair back from her cheek, his fingers lingering on her skin as he moved closer. His lips touched hers, his soft kiss tasting of gummy bears and tears.

"A dream, or a nightmare?" he whispered.

She gazed up at his wide gray eyes. "Definitely a dream."

"Hazel, where's Micah?"

She didn't answer.

"He got shot, didn't he? Last night, helping me, right?"

She nodded. "Just a little hole. He said it didn't hurt, but I told him he had to see a doctor."

"And he left you alone?"

"It wasn't his choice."

"What's with the gear in the cockpit?"

"I'm going fishing."

"For what?"

"Little fish. To catch big fish, live bait works best." She stretched, her fingers grazing his. "Why are you following me? What do you want, really?"

"You." Color rose in his face. "To stay with me forever."

Hazel smiled. "Micah was right." She reached up, pulling him toward her, taking charge this time with a kiss. Only too soon she'd wake to the nightmare her life had become, but at least for the moment she could give in to this little bit of escape. She pulled Hammon closer, and he shifted himself onto the bunk, lying beside her, holding her protectively. She pressed her face to the heat of his throat, feeling his pulse, and twined her fingers into his, remembering how he'd jumped the first time they touched. Safe in his arms, safer than she'd felt for so long, she closed her eyes and drifted off.

Her dreams dissolved as Hazel woke, leaving only a vague, bittersweet ache. The alarm hadn't sounded yet, but it was growing dark outside. She lay half-awake, staring at the faint constellations on the ceiling, hearing distant fireworks. The bunk was empty, the cabin was empty, she was alone, and she squeezed her eyes shut, trying not to think about it. Not yet at least; there was still work ahead.

First order of business: check that all was clear. She headed outside, half expecting to see *Temperance* nearby, uncertain whether she'd be furious or relieved. But all she saw were distant running lights farther offshore, all underway. The park she had anchored east of closed from dusk to dawn, and only those with fishing permits could enter. With the night scope, she scanned the area, confirming the only movement was a single raccoon foraging for scraps of discarded bait. That was good. The raccoon wouldn't stay if anyone was around, hidden or otherwise.

Taking offerings from the galley for her four-legged security, Hazel loaded a child-sized inflatable raft, leaving no room for herself. That was fine; she'd bought it specifically to ferry the necessary gear to the beach. She lit the hurricane lantern, hanging it from the boom and setting the flame just bright enough to guide her back to the boat. Then, wearing only her tank top and panties, she slipped on a snorkel and fins then eased into the cool water, swimming to shore with the raft in tow. With everything prepared in advance, setting up didn't take long at all. She left the raccoon treats by a stretch of low grass then returned to *Revenge*, deflated, and stowed the raft. She stripped, shivering as she pulled on dry clothes she'd left waiting, along with Hammon's trench coat, the Glock's reassuring weight tugging in the pocket. She positioned three fishing rods, each set with eighty-pound test multi-strand nylon-covered wire, and checked her watch. It was eight fifty-five. There wasn't a car for miles. Everything was set to go, right on schedule. Now, it was a matter of sitting back and waiting. In the distance, fireworks rose spectacularly above Manhattan.

"I see piracy is alive and well off the Jersey shore."

Hazel whipped around, her mind racing as Hammon materialized like an apparition, stepping down from the shadows of the side deck.

"What are you doing here?" She pulled the Glock from the coat pocket.

He broke into a broad grin, all fangs, and pushed his hair back. "I came for my boat. And you. Mostly you."

She couldn't imagine how he'd gotten there but that didn't matter. What mattered was staying on schedule. "I don't have time for this. Not now." He wasn't her immediate target; in fact, she wasn't sure whether he was a target at all. She only knew whenever he was around, things never went as planned. "You have to leave."

"That's some rig you set up." He studied the rods, plinking a wire line. "But you should check the restrictions and size limits on humans."

He wasn't going to listen. She leveled the gun at him. "I said leave."

"You know, I'm getting some real mixed messages. You're still wearing my jacket. I like that. I like you even better in nothing at all. I guess the water's still pretty chilly, this time of year."

"Otto, I'm serious. I'll shoot you."

"No you won't. You don't want to. I see it in your eyes." He stepped forward, ignoring the gun, his thigh brushing hers, his arm sliding around her waist, pushing the gun away. She thought he meant to kiss her, but his ankle pressed behind hers, and he shoved her off balance. She fell backwards; the deck came up, knocking the wind out of her, and Hammon dove down, pinning her arms to either side.

"Go ahead," he coaxed, holding her wrist firmly. "Pull the trigger now; you'll put a hole in the side of your boat. My boat, technically, but I'm willing to share. Sweet dreams before? We were in pretty much the same position, only you were way friendlier."

"Otto, please!" She twisted around, pinned beneath his weight. "Let me go!"

"No." He squeezed her wrist until she cried out, releasing the gun. She fought him, sinking her teeth into his arm as he fumbled to bind her wrists with duct tape. Layers of fabric blocked a direct hit, but he yelped in pain and sat up, still straddling her. He stretched for the gun and placed it on top of the freezer, beyond her reach. Twisting around, he wrestled her ankles together, binding them as well. "Sorry, dear." He rubbed his arm and pushed his hair back from his face. "I never meant for it to end up like this. All things considered, you can't blame me."

Hazel looked around, panic building. The dart gun was in the backpack, close by, but it was a clumsy reach she couldn't make without tipping off Hammon as well. He rose, stepping back, and flipped open his cell phone, casting a circle of dim blue in the darkness.

"Hi, Gary. Yes, we're good…You can head back. I think we could use some time alone, just the two of us." He knelt beside her, gently brushing the hair from her eyes. "You know, to talk and all."

I'M LOSING IT

Hammon looked around the cockpit, completely disoriented. Sweat soaked his clothes and plastered his hair to his neck and forehead.

He was aboard *Revenge*, he knew that much. He could hear Hazel's anxious breathing, he could feel her fear. But he couldn't remember any of what he'd done.

"You haven't done anything," Annabel said. "Aside from panic before, when you had her safe in your arms."

"Oh God…" Suddenly he remembered. She'd been lying against him, so warm and soft and vulnerable, so utterly unaware of the conflicting thoughts racing through his head. He held her, torn between feelings of overwhelming protectiveness and unspeakable desire, certain he was on the verge of doing something he'd regret. The more he tried not to think about it, the more the perverse, unforgivable thoughts invaded his brain. How could he even think like that? It was so wrong. Finally, for her sake as well as his own, he retreated to the darkness of the bridge.

"So," Annabel said. "If you plan to fail, and succeed, which did you do?"

He didn't have time for her head games. "You're not helping."

"Otto, please." Hazel tugged futilely at the duct tape binding her wrists. "Let me go."

No. That was the only thing he knew for sure. Now that he had her there, he could never let her go or he'd lose her forever. And he couldn't let that happen.

Annabel sat beside Hazel, looking down with concern. "Talk to her. Tell her you want to help. I did all the dirty work. Now you can tell her you love her and you can live happily ever after," she said sarcastically. "Tell her the truth."

How? He couldn't even remember half of it himself, much less explain it to her. She'd never believe him. But the silence was unbearable. He had to say something. He knelt beside her. "I don't want to hurt you," he mumbled, touching her cheek. She flinched and pulled away.

"Please, let me go."

"Not yet. You were talking before with Micah. He got shot, right? Where is he?"

"Let me go."

Hammon could see she was at the edge, fighting not to panic. She squeezed her eyes shut, a tear slipping out between the lashes.

"Look at me." He gently turned her head. "Where's Micah? I just want to talk to him."

Beneath the tears, anger flared. Was that it? Did she blame him for Micah getting hurt? His brain was coming unglued, pieces of mercury shifting, and he wanted to shake them back into place but he couldn't, not with Hazel staring at him like that. His hands lingered on her wrists, tracing over the delicate skin. If he released her she'd leave.

"Please," she asked, her voice so soft it gave him chills.

"No." Hammon shook his head, hair falling in his eyes, and he pushed his glasses up. He'd made up his mind. She would stay. It wasn't her choice anymore. She might not understand, but in time he'd make her see it was for the best. "You're not leaving. Not ever."

Hazel pulled back, tucking her bound arms against herself in a modest, defensive way, and Annabel sighed.

"Knock off the 'forever' crap. You already qualify as a stalker, now you sound like a freakin' serial killer."

Hammon swallowed, feeling his hair sticking to his neck. He had to say something, anything, but everything came out wrong. Water lapped along the hull, the sound magnified against the silence. Hazel's lips parted as if to speak, but she only gazed at him, her eyes wide and beautiful. Why was she looking at him like that? What did she see? She swallowed, her expression strangely uncertain.

"What are you thinking?" he asked, dreading her answer.

She almost spoke, then hesitated, wincing. She was trembling the slightest bit, and Hammon wondered if it was fear, anger, or adrenaline. She took a deep, shuddering breath, breasts pressing against her shirt, momentarily drawing his attention...and then he saw blood on her wrist, seeping beneath the tape bindings.

"Oh God. I hurt you."

"No." Hazel pulled away, abruptly looking confused.

"Lemme see," he insisted, reaching for her hands.

"Stay back!"

As he touched her something shifted in her eyes. Her right hand, no longer bound, whipped outward, and pain seared through his palm as he reached to grab her. He threw his weight on her, and they both went down. She stared straight into his eyes with cool anger, and he realized that while she'd been pleading with him she'd also been cutting the tape, and herself, with that same knife she'd once held to his throat. His palm stung and blood flowed between his fingers, wrapped around her bleeding wrist. Hazel stared back, eyes glowing with murderous fierceness, breathing heavy.

"That hurt," he said plaintively.

"It felt good to me." The tears had been replaced with scathing hatred.

"You tried to kill me," he mumbled, amazed, scared shitless, and more than a little turned on. "The fear, the crying…that was just an act."

"Sorry to disappoint you."

Hammon grinned. "Oh, this is way better. You're not so helpless; you just let me think you were so you could kill me."

She glared back; knife in hand, defiance in her eyes as she tried to pry his fingers from her wrist with her left hand. "You're surprised?"

"Impressed." He turned his attention to the little blade. A worn Spyderco, half straight-edged and scalpel sharp, leading into a vicious serrated pattern. Years of use wore the handle smooth.

"Nasty little thing," he observed. "I'd bet it could do some serious damage."

"I'd be happy to demonstrate."

"Wow." He laughed, feeling a rush of lust. Was it wrong that he found her desire to kill him a turn-on? "I think I see how Stevenson ended up the way he did. He underestimated you, didn't he?" Carefully he started pulling her fingers back from the knife. Her left hand locked around his.

"He's paying you, not me. Ask him yourself. Or does he have you on a need-to-know basis?"

Hammon froze. "He's *not* paying me!"

"So it's just a coincidence that you've got an envelope full of money from him."

He tried to think of how to explain, but his brain wasn't getting enough blood. The pressure of her thighs against his, her smooth, warm skin beneath his fingers, was unbearable. "It's not what it looks like."

"It looks like you're getting a little too excited," Annabel observed, and a flash of pain blurred his vision, distracting him from the X-rated images playing in the back of his head. "Stay focused."

It was hard.

"Well, that's apparent," Annabel grumbled.

To think. It was hard to think. And that too. He couldn't help it, wrestling with Hazel beneath him like that.

"Then what is it? Why are you following me?" Hazel said, still fighting his grip. "What do you want?"

What did he want? Other than the obvious, unspeakable things, he wanted her to understand he'd die for her. He wanted her to stay and never leave.

"Then tell her," Annabel said.

His hand throbbed, his clothes were soaked with sweat, and the air around him was suffocating. He wiped his face on his shoulder, not taking his eyes off her for a second. He was exhausted and sore, his arm was starting to cramp, and he could feel her straining against his weakening, slippery grip. He couldn't hold her like that indefinitely, and once she was free he'd be helpless to prevent her from slicing him into neat little ribbons. Harsh language. Yeah. He could try harsh language; then again, even that wasn't like him, and he'd never pull it off convincingly.

Annabel sighed. "Tell her the truth."

He couldn't. He'd only make things worse.

"I don't think that's possible," Annabel said.

The knife moved toward his throat as her leverage increased.

"Hazel, I want to help you."

"Then let me go."

"But then you'll leave…"

The lethal little blade grazed his neck and he swallowed. Everything seemed frozen in the lamplight, with only the sound of waves lapping against *Revenge*'s hull. He could feel every beat of her heart, every breath, and beneath her anger he could still see that gentle child that touched his hand and his soul. He'd failed, completely, absolutely, and he knew it. There was nothing he could say or do to win her trust. His strength was gone, both physically and mentally. She'd get free and she'd leave. Maybe she'd kill him first, but either way there was nothing he could do to stop her.

Close by, the sound of a large powerboat quickly came and went, never slowing. Hammon sensed impending danger as he stared into the depths of her eyes, fascinated by the darkness, pulling him under, drowning him. His grip went slack, his fingers lingering on hers as she turned the blade, still between them, away from his skin. Time seemed to stop as she gazed back at him as though she sensed his surrender, she understood all he couldn't say, when suddenly the powerboat's wake slammed into *Revenge*, throwing the boat violently against the anchor lines. Hammon was crushed down on top of her as Hazel cried out. The cabin door banged back and forth, the lantern above them swayed wildly, light and shadows dancing across the deck as halyards slapped the mast, and the gear on the freezer showered down around them. Hammon tried to brace himself as *Revenge* lurched beneath them a second and third time, finally settling enough for him to back away and give Hazel some air. She sat up, knife in one hand, her other hand to her throat, and Hammon stared in horror as blood covered her fingers.

21:20 SUNDAY, JULY 4

40°28'17.43"N/73°59'34.76"W

SANDY HOOK, NJ

Hazel took a deep breath, willing herself calm. Panic wouldn't solve anything. How bad was she cut? As Hammon watched in despair, she found her pulse, racing faster than blood flowed from the wound. In the corner of her eye she spotted his vivid gun lying among her wet clothes. He looked over at the Glock but made no attempt to pick it up.

"I'm so sorry," Hammon said, his voice breaking. "I never meant to hurt you."

Hazel grabbed the gun, leveling it at his chest. She expected he'd try to wrestle it away from her but he didn't. He only sat motionless and sighed.

"So this is it, huh?" He smiled weakly. "Okay, I guess. Go ahead; get it over with."

It wasn't a dare or a challenge; it was an offering. Still she didn't move, locked in his eerie gaze. This was her chance. Just shoot him. But Micah's words echoed in her head, and she wondered if there might be another option.

"How much is Stevenson paying you?"

"I already told you, he's…" Suddenly he brightened. "Why? You want to make a counteroffer, right? You want my help and, you really don't want to kill me!"

There was no point in denying it. "I know who has the money. I don't know how much, but it must be a lot."

"I help you, I get a cut?" Hammon paused, looking from her neck to his bleeding hand. Ignoring the gun leveled at him, he reached across and pulled some White Castle napkins from his coat pocket. "Is that it?" He blotted his palm and winced. "In exchange for my help, I share the spoils of this war."

"Yes."

"No." He gazed at her, his odd, colorless eyes magnified through the glasses, a strange tranquility barely veneering the madness. "I want more."

"You can have it all. I don't want it."

"That's not what I mean." Again he reached past the gun as though it wasn't there, softly dabbing her throat with a napkin. "I want you." His eyes almost glowed. "I help you, you stay with me. You can't leave. Not now, not ever."

"Stay?" she repeated.

A trickle of sweat ran down his cheek. "Yeah. Forever. Stay with me or shoot me. That's your choice." Hammon leaned forward, reaching down, cautiously untaping her ankles. "I know I'm insane, but I'm not crazy. I can't lose you. Without you I might as well be dead. I love you. I'll never leave you. I'll die for you. Maybe you hate me, but I'll take that chance."

It was insane, he was insane, and she was insane to even consider it. Slowly, with infinite care, he lifted her chin, his hand trembling the slightest bit. Hazel squeezed her eyes shut, laughing quietly when she imagined what Micah would say. Hammon gently held her face, taking another napkin and wiping away the blood. She laid the gun down beside them and took his other hand, turning it, inspecting a deep slash cutting through layers of scars, still bleeding but not seriously. He flinched and fidgeted, biting back a whimper as her grip on his fingers tightened. Hazel checked her watch. It would be slack tide soon. Too soon. She had so many questions, and time for only one.

"Otto? Yesterday, why did you shoot me?"

"I didn't know what else to do. You were in danger, and I knew you wouldn't trust me. The only way I could keep you safe was to kidnap you. I had to protect you, even if you wouldn't understand."

There was no mistaking the pure, childlike devotion in his eyes. Micah was right. It made no sense, but nothing did anymore. Trembling, she moved forward, kissing him tenderly.

"I do understand." Her lips brushed his while her hand found the dart gun in the backpack. "And so should you."

21:40 SUNDAY, JULY 4

40°28'17.43"N/73°59'34.76"W

SANDY HOOK, NJ

Hazel sat alone on *Revenge*'s unlit bridge and watched the beach. The moon was a thin crescent, barely visible in the dark sky. From her vantage point, she scanned the empty length of Sandy Hook, spotting the approaching headlights. Through the night scope, she could clearly see Keith park, looking around anxiously as he stepped from the Jeep. She switched on the digital recorder, the tiny LED flickering as it picked up *Revenge*'s quietly burbling engine, and dialed the cell phone. She set the phone to speaker, tucking it and the recorder in her pocket.

"Okay, Micah," she said softly. "Here goes. Let's see what we catch."

Meeting Keith was risky; there could be someone else in the shadows, ready to gun her down on sight. It was naive to expect anything less. Walking onto an isolated pier would be suicide. Meeting somewhere public and crowded might have been safer, but it wouldn't work for her plans. She was sticking with a lesson Joe taught her long ago. The safest defense was to stay out of range.

Inches above the high-tide line, a folding beach chair waited in the sand, a colorful towel draped across the back and a yellow plastic bucket to the side. An innocent arrangement, as though merely forgotten at day's end. Hazel watched Keith trudge across the sand, guided by the glowing display on his handheld GPS, head swiveling like a frightened rabbit in an open field.

The stretch of beach left no spot for hiding, not for her and Micah or anyone else. And though the chair faced the ocean, as he hesitantly dropped into the low fabric seat, Keith watched over his shoulder. Due to the height of the chair, getting to his feet would be awkward; he leaned forward, visibly nervous as he scanned the surrounding beach. For a moment he turned toward the empty darkness of the ocean. The surf masked *Revenge*'s softly idling diesel, and her unlit black transom blended seamlessly into the night. Keith removed the flashlight from the bucket, following Hazel's instructions, shining it on his face, identifying himself, signaling Hazel and effectively cancelling any night vision he had.

Hazel smiled coldly. This was it. This was for her father and Micah.

She yanked up on the line leading down to the cockpit, which pulled free a screwdriver serving as the pin securing two toggle hitches together. Simultaneously the two anchor lines which had held *Revenge* with her stern facing the beach were released. Hazel pegged the throttle; *Revenge* surged forward, drawing tight the three hundred feet of line trailing from the three game-fish rods. Each line, weighted along the bottom and buried under a foot of wet sand on shore, formed a large, sliding loop, the outer edge taped smooth against the frame of the chair, hidden by the towel and the darkness. In the simplest sense it was a giant snare, with Keith perfectly positioned as the loops closed at his chest, waist, and knees, jerking him from his seat and into the breaking surf, leaving only a tilted chair and a flashlight in the sand. A perfect ten-point catch. Hazel only wished Micah could have seen it.

She flipped on the spreader lights and went below, easing the throttle at the cockpit station, giving Keith a chance to catch some air as she dragged him out to sea. He immediately began screaming sputtering threats, and Hazel pushed the throttle until the wake covered his face, forcing him to shut up or drown. That silenced him, but she knew if he was dead he'd be no use to her, so she put *Revenge* into neutral, reeling him alongside, then brought in the line snaring his legs. Ignoring his thrashing, she swung the boom over the water and pulled the heavier line down, tossing a loop around his tangled feet, then powered the winch and hauled him up, dangling head-down like a flailing game fish.

"Hello, Keith."

It took every bit of willpower she could muster to suppress her loathing at the sight of him, but she knew it was vital she stay with the script. Only, without Micah there, she wasn't sure whether to play good cop or bad cop.

"Micah!" he bellowed, untangling fishing line from his arms and twisting to reach a pistol secured in a holster beneath his shirt, hanging halfway over his face. "Where is that bastard?" He managed to unclip the gun and search for his target while the boat rolled, alternately swinging him through the air and plunging him headfirst underwater. She gave him credit; he never dropped the gun.

"Please, Keith, lose the gun," Hazel advised. "Don't force me to do something you don't want me doing."

Through two more rolls and dips he refused, his face contorted with rage each time he came up for another gasping mouthful of air.

"I asked nicely." Hazel lowered the boom, keeping Keith below the waves. He used all those well-defined muscles to raise his upper body, fumbling and dropping the gun as he struggled to remain above sea level.

"Where's…Micah…"

"You'll see him soon enough. First you talk to me." Hazel began reeling in the now slack wire lines. She didn't want them fouling the prop. "It seems you've broken a whole lot of those commandments you were teaching me. Thou shalt not steal, adultery, and I'm pretty sure you mentioned one about killing. I'm not one to judge; only why else did you have a gun? It's truly disappointing."

The backpack had slipped down, dangling behind his head. Hazel leaned out with a boathook and snagged it. Keith clung to one strap and Hazel submerged him further, waiting until he let go. He tried the impressive curl with less vigor, splashing down like a bag of sand. Hazel hauled the backpack into the cockpit, giving Keith another moment to contemplate his situation, watching while his arms flailed wildly before raising him into the air. Coughing violently, he vomited saltwater while she opened the backpack, peeling apart soggy sections of the Sunday *Bergen Record*, stuffed with flyers and advertisements.

"Oh, look. There's a Fourth of July sale at Nelson Appliance." Hazel sighed, shaking her head. "Micah said you might try something like this. I hoped you wouldn't. You know, I wanted to be forgiving and give you a chance to redeem yourself, but you're not making it easy."

Keith retched in spasms, struggling to speak.

Hazel leaned against the transom. "I didn't want to do this." No, she wanted to use treble hooks on the lines and drag him over some oyster beds first, then question him. "But you're leaving me no choice. Will you just talk to me?"

He gagged, strings of phlegm trailing from his mouth.

"I'll take that as a yes. You know, I didn't even want the money, just the truth. You told me I must seek the truth. But now I'm not sure I can trust you. Can I trust you, Keith?"

"Where's Micah?" he choked.

"I already told you, first you talk to me. You're going to tell me where you fit in this whole mess and who else is involved. Then I confirm facts. Wrong information results in more unpleasantness. You decide just how bad this gets."

"Let me aboard and we can talk," he pleaded.

"After you showed up with the Sunday paper and a gun? I don't think so."

"I wasn't going to shoot you."

"Who, then?" she asked, her voice tight. "Micah?"

"He's a sinner, Hazel. I know you don't see it, but he is."

And down he went. Hazel eased *Revenge* into gear, gunning the engine. The sound of the prop biting water would send a clear message: he was dangling beside a diesel-powered Cuisinart. Hazel dropped the boat back to idle and shifted to neutral, hauling Keith up, waiting as he expelled more of the Atlantic. She took a moment to admire the terror in his face.

"Here's your options, Keith. You start talking, or I test reverse. I've heard confession is good for the soul. Who else was involved?"

"It's Nelson's operation," Keith admitted. "They moved drugs. Him, Kessler, and Atkins, polluting the world with their evil, profiting on the weaknesses of others. I was going to purify the money by using it for the Lord's work. Atkins was supposed to be driving," he insisted. "He's a sinner and a blasphemer. He's damned anyways. They're all damned, and their greed would be their downfall."

"Who else?"

"That was it. Nelson kept it small: Kessler handled the dealers, Atkins drove." Keith coughed. "I heard Nelson and Kessler talking. I knew if the money never arrived, they'd turn on each other. I'd use the money for good and let the evil be punished at their own hands. This was my chance to truly serve the Lord and prove my faith to Him. I followed the truck; when Micah stopped, I took it. You have to understand, it was supposed to be Atkins. But Micah was knowingly associating with sinners."

"Did you even consider that stealing the truck was a sin? Or does that not apply if you do it for God?"

"I knew Christ would forgive me. I told you, if we confess our sins, He is just and will forgive us and cleanse us from all unrighteousness."

Hazel's hand hovered over the winch switch. His twisted zealousness infuriated her, but she restrained herself from submerging him. "Look, Keith, I know you didn't pull this off alone. I know there's others involved. Just tell me who."

His expression clouded and he shook his head. "No one…"

"Wrong answer." The winch whined as he descended. She lowered him until waves smacked his head and each roll of the boat dipped him briefly.

"I want names…now!"

Keith twisted frantically, whimpering.

Hazel's hand hovered over the throttle. "You're not going to make me go backwards, are you?"

She waited for his reply, and through that pause came a faint squeak, almost like a mouse. Or a hiccup.

"Do me a favor," she told Keith. "Just hang there a minute." She stepped into the cabin, closing the door.

Hammon was right where she'd deposited him, taped up and sprawled across the cabin sole. She wasn't happy about leaving him like that, but she was certain he'd get in the way or get hurt if she didn't. He blinked with the sluggish, disoriented look of a sedated puppy.

"Annabel." He gazed up helplessly. "Hazel's gone again, isn't she?"

She said nothing. It was impossible to imagine the effect ketamine had on a damaged brain like his.

"She hates me," he moaned.

Hazel sighed. "She doesn't hate you."

"But she shot me."

"You shot her first."

"To protect her."

"Exactly."

"I have to help her. I'd die for her."

"And that's precisely what we'd like to avoid." She knelt down, brushed the hair back from his face and placed a soft kiss on his forehead. His eyes grew wide, and he smiled a trusting, childlike smile.

"Hazel? You stayed! I don't feel so good. My head feels weird."

"I'm sorry." She ripped off a strip of duct tape, covering his mouth. "Trust me. It's for your own good." She returned to the cockpit, shut the door, and regarded Keith, swinging like a pendulum with each roll of the boat.

"So, what to do with you? No offense, Keith. It's not that I don't trust you…No, actually that's exactly it: I don't, and I can't. There's something you're not telling me. But if you're not going to, there's not much I can do."

"You're going to kill me," he choked.

"Do I have to? Personally, I'd rather not. I'm not the devout Christian you are, but I do know killing is wrong. Then again, you said I'm going to burn in hell anyways, so I might as well just run this boat back and forth till you're chum." She reached for the winch. "You've already got your reservations booked in heaven so you've got no worries, and we'll certainly make the striped bass happy."

"No!" Keith sputtered.

Hand on the switch, she paused. "Why not?"

"I can get you the money, it's in a storage center!" he shrieked between waves. "I know where, but I don't have the key."

Now she was getting somewhere. "And what trusting soul does?"

"Valerie," he said, his voice awash in humiliation.

That wasn't the answer she'd expected, though in hindsight it did connect a number of dots. "I'm listening."

"She told me about Nelson's operation. She had a copy of the route Atkins was supposed to drive. She said if I took the truck we'd have their money and it would destroy Nelson." Keith stared across at Hazel, ashamed. "She came to me after you rejected me. She'd learned her husband was unfaithful, she was crying, and..." His voice faded.

Hazel sighed. "Let me guess. She wanted to get even with Nelson, and she put her hand down your pants."

"I was weak," he sobbed.

"No." Hazel grumbled, furious with herself for not seeing it sooner. "Valerie needed a driver and she used you. You were set up. She tried the same act with Micah, but he didn't go for it. All she wanted was the money. We don't. It's caused nothing but pain. All Micah and I want is to set things right and be safe again."

Her hand dropped from the winch and she turned away. She knew what she had to do and it wasn't going to be easy or pleasant. It was Micah's idea; he insisted she could pull it off. She turned back to Keith.

"I'm so sorry. I didn't want to do this, but I didn't know what else to do. I've been so scared. Everyone is trying to hurt us. I didn't know where to turn anymore. And when I came to you... hoping you could help me, protect me...*needing* you..." Her voice wavered, and she wiped imaginary tears.

"You were with...with *her*." She looked to him in anguish. "I want to trust you, Keith, but I'm so scared. I need you, I realize that now. You told me once if I open my heart to Jesus, he'd forgive me. But can you? Is it too late for us? Could you show me the way of the Lord? Can you be like Jesus?"

She wasn't sure whether it was too much inhaled seawater and prolonged upside-down dangling affecting his brain, or, as Micah theorized, Keith was genuinely obsessed with winning her undefiled body and heathen soul. She never believed she'd pull it off with a straight face, and she never figured Keith would buy it, but as Micah predicted he took the bait, hook, line and sinker. His face glowed with rapturous delight. "Yes!"

"Truly?"

"Yes! Do you know how long I've prayed to hear you say those words?"

"Oh, Keith! You can't imagine how much that means to me!" She removed the phone from her pocket. "Did you hear that, Micah? You were right! Everything's going to work out just fine!"

With everyone at the beach or anchored on the water to watch the miles of fireworks shows visible from the bay, the Leonardo docks were all but vacant. *RoadKill* waited, reassuring in its offen-siveness, and Hazel smiled when she read the side of the trailer, where reflective red letters stated: "SAFETY IS MY GOAL."

"Is that Micah?" Keith's clothes were beginning to dry, but he was still shaky and his voice hoarse from his ordeal, which included a bout of seasickness on the way in.

"It looks that way." Hazel guided *Revenge* alongside, snub-bing off the spring line. She secured the other lines, shut the engine, and went ashore, opening the trailer. The light from the docks slanted into the empty interior. Perfect. But where was Atkins?

In the distance, the sky flashed green. A whistle shrieked and the air shook with the deep thumps of reports.

"Keith," she called sweetly, climbing up into the trailer. "Come give me a hand with this."

Outside the truck, the sky crackled magnesium-white. Keith climbed up beside Hazel and looked around the trailer in confusion.

"There's nothing here." He backed up nervously as the wrecked Dakota pulled up, a single misaligned headlight flood-ing the trailer. Hazel cursed under her breath; she'd been so dis-tracted, she totally forgot about the damned tracker in the boat. Gary stepped out, looking from her to *Revenge*.

"Where's Hammon?"

Uneasy, Keith looked from Gary to Hazel, eyes widening as he spotted the pistol and a dart struck his thigh. He yanked it out, holding it up. "What's going on?"

"It's called Karma." Hazel stepped back as he staggered toward her. "We've been hunted, my dad nearly died, and the whole time you stood by and did nothing. Far as I know, Jesus never said 'screw onto others.'"

Keith crumbled to his knees, fury building in his eyes. "You… lied…"

"Casting stones? I really don't think you're qualified, and I'm pretty sure salvation isn't a license to sin." Hazel pulled duct tape from her backpack, wrapping his wrists, ankles, and mouth as he stared up, eyes glazing. "Christ may forgive you, Keith, but I don't."

She jumped down, her attention turning to Gary, who scrambled backwards.

"Relax," she told him. "I'm running low on darts. I'd rather not waste any on you if I don't have to."

He glanced nervously at Keith. "Who's that?"

"My ex-boyfriend. What are you doing here?"

"Zap texted me, sort of. He said 'hekp.' Where is he?"

"Safe and sound aboard *Revenge*." She peaked into *Road-Kill*'s cab. Keys hung in the ignition but Atkins wasn't there. The back of her neck prickled as she scanned the shadows while Gary watched her warily.

"Zap just wants to help you."

"And he's going to get himself killed in the process."

She walked past, and Gary's protest fell silent as he turned to find Atkins's discolored eye fixed on him and a rifle aimed at his skull. Behind them, the air rumbled with thudding explosions, triggering distant car alarms. Atkins remained rock-steady.

"You want I shoot him, kid?"

Hazel shook her head. "This poor guy's just an innocent bystander. He won't cause trouble." She glared at Gary. "Right?"

Atkins lowered the rifle, and Gary scrambled aboard *Revenge*. Hazel looked to Atkins. "Where were you?"

"Watering the bushes. Looks like you had things under control." Atkins peered into the trailer. "Preacher Keith, eh? Never did trust that holier-than-thou jackass." He glanced at the pistol in her hand. "You killed him?"

"No." She held the tranquilizer gun up to the light for Atkins to examine. "He's more useful alive." Hazel jumped down to the dock and climbed aboard *Revenge* as bursts of light filled the sky.

"What's with your neck? Keith done that?"

Hazel touched the shallow slash. "No. It was an accident."

Atkins climbed aboard. "Where's Micah?"

"Let's get moving and we'll talk. Give me a hand with this." She disconnected the power and removed bolts locking the freezer to the deck chocks, passing dock lines beneath it. "I need to load it in the truck." She lowered the block from the boom. She could feel Atkins watching her even as she stared down, concentrating on securing the lines. He started to speak when Hammon stumbled out of the cabin with Gary behind him. Atkins raised his rifle and Hazel pushed it down. "Leave him be. He's harmless."

Hammon looked from Atkins to Hazel in bewilderment.

"I'm leaving," she whispered.

Hammon flinched as the sky flashed blue-white. "But...you can't go."

Hazel turned away. She couldn't bear seeing the pain in his eyes. "I have to. Don't stop me, and don't follow me." Her throat tightened. "I don't want to see you again, ever."

"You can't go," Hammon choked, stepping between her and the freezer. Sparkles of white shot over the trees.

Gary looked uncomfortably from Hazel to the freezer. "Zap, just let her go."

He didn't move. Atkins raised his rifle, taking aim at Hammon's heart. "I'd listen to your friend there."

Hazel grabbed the barrel, pointing it away. She turned to Atkins, eyes damp. "Please, don't. Let's just load the truck and go."

The air resonated with thumps, and brilliant flares of color reflected off the water. Hammon's eyes flickered from Hazel to nothing. "But…" He stared into the darkness. "I told her…" He reached for Hazel's hand. "Please…"

She pulled back, shaking her head as the sky burned red.

Atkins said, "Back off, son. Now ain't the time."

Hammon looked at the freezer, the lines beneath it forming slings, then he stared into nothing, color draining from his face. "No…" He turned to Hazel as she blinked back tears. "Annabel says…" Dread reflected in his face. "When you were talking to Micah, you weren't on the phone, were you?"

"NO!" she cried, trying to pull him back as he lifted the lid.

"Holy shit." Gary staggered backwards. Atkins pulled his baseball cap off, shaking his head. "I was afraid of that…"

Eyes closed, head resting on a box of Popsicles, surrounded by daylilies and wild roses, Micah looked almost tranquil. Hazel fell to her knees beside the freezer, trembling as the sky erupted in color.

"He said he was fine." A sob escaped her lips, tears welled up, and she squeezed her eyes shut, fighting the agonizing memory. "He wouldn't listen to me! I tried to…I couldn't stop the blood."

She couldn't hold it together anymore as she remembered Micah laughing. Just a little hole, he'd said, nothing serious. But under his back, warmth pulsed from him. She could still see the lightning cracking overhead, illuminating the darkness spreading over the cockpit as she cradled him across her lap. She begged him to get up; she couldn't lift him. She tried to call 911, shielding her phone to keep it from shorting in the torrential rain, but the signal was too weak to complete the connection. The cockpit was slippery with blood, but Micah didn't see it. He grinned, squeezing her hand weakly. His touch was ice, the chill running like a current between them. She couldn't find where to put pressure, and she couldn't stop the bleeding. Micah leaned back across her legs and closed his eyes, a lazy, relaxed smile drifting across his face. She knew he was dying, and she was dying with him; her heart was being crushed, and she was helpless to hold him back. His blood ran through her fingers, running until his heart stopped while she held him, rocking him, begging him not to leave her, screaming in anguish as rain pounded down, draining through the scuppers, washing the cockpit clean, leaving her there alone with that sickening emptiness.

"Hazel…?" Hammon said, pulling her violently back to the present. There was no more denying the awful reality or the crushing helplessness she'd been blocking. A cascade of stars shot overhead, showering fading trails across the water. She stared at Hammon, tears streaming down her face.

"*Just let me go!*" she shouted. She knew she was only lashing out in pain, but she also knew if she broke down now, if she ran to him and buried herself in his arms, she'd never resurface. It wasn't over yet. There was still too much to do. She stroked Micah's icy cheek, then closed and latched the lid.

"Hazel…" Hammon said.

"Stay away from me, Otto," she said through clenched teeth. "You'll live longer that way."

She started the winch. The freezer rose into the air, lit by the backdrop of crackling red stars, and Atkins guided the boom across to the trailer. She lowered the freezer, and Atkins unhooked the block, swinging the boom back and closing the trailer. Glock in her right hand, dart gun in the left, Hazel climbed off *Revenge*, and Hammon scrambled clumsily ahead, blocking her path. She wiped her eyes, trying to rub away the stinging.

"Otto, get out of my way. I'm leaving and I don't want you following me."

Hammon blinked, eyes flickering from her to emptiness and back, and he stiffened as the air shook and thumped. "I won't let you go."

Gary tried to pull him back. "Stop, Zap. You're playing with lightning, and you're too dense to see it."

Overhead, the sky echoed with explosions.

"I'm sorry." Hazel raised the Glock.

"Shit!" Gary ducked. Hammon winced but stood fast, resisting Gary's efforts to pull him clear. Hazel fired three rapid shots, and the Dakota settled lower as three tires deflated. She turned to Atkins. "Let's go."

They started toward *RoadKill*, freezing as a figure bolted out from behind the cab, out of breath, gun raised.

"Joe!" Hazel gasped. How did he get there? He must have tailed Atkins. She'd planned to face Joe, but she wasn't ready yet; this was too soon. Hammon grabbed her and pulled her against him.

"That's the guy I took the dart gun from. He's got a sea monster on his arm."

"Jesus H. Christ." Atkins raised his rifle. "Who in hell didn't get an invitation to this damn funeral?"

"You two again." Joe looked from Atkins to Hammon with disgust. "You, drop the gun, and you, give me Hazel."

"Like hell," Atkins said, advancing.

"Last warning," Joe said.

"Likewise," Atkins replied, remaining steady.

Joe let out a sigh and lowered his gun and raised his left hand in what appeared to be surrender, then sprayed Atkins with a small canister. Atkins doubled over, eyes squeezed shut, gasping and coughing convulsively.

"It's pepper spray," Joe said, pistol raised and aimed toward Hammon. "He'll live. Give me Hazel and you will too."

Hammon moved around her and acted as a shield. "You'll have to shoot me first."

"Fine by me, sport." Joe advanced, sights on Hammon.

Hazel pushed Hammon aside and leveled the Day-Glo Glock at Joe. She was furious that her hand was unsteady, furious that she felt so emotional. She couldn't afford to be, not now.

"*Why*, Joe?" She was shaking, and tears streamed down her cheeks despite her anger. Still blinded and coughing uncontrollably, Atkins struggled to stand.

"Haze, settle down," Joe said with the same patient tone he'd used when she was little. "You're upset."

"Upset?!" She almost laughed in spite of everything, and strangely that helped her regain some composure. "You're working with Stevenson! You're damned right I'm upset!"

He didn't even trying to deny it. "There's more to it than you understand."

"Then explain it to me, Joe. Help me understand why you'd betray us." She stepped toward him, gun no longer trembling. "Explain to me why Micah had to DIE!"

Joe's gun dropped ever so slightly. "Micah's dead?"

Hearing him say that only seemed to drive home the truth she'd been trying to block, and all the pain and rage she'd held back. Hazel took a deep breath, steadying herself. She planted her feet the same way Joe taught her so many years ago, and she pulled the trigger. A stunned look crossed his face as he went down.

"Yes, Joe. Micah is dead."

She turned to find herself looking at three shocked faces. Hammon's mouth hung open but no sound came out; Gary's eyes were on her, wide with horror as he yanked at Hammon's arm, trying to drag him back; Atkins was still on the ground coughing uncontrollably, leaking profusely from his eyes, nose, and mouth, but beneath that Hazel could still see the shock in his expression.

Beyond the trees the sky erupted in a finale of colors and noise. Hazel bolted to *RoadKill*; she had to get away from there. She started the truck, released the brakes, and put it into gear. She didn't look back.

IT'S ALL MY FAULT

Hammon watched the Kenworth disappear into the night, and he knew he'd failed. He fell back against the wounded Dodge and screamed. Nothing in particular, just screamed. And continued screaming until Gary tried to grab him.

"Christ, Zap, hold it down!"

Hammon howled, swinging blindly, striking out at Gary as every ounce of frustration boiled over.

"Stop it!" Annabel shouted. "What the hell are you doing?"

Fist raised, he froze, then staggered backwards.

"Don't you get it? Micah got shot helping me! They were safe. They weren't supposed to turn back." He sank to the ground beside the Dakota. "*I* should be dead, not Micah. If I was dead, things would be better."

"I'm not so sure," Annabel said. "Once you're dead you wouldn't be able to help."

"She doesn't want my help; I'm useless." He banged his head against the door. He needed to feel something, anything, beside the sick emptiness sucking him under.

"That isn't helping," Annabel snapped, fading slightly with each impact.

"Don't start that shit." Gary grabbed his arm, dragging him clear of the Dodge. "There's enough dents already. And stop being stupid. When she shot that guy…" He gave a queasy glance at the body on the ground then circled to the other side of the Dodge. "She was protecting you."

Hacking, Atkins struggled to his feet and joined Gary. "He's right. If you still got a pulse, that little girl must like you. And trust me, she don't like most people."

Gary turned to Atkins. "Who are you? Who," he pointed toward Joe, "was that? Who's she got in the trailer? Would someone please tell me what the fuck's going on?" He paused, looking everything over. "On second thought, don't tell me. I don't want to know, I just want to leave."

"You!" Hammon sprang to his feet, clutching Atkins by the shirt. "You were helping her! You know where she's going!"

Atkins rubbed his tearing eyes. "Sorry, son. I wish I did. She never got round to telling me. I don't think she knows anymore." Atkins looked over the Dakota. "And unless you got three spares, we ain't goin' nowhere."

"We've got to find her." Hammon limped between the dock and the pickup. "She needs help."

"Why us? Why not call the cops?" Gary pulled his phone from his pocket.

"You can't!" Hammon jumped him, grappling frantically to pry the phone from Gary's hand.

"Why in hell not? What's wrong with you? There's a dead guy right there…that girl's driving around with a corpse in a *freezer*, for God's sake, she's got some other bastard knocked out…god only knows what she's got planned for him, and I'd put money on it before this night's over she'll be hunting down Stevenson. Any sane person…" His voice faded as he looked from Hammon to Atkins. "Well, *I'm* calling nine-one-one."

"And you'll tell the cops what, exactly?" said Atkins, picking up his rifle.

"You really think you're helping her?" Gary shook his head in disgust. "Count me out. Soon as I figure a way to get out of here, I'm gone. You two can have fun chasing that lethal pile of PMS around. This is none of my business, and I don't want it to be." He regarded his disabled truck in disgust. "I wonder how the dead guy got here?"

Atkins shrugged. "I can ask, but he ain't gonna…" He looked back. "What the fuck?"

Hammon turned and studied the empty ground. Joe was gone, gun and all.

"But he was dead…" Gary wondered. "Where…"

Across the lot an engine roared and lights flared as the yellow Chevelle screeched out, never slowing as the taillights disappeared around the bend.

"But she shot him," Gary said. "We saw her shoot him. And that wasn't the dart gun."

"Kevlar," Hammon said. "Stevenson was wearing a vest when he got shot."

Atkins nodded grimly. "Likely. Joe'd know better than anyone the risk of just walkin' up to Hazel."

Hammon stared at the dark road. She was out there alone, with the sea-monster guy close behind. He had to warn her. He dialed the last number she'd called him from, but he knew she wouldn't answer. Of course not. Why would she? He had no idea where she went and no way to track her. He only knew he'd sell his soul to save her.

"I'd say that's your best option," Annabel said. "Hell's officially frozen over. Summon the Evil One; beat some answers out of him."

Hammon pushed his glasses up and stared at the phone in his shaking hand. Seven years ago he'd called Stevenson. It destroyed his life. He lost everything.

"And now he's destroying her life. You have to stop him," Annabel said.

Hammon took a deep breath, swallowed, and entered Stevenson's number. His finger hesitated over the "send" key. Hitting it would be equivalent to signing a contract in blood. But the consequences of not doing it were far worse, and with every second the distance between him and Hazel grew. He pressed down, waiting that eternity for the connection to go through when, as though supernaturally summoned, cool white high beams rounded the corner and the black Mercedes glided up beside the Dakota. Stevenson climbed out, took a drag from his cigarette, and flipped it to the side.

"He truly is evil incarnate," Annabel said in awe.

Stevenson glanced at his ringing phone and silenced it. He regarded Gary, Atkins, and Hammon, the expression on his bruised face grim.

"Where's Hazel? Where's Joe?" He turned to Hammon. "And what the hell are *you* doing here?"

"Stay in control," Annabel whispered.

Hammon stood frozen. Since that fateful call seven years back, he hadn't uttered a single word to Stevenson. Hatred, fear, and anger seethed inside his brain, heating the mercury, itching, burning, reminding him of all he wanted to forget. Stevenson was there—

"Stay in control," Annabel repeated.

—looking for Hazel.

"Stay in control!" Annabel shouted as Hammon lunged, toppling Stevenson backwards and landing several good swings into his Kevlar-armored gut before Gary dragged him off, kicking and flailing.

"Lemme go!" he screamed. "Hazel's right, he sent Joe to get her! Why else is he here?"

Stevenson climbed to his feet and dusted himself off. "You're absolutely right." He scanned the lot and the docks. "Now, where is she?"

"Gone!" Hammon snarled. Stevenson was a dead end; the Evil One had no more idea where she went than the rest of them. "She's gone," he repeated, his last desperate hope shattered.

Stevenson looked from Hammon's scraped-up face and blood-stained clothes to the mangled Dakota, and he broke into a broad grin. "I take it she's upset. Amazing. You two actually managed to find each other, almost without my help, yet I'm betting neither of you know what this is really about."

"I know she's in trouble, and I know you have something to do with it."

"True. Then again, Hazel, by definition, IS trouble. You'll have to be more specific."

Hammon glared at Stevenson. "Micah's dead."

Stevenson's smile vanished. "Dead?"

"Shot," Hammon said, his voice breaking. He turned to Atkins. "Last night they met with you but someone followed…I ran him off the road so they could get away. They were supposed to keep going." Hammon sagged against Gary, the weight of the memory bearing down on him. "They weren't supposed to turn back to help me."

Stevenson grabbed him by the collar. "Who followed them?"

"She's gone." Hammon turned to Annabel. "I don't know where."

Stevenson shook him roughly. "Who followed them? What did he look like?"

"I don't know," Hammon moaned. "It was dark, and there was lightning…lots of lightning, and he was beating the crap out of me. He smiled a lot like, one of those TV news people."

Atkins stepped forward. "Wha'd he drive?"

"Ford Three-fifty pickup, blue, Jersey plates."

"Boat prop on the trailer hitch, right?"

Hammon nodded excitedly. "Yeah!"

"Son'vabitch!" Atkins hacked. "I know where she's headed."

Hope rose in Hammon. "Then we can find her! We'll take his car." Hammon shoved Stevenson away and limped to the driver's door, only to find it locked. Stevenson hit the unlock for the trunk and removed a rifle. Atkins aimed his barrel at Stevenson's head, fixed a watery eye on him, and spat at his feet.

"You heard the kid," Atkins said. "We're takin' your car, whether I got to shoot you to do it or not."

"Keys," Hammon said. "Tell him to give us the keys."

"You heard'm. Keys."

"I thought so," Stevenson replied. "You were helping them. Very noble of you."

Atkins spat again. "Go to hell."

"Later. First we need to find Hazel." He handed Hammon the rifle. "I trust you remember how to use it."

A bitter taste rose in Hammon's throat as he lifted his old competition Anschutz, feeling the balance. He took aim at Stevenson. "I want to know what's going on."

"You're not going to like it," Stevenson walked between the rifles, both aimed at his skull, and unlocked the Mercedes. "Get in and I'll explain. Feel free to shoot me."

22:32 SUNDAY, JULY 4

40°29'53.19"N/74°17'57.54"W

ROUTE 9 NORTHBOUND, SOUTH OF

THE DRISCOLL BRIDGE

It seemed like an eternity though in reality only eight days had passed since Hazel had last driven *RoadKill*. Shooter Jennings still looped in the stereo, ironically back to "4th of July." Her eyes stung as she watched the dark highway unwind in the headlights. She felt bruised and drained, every fiber of her being hurt, but she had to go on, just a little longer. If all went right, by sunrise everything would be over and she could break down. That, or she'd be dead.

Her life had disintegrated, undeniably and irreparably. Micah was dead. She'd never have him tease her again, never hold his hand or listen to him crack jokes and butcher song lyrics. He wouldn't be there to share the future they were supposed to have together. He was gone, and she'd never have the chance to tell him all he meant to her. And Joe…how could he turn against them? She rubbed the tears from her face and recalled Joe's expression as she pulled the trigger; burned forever in her memory. Damn him. It was his own fault. He should have known better.

High beams flashed in her mirrors: a car coming up fast. Her heart went to her throat. She tried to stay calm; not everyone in the world was after her, it only seemed that way. But to her horror Stevenson's yellow Chevelle pulled alongside her left door, horn blasting. The interior light switched on and Joe leaned across, waving for her to pull over. It took her a moment to process what she was seeing, though if there'd been any question left in her mind as to his betrayal, the bright yellow Chevelle he was driving settled it. And he may have known enough to wear body armor, but apparently Joe wasn't smart enough to keep clear of *RoadKill.*

Hazel swung the wheel, crowding him into the median, *RoadKill's* front wheel lugs jackhammering the car's door. Joe gunned it, barely pulling ahead, and she rammed the car, pushing it sideways in front of *RoadKill's* headlights. She jerked the wheel and sent the Chevelle into a spin, skidding down the shoulder, burrowing into the underbrush. She locked the brakes and fought the wheel as the trailer hopped and the cab shuddered, coming to a stop in a cloud of tire smoke.

She grabbed the Glock, watching the Chevelle for reverse lights or an opening door. This time, she resolved, she'd aim for the shine on his bare skull. A single taillight cast a dim red glow on the torn-up grass, otherwise all remained still.

What was he thinking? She would have figured Joe to shoot out her tires or pepper-spray her when he'd sprayed Atkins. It made no sense. Multiple times he'd broken the one rule he'd drummed into her since childhood: the safest defense was to stay out of range. Then again, nothing made sense anymore, and she was too numb to think straight.

Still there was no movement from the car. Was he trying to lure her into the open?

23:49 SUNDAY, JULY 4

40°57'12.77"N/74°04'05.10"W

PARAMUS PARK MALL, PARAMUS, NJ

On the moonless night, it was easier to hide in plain sight than try to conceal the Kenworth. Parked beside the Sears Auto Center at the Paramus Park Mall, *RoadKill*'s silhouette blended with the other rigs and trailers. From the dark cab, Hazel had an unobstructed view of all approaches. At that hour the mall was vacant aside from a lone white sedan, labeled "SECURITY," distinguished by a flashing amber light, slowly making a sweep of the lot.

A silver BMW convertible glided in and parked near the south Sears entrance. Valerie Nelson climbed out and looked around anxiously. It didn't appear she'd been followed. Hazel fired up *RoadKill*, flipping on the high beams, and Valerie spun, eyes wide, as the truck approached. Hazel stretched across the cab, swinging the passenger door open. "Get in."

"What's this about?" Wariness tightened Valerie's features. "What couldn't you discuss over the phone?"

"What Keith told me. We had quite an interesting talk earlier this evening. It took some persuasion, but eventually he explained everything."

Valerie's face wilted. "Where's Keith?"

"He's waiting with Micah. I recorded the whole conversation, if you'd like to hear it. And if anything happens to me, you will. You, Tom, the police, the entire tristate area, tomorrow morning, when a digital copy gets e-mailed to every news network. So here's the deal: our silence in exchange for half the money. Micah and I disappear along with your little secret, and Tom's cash remains lost forever."

It took a moment, but to her credit, Valerie regained some composure. "Sounds fair to me. But I don't think Keith will agree…"

Despite herself, Hazel giggled, which she realized wasn't exactly reassuring. She smiled. "Don't worry, Keith's very agreeable. Get in and we'll talk."

Valerie hesitated, weighing her already limited options, then climbed up, glancing into the empty sleeper as she closed the door. Hazel pulled *RoadKill* onto the service road and turned to Valerie.

"To be honest, woman to woman, I'm impressed. You really screwed over your scumbag husband. Still, I'm curious: how'd you know enough about the operation to pull this off?"

Valerie sat watching the road pass by, her shoulders tight, and her fingers drummed on the door. Finally she leaned back in the seat.

"It's his own fault. Tom brought it on himself; if he'd just kept his fly zipped, none of this would've happened. I've known Tom was cheating for years; it only goes to figure, the prick cheated on his first wife with me. What goes around comes around, but I had a feeling he was getting ready to trade me in. Every night he's down at Hooters, shopping for a newer model. I'm too old to go back to working at that place, and I'll be damned if after the twelve years I've put in I'm going to wind up in some crappy apartment, eating mac-n-cheese while Tom's latest piece of ass moves into the house I remodeled, drives my car, and swims in my pool."

Valerie's words came louder and faster. "If he wanted a divorce, I'd make sure it cost him. Catching him with his pants down was easy; I bought some cell-phone spyware right off the Internet, well worth every cent. I heard a few bimbo calls; I knew where he'd be and when, and I kept records of it all. Then one night I heard Tom arguing with Kessler."

Hazel wove *RoadKill* through local roads running parallel to Route 17 while Valerie clutched her Coach bag and stared at the passing streetlights. Her voice was steady, but she picked unconsciously at her manicured nails. "Kessler was furious, screaming about Tom wasting money and coming up short. From what I heard, they were moving something with appliance shipments, using the stores to make the money—*lots* of money—look legitimate. At least that's how it sounded. I wasn't sure, it was rather cryptic."

So where did Stevenson figure in, Hazel wondered, and why the decoy truck? She'd ask him when his turn came. Valerie continued, looking somewhat pleased.

"All I knew was that Kessler said if Tom ever came up short again, he was dead, and Kessler made it clear he meant that literally. So I watched and waited and listened for more details. And polished the furniture." She grinned. "Lucky thing."

Hazel glanced over. "I don't follow."

"Tom's a slob. You think it'd kill him to put a cup in the dishwasher or use a placemat." Valeria gave a snort of contempt. "He's ruined more furniture with scratches and water rings…One day I'm cleaning up some plates and beer bottles he'd left on the dining room table, and I see faint marks in the finish. He must have written on a sheet of paper, and it transferred straight through.

Locations, times, everything." She laughed derisively. "It was just what I needed; a front-row seat to watch Tom crash and burn, not to mention a nice pile of cash. They had Wayne Atkins driving the delivery. I always wondered why Tom ever hired that disgusting man, but I suppose you need someone like that for these sorts of tasks. I just needed someone to intercept the shipment."

"Keith," Hazel said. Or Micah, but she didn't imagine Valerie would mention that.

"That should have been the simple part. Keith could drive the truck, and he was easy enough to persuade. I told him we'd split the money; I had no idea he had his own agenda."

Hazel nodded. "Ah, yes. Keith's agenda. Praise God."

Valerie fussed with her hair like an anxious cat grooming. "It's the Lord's money now," she said, imitating Keith's tone quite well. "He's *sick*. You were smart—that, or just plain lucky—steering clear of him. He said back before he was Born Again he killed a woman. They met at a club and left together, they were drunk and ended up fighting. He started hitting her, and he didn't stop until she was dead. He said even though police never knew he did it, the guilt was unbearable. And that's when he found Jesus."

Valerie shook her head. "He said Christ forgave him for killing the harlot, and he vowed he'd serve Him from that day forward. I didn't know whether he was confessing or trying to scare me, but either way…" She shuddered.

"Psychos for Jesus." Hazel downshifted, swinging *RoadKill* onto 17 north.

"I was in over my head and I knew it, but I didn't know what to do anymore. Keith made it clear I'd never see one cent; he said he'd make sure that money was used righteously, and I could see he was starting to think I didn't fit into those plans anymore."

Hazel nodded. "Yeah, Keith told me something similar. I guess he figures if Christ paid for our sins, He might as well get His money's worth. He said he realized you manipulated him for your own greed, that you were a whore sent by Satan to lead him astray."

Valerie laughed darkly. "Ah, yes. Whore. He was using that term more and more to describe me, especially after that night you showed up. Until then he was sure you were dead. He was obsessed with you; he'd talk about you constantly, how pure you were, just misguided. And once he knew you were still alive…let's just say our little honeymoon was over. But he's not going to just give up," she warned. "Not with me, not with you, and not with the money."

"Don't worry," Hazel assured her. "The less you know the better, but here's how this works: I take Keith's share, you keep yours, I tell Micah we're all set, and no more Keith problems. Nice and simple. The way I see it, it's a win for everyone. Oh, except for Keith, that is."

"That sounds fair." Even in the darkness of the cab, Valerie's expression visibly brightened. "You know, if anything unfortunate happens to my dear husband, he's got five million in life insurance."

"Your point?"

"Just that if Tom had some sort of accident and I had no more Tom problems, I'd happily share the wealth. Think about it. I can't think of any problem money like that won't solve."

Hazel's grip on the wheel tightened. "I know one."

Valerie laughed bitterly. "Right. Love. Trust me, it's way overrated."

Hazel downshifted and pulled onto the shoulder outside the entrance to a self-storage facility. It was exactly as Keith had described it and would work perfectly for her plans. She set the brakes. "Give me your gate key and wait here," she told Valerie. "Keith said there's only cameras, no guards, but I'd rather not end up on the security tape."

Hazel scouted the front of the building, then slipped out the paintball gun and blinded each security camera. She swiped Valerie's pass card and disabled the rest of the cameras, then returned to Valerie and *RoadKill* and pulled the truck through the gate.

"Right down that row," Valerie directed. "Number seventy-one. There."

Hazel parked beside the unit and killed the engine. She grabbed the backpack and followed as Valerie dug out her keys, unlocked the padlocked unit, rolled up the door, and switched on a fluorescent light. Random appliances were stacked inside and foam fragments littered the floor. A plastic Home Depot bag sat beside *Tuition*'s emergency roadside kit. Hazel opened one of the refrigerators but it was empty.

"Don't worry, it's here." Valerie rolled the refrigerator around, taking a screwdriver from the roadside kit. She pried away the back panel then hacked at the foam insulation beneath. "They hid the money inside the insulation then resealed them with spray foam. I think that's how they moved whatever they were selling as well. Originally, Keith and I planned to leave this all here until after things cooled down or Tom wound up as landfill in the Meadowlands." Valerie removed ten ziplocked bricks of cash, lining them up on top of the refrigerator. "Each one's fifty thousand. Not bad for one night's work."

Five more minifridges and eight air-conditioners lined the back wall. Hazel stared at the stacks of drab green paper, revulsion rising. That miserable space could have been filled to the ceiling and she'd still never hear Micah's laugh or see his grin again.

"And you'll get rid of Keith and Tom?" Valerie turned, gasping as the dart hit her thigh. "What are you doing?" She yanked it out, confused. "But we agreed…" she stammered, panic rising in her voice.

"I never agreed to anything." Hazel put the pistol away, pulled out the recorder, and shut it off. "But don't worry. I'm not taking the money."

Valerie sank to the floor.

"You thought it all out, didn't you?" Hazel said. "Did you ever consider what would happen to Micah when the truck vanished? Or would that mess up your plans?"

"It was supposed to be Atkins," Valerie slurred.

"So I've been told." Hazel reloaded the dart gun, slipping the last two capped darts into her pocket. She picked up the Home Depot bag. Six cans of spray foam, two still full. "But you really didn't care either way, did you? So here's how this works: I'm leaving now, and," she held up the recorder, "I'm calling Tom."

Valerie's lips twitched as she made a futile attempt to speak.

"Oh, one last thing," Hazel said. "You know what all the money in the world can't do?"

She stepped over Valerie's limp body and stared into her semiconscious, slowly blinking eyes. "It can't bring back the dead."

Hazel rolled the door down and locked it.

I'M "IT"

Stevenson was right. Hammon didn't like what he had to say. Hammon listened, saying nothing. This went so horribly beyond the worst he could imagine, it left him speechless even as his brain boiled with all he wanted to say. He lowered his window, watched the passing darkness, and fought to hold down his churning stomach. Any second now he might hurl, but not out the window. Puking inside Stevenson's Mercedes would more accurately express his current mood.

"It does explain a lot," Annabel said, sitting between them.

"That's why I didn't want to tell you," Stevenson said. "You couldn't handle it."

Hammon glared back at him. "Screw you. First we find Hazel. Then we discuss…this." Not that there'd be any discussions. He'd made up his mind; there was nothing to discuss. He wouldn't be a part of it.

"I don't think you have a choice," Annabel said. "Like it or not, you *are* IT."

"We'll see about that."

"See about what?" Atkins said from the backseat.

Stevenson shook his head. "Don't ask."

"That boy's seriously confused, ain't he?"

"I'm not saying a word," Annabel said.

"No one asked you," Hammon said.

Stevenson and Atkins exchanged looks in the rearview.

Annabel said, "Tell them this is a private conversation."

"What conversation? I'm not talking to you either."

"Whoa," Annabel said. "Chill. I'm on your side."

"Trouble in fantasy land?" Stevenson asked.

Head down, Hammon hunched his shoulders. "That'd screw up your plans big time, eh? You're worried I've slipped one gear too many, and you'll never get what you need."

Hammon tried calling Hazel again, but she still wasn't answering, not that he expected she would. The car swerved abruptly, and Hammon looked back to see a chrome bumper lying in the road.

"Looks like that came off a Chevelle, don't it?" Atkins observed.

"A sixty-nine SS, I'd bet," Stevenson replied grimly. "That's my girl. At least we know we're headed the right way."

Hatred surged in Hammon. "She's not your girl."

Ahead, black streaks of rubber led to torn-up grass. Beneath the overgrowth, a single taillight glimmered faintly.

"It's like chasing a tornado," Stevenson said. "Just follow the trail of destruction." He pulled onto the shoulder and rushed over to the Chevelle, wedged within some small bushes, tires slowly revolving in the soft mud. The worst damage was concentrated around the sides and the windshield, which bore a clear imprint of Joe's forehead. Bloody and disoriented, Joe struggled with the door. He looked from Hammon to Atkins and fumbled for his gun.

"It's okay." Stevenson reached in, shifting the car to neutral. "They know the situation."

Joe slumped back in the seat, wiping his face. "Sorry, man. I messed up your ride. Tried to stop Haze but she got away."

"You need a doctor." Stevenson turned to Atkins. "Give me a hand. Let's see if we can get this thing back to the road; maybe it's still drivable. Joe, slide over."

"Stevenson left the Mercedes running," Annabel whispered. Hammon nodded, slowly backing toward the car. Stevenson reached back and grabbed his shirt.

"Where do you think you're going? Get in the Chevelle, and when I say, put it in reverse."

Hammon stood firm. "I'm not taking him anywhere. I'm going after Hazel."

"No. He…" Stevenson pointed to Atkins, "is taking Joe to the hospital, and WE are going after Hazel. Now get in the damned car so we can push."

Arguing was only wasting time. Grudgingly Hammon climbed in, glaring warily at Joe.

"Now!" Stevenson yelled. Hammon put the Chevelle in reverse, gunning it as Stevenson and Atkins shoved the crumpled hood. Tires spun, flinging clods of dirt, then grabbed, jerking and hopping the car over the branches and soft ground. Hammon eased it onto the shoulder, climbing out for Atkins and returning to the Mercedes as the Chevelle clattered away.

The next twenty miles passed without a word. Even Annabel remained silent; Hammon wasn't sure why, but this only made things worse. He drummed his fingers on the dashboard then reached for the radio, only to discover it had been dismantled. He began humming Hampsterdance.

Stevenson looked over, irritation simmering in his eyes. "You just don't get it."

"Get what?" Hammon picked at his fang with his middle finger. "Your obsession with revenge, or the fact that Micah's dead? Was that part of your plans? Then again, what's one more life?

Destroying them is what you do. How about you do everyone a favor and go kill yourself."

It should have been more satisfying seeing Stevenson wince, but it was a hollow victory.

"At least he still has a few nerves to strike," Annabel said.

"Like it makes a difference. He doesn't care; he gets off on manipulating people. He hasn't changed, he never will."

Stevenson's knuckles whitened on the wheel. "Same could be said for you. Still got those demented fangs, still pulling juvenile pranks and talking to imaginary friends. I hoped you would've grown up over the last few years. I should have known by the crickets, nothing's changed."

Hammon turned away. "Everything's changed. Micah's dead. They were safe on the water; they weren't supposed to come back. He came back to help me. I didn't know. She…she talked like he was still alive…"

Stevenson let out a weary sigh. "She's blocking her pain, not letting it stop her, not while there's still work ahead. When she runs out of people to kill, then it's time to worry."

"So her wanting you dead is a good thing."

"You could say that. Apparently she has trouble dealing with loss."

"Asshole. Now I remember why I stopped talking to you."

Stevenson laughed coldly. "You stopped talking to me when you found out I had you killed."

23:45 SUNDAY, JULY 4

40°56'52.89"N/74°04'20.27"W

ROUTE 17 SOUTH, PARAMUS, NJ

With the storage unit locked and the trailer uncoupled, Hazel headed out, driving *RoadKill* bobtail. She hated leaving Micah behind, but she needed to travel light, and the unpleasant truth was that it wouldn't matter to him anymore.

At midnight nearly every trace of central Paramus's vibrant economy had curled up and gone to bed, with one glaring exception: Hooters. Lights glowed bright, through the windows Hazel could see the building was packed to capacity, and the parking lot bustled with an overflow of activity.

She killed the truck's lights and switched off the engine brake as she coasted past and pulled between buildings one lot away. Valerie had confirmed Micah's claim that Hooters was Tom Nelson's favorite haunt. And sure enough, Hazel saw Nelson's dented 350 parked in the reflection of the orange signs.

This was a risky step; if Nelson spotted her, at best it would throw her plans off, and at worst Hazel only hoped the public setting might keep him from shooting before she said her part. Fortunately, no one took notice as she approached the smashed-up Ford 350. Heart pounding, she tucked a note under the pickup's wiper which read MORAN TRUCKING and her cell phone number. She duct-taped a ziplock bag into the corner of the truck's bed then sprinted back to the relative safety of *RoadKill*'s cab, watching her mirrors as she pulled away. It was time to return to the storage unit, finish setting up, and wait.

But not for long. As she backed *RoadKill* into position, the phone lit up, vibrating. This was it. She knew what she needed to say but her stomach fluttered with panic. She took a steadying breath.

"Moran Trucking," she answered in a neutral tone.

There was a nervous hiccup. "Hazel…?" Hammon said, his voice breaking along with her heart.

She slumped back in the seat. "Otto, leave me alone."

"Where are you?"

"You really think I'll tell you that?" She laughed, squeezing her eyes shut, blocking the pain in her chest. "Trust me. You're better off without me."

"Hazel, please. Listen to me. There's something you don't…"

The phone beep-beeped, call waiting. "Good-bye, Otto." She hit END. The phone buzzed like an angry hornet. She hit SEND.

"Micah? You little bastard, you think this is some game?"

"Hello, Tom. I'm going to say this once so shut up, pay attention, and listen carefully. Micah didn't take your shipment and neither did Atkins, but we know who did and where it is. In fact, we have the whole mess locked away in a nice, tidy package. If you'd only worked with us from the start, we could have avoided all this trouble."

"And?" He was suspicious, but listening.

The phone beeped insistently. She ignored it.

"Obviously, you want it back. We want you to go away and leave us alone. We figure the only way that'll happen is if we tell you where it is. And considering the aggravation you put us through, a small finder's fee is in order…say, oh, fifty percent. That's fair, wouldn't you agree?"

She could hear him breathing.

"Consider it a salvage fee," she continued. "Half of what you lost plus our silence is better than all of nothing. The way I see it, you owe us big for what you did to my father, our boat, and Atkins's trailer. So it's fifty percent; either you agree, or we take this information to the police and let them sort it out."

The breathing quickened. Hazel imagined he was working out how he'd go around her little split. Finally he said, "Fine. You want half, you'll get it."

"I figured as much. So here's how it works: We already took our share. The rest, along with the 'masterminds' behind this unpleasantness, are locked up and waiting."

"Where? Who are they?"

The phone beeped again.

"And spoil the surprise? What fun is that? But you'll love this part. You're not on the road yet, are you? Look in the front left corner of your truck's bed. There's a bag with a recorder inside. See it?"

There was a moment of shuffling. "Yeah."

"Listen to it. They give directions and everything. The gate card and keys are in a plastic bag by the gate. We've disabled the security cameras. I'd advise you hurry, before either of our friends get free or make enough noise to attract attention."

"And you and Micah?"

"Already long gone. I told you. You don't bother us, we don't bother you. But try anything stupid, and duplicate recordings go to the police, the news, the Internet; you get the idea. If we go down, we're taking you with us."

I DON'T MEAN THOSE!

"She's not answering," Hammon said in despair. "She won't talk to me."

Stevenson looped the Mercedes around the Nelson & Sons Appliance and Electronics Supersaver Store lot. There was no sign of Hazel or the Kenworth.

"Now what?" Hammon asked Annabel.

"I wish I knew," Stevenson admitted.

Hammon shot him a dirty look. "I wasn't talking to you."

Stevenson sighed. "I see. So what does Annabel suggest?"

"That he go fuck himself. Some help he is." She leaned toward Hammon. "Atkins said she's got that Keith guy in the back of the truck. Why? I think that's the live bait she was talking about."

"That's what worries me."

Stevenson looked over. "Care to include me in the conversation?"

"No." He turned to Annabel. "Didn't Micah talk about somewhere in Paramus his boss hung out?"

"You're asking me?"

"Usually you remember these things."

"Yes. But I wasn't the one banging our head against a Dodge."

Stevenson said, "Where in Paramus?"

Hammon rubbed his forehead. "I can't remember."

"I guess that hasn't changed either."

"And whose fault is that?"

Other than Dunkin' Donuts and the Suburban Diner, that stretch of Route 17 was empty. But farther ahead Hammon saw signs of life. Cars, trucks, and motorcycles filled the lot; through the windows a crowd was visible. Out front, several girls in snug tank tops and orange shorts waved enthusiastically to passing cars, beckoning them to pull in.

"Hooters! Hooters!" Hammon jumped up in his seat, swiveling and pointing as they passed.

Stevenson's jaw tightened. "Really? I expected a little more maturity from you, considering."

"Truck…Hooters…" Hammon stammered, struggling to form a coherent sentence as the bashed-up 350 pulled from the lot. There was no mistaking the Ford; he recognized every dent he'd inflicted.

"Say 'U-turn,'" Annabel calmly directed.

"You turn!" Hammon yelled.

Annabel said, "Say 'The psycho that shot Micah is pulling out of Hooters right now.'"

"That psycho shot Micah!" He pointed frantically. "There!"

Stevenson floored it, whipping through the jughandle. "You're sure?"

"Positive. Faster…you're losing him."

"I'm not losing him. I'm staying back. I suspect he's headed right toward a certain helpless little girl and a very nasty trap."

Lying on top of the disconnected trailer, set parallel to the vine-strewn eight-foot chain link fence bordering the lot, provided Hazel an uncomfortable but unobstructed view of the entrance gate and unit seventy-one. From ground level her prone silhouette would blend into the backdrop of trees that bordered the property's overgrown perimeter. Darkness covered much of the lot; she'd shot out all but one of the flood lights, leaving only a deliberately small circle of light illuminating the drive separating the trailer from the building. Behind the trailer, outside the fence, four saplings bent downwards, their straining trunks bowed over with the aid of *RoadKill*. Beyond view, the Kenworth waited on the far side of the building, buried in the shadows between two RVs.

The trailer shook faintly as Keith indulged in one of his occasional struggles to free himself, and an odd sound, almost like a cat wailing, carried across the lot. Valerie was coming around, moaning for help.

Leaving the money went against the Travis McGee code, but Hazel didn't care. This had never been about the money, not for her. It had been about protecting her family, and there she'd failed. Now it was about avenging them, taking down everyone responsible for what had happened to her father and Micah. Once she had Nelson, she'd decide what to do about Stevenson and Joe; she still hadn't figured their places in this operation, but she was determined to see things through to the end, whatever that might be.

A set of lights slowed on the highway, breaking from the sparse traffic, and Hazel sank down as the 350 pulled up to the gate. The driver's door opened and the interior light came on as Nelson stepped out to retrieve the gate pass. There was no one else visible inside the truck, which still didn't guarantee he was alone. Nelson's left arm was bandaged, likely from Micah's gunshot, but the injury looked minor.

Nelson drove in slowly and parked beside the unit. Hazel slid back, listening as the 350's door slammed. Beneath her Keith thumped around like a fish in a cooler as one set of footsteps approached. In the corner of her eye, she saw movement near the gate; by the time she turned it was gone. Had Nelson brought company, perhaps even Stevenson? It was possible, not that she was worried. There were enough snares to go around. She heard Nelson open the trailer and laugh.

"I'm impressed, Keith. Screwing my wife right under my nose and fucking me over. I didn't know you had it in you. And you almost pulled it off, but it looks like that little Moran girl played you good."

Nelson only had to step inside and she'd have him. Hazel waited for the sound of the sapling snapping straight. Instead, a gunshot echoed and the thrashing ceased. Footsteps moved away.

Nelson had dealt with Keith more abruptly than she'd expected, and unwittingly dodged her first trap in the process.

Still, three other snares awaited, and she had the Glock and the dart gun. Hazel didn't want Nelson's end to come from an unseen bullet: that would be too easy. She wanted him to suffer, and she wanted him to know why. It was vengeance now, pure and simple. It would never bring back Micah, but that wasn't going to stop her. She wondered if she was turning into something worse than those she hunted. If by night's end she'd finished off Nelson, Joe, and Stevenson, what would remain of the person she once was? But she couldn't dwell on that, not while she still had work ahead.

Inside the storage unit, Valerie, no doubt fully awake now and panicked by the sound of gunfire, began screaming, luring Nelson straight toward another snare. In her peripheral vision, Hazel saw movement: a figure hobbled through the shadows along the fence, a faint light reflecting off his glasses as he stalked Nelson. Hammon was moving toward the trailer and the unit, heading straight into a minefield of high-tension snares. He was going to get himself killed trying to rescue her.

She should have disabled him when she'd had the chance; then he wouldn't have followed her and at least he'd be safe. She could shoot him with a tranquilizer dart, but even if it did penetrate his layers of clothes, it wouldn't immobilize him fast enough and he'd be left helpless and exposed.

Nelson was walking toward the storage unit, drawn by Valerie's frantic pleas, as Hammon slipped beside the trailer stalking Nelson. Hazel silently slid herself to the edge, peeled off a strip of caulking, and winged it at him. Hammon paused, glancing around anxiously.

"Otto," she whispered, praying he'd hear and Nelson wouldn't.

"Not now." He rubbed his forehead.

Hazel's voice caught in her throat as Valerie's cries amplified. Nelson would be steps away from one snare; once

Hammon cleared the trailer after him, he'd be closing in on Nelson and another. She could shoot Nelson, but if Hammon ducked for cover in the shadows, odds were he'd end up horribly snared. She put the dart gun into the backpack, tucked the Glock into her coat pocket, and eased down the back of the trailer, pulse racing as she stepped in front of Hammon.

"Otto, stop," she said, barely audible.

He looked at her, shaking his head, then slipped past as though she didn't exist. He narrowly missed the closer snare but headed straight toward the next. Nelson was only ten yards away, his back to them at the unit's door as he pulled the card key from his pocket. She circled around Hammon, blocking his path.

"Stop," she mouthed, eyes on Nelson as she drew the Glock.

"Annabel, quit it. Hazel's…"

Over Valerie's screams, Nelson still hadn't heard them. Hazel stepped against Hammon, pressing her fingers to his lips. His eyes widened, and she could see the gears shifting.

"Hazel…"

She leaned toward his ear. "I told you not to follow me."

"I had to find you," Hammon said—a bit too loudly, at the very moment Valerie decided to stop screaming. Nelson spun, gun raised, to find himself staring into the barrel of the Day-Glo Glock Hazel aimed rock-steady at the center of his head. With only five yards separating them, neither would have any trouble taking the other out. Time seemed to freeze, and a cold sweat ran down her back. She hadn't planned for this; she was no longer hidden or out of range, and in that millisecond when Nelson's focus shifted and the smell of cigarette smoke drifted past, she knew she'd failed. An arm closed around her throat and pulled her backward as the Glock was yanked from her grip. The cool muzzle pressed beneath her jaw, forcing her to look up at Stevenson's chilling smile.

"Good work, Hammon," Stevenson said. "I had my doubts at times, but you came through in the end." He turned his attention to Nelson. "Tom Nelson, right? You mind lowering your gun, considering I just saved your life? I knew this," he stroked Hazel's cheek with the barrel, "was hiding somewhere. It was simply a matter of using the right bait to lure her out."

Was that why Hammon was there? She didn't want to believe it, but as he stood by, watching with detached indifference, clearly unconcerned by the gun to her head, her heart sank.

"Poor thing." Stevenson's strangle hold remained firm. "You almost pulled it off, didn't you? Things were going perfectly until you risked your pretty little neck to save Hammon's. Don't feel bad, we all have our weaknesses."

A low roar had been building inside her skull, like a distant waterfall, and the sweat from Stevenson's arm burned the cut on her throat. Her fingers found her knife and she flicked it open as Stevenson squeezed harder and everything turned a dim red.

"Hammon," he said wearily, "she's still armed."

Hammon removed the knife from her hand as her grip slackened and air became more a priority than a fight.

"I'll take this too," Hammon said, reclaiming his backpack as the roaring in her head grew deafening. Her lungs ached, the ground tilted, and only Stevenson's choke hold kept her from falling as her world swam into grayness.

"Behave," Stevenson warned, his arm loosening just enough for her to breathe. Hazel gulped and coughed, filling her starved lungs. Hammon inventoried his backpack, removing the dart gun.

"Who *are* you people?" Nelson demanded. His gun remained fixed on them, his expression suspicious and uncertain.

"Jake Stevenson. And I understand you've already had a run-in with my associate, Hammon. I've been trying to speak with you regarding some business, but this delightful little creature kept complicating matters."

Nelson scanned the shadows uneasily. Other than the sound of Valerie scraping at the door with something metallic, trying to pry it open, all was still. "So where are Micah and Atkins?"

"I've already dealt with Atkins," Stevenson assured him. Hazel's eyes stung and she squeezed them closed; Atkins was only trying to help, and now he'd paid for it. "And Micah's lying dead in the freezer in that trailer over there, shot by you last night, I'm told. Truly heartbreaking; he died in her arms. Why do you think she set this little ambush?"

"Is that so?" Nelson grinned at Hazel. "I should thank you, catching that dumb bitch and Keith for me. So let me see if I understand. I kill them, you kill me, get yourself some payback and the money. Was that your plan?"

"Go to hell," she said softly. "All of you."

Stevenson laughed. "Enchanting, isn't she?" The gun moved from her jaw as he touched the blood on his arm, still loose around her neck, then lifted her chin, inspecting the cut. "Hammon, care to explain?"

He shrugged. "It was an accident."

"You wanted to talk business," Nelson said impatiently. "So talk."

Stevenson nodded. "This operation of yours: it's obvious you have distribution connections but you also have management problems. If a little thing like this," he lifted a lock of Hazel's cropped hair, "can disrupt things to this extent, you obviously lack a disciplined team. I believe with some restructuring, we could both profit very nicely."

The nearest snare was off to their right, a few feet back. Stevenson had relaxed his hold and Hazel made a quick jump to escape, knowing his arm would only tighten back into a controlling choke hold, pulling her back against his chest. But now she'd shifted their angle to where she wanted, and she shoved backwards with all her strength, hoping he'd catch the tripwire. She almost succeeded; Stevenson took a quick step to keep his balance, but not far enough. She tried again, managing to inch him further back. Stevenson squeezed her throat and pressed his face to her cheek, his stubble coarse and painful. "Stop the nonsense or you'll regret it."

She pushed back again, but he was ready and it was like trying to move a wall. He lifted her chin, twisting her head painfully.

"Such a fierce little thing. Look at the intensity of that hatred." He smiled darkly. "You need to watch your step around her. Isn't that right, princess?"

"She's a problem," Nelson said. "We have to get rid of her; she knows too much."

"True." Stevenson caressed Hazel's cheek. "But I have some personal plans for this one first. And besides, she's still useful in other ways. I hate to say, you've left one hell of a sloppy trail. Burning that old sailboat, Atkins's trailer, shooting her father, her cousin, and Keith; those things draw unwanted attention."

Stevenson paused for a moment, considering. "Now, our sociopathic little friend here could write a suicide note explaining how she killed her disapproving family, only to learn that her beloved Keith was unfaithful. Poor thing, she already has a documented history of instability and violence; a multiple-murder/suicide would seem perfectly believable."

"You'll never make me write that," Hazel informed Stevenson, her voice strained with loathing.

His fingers traced tenderly along her chin. "Princess, you can't begin to imagine the things I'm going to make you do. We're going to have so much fun together, you and I."

She squeezed her eyes shut, fighting not to let herself cry. Backed to Stevenson as she was, he couldn't see her tears, but she knew he could feel her shaking with rage and frustration.

"We'll need to hammer out a few details," Nelson said, "but I think we can work together. From what I understand, the cash from the last shipment is supposed to be in that unit over there with my lovely wife," he motioned toward the building. "Unless our friend here is pulling another cute stunt. I'd like to inspect it all and make sure everything's in order."

"Good idea." Stevenson turned to Hammon, still holding the dart gun. "That loaded?"

"Yup."

"Perfect. Stand right here and don't move one inch. Watch her. She tries anything, shoot her."

Stevenson nodded to Nelson. "After you."

Hazel rubbed her bruised throat. "Otto, please…" She searched his eyes for any trace of the boy she'd met under the stars, the one who more than once stood on the wrong end of a gun to protect her, but he only watched her with disinterest.

"You promised you'd help me," she said, not sure whether she meant it as a plea or an accusation.

He merely shrugged. "And you believed me."

Hazel froze, stunned. He might as well have struck her.

Valerie must have given up on trying to pry her way out; she began pounding futilely on the door, the clattering drowning out Stevenson and Nelson's hushed discussion, which concluded with a handshake. Stevenson glanced at Hazel, his face lit momentarily by the flare of the match raised to his cigarette. He stood back, waiting as Nelson unlocked the storage unit and rolled the door up. Valerie shrieked hysterically, Nelson fired, and there was silence. Nelson started to step through the unit doorway and was whipped backwards twelve feet by the stored force of the bent sapling, the snare slicing into his flesh and pinning him against the trailer, where the wire leading to the tree ran between the tires. He tried to scream, but the pressure compressed his chest and left him barely able to breathe. Stevenson took a long drag on his cigarette as a puddle spread beneath Nelson.

"Wow," Hammon said. "That's gonna leave a mark."

This was her chance to run; Hammon was distracted and the dart gun only worked at close range. She knew where the other traps were, he didn't. But Stevenson was watching her, an icy gleam in his gold eyes, and she knew she wouldn't get far. "That," he told Hammon, "could have been either of us."

Stevenson walked to the opposite side of the trailer, and Hazel heard each sapling spring free as Stevenson safely released each remaining snare.

Nelson looked to Hammon. "Hel…mm…"

Hammon said, "I bet he'd give up all that money right now just to live."

Nelson's eyes widened and he nodded feebly.

Stevenson considered and turned to Hammon. "How much do you think is in there?"

"A lot. A whole lot."

Stevenson turned to Hazel. "And you? What do you think?"

There weren't words to express her thoughts, and her mouth was too dry to spit. Slowly she approached Nelson, studying how the wire sliced clear to the bone on one arm and buried itself within his chest on the other side. A little more tension might have cut him clean in two. Nelson's head bobbed weakly, desperation in his eyes as he gasped like a dying fish.

Stevenson rubbed his face. "So, princess, now what?"

She didn't reply, and he made no attempt to stop her as she walked to the unit and picked up a can of spray foam lying on the floor next to Valerie's corpse. The horror in Nelson's eyes as she approached, the nozzle raised toward his gaping mouth, almost brought a smile to her face. He thrashed feebly and tried to scream. Stevenson let out a long sigh and pulled Hazel's arm away.

"Interesting choice, but I can't let you do that." He took the can from her and wiped it down with a rag.

"Why not? He's dead either way, and you've got your damned money."

"You think this is about the money? You still haven't figured it out, have you?"

"Then what is it about?"

Stevenson smiled the same chilling way she'd seen in her nightmares; that eerie cemetery smile. "You."

Run, her mind screamed. But like the nightmares, she couldn't move.

"There's something else you should know." He pulled on a pair of latex gloves.

She couldn't speak.

"This," he held up the can, "works better when you shake it." He turned to Hammon. "You're positive she disabled the cameras."

Hammon nodded. "Every one I saw."

Stevenson stepped over to Nelson and patted him down, retrieving his cell phone and the recorder Hazel had left for him.

He listened to the recorder for a moment then passed it to Hammon. "Get her in the car and stay there with her. Now."

Hammon grabbed her arm again and pulled her. She stumbled along, feeling in her pocket for a dart, slipping it from its cover. She could easily outrun Hammon, and while one dart might not knock Stevenson out, it would slow him enough for her to reach *RoadKill*.

Hammon stopped to watch as Nelson tried to resist the nozzle Stevenson forced in his mouth. Nelson's gurgling moans faded to a sickening hiss and then nothing. He writhed, nostrils flared, eyes bugging, mouth moving silently as foam extruded from his mouth like slow, sticky vomit. Hazel's fingers closed cautiously around the shaft of the dart.

"That stuff expands," Hammon remarked as a glob bubbled from Nelson's nose. "A lot. And it hardens."

Stevenson glared at him. "I said get her in the car."

Hammon still stood, watching in curious disgust as Nelson's face turned purple and he convulsed, bucking violently. Stevenson charged over and grabbed Hazel by the arm, yanking her hand from her pocket and turning her forcibly away. She gasped as the sting in her hip registered and the familiar burning, tingling numbness began to spread.

"And him?" Hammon asked behind her.

"Leave him," Stevenson snarled.

He bumped the gate release with his elbow, revealing the Mercedes parked off to the side. Stevenson opened the trunk and Hazel pulled back in a panic, scratching at his hand to get free. He chuckled darkly.

"That's probably not a bad idea." Stevenson laid the guns in the trunk. "But I figured you'd be more comfortable in the backseat." He held the door open. "Get in the car, princess. It's over."

I WANT TO DIE

Hammon stared ahead as his world unraveled, shredding like a tattered flag in a hurricane. Each death he'd died—burning, bleeding, drowning, lightning—had been mere practice for this moment and the pain of his heart slowly ripping itself apart.

"Where are you taking me?" Hazel whispered faintly from the backseat, as though it took all her strength to ask. She sounded so diminished. Hammon had to turn away so Stevenson wouldn't see him cringe.

"Tell her," Stevenson said.

Hammon's hand clenched into a fist. He stared out at the road, fighting not to look back or acknowledge her presence. "This was your brilliant idea. You tell her."

He could hear her rapid breathing and he could feel her confusion radiating through the car. He wanted to hold her and tell her this wasn't what it seemed.

It was worse. Much worse.

Stevenson glanced into the backseat then dialed his cell. "It's done," he said tersely. "Yeah. We've got her...No, nothing to discuss over the phone...Okay, good. We'll talk later." He snapped the phone closed, staring ahead.

Pain boiled through Hammon's brain, and he writhed in his seat. He knew not to turn around and look at her, it would only make things worse, but he couldn't help it. She seemed so small and fragile, eyes closed, curled into a defensive little ball beneath Stevenson's jacket, and the stabbing in his chest overrode the pain in his head.

Annabel glared at him. "Talk to her, you heartless bastard."

He couldn't. If she hated him, if she never forgave him, he could live with that. It was better that way. He winced as the mercury seared within his skull.

"Better for who?" snapped Annabel. "She's terrified, you sadistic son of a bitch. She trusted you. How can you do this to her?"

The temperature must have risen another fifteen degrees. Sweat soaked his hair and clothes as he fought to block Annabel from taking control. He knew that was what she wanted, to take over, to tell Hazel everything, but he couldn't let her. He was going to pass out if he didn't get out of there soon.

"You can end this," Annabel whispered. "Just tell Stevenson it's in the snow."

"*What* snow?" Hammon clapped his hands over his ears. "It's the goddamned Fourth of July!"

Hazel didn't move and Stevenson stared ahead, focused on the road, not speaking for the rest of the drive back to his house. He parked roughly beside the kitchen door, shut the car, and glared at Hammon.

"Knock off the damned humming; it's getting on my nerves." Stevenson turned to the backseat. "Ride's over, princess."

Hazel blinked and gazed around with a disoriented expression, shaking ever so slightly. Hammon stared out the passenger window.

"Let's go," Stevenson snapped at him.

"You don't need me for this."

"No, you dense little shit." Stevenson looked like he wanted to hit something. Or someone. "I don't. But you're coming anyway."

"You seem to have the situation well in hand. As usual."

"Don't start."

Hammon climbed out, slamming the door. "What makes you think I ever stopped?"

Stevenson opened the back door and waited, but Hazel didn't move. Finally he reached in, guiding her out and to her feet. Eyes unfocused, she swayed and stared around the darkness passively, stepping toward Hammon, reaching out for him. He backed away and she stumbled; Stevenson grabbed her as she went down, and she didn't resist. All her fight was gone. She squeezed her eyes shut as Stevenson picked her up, cradling her in his arms.

"It's all right," he told her, sounding almost compassionate. "It's over."

Hammon couldn't watch. He had to leave. Leave, and he wouldn't have to see where this was leading. He wouldn't be a part of it. Leave, and it wouldn't be his problem.

"Sure," Annabel said. "Take the easy way out."

Easy? Ripping out his own barely beating heart? He should have died instead of Micah. Then none of this would be happening.

"But you didn't and it is," Annabel insisted. "You can't let him do this."

"Yeah," Hammon said. "You're right about that."

01:03 MONDAY, JULY 5

41°01'48.76"N/73°55'09.91"W

PIERMONT, NY

Hazel didn't speak as Stevenson carried her into the house, sitting her on a kitchen chair. The effects of the dart were starting to subside, and she wondered groggily what occurred while she was out. Head bowed, she stared down. In the reflection on her watch crystal, she could see Stevenson, and with a minute shift of her wrist, Hammon staring into nowhere.

"Hazel?" Stevenson snapped his fingers. He studied her grimly. "When was the last time she ate or slept?"

Hammon shrugged. "Damned if I know."

She gazed at the slow-motion sweep of the second hand while her brain gradually reconnected with her body. She would wait. Wait to see what lay ahead. Wait to see what they had planned. Wait for the tranquilizer to wear off. Wait for her chance to kill Stevenson.

As the fog in her head cleared, the events of the night replayed through her mind, reviving the horrible ache in her chest. It was as if her heart had been torn in two, and half remained behind with Micah, dead and frozen. Beneath her hand she felt the shape of the darts in her pocket, one still capped, one empty. She wasn't sure how long she'd been out, and she knew she couldn't stand or walk more than a few steps, if that. Hammon watched from the doorway, his expression unreadable. Was the boy she'd met that night by the river, the one who'd trembled at her touch, anywhere behind those cold eyes?

Stevenson knelt beside her. "Hazel?"

She didn't answer. There was no answer. There were only the passing seconds and minutes and the reflections on her watch.

Hammon stepped to the sink and washed the dried blood off his hands: his blood and hers. "Nice work, Jake. She's gone. All trains of thought have stopped running. The tracks are shut, and service's suspended till further notice. Kinda screws up your plans, don't it?"

Stevenson's hands closed in fists, tendons rippling up his arms, and Hazel flinched. In a voice surprisingly steady for someone who looked ready to kill again, Stevenson said, "Talk to her. You might be able to reach her."

Hammon shut the faucet, wiping his hands on his pants. "It's over. I'm done. You're on your own with this."

He turned and walked out, the kitchen door slamming behind him.

Until that moment, Hazel didn't think she had a shred of hope left to crush, but as the rumble of the Viper broke the silence and tires screeched away, fading into the distance, a fresh wave of pain flooded through her. Her face burned and her throat tightened as surely as if it were still in Stevenson's grip. What had she expected? She'd known Hammon was working for Stevenson, yet she'd let herself trust him. She tried to tell herself it didn't sting, but there was no more pretending or wishing or hoping. This was a nightmare she wouldn't be waking from, safe and sound in her bunk aboard *Witch*, back in her familiar, secure world. That world was gone, forever destroyed. Her father was lying shattered in a hospital, Micah was dead. It was all for nothing.

The air hung heavy with tense silence, punctuated only by the ticking of her watch and random chirps of crickets. Hazel wanted to scream, to beat Stevenson until he was reduced to a bleeding mass of agony, but she was barely able to stand, let alone attack. A single tear of frustration escaped, dropping to the tile between her feet.

Stevenson slammed his fist on the counter. "Son of a bitch."

She couldn't let herself cry. If Travis McGee could do this then so could she, and Travis sure as hell wouldn't be crying. Her hands stayed on her lap, her eyes on the watch, her mind set on that last sealed dart. The night and this nightmare were far from over.

Stevenson offered her a napkin, but she stared through it. And she didn't flinch or blink when he cupped her chin, lifted her face, and gently wiped her cheeks, the fury in his eyes mixed with something that almost passed for sympathy. With a weary sigh he rose, taking orange juice and eggs from the refrigerator and pouring a glass of scotch.

"You need to eat," he said, more to himself than her as he lit the stove.

Hazel felt her way into the pocket, easing out the sealed dart, hiding it beneath her hand.

"Sorry I was so rough on you before." He downed the scotch. "There wasn't time to explain, and I figured it was better I be a bastard than risk Nelson shooting you." Metal banged sharp against metal as he dropped an iron skillet on the burner.

While his back remained to her, Hazel moved her right foot the slightest bit, testing her reflexes. Pins and needles coursed through her veins. She tried her left foot, pausing as Stevenson

turned. She continued to gaze down blankly while the muscles in her face tingled as feeling returned. She kept her expression slack and fought the impulse to wipe another escaped tear, itching unbearably all the way down the side of her nose. Stevenson studied her, his features hardening.

"Goddamnit!" He struck his fist into the wall, cracking the plaster, leaving a bloody smear. "Show me Hammon's wrong. Show me you're still in there."

He picked up another napkin and blotted his knuckles. "I know you're in shock and things haven't sunk in yet. Unfortunately, it's only going to get worse. Right now you're running on hurt and hate; they're powerful emotions and they'll keep you going for a while, but they'll consume you eventually, leaving nothing but bitterness. Trust me, I know." He shook his head. "We're already more alike than you realize."

He knelt down and lifted her chin again, gently drying her tear. As his hand brushed her cheek, her eyes locked onto his and she buried the dart deep into the underside of his arm. He winced and carefully pulled it out, studied the now-empty cylinder...and began to laugh.

"That's my girl. You were starting to worry me." He eased himself to the floor and sat back against the cabinets. "I should have known better, right? Pretty careless, not checking if you were still armed." He regarded the dart with amusement. "So this is it."

"It is." She moved to the edge of the chair, testing her balance. "This ends here, tonight."

"I see." He gazed at her and massaged his arm. "Now what?"

"To start with," she rose unsteadily, "you're going to give me answers."

Stevenson yawned and tilted his head back against the door.

"Why. That's the big question, isn't it? Why was I following you, even before I showed up in Bivalve, and why did I walk away from all that money? Why was Joe helping me? And why would Hammon leave you with a scumbag like me when it's obvious how desperately he loves you?"

Contentment filled his face, infuriating Hazel beyond words. He was supposed to be panicking; he was supposed to be terrified.

"Revenge. It's all about revenge." He sighed. "And I'll bet you think I mean that goddamned boat. Poor thing. Your world's been shattered, your heart's broken, nothing makes sense any-more." His words were beginning to slur. "Before you start slic-ing, you might want..." He tried to motion but his arm flopped uselessly. His eyes fixed on his limp hand and he smiled faintly. "Complications."

His head drooped and his expression softened, but Hazel stood back, waiting. She hadn't expected one dart would knock him out entirely, but combined with the alcohol in his system, it might. She kicked him with all her strength, which still wasn't much, but enough for him to feel it. One eye half opened.

"Not quite dead yet..." he mumbled, the corner of his mouth almost curling. "Go look."

"At what?"

His face relaxed, his body sagged, and he lay there like a sedated lion, breathing slow and even. Hesitantly Hazel approached, watching. She slapped him across the face, hard. It felt good, but he only grunted and her hand stung, diminishing her satisfaction. Using kitchen aprons, she tied his wrists together securely and bound his ankles. Then she gathered the knives.

I'M DONE

"You know she'll try to kill him," Annabel yelled over the Viper's rumble.

"Likely. That'd solve lots of problems."

Hammon stared up at the red light, casting the same soft glow in the darkness over the same intersection where he'd first seen Hazel. Beside him, Annabel tore at his brain as she fought for control, trying to hijack his consciousness the minute he lowered his guard. He wouldn't let her; she'd only go straight back to Hazel and undo all the heart-wrenching damage he'd done, making things infinitely worse in the process. The light turned green, and he struggled with the clutch. The Viper lurched and stalled. This time there was no one around to notice or care as they sat in silence.

"You can't let her," Annabel said, more softly now.

He pulled off his glasses and wiped his eyes. "That's where you're wrong."

There was still time to turn back. It wasn't too late. Start the car, go back, walk in, take her from there, from Stevenson. Tell her he loved her and couldn't live without her.

"Then do it."

It wasn't that he didn't want to. More than life itself he wanted to go back, take her, hold her, keep her forever. But he wouldn't. He couldn't.

"So you're just leaving her there? She's all alone. She lost Micah. She needs you."

"She lost Micah because of me. If he hadn't come back to help me, I'd be dead, not him. I'm doing what I have to. She hates me anyways."

"She doesn't hate you."

"She should. It's better that way."

"You really believe that? Or are you trying to convince yourself? I think you're a coward and you're running away. You swore you'd help her."

"And that's what I'm doing." He had to let her go, even if it killed him, and he knew it would. There was no way his heart could withstand damage of that extent for long.

"You told her you loved her. That you'd die for her."

"Exactly."

He shouldn't have said that. It took the right side of his brain a few seconds to process that thought and set off a barrage of questions he had no intention of answering. He restarted the Viper, the engine's roar making it nearly impossible to hear himself, or anyone else in his head, think. With his damaged leg, driving that car demanded his full, undivided attention, allowing him to ignore his intangible passenger. Not surprisingly, headaches followed, distracting him from the agonizing ache in his chest. Unfortunately, they also left him disoriented and lost. He looked around for signs. It was New Jersey: there were signs everywhere, only none pointed toward the Parkway. He glanced at Annabel for a second and his heart twisted. She knew what he was thinking. She always knew.

It wasn't that he wanted to do it, but he had to. He was keeping his promise. His hands were shaking from adrenaline, yet he felt strangely tranquil. Was it peace, absolute despair, or both?

Once he reached the Parkway, he'd see what the Viper's top speed was. Then he'd see how quick it could stop by swerving into an overpass abutment. It was the only way. If he ceased to exist, Hazel would be safe. Sooner or later Stevenson would use her to get to him, to get answers. And those answers were deadly. Far better they remain questions.

Hammon rounded an unfamiliar bend as train crossing signals flashed, and he coasted to a stop as the gates dropped in his path. The train whistle sounded through the darkness.

"You can still turn back," Annabel said. "I know the way, it's not far. Go back for her, get her out of there. Get her away from Stevenson."

The whistle sounded again, sharper, louder, approaching fast. Hammon sat, watching the reflections of the gate lights flashing across the black paint on the hood, waiting.

"Don't even consider it," Annabel warned.

Ironically, the thought hadn't even entered that side of his mind until she mentioned it. He wouldn't need the Parkway. The whistle cut the night air. The wobbling gates formed little more than a symbolic barrier between the car and the tracks, one the Viper could easily slip beneath. He was still in gear, his left foot holding the clutch to the floor. He was facing the wrong way for the full benefit of the impact; the train would hit the passenger side first, not that it'd make much difference. In an instant the passenger side would be the driver's side. Crushed like a soda can, the Viper would all but vaporize beneath the first engine and be scattered in the bushes and trees while the train screeched and braked for a quarter mile, maybe more, dragging bits of debris the whole way. It would make interesting headlines in the local papers for people to read over their morning coffee. Hammon grinned coldly, imagining Stevenson reading the news, a grin that faded as he thought of Hazel seeing the paper. Maybe she'd be glad.

"I'm sorry," he told Annabel, his voice drowned by the piercing whistle. The ground shook and the engine's light broke through the trees to his right. Hammon started to lift the clutch. It would be over before the engineer had any hope of stopping.

"I won't let you!"

His brain throbbed and he blocked the agony, focusing only on lifting the clutch. "You won't stop me. Not this time."

The Viper inched forward, ready…ready…

A searing cramp shot through his left leg, locking it down as the ground quaked and four deafening locomotives blurred past the headlights. The freight cars, a wall of rushing metal and colors, roared along, drawing up stray leaves and paper to swirl in confusion in his headlights. And then it was gone. The gates lifted, their red lights snuffed as they returned to upright, leaving an empty silence.

The flashing light on the rear of the train receded, along with the cramp in Hammon's leg. "Thanks for nothing."

Annabel's dark eyes fixed on him with a merciless hatred. "You're welcome. You know, you used to be someone I liked. I can almost see why she'd be better off without you."

"Yeah, angel. That's what I love about you, how you always manage to make me feel better."

"I didn't see that on my job description."

"Why won't you just leave me alone?"

"That's what you want? Fine. Remember: be careful what you wish for."

02:16 MONDAY, JULY 5

41°01'48.76"N/73°55'09.91"W

PIERMONT, NY

Hazel knelt beside Stevenson, watching blood rise in the thin slice she'd made along his bound arm. A small cut; nothing life-threatening…yet. She thought about Micah lying lifeless in that freezer and she pressed harder. Stevenson jerked and she stepped back.

"Hello, Jake," she said softly. "Ready to play twenty questions?"

His head swiveled, zeroing in on her voice. His mouth moved but no words came out.

Hazel rose as the kettle reached a boil, and she made herself a cup of tea. She lowered the flame, leaving the water at a slow sim-mer, then returned to Stevenson, sipping her tea as he stared up, awareness growing in his fogged eyes.

"God you're young." He blinked, unfocused, and suddenly he looked excruciatingly sad. "Years ago," he slurred, "in a king-dom by the sea…lived a maiden you may know…by the name of Annabel Lee."

Anger welled up inside Hazel. It was the ketamine talking, but she didn't care. "Annabel isn't real, you son of a bitch!"

"Oh but she is, realer than you can imagine," he mumbled. "Annabel…is you…and you are Annabel." His eyes closed. "The moon never beams, without bringing me dreams of the beautiful Annabel Lee. The stars never rise but I feel the bright eyes of my beautiful Annabel Lee." He sighed. "Tragic. She dies in the end. But you didn't die, dear Annabel. He did."

Her hand shook and it was all she could do not to run the knife straight through his heart. "Damn you!"

"Too late. Already damned." His head rolled sideways. "Wake me when we get there."

Hazel traced the knife along his bicep, slicing through the fabric of his shirt, watching as a stain of blood spread. He winced but remained still.

"Tell me, Jake, who were you talking with that night about me and the truck?"

He grunted. "You won't believe me."

She pressed the blade into the meat of his shoulder. "It was Joe, wasn't it?"

He flinched. "No, princess. It was your father."

"Don't lie to me!" She twisted the knife hard. "I heard the whole conversation; that was NOT my father. Tell me who it was!"

Stevenson choked back a groan and nodded. "Your father," he hissed through clenched teeth. "Set a trap… duplicate truck and cargo…and me playing the part of…well, me. Quite convincingly, it seems. The plan was to get both you and Micah somewhere safe, along with *Witch*."

Hazel pulled the knife back. "Why didn't he tell me?" she challenged, not wanting to believe him, even as part of her knew it was precisely the thing her father might do.

Stevenson regarded the blood on his arms, trying to focus. "He said you wouldn't listen. I thought we should, but he said if you had no idea what we were doing, then you couldn't try to help or do anything risky… playing 'salvage consultant,' he called it, whatever the hell that means."

There was a rushing in her ears, and her hands fell to her sides. "Go on." Her voice was a whisper; she couldn't manage more.

"He didn't want anyone else involved; it was supposed to be just me and him. Even Joe didn't know the details until after your dad got shot. Plausible deniability, he insisted. If he wound up in jail, he wanted Joe around to keep you and Micah in line. It took me all night to track down a matching truck. Fortunately the graphics shop that did *Tuition*'s logos still had the design on file. Your dad picked up the truck, drove it to the warehouse, dressed it up, and e-mailed me the pictures. Everything was coming together until you overheard that conversation.

"When you attacked me, your dad was more worried about covering your tracks and finding a place to dump my body." Stevenson tried to grin. "He was sure you'd killed me. We agreed it was probably better if you thought you almost did. You were supposed to stay at Forelli's boatyard. Hidden. Safe." He was more alert now and he shifted, managing to sit straighter. "Yes, I knew you were there; I didn't know you took Hammon's boat."

Hazel listened, taking in all he was saying, processing it. "What was my dad doing the night he was shot?"

Stevenson stared down at his bound hands. "He'd gone down to Bivalve to talk to the police. They had some questions regarding 'human remains' they found wrapped around your runabout's prop. He went alone. Nelson must've tailed him on the highway afterwards.

"Joe tracked me down, told me what happened." He half smiled. "Scary bastard, that Joe. He made it clear he had some doubts about my involvement. Once he knew the whole story, he insisted on stepping in. Said you were his family, he owed it to all of you."

Stevenson made a sound that might have been a laugh but sounded more like a moan. "When you shot Joe, he was only trying to protect you. Joe saw Atkins negotiating with me over the decoy truck, and apparently Hammon ambushed him pretty good, so he figured those two were working together. Joe saw Atkins take your old truck so he tailed him."

Hazel gasped as it all sank in. "JOE! I ran him off the road!"

"We saw. He's fine, just a concussion." Stevenson shifted uncomfortably. "Atkins brought him to the hospital. I guess that's what your father meant about you getting involved. He said things…how'd he put it…tend to 'escalate' around you. Joe said to tell you he's impressed, he taught you well." His eyes narrowed. "But you owe me a new Kevlar vest and repairs on the Chevelle."

"My father…" Hazel began, her voice faint. "Does he know about Micah?"

Stevenson shook his head. "No. Last time I spoke with your father was yesterday, right after you called the ICU. I'm sorry, but you can't tell your father until after the police notify us first. As far as you know, Micah left you behind at the boat two nights ago, and you haven't seen or heard from him since." He paused, contemplating his bound hands for a moment. "You should take Joe with you when you visit your father; you shouldn't go alone."

Hazel's stomach was in knots; she sat on her heels on the floor holding her knife limply. It all made perfect, horrible sense: her father keeping her in the dark like that, and everything had gone so wrong. But one detail still didn't fit. Why was Stevenson involved to begin with, and why would her father trust a total stranger when he wouldn't even include Joe?

"There's something you're not telling me," she said. "I saw that file, you had all those things on me, even those photos from long before you hired my dad to move your boat. You've been following me since right after *Tuition* vanished."

He nodded. "Exactly. *Tuition* vanished, and instead you had to drive that old Kenworth for your next delivery. After all these years of searching I thought I'd never find that god-awful truck—I'd pretty much given up—I figured it'd probably long since rusted away—and then it pulls into that marina in Cape May, with you at the wheel, no less. Talk about dumb luck."

"What does that have to do with anything?" A shiver ran down her spine, and Hazel rose, moving back. "What is this really about?"

"Are you sure you want to know?" Stevenson frowned. "Yes, of course you are. Maybe you should have known all along." He tugged at his bound hands and sighed. "I really could use a drink and a cigarette right now, but I guess untying me is still out of the question. Remember your first night here, I said there'd be a prize. You want your answers? Open the cupboard below the stairs. There's a latch beneath the middle shelf; release it."

It might have been a trick, but she couldn't see how. She followed his instructions, and the cupboard wall swung inward to reveal a hidden closet her initial exploration of the house hadn't uncovered. Light slanted across cobweb-laced shelves, stacked with shoeboxes and papers.

"Bottom shelf," Stevenson called, his voice weary. "Right side. Brown manila envelope."

It was there beneath a layer of dust that hadn't been disturbed in a long time. She took a seat at the kitchen table, sliding out several brittle newspaper clippings. A chill washed over her as she recognized the first headline; the cover page of the *Bergen Record* from nearly seven years back.

FAMILY OF 4 KILLED IN TRAGIC PARKWAY CRASH

Below the headline was the image of a charred, mangled Mercury station wagon smoldering in a blackened crater on the shoulder of the Garden State Parkway. In the background, a bright yellow sign stated ominously, "LAST EXIT IN NEW JERSEY."

The inset photo of Jeremy Matthews, permanently frozen at age fifteen, grinned brightly beside his big sister Helen and their parents. Hazel sucked in her breath as she stared at the boy. It was *her* Jeremy. She'd met him only two weeks earlier, while he was on vacation in Cape May. He'd seen *Witch* sail in at dawn and went down to the docks for a closer look, fascinated with the ancient schooner and even more so with Hazel. He was awkwardly sweet and disarmingly funny, and he had the bluest eyes she'd ever seen. They'd spent every moment of that day together, walking on the beach, eating ice cream, sailing in her dinghy. She remembered laughing when he claimed that they were meant to be together forever. It was the same day she'd had her first kiss, and he gave her that ring, the one she still wore. By night he had to leave, heading back to north Jersey in an over-packed station wagon, but not before they exchanged numbers and addresses, promising to write and to call. Her father assured her they could visit him in a few weeks when they would be passing nearby.

"The funeral ran late." Stevenson interrupted her thoughts. "Private ceremony. Toward the end, a distinctly ugly old Ken-worth pulled in and parked a respectable distance back…too far back to read the name on the door. You waited until everyone was leaving and then you came over." He frowned, his expression distant. "I remember…you had wildflowers."

Hazel remembered as well, as though it was yesterday. She and her father were on the Turnpike in *RoadKill*, listening for the traffic report to roll around, when they heard the tragic news about the funeral for a family that died on the Parkway. As the names of the victims were announced, Hazel's father pulled over. They sat in silence for a bit, and he promised he would take her to the cemetery so she could leave flowers.

Hazel shuddered as she dropped the clipping to the table and stared at Stevenson.

"I know. You have questions." Stevenson nodded to the clippings. "Keep reading."

She returned to the stack; the next one was dated three days before the Parkway accident:

ARSON SUSPECTED IN MONTVALE OFFICE FIRE

The building's occupants were listed as Spirig Insurance and Benjamin Matthews, CPA. Hazel held up the clipping toward Stevenson so he could see what she was reading.

"That was the first try. Jeremy's dad's office. The ground-floor office was vacant," he explained. "Someone placed an accelerant and a timer in it. Ben had a new client meeting that day, a nonexistent one, it turned out, but he got stuck in traffic and ran late."

The next, dated ten days later, read:

PARKWAY CRASH CAUSED BY EXPLOSIVES

Hazel held that up as well.

"Try number two did the trick. Enough explosives to take down a small building," Stevenson said. "Enjoying my scrapbook? You wouldn't have any more of those darts? Good stuff. Better than scotch. I'm nice and numb. Wears off too fast, though. I think I need a higher dose."

Ignoring his request, she held up the next clipping. This one was from four months before the fire and accident, and mentioned a golf outing to benefit mental health services.

"Other side," Stevenson whispered, looking away.

Hazel read:

HELEN CHRISTINE MATTHEWS & JAKE EDWARD STEVENSON TO WED

Leaning against the white Mustang, a younger, trimmer, more carefree version of Stevenson grinned beside a young woman with a mischievous sparkle in her blue eyes. Jeremy's sister. The clipping announced their upcoming October wedding.

Stevenson shifted and winced. "I could really use a drink right now. I'm starting to get feeling back, and I don't like it."

Hazel stared at the clippings, mystified. "I'm sorry about Helen. But I don't see what that has to do with me. There's a reason we're having this conversation, and I want to know what it is."

"I can see that." Stevenson dropped his head back against the cabinet. "I'm serious about that drink, and you might want one too." He looked at her. "No? Okay. Helen and Jeremy's old man was born to be a CPA. Very orderly guy. Liked to keep all his documents up-to-date. Guess who old Ben had just happened to name Jeremy's legal guardian if anything ever happened to them? Helen and yours truly." He gave a tired laugh. "We're scrambling, getting ready for the wedding, and he springs it on us. We say yeah, sure. Whatever. I'm thinking it's weird, but also kind of a nice gesture. He trusts me."

"But Jeremy died," she said, staring down at his picture.

"Did he?" Stevenson laughed humorlessly. "Do the math, princess. Throw in years of reconstructive surgery and take a wild guess who our singed friend Hammon is. Or, more accurately, was."

Hazel stood so abruptly the chair fell over. She'd been there at the cemetery; she'd placed flowers on Jeremy's grave!

"Yeah. That's the same look your father had. You need a minute, or should I continue?"

Hazel righted the chair and sat down, feeling her earlier dizziness returning. There was so much to be confused by all at once. "Go on."

Stevenson nodded.

"Jeremy had a real talent with computers, and he usually worked for his dad after school. One day he called me bragging about how he'd found something strange with one of his dad's clients, some sort of error in their records; he was quite pleased with himself." Stevenson smiled the slightest bit. "He was saving up for a car, and he figured this was worth a guaranteed raise. His dad said he'd look into it, talk with the client, and give the kid a bonus if he was right.

"After the fire, Jeremy had a hunch it wasn't just a simple error, that the arson was intended to destroy what he'd found. He told me he'd backed up a copy before the fire and put it somewhere else, and he wanted to show me everything. They were going out to dinner, the whole family. I was supposed to go too, but couldn't make it. I told him I'd come by after I got off work and we'd talk. He was a sharp kid, real sharp, and I had a bad feeling he was right."

Stevenson swallowed and a strained expression crossed his face. "Two hours later the police are on my doorstep telling me Ben, his wife...and Helen are dead, with Jeremy not far behind. I get to the hospital...the poor kid's...unrecognizable, just burned flesh and shattered bones. His heart had already stopped once;

they didn't think he'd last, and I was getting hit with whether to revive, organ donation and all. I'm still numb, and I'm thinking, Thanks for the gesture, Ben. They said Jeremy suffered so much damage that even if he did survive, he'd never be right again. There were metal fragments from the car too deep in his brain to risk removing."

Stevenson turned away, leaving Hazel to study his weary profile, his defenses down and the underlying pain exposed.

"I couldn't forget Jeremy's phone call. There's one cop, he's already working the investigation on the arson, and he must've believed me when I told him the kid knew something, and IF Jeremy lived, someone would try again. Paperwork was altered, Jeremy was declared dead, John Doe went into surgery, and Hammon came out."

Hazel sat across from Stevenson, knees pulled to her chin, arms wrapped around her legs, listening in silence. It wasn't the time to comment even if she could imagine what to say. Stevenson looked grim.

"I don't know what did more damage: the accident, or surviving to learn everyone including him was dead and buried. Those surgeries, skin grafts, the therapy, it was hell. It changed him. The more they reconstructed, the more Jeremy disappeared. It wasn't just the new identity; he went into a cocoon of bandages and came out someone else. He couldn't, or wouldn't, remember anything. Not the accident, not the phone call, not the backed-up information, and he wouldn't even speak to me. His doctors said frontal lobe damage could wipe out recent memories. They said that part of his mind was gone."

He looked up, smiling grimly. "They were wrong. When his therapist told me about his imaginary friend, I knew it was the girl at the funeral, the one in the truck. You. Only there were no records of anyone named Annabel, or anyone else you could have been. No classmates, neighbors, relatives, no one. If he'd had any name or address for you, it burned with him. I searched for years with only that moment from the funeral and the memory of that ugly old truck to work with."

Stevenson shifted his weight, clearly uncomfortable but resigned to the fact that she wasn't freeing him just yet. "His doctors said he blamed me for everything. He decided I was covering something up, that their deaths were my fault. The more I tried to fix him the more he fell apart. I watched him disintegrate, and I couldn't do a damned thing to stop him from self-destructing. He nearly killed himself a few times; I had to have him supervised constantly. When he was seventeen, he managed to disappear; for six months I couldn't find him. I thought he was dead until Gary found him holed up in that boat, and he started tapping my bank account."

Stevenson smiled to himself. "Him and that damned boat. I finally had some way I could help him. That, and leaving 'hidden' cash lying around. It's his money—his parents' life insurance and the money from selling their house—but the only way I could get it to him was letting him think he's stealing it from me."

Stevenson took a break and Hazel waited silently. She didn't know what to say. He continued. "You didn't know him long, but you made some impression on him. Enough to create Annabel, enough to hold him together and keep him going. Enough for someone terrified of water to take up living on a boat. I'd given up hope of ever finding you...and then, all these years later, that truck rolls into Cape May and you climb out. I had to find out if you were the real girl to Hammon's fantasy Annabel. But you turned out to be hostile, unsocialized, uncivilized, utterly unmanageable, and even more hell-bent on disliking me than him." Stevenson grinned.

"But why? You think I know where this data is? I don't."

"I didn't expect you would. But if he remembered you and fixated on you the way he did, then it's possible he remembers other information, and reconnecting with you could trigger those repressed memories. And more than that, you might be the key to reaching him, helping him before it was too late. So yes, you were absolutely right. I was following you, and hiring your dad to move my boat was just an excuse to meet you face-to-face and see who you *really* were. When the time was right, I planned to explain all this and reintroduce you two. Then everything went to hell."

Stevenson looked around the room. "So here we are, right where we both would have been seven years ago, if my life hadn't been destroyed." Stevenson's chin dropped and he gazed down at his bound hands. "Helen loved this place. It was vacant, abandoned, and she would drive me past all the time and tell me how unbearable it would be seeing it torn down. I told her it was too far gone to save. She had no idea I'd bought it, I had crews inside doing a full restoration, planting the gardens out back. From the street you couldn't tell a thing. She thought the wedding was going to be at her parents' house. This would have been my surprise, my gift to her."

As unimaginable as it all was, it made perfect twisted sense. Stevenson's questions and comments from those first days all fell into place, and it explained so much of Hammon's baffling behavior. Micah would have found it all very amusing, and for Hazel that was strangely comforting. It validated everything Micah believed right to the end. She knelt beside Stevenson, untying his hands.

He rubbed his wrists. "I won't try to say I know how you feel right now over what happened to Micah. But I do know how it feels to lose everything you love."

I'M DOING IT AND THIS TIME
NO ONE'S STOPPING ME

In the predawn darkness, *Revenge* cut through the offshore Atlantic swells, heading due east on autopilot, nonstop until the fuel ran out. Then Hammon figured he'd take every sleeping pill he had aboard, slice every hose, and take a nice, permanent nap as the boat went down.

He was truly alone and losing what little mind he had left. Annabel had vanished hours earlier, leaving him lost and disoriented. He was barely able to drive the Viper and too afraid that in his attempt to crash he might hit someone else in the process. He already had Micah's death on his conscience and that was enough. Going down aboard *Revenge* seemed the best option. It took hours of stubborn determination to find his way back to the boat, still waiting dark and silent at the Leonardo docks. By the debilitating headaches, he suspected Annabel was still lurking somewhere in the back of his mind, but he couldn't be sure. He wasn't talking to her and she wasn't speaking to him, which was either really good or really bad. Not like it would make much difference. Not this time.

It was too quiet. Too quiet on the boat, too quiet inside his throbbing skull. He leaned back, staring up at the fading constellations as *Revenge* rolled beneath him.

"I did the right thing," Hammon told the stars.

"Are you sure?"

Hammon turned to the vision beside him, smiling weakly. "Annabel. I thought you weren't talking to me."

She stared ahead, not meeting his eyes. "Who else do I have?"

"True. I guess it's just the two of us again." At least for what little time they had left. But he didn't have to tell her that. She knew. She always knew. "You still pissed at me?"

"Do I really need to answer that? You said you'd stay with her forever. Then you left."

"Do you know how painful that was?"

"For you or her? You pushed her away when she needed you most. She didn't know why."

"I had to. Stevenson wants revenge. I do too, I lost everything, but it's too dangerous for Hazel. You heard Stevenson, he says I knew Hazel when I was Jeremy; I even gave her that ring she's wearing. But I don't remember any of it, not one thing. Stevenson thinks if I'm with her it'll come back to me, but I don't want to remember what he wants me to remember. Look what happened the last time because of what I knew. This ends with me. Once I'm dead there'll be no me to remember anything, and she'll be safe. And I should be dead. It's my fault what happened to Micah."

She stared into the darkness and took a deep breath. "You risked your life trying to save them both. You didn't pull the trigger, but if you kill yourself, you make Micah's death pointless."

"She doesn't need me. She's better off without me."

"Is that what you really think?" she asked, regarding him in a strange way.

He turned away. "No matter what anyone says, I'm not Jeremy anymore."

"She never thought you were to begin with. Do you love her?"

"Yeah. But I'm also insane."

"That doesn't change the fact." She laughed softly. "True love is insane at best, especially under the worst conditions."

"It's too risky. I stay with her, one day we'd lift the wrong rock, I'll remember the wrong thing, and it'll all start over. I can't take that chance."

"Then don't lift any rocks. Leave the past where it is."

"It's inevitable. I'm already remembering things I shouldn't." Hammon stared ahead. The faintest pink strands of dawn began to separate the dark sky from the black water. "I was starting to think there was some hope on the horizon. But you know what the horizon is, right? It's an imaginary line you can never reach."

She slumped back, aggravated. "How about this? You remember anything you shouldn't, I'll just whack you over the head."

"If only it were that simple."

She smacked him hard across the back of the head.

"Ow!" he whined. "That hurt."

Then it sank in. That hurt. He broke into a grin, beaming. "That hurt! It really hurt!"

"No," Hazel said, smiling slightly through her tears. "That felt good."

Hazel, Hammon, Annabel, and Stevenson
will all return in *No Wake Zone*.
For a sneak peak at Chapter One, keep reading!

~ ~ ~

No Wake Zone

14:34 Saturday, September 18

41°03'31.63"N 74°06'03.23"W

Lake St, Upper Saddle River, NJ

"Pull over," Jake Stevenson said, looking grim.

Hazel Moran slowed Stevenson's black Mercedes and eased onto the shoulder, feeling the car lean as the tires sank into the grass. She took the sedan out of gear, switched on the hazard lights, and turned to Stevenson.

"Is something wrong?" she asked, as though she didn't know.

He regarded her with that weary, strained look of his. "I want to be sure you understand where we're going and why."

Hazel smoothed her silk dress and leaned over, peering into the rearview mirror to check her hair, which was subdued into tidy finger-waves. She studied Stevenson's perfectly tailored tuxedo and neatly trimmed blond hair for a moment, then reached across and straightened his tie.

"Casino Royale." She smiled sweetly. "We're off to a high-stakes poker tournament, yes?"

The muscles beneath his clean-shaven jaw tightened. "Funny. You going to be able to focus, Miss Moran?"

"Just trying to lighten the mood." Actually, between his black attire and somber expression, he looked as though he was heading to yet another funeral, but she refrained from voicing that observation. She could see he was having second thoughts about bringing her. She'd better pacify him or he'd have her turn back to the house.

"It's a wedding for one of George Dulawski's daughters," Hazel said, reciting the pertinent facts she'd memorized. "Stepdaughters, technically. Second wife Barbara's kids. George Dulawski heads Metro Construction Management, which recently purchased property along the Passaic River for which you are bidding for a sustainable redevelopment. You've done a number of projects with Metro over the years." Including the year the Matthews family met their untimely end, though she omitted mention of that detail.

"You've pretty much sold George's partner, Roger Newman, on the project," she continued, "but George has his reservations." And according to Stevenson that was the reason he'd chosen to attend this joyous occasion. Stevenson made a point of avoiding social situations, and most invitations wound up in the recycling bin without so much as an RSVP. "And you requested I accompany you because you're a shallow jerk that no other self-respecting woman would be seen with."

That brought a momentary flicker of amusement to his pale gold eyes and Hazel smiled. "I'm here as arm candy," she said, "and to run interference and pretend we're a couple while you talk business. But mainly I'm here so that, the moment you give the signal, I can claim a terrible headache and we can graciously exit. And…" She passed Stevenson the elaborately printed sheet of ivory paper. "You are fully aware that the wedding was at one o'clock." She checked her watch again; it was well past two thirty.

"Such a shame we were unavoidably delayed," he said flatly.

Delayed by him meditating over a glass of scotch before they left, which was also the reason he wasn't the one behind the wheel. "No. You're deliberately stalling. The sooner we get there the sooner you can talk your business. So what's my story? Family fortune, finishing school?"

Stevenson chuckled. "Like you could sell that. There's no story; you're you. Your father runs a small trucking company; I hired him to move my boat. We met, you hated me on sight, said I was a creepy old rich guy, which I am, but you've gradually come to appreciate my more sensitive side."

"Ah. So you're dating the chauffeur's daughter. How very democratic. But I thought you wanted to make the right impression."

"And this will. These people know me. Just be yourself and you'll be fine." He paused, considering. "A better-behaved version of yourself. Don't maim or kill anyone. No playing with sharp objects. Try not to talk like a truck-driver. Avoid any mention of murder, mayhem, all other unsavory details such as Hammon, and that's about it."

Hazel offered the sweetest smile she could manage. "The moment we have an audience, I'll be on my best behavior."

He eyed her skeptically. "That isn't much to speak of."

"I promise," she assured him. "I'll be a perfect lady. Cross my heart."

She reached to put the car back in gear. He caught her hand and she stiffened. "What?" She looked uncomfortably at his fingers, still wrapped around hers.

"For one, try not to flinch when I touch you. It'll be more convincing that way."

"Understood." Stevenson's hand remained on hers. "We really should get going," she said.

"You're being far too cooperative. And when you get cooperative, I get suspicious."

"Really, Jake!" She stared back with the most sincerely wounded expression she could manage. "You asked for my help. After all you've done for me, it seemed only reasonable."

"Reasonable, or convenient? I saw how quickly you agreed to come once you learned who would be there. You're distressingly easy to read at times. Trust me, princess, there's nothing you can learn from these people that I don't already know, and I don't need some little girl playing detective for me. Understand?"

Heat rose in her face. She knew that some of what she'd learned from Hammon had opened his eyes to new leads. She thought that was the real reason he'd chosen to attend this wedding, even if he claimed otherwise, and why he'd asked her to accompany him. She took a deep breath and turned away. "Understood."

"Hazel," he said, his voice softening, "I appreciate your intentions, but I'm serious: there isn't an angle you can think of that I haven't already explored to exhaustion. I've wrecked a chunk of my life going down that road and back; I won't stand by and watch you take that same path."

She stared ahead. "So what exactly am I supposed to do?"

"Smile, be pretty, make nice. Do not, under any circumstances, snare, stab, or shoot anyone. Don't make any waves. And remember just for today, no matter how insane it might seem, you truly love me with all your heart. In other words, just pretend I'm Hammon."

She smiled sweetly. "Whatever you wish, dear."

Despite what he claimed, Hazel knew Stevenson had been digging into the past, lifting rocks. And things that reside under rocks are rarely happy when exposed to the light of day. She put the car in gear and pulled her hand free of his, discreetly running it across her purse and the reassuring shape of Hammon's colorful little Glock concealed within. For one afternoon she would be charming, gracious, and polite while she mingled among developers, trophy-wives, socialites, and possibly a murderer or two.

ABOUT THE AUTHOR

C. E. Grundler is a native Jersey girl who has been sailing the region's waters single-handedly since she was a child. Needless to say, she knows her way around a boat, having done everything from restoration and repairs to managing a boatyard and working in commercial marine transportation. Her "how to" articles have appeared in several boating magazines. When she's not writing, she spends her time messing around aboard *Annabel Lee*, her thirty-two-foot Cheoy Lee trawler. She lives in northeast New Jersey with her husband, three dogs, and an assortment of cats. *Last Exit in New Jersey* is her first novel.